TWO NOVELLAS

RUTH –
Suppression and Redemption

BYBROOK IMAGES –
More Things in Heaven and Earth

Stephen Constance
Stephen Constance

THE CHOIR PRESS

Copyright © 2025 Stephen Constance

All rights reserved. No part of this publication may be reproduced or transmitted in any form or by any means, electronic or mechanical including photocopying, recording or any information storage or retrieval system, without prior permission in writing from the publishers.

The right of Stephen Constance to be identified as the author of this work has been asserted by him in accordance with the Copyright, Designs and Patents Act 1988

First published in the United Kingdom in 2025 by
The Choir Press

ISBN 978-1-78963-524-9

For all those indoctrinating and those oppressed by hypocritical religious belief, or deluded by the questionably existing occult, that they may be englightened.

ACKNOWLEDGEMENTS

Many thanks to Jonathon Lomas, Editor and all at The Choir Press, and to daughter Sophie, Tom, Big Ant and Roger, for often sorting out my computer problems.

RUTH
Suppression and Redemption

CHAPTER ONE

It was the time when you could suck the honeysuckle and taste its sweetness, and the perfume from the roses overwhelmed. She ought to be content out here, not far from the city in a situation that some would call a rural paradise. Yet she felt becalmed, trying not to rebel against the constrictions imposed upon her by an upbringing that did not fit one for the modern world. No TV, no radio, computers for business only and as a female, not permitted to work. Still classified as the inferior sex and – thanks to chauvinistic St Paul – compelled to wear your hair in an unvarying chignon. All aspects of life were based on biblical teaching: straying from the 'true way' could incur swift punishment, and more serious transgressions, permanent exclusion from the sect.

And since the swarthy and attractive young man had come to build the extension, Ruth had experienced an air of disquiet that was hard to quell. Gareth was very Welsh, ruggedly handsome, partially unshaven in the current fashion and fascinated her with his pigtail and muscle-bound torso.

Ruth had been born in South Africa, married Elisha under the towering Table Mountain and strictly adhered to the local fundamentalists' strict code of conduct. Back in the day the fundamentalists had been willing proponents of apartheid and the possibility of her choosing a partner outside the sect was not an option that would ever be tolerated. Indoctrinated from birth, Ruth had duly complied with all the rules the sect imposed, but in frighteningly more rational moments, felt she'd been a ritual lamb to the slaughter.

The city had a big industrial estate and the fundamentalists had taken over a large part of it. Like the Jews, they had a keen eye for business and bringing his bride to England, Elisha had leased a warehouse next door to his father's wherein he manufactured a product that Ruth knew nothing about. A 'prototype' follower, Elisha nevertheless treated her tolerably well, and it she'd managed to banish her misgivings and conquer the guilt engendered by them, the days might have passed pleasantly by.

The bungalow they inhabited was lengthy, painted in unrelieved white and rectangular in shape. It complimented an already picturesque setting, had large rooms and in her unsought opinion, was far too big without an extension being added on. Like all the sect's properties it came with pre-conceived décor, which was abysmally unattractive and in Ruth's considered opinion, invasively depressing. And not enhancing things further, the uniform black leather chairs and the shelves of brown hardbacks written by a long-deceased elder were an imposition: the possession of both being quite arbitrary. Ruth had no illusions as to why the bungalow had to be so spacious, for where the sect was concerned a woman's main purpose in life was an age-old one. Children would ensure the continuation of the order and she could not view this part of 'wifely duty' as becoming anything less than onerous.

Friction had been caused by Gareth's radio and words had been exchanged. Elisha objected to the strains of Radio Two profaning his dinner hour too loudly from the new annex and this had led to some complicity between his wife and the young Celt. It was fortunate that Elisha always rang to inform Ruth of his pending arrival for lunch and with the bungalow situated a couple of miles from the city, there was time to silence the radio before he appeared.

Upon taking Gareth's mid-morning tea, Ruth had found herself enjoying what was being broadcast by the small paint-besmirched radio that sat amongst various pots and brushes on a side table. Should they be an essential aid to improving life, you were permitted to provide non-believing tradesmen with sustenance, and inclined to lapse in her thoughts when confronted with the engaging young Welshman, she had to concede that he was challenging her beliefs. Taking him tea was one thing, but having lengthy discussion another, though his refreshing personality made it hard to resist.

'Not from round 'ere, are you, girl?'

He was very direct, even a trifle impudent, and this caused her to speculate over what it must be like to live in the world he inhabited. She tried to dismiss this inviting flirtation with apostasy immediately but found it difficult not to answer him eagerly.

'No, I'm actually from South Africa.'

This made him abandon his brushwork and with a smile, he took the proffered cup of tea. He then sat astride a chair backwards, rather than on it, and gave her his full attention. This totally disarmed her, and she knew he was aware of the effect his direct manner had induced as he proceeded to talk about his great-grandfather who'd fought in the Boer War.

'Did you know it was the British who invented concentration camps?'

Slavishly attached to the Bible all her life, her knowledge of history was sketchy, and she was only vaguely aware of what he was talking about.

'Are you saying the British put people in the same sort of camp that the Nazis did during the Second World War?'

'Yes, indeed,' he said, and did not avert his gaze from her face for a moment.§

'And when would that have been?'

"bout 1890. The Boers were the very first guerrilla fighters. They left their farms and made sudden sorties on the British. The British retaliated by rounding up the Boer women and incarcerating them prior to setting fire to the Boers' farm buildings.'

As he related these grim historical facts, she became wide-eyed and this enhanced her attraction, causing his heart to lurch and lascivious thoughts to invade his mind. He tried hard to dismiss them, but found he could not do so. This was another man's wife, yet it was almost a tragedy that the lovely creature had been tamed and subdued, sullied by the fundamentalists' repressive doctrine and having to submit to the gormless Elisha.

Then the phone rang, and she left to answer it.

CHAPTER TWO

Gareth's mam had come up from the valleys with his dad at the time the big metal company was offering plenty of employment in the city. She had always been a staunch member of the Church of Wales and this defined her in Risca as something of a religious reactionary, a label she was glad to be relieved of when coming over the border to live in England. She found the litany of St Mark's Church in the city suburbs undemanding, the people friendly and on special occasions she could even persuade skeptical Da to attend. Perhaps surprisingly, young Gareth would spasmodically grace the church with his presence and his mam reckoned it was because he had a keen eye for the girls who came rather than any strong religious conviction. He still chose to live at home with his parents and Da reckoned he was too comfortable, and bearing in mind that his Mam still catered for his every whim, produced the best pastry outside Wales and baked the most delicious roast potatoes after church on a Sunday, this could not be very far from the truth.

But something had been troubling him lately and Mam knew it was only a matter of time before he confided in her: her infallible woman's intuition telling her that something was amiss.

Nearly everything that went on in the Jones household took place in the kitchen. A staunch socialist, Da read the *Daily Mirror* from the depths of an easy chair in the far corner and when not occupied in cooking or keeping the house in pristine condition, Mam simply held court at the kitchen table. The kitchen table had a floral-patterned covering which just required wiping between meals these days, though 'dew', it wasn't as nice as the 'old tablecloths, see,' but there's less washing you had to do.

And Mam's greatest aid to culinary excellence was her all-purpose Rayburn which took up space near the airing cupboard. The Rayburn remained active most of the year and from a male perspective had its drawbacks. It had to be constantly made up with logs and anthracite and this recurring task produced grumbles from both Da and Gareth, particularly when they were watching something on the kitchen's large 'tele'. The TV set sat on a stand in front of the window and Gareth could never understand why it had to be sited there, but as he liked to watch a 'soap' whilst having his tea, he hadn't demurred when his parents claimed there was nowhere else to put it.

Beyond the kitchen was the scullery, a hotch-potch of a place containing a washing machine, various items of wet weather apparel, a small sack of birdseed and sundry tools that Da averred it was essential to keep, but never used. To complete the picture, several piles of old newspapers adorned the floor, and were it not for the fact that Gareth's married sister, Gwyneth, came every so often to claim them for her guinea pigs, the space they took up would have been even greater.

When not 'affixed' to the Rayburn, Barnaby the cat took his repasts in the scullery and not earning his keep, had proved to be a useless deterrent where one or two resident rodents were concerned. Mam asserted that these invaders came from 'that shambles' next door, a neglected property containing half a dozen unruly kids, who alternated between being quite endearing and what Da termed 'a bloody nuisance'.

With ominous determination, Ma sat down at the kitchen table and gave Gareth one of her inquisitory looks.

'Anything the matter, boy?'

Gareth knew it would be useless to resist.

'Sort of.'

This was not good enough. Ma took a sip of her tea and allowed him to swallow his mouthful of cottage pie before returning to the attack.

'There now, is it a girl? You can tell your mam, boy...' Gareth put down his cutlery with a clatter and sighed. He thought the world of his mam, but sometimes it seemed that in her eyes, two decades had not elapsed since he'd been the curly headed infant she'd doted on day and night.

'Well.'

'It is, then?'

'It's not like that.'

Mam's eyes suddenly crinkled, and he knew the matriarchal inquisition was about to become more insistent.

'Go on with you, boy. Most girls are the same. Pure dynamite. Don' touch the fuse until you're sure she's what you want. And then do it proper. No livin' tally. Get married, see. 'oo is she? What does she look like? You can always bring 'er 'ome, you know that. We 'aven't got a lot, but I could make some cakes and she'd be most welcome.'

An unexpected distraction was caused by Barnaby's decision to jump on the table. Irate at this blatant feline insurrection, a flouting of a strictly imposed taboo, Mam swept him imperiously off it with her right arm and prepared to resume the remorseless questioning of her captive son. The cat slunk away to seek solace on the Rayburn and having had a slight respite from the ceaseless interrogation, Gareth decided to tell the truth.

'Mam, it's not that simple. She's a married lady.'

Mam's face had turned gravely sour, and this could only presage a sudden eruption.

'Now, boy, you know that's unwise. I'm not chapel, but that's forbidden fruit. She's another man's and you mustn't meddle there. Are there any children, then?'

Gareth raised his arms in a gesture of protest. 'No, Mam, it's not like that. I just feel sorry for her. They're fundamentalists and she doesn't have much of a life.'

This obviously didn't mean anything to Mam.

'Fundamentalists? What on earth are fundamentalists, boyo?'

A trifle reluctantly, Gareth proceeded to explain.

CHAPTER THREE

On Wednesday it rained. This curbed any intention she had to garden, an activity that maybe unconsciously Ruth found a solace. In one of her furtive dissenting moods, she reflected that this at least was something which would not warrant the fundamentalists' disapproval. Did it not say in Genesis something about stewarding the earth? Mankind had not heeded this and according to the environmentalists, mankind was well on the way to extinction.

Right now, she was trying to ward off depression, a condition the sect disregarded, attributing it to the ludicrously primitive idea that anyone suffering from it could be possessed by demons. Any mental condition could apparently be attributed to the sufferer's shortcomings. You were instructed to have faith, examine your soul, repent and trust God to cure your assumed transgressions. This attitude also applied to sexuality. Deviance from the 'norm' could be rectified by prayer and self-determination. The 'treatment' included laying on of hands and a preposterous notion that those of gay and other 'abnormal' inclinations could be 'cured' and saved for eternity.

The rain showed no signs of abating and descended from dark, lowering clouds, the like of which she had never experienced in Africa. She tried to tell herself that her adopted country had compensating contrasting seasons but found the sun in too short supply and the winters hell.

The phone rang and she persuaded herself to answer it. Sometimes she didn't bother, then felt ashamed because she found the usual conversation about prayer meetings or the new special school the fundamentalists were building in the city to make sure their offspring were not sullied by the outside world, merely engendered a feeling of disinterested ennui.

But this call lifted her spirits and then almost immediately quashed them. Gareth wouldn't be coming today. Had to go to another job with his boss. Was she all right and he'd be back tomorrow? What she wanted to reply and what – after a moment of tremulous hesitancy – she actually said, were two polarised things. She wanted to tell him she'd miss him, felt like shit and was so disillusioned with the fundamentalists that she was tempted to walk beyond the thistles on the riverbank and into the river itself. Most assuredly, this would assuage her depression and eliminate her dreadful misgivings once and for all.

'Fine, thank you, and where are you today?'

And how many times when depressed had she gritted her teeth and affirmed that all was well when it wasn't? It did not do to look people frankly in the face and declare something like, 'I feel dreadful. I suffer from clinical depression.' The reaction from the few people she encountered in the outside world like the postman and the dustmen, all of whom were otherwise perfectly amenable, would probably produce blank stares and cause them to hastily discuss the weather, or rapidly go on their way without further comment.

And as for the fundamentalists.

'The barn conversion. The boss has got a bit behind and I'm helping out.'

He didn't sound as if he was enjoying it much and she dared to hope that her feelings were not unrequited and with a pang of conscience, immediately tried to quell them.

'Oh. Oh, well, I'll make sure the tea's ready first thing tomorrow. What time will you come?'

How trite that sounded, but it didn't seem to have any other effect on him other than to make his speech jauntier.

"bout half-eight. I look forward to it!'

Elisha would be gone by then and perhaps they could have the tea and a chat in the kitchen? On the other hand, what on earth was she thinking of? Startling her, the doorbell rang, and she used it as an excuse to ring off and answer the door. She'd forgotten her mother-in-law was coming for coffee and to discuss plans for the weekend fundamentalist gathering in the church hall. Both buildings had been cleverly converted from industrial usage and were now ready to host fundamentalists, who would attend from a wide area.

As a 'dutiful' wife, Ruth would be helping with the catering, and a stickler for correct procedure, her overbearing mother-in-law was calling to make sure Ruth knew what was expected of her. Unlike her biblical namesake, the young wife was not enamoured where her mother-in-law was concerned but could bake and prepare food in a highly satisfactory manner and would make sure she'd not be faulted on that score.

'Hello dear. Not a very wholesome day, is it, but we have to take what the Lord chooses to send, don't we?'

That excruciating smile. Ruth wondered what would happen if she gave that smug face a good slap. Gareth had told her the barn conversion was at Dinedor. Only a mile away. Maybe when mother-in-law had left in her obscene great Volvo – some were allowed better cars than others – she'd take a walk down that way. It couldn't do any harm and if several of them were working on the barn with Gareth, it would be better than seeing him on his own.

By some miracle it stopped raining and her mother-in-law having left, Ruth cast any doubts to the back of her mind and set out.

CHAPTER FOUR

Hugo made an imposing figure. He stood on one of the supporting beams of the unfinished barn conversion, his muscular torso bare, his binoculars trained on the young woman who was walking down the lane which skirted the pig farm. What he discerned obviously met with his salacious approval and he nearly lost his footing when Gareth snatched the binoculars from him and proceeded to berate him in a surprisingly harsh manner.

Down below, Tony the boss ceased the strenuous efforts he was making with a lump hammer, sauntered out onto the newly constructed terrace and gazed upwards. The altercation drifted down to him from above. It was an unusual thing to occur, and it did not worry him unduly. Gareth and Hugo were usually firm friends and for all his macho appearance, Hugo was just a big pussy cat and wouldn't hurt a fly.

'Somethin' wrong?' A wiry, slimly built and slightly taciturn character, Tony ran a good ship, and his men were always left in no doubt over who was in charge.

The girl was now only a couple of hundred yards away and descrying her, he could see why she could well be the cause of the aerial dispute. It did not take long for her to come up to him and he answered her greeting with a nervous smile. He had met her briefly when they'd started on the extension, and he assumed she'd come to talk about it. He thought it highly unlikely she'd come to complain of some impropriety by Gareth, but if it was to do with some flaw in their workmanship, he was surprised she'd come and not her husband. He didn't think fundamentalist women had anything to do with that side of things and couldn't imagine what she wanted otherwise.

Making a swift and noisy descent, Gareth and Hugo soon joined the couple on the terrace and their sudden incursion caused an awkward interval to ensue. Eventually Gareth summoned up enough initiative and courage to speak.

"Ello Ruth. Nice to– to see you. Was there something you wanted, then?'

The girl blushed in a delightfully old-fashioned way and even the lecherous Hugo had to admit to himself that she was not the type with whom you'd take liberties. Her hesitancy was palpable, and Gareth had to resist a strong inclination to dispel her slight timidity by inappropriately putting his arm around her.

'I– I just– uh– just fancied a walk, so I thought I'd get some exercise and see what you guys were up to. I must say it certainly looks like it's going to be a magnificent home for someone…'

Gareth was pleased to hear her use the word 'guys', a surprising deviation from what he imagined was approved fundamentalist terminology.

She soon had them eating out of her hands and Gareth could not help noticing that her chignon had gone, and that her hair hung down in an untended fashion to her shoulders. She accepted the offer of builder's tea made on a primus stove and tried not to contort her face as she drank it. Some of the discussion that concerned TV programmes, politics and world news she found largely beyond her understanding and Hugo's interest in what might win the 3.30 at Haydock to her, was utterly incomprehensible.

Tony came out of his shell to talk about his children and Gareth detected a moistening in Ruth's incomparable eyes. He knew she'd been married three years and though his thoughts were entirely without foundation, he suspected that Elisha had a 'fundamentalist' attitude towards sex. He didn't think Elisha would have much imagination where that was concerned and wondered how satisfied Ruth could be with the situation. Realising that he had now become hopelessly smitten, Gareth had the wayward thought that despite Mam's admonishments, he'd take his chance if the opportunity arose.

With a slight panic, Ruth consulted her watch and realised the interesting company and conversation had made her loiter for longer than she had intended. It was now 12.30 and Elisha usually got home at one. He had probably rung, been puzzled when no answer had been forthcoming, and would most likely fulminate at length upon discovering his dinner was not on the table.

13

Gareth proposed to conduct her home, an offer she refused, and aware that this attempt at gallantry would have taken place in his time, Tony quietly suggested they all return to work. There were no hard feelings between the two employees and Hugo opted to put his binoculars back in his car. Thus placed, they would be ready for tomorrow night's bird twitching: an unlikely pastime for one of such macho tendencies, but as Tony had said of him in his broad Herefordian brogue, 'You shouldn't judge a book by its cover, mind!'

CHAPTER FIVE

Hot and bothered, she stumbled up the driveway to find Elisha awaiting her in the porch. He was obviously in a very agitated state.

Without waiting for an explanation, he launched into a withering and unrelenting condemnation of her, and not allowed any respite in which to defend herself, she burst into tears.

What happened next became a hideous memory that haunted her for the rest of her existence. Elisha forced her arm behind her back, compelled her to walk inside and virtually made her crawl into the master bedroom.

*

It is sometimes said that a good number of people with bigoted beliefs are permanently on a knife edge. If something arises to challenge their purblind creed, they may not accept it at first, but when the penny drops, it destroys them, and they seek refuge in completely contrasting worldly philosophy.

Elisha was not naïve. He had noticed a change in Ruth and was aware that it had happened since the building of the extension had brought Gareth into her life. Conflicting emotions enveloped him. Anger and remorse: anger about what he was convinced she had done and remorse at his subsequent treatment of her. She'd denied any wrongdoing, but he didn't believe her and the discarded chignon which she'd neglected to restore, in his view, had given her away. Nevertheless, his appalling abuse of her had been inexcusable. Panic stricken; he wondered what the fundamentalists' elders would do if she appealed to them about his behaviour. They'd probably take the hypocritical biblical stance that asserted a man had every right to expect his wife to accede to his demands regardless of her lack of consent and not believe or disregard her accusation of assault.

Elisha hadn't waited to find out. He didn't really know if the law could condemn you for raping your wife and wasn't prepared to wait for any potential recriminations. He'd departed the scene in his powerful motor and sped to Abergavenny where he caught the Welsh Government train for Holyhead where he hoped to embark on the ferry to Ireland. He'd cunningly decided not to be seen leaving Hereford station and left his car in a back street of the Welsh border town. He had an undisclosed bank account in Dublin, and he hoped it would keep him going for a while until he decided on what he might be able to do in the future. He also knew of a cousin who had defected from the sect and with whom, against all the rules, he had kept in touch. Now conceivably quite deranged, he imagined his flight would ensure his damnation in the sect's eyes, but as he now barely believed, he was more intent on avoiding a long stretch in HM prison than contemplating an afterlife in an implausible hell.

*

Still trembling with shock, Ruth had somehow managed to ring her in-laws. In answer to their invasive probing, she clammed up and requested they come round as expeditiously as possible.

Elisha had a 'business' laptop in his small home office and the password was carelessly and unwisely displayed on a piece of paper nearby. She'd been tempted to use the laptop during his absence on other occasions, had resisted the temptation, but now had no qualms about doing so. She booted it up and discovered that an act of 1991 established that a man could indeed be prosecuted for marital rape. This included penetration of the anus, mouth or vagina when consent had not been granted and with Elisha having also assaulted her, she thought the next move would be to contact the police.

Of course, she hadn't allowed for the attitude of senior elder and father-in-law David. He arrived like some Old Testament prophet, declaring that the matter should be dealt with internally. He seemed more concerned that the fundamentalists avoid adverse publicity than he was with Ruth's obvious distress. His customary elder's beard almost bristled as he insensitively questioned her, and she could tell he did not believe her accusation of rape.

To give her credit, mother-in-law Sarah looked dismayed, but knew it would be pointless to intervene. David was the senior elder and what he decided was usually deemed sacrosanct and not subject to dispute. Not so Ruth who, though traumatised, still had enough gumption to defy this patriarchal and chauvinistic stance. At the same time, she managed to tolerate her father-in-law's hypocritical ranting with some forbearance but decided she might take what must be an unprecedented step for a female fundamentalist and contact the police herself.

With preposterous unconcern, David opined that he thought Elisha would soon return and if he didn't, Ruth might be asked to leave the sect and lose everything. He stated that the scriptures did not accept that a woman could be defiled within marriage and that her 'false' accusation alone could be enough to convict her and cause her exclusion from the fundamentalists. He would consult the other elders but didn't hold out much hope.

With almost callous disregard, David left her to it and Ruth had some small satisfaction in noting that her previously despised mother-in-law, revealing herself to be more of a woman than a diehard fundamentalist, was close to tears and could not bid Ruth farewell.

Following their departure, Ruth flung herself on the grotesque brown couch and wept without restraint.

CHAPTER SIX

Gareth hadn't expected the reception he received at the bungalow the next morning. He tried not to respond when Ruth warmly embraced him, but to no avail. He became a victim of conflicting emotions. The spectre of Mam chastising him slowly vanished, and it did not take much to relish the unexpected fervour of Ruth's welcome; at the same time being bewildered by it. Something must have gone drastically wrong between Elisha and herself. He did not demur as she clutched his hand and led him into the kitchen where she invited him to take one of the high stools whilst she made the tea. He noticed her face had become the colour of vellum and had a distinctive bruise upon it. Her hands shook as she performed the motions necessary to fill the kettle and she did not take down the stark black mugs from their hooks without difficulty. She had this thing about loose tea and insisted it tasted better than teabags. He had to agree, especially as his mam had exactly the same take on the subject. But the process required a teapot, and she nearly dropped the highly decorated vessel as she removed it from the shelf.

He made to help her and Jesus, this evolved into another clinch and with helpless resignation, he succumbed: savouring her unbridled response and thinking it a preferable sort of heaven to the one he purported to believe in. This earthly nirvana lasted some time, but eventually concluded and he held her at arm's length in an enquiring manner.

'What on earth has happened?' he asked, already having a suspicion that she'd somehow been a victim of Elisha's ire.

In reply, she gently sat him back on the stool, and fetching the singing kettle from the stove, poured its contents into the teapot. Not without some hesitancy, she proceeded to make him au fait with the horrific happenings of the previous day and aghast at this revelation, he wanted to comfort her once more, instead of which she persuaded him to pour the tea.

'An' where is Elisha now?'

She shrugged and pulled a face.

'Heaven knows, or if you'd believe all the crap I've been indoctrinated with, maybe Hades is his destination? He just shot off in the car. I wouldn't know where he is. I don't care and as far as I'm concerned, he can rot in hell!'

Gareth reflected that the 'old' Ruth would never have come out with a word like 'crap.' It seemed things had changed dramatically.

'Dew, girl. And has your father-in-law contacted the police?' Cognisant of how serious Elisha's unbelievable defilement was, Gareth was convinced that the help of the law should now be sought and passed his arm across his brow where tension had caused perspiration to gather.

Ruth laughed derisively. 'Him? That fat, autocratic old bastard! According to the holy book, rape within marriage is not possible. He won't involve the police. Amazingly, he won't accept that his precious son has done anything wrong! The matter has to be settled internally, you know, and I shall probably be chucked out for making an unfounded accusation!'

Gareth found his own choler rising.

'But that's heinous. Surely the fact that Elisha's done a runner proves his guilt?'

Ruth gently put her hand over his. 'Ah, but you don't realise how narrow and hypocritical they can be. Elisha has a distinct advantage. The fundamentalists are a patriarchal movement, and Elisha is a man and furthermore, the son of the senior elder. They'll brush it all under the carpet and if he turns up, nothing will be said and even more unbelievably, I will be expected to resume my supposed marital obligations without further dissent. That is, if I've not been kicked out before the "prodigal" returns!'

Gareth could hardly contain himself.

'For God's sake! You can't allow that to happen. You must go to the police yourself. Expose the bastards for what they are!'

Those glorious eyes of hers conveyed a hint of fear and he was prepared for her to appeal to him. To contact the police would most likely instigate a manhunt and he didn't know if she had the courage to go through with it without his support.

His anger under control, Gareth left the stool to its own

devices and put his arm around her. He kissed her again and addressed her positively. It hadn't taken a moment for him to make up his mind. He would be her knight in shining armour and put the infidel fundamentalists to flight. It would be all over the city's local newspaper and with luck, finish them off for good.

'How would it be if I came with you?'

'Come with me?'

'To the police.'

'You'd do that?'

'Of course...'

Another long embrace and he had to tell her something that, by now, must be obvious to her.

'I– I love you...'

She gave him her radiant smile. 'What makes you think I didn't know that, but it's nice to be told.' She entwined his work-ravaged digits with hers and said, 'And please be assured, Mr Jones, that I feel exactly the same way.'

His expression became rueful. 'Mam won't like it at first, but she'll come round. She 'as a heart of gold and won't be able to resist you.'

'You've not talked of her before. I'd like to know more about her.'

Before answering, Gareth amused himself by dismantling her recently restored chignon and she did not protest. The fact that the fundamentalists would consider his action an act of flagrant desecration did not concern her anymore, and she revelled in the attention he was giving her.

'You'll like my mam. She's a Christian, but a compassionate one.'

Ruth's laugh was again derisive. 'Huh– I don't think the fundamentalists know what compassion is and they don't seem to have heard of "judge not lest ye be judged".'

Her expression suddenly turned to dismay. She became highly agitated and regarded Gareth with a redolent look of indecision.

'Gareth, I have to tell you... I'm sorry...' He showed concern as she continued. 'It might be a while. It was an horrendous experience...'

He patted her shoulder and was all assurance.

'Oh that,' he said, 'I can wait. Let's put first things first. Would you like me to take you to the police station in my old van? It's laden with bricks and other building stuff, but it'll get us there and I think the sooner we make a move the better...'

CHAPTER SEVEN

The police sergeant was very sympathetic, but unaccustomed to having a married woman complain of rape. She questioned Ruth extensively and concluded that something must be done.

A manhunt would have to be set in motion and despite Ruth expressing fear at what the fundamentalists might do in the way of retribution, a kindly inspector insisted that a search for Elisha would have to happen. He intimated that the sect were the ones who would have to worry. For once, they would learn what it was like to be on the wrong side of the law and the only worry he had was over Ruth's continued occupation of the bungalow. Her explanation that she was only allowed to reside there with her husband per favour of the elders, caused the senior officer some disquiet. The fact that rent was not paid could be a stumbling block and might mean she had to leave. This would be compounded by her 'perfidy' in getting the police involved against her father-in-law's wishes and now her only hope could be Gareth.

Gareth assured her that his mam would come round. Ruth could have the spare room. They'd go and see Mam after leaving the police station. He'd then take her down to the barn conversion to ask Tony for the time off to help her move in a hurry. There would only be her personal things. The furniture and fittings, being the property of the fundamentalists, would have to remain there and though afflicted by recurring doubts, she felt unable to raise any serious objections and went along with Gareth's proposals.

He poured scorn on her fears that Elisha might return and further molest her and pointed out that whilst friend Hugo was normally the most even-tempered guy on earth, when sufficiently roused he could be a formidable opponent. She would have enough people protecting her, including the police, and displaying a bravura he did not entirely feel, Gareth drove her back to the bungalow to collect the meagre 'goods and chattels' she claimed as hers. He then diverted to inform a surprised Tony of his intentions and from there, quickly departed to confront Mam.

CHAPTER EIGHT

Gareth had never known his mam speechless. Taciturnity and Mam were not bedfellows. Quietly ensconced behind his *Daily Mirror* in the corner of the kitchen, Da tried hard not to be amused.

But Mam was also soft-hearted and was soon inviting the 'girl' to sit 'over by there' whilst uttering repeated 'Dew, Dews' and 'Ych a Fi' as she made the tea and listened to Ruth's horrific story.

Yes, Ruth could have the spare room for now – this with a severe look at Gareth! – though thought it fruitless to hope it might not become an annex for the two of them. She did not approve of people living 'tally', a word they used to describe unmarried liaisons in South Wales, and hoped that her son knew what he was letting himself in for.

Given an explanation of the fundamentalists' creed, Mam was appalled. These people were far worse than her chapel-going neighbours had been with their non-conformist attitudes to 'demon' drink and licentious living, but at least they'd showed some tolerance and compassion, and if you were hard up, made sure you didn't go hungry. 'Ych a fi', but these – what were they? fundamentalists – were beyond her comprehension. To outlaw your own family for dissention? That was beyond belief and utterly inexplicable to her.

'Come over by 'ere, girl,' she said, 'come and have a cwtch!' and standing up, enfolded the lovely, violated young girl in her arms.

Relieved, Gareth knew the first hurdle was over. There would be others, and he idly began to speculate what the future could hold. He even mulled over the idea of her obtaining a divorce and wondered what complications this would cause with the fundamentalists. They probably wouldn't acknowledge it. They would almost certainly 'cast out' adulterers and other supposed malcontents without qualms or have any notion that their half of the marriage breakdown could possibly be at fault.

Their dogged stance on such matters was born out the next day. It transpired that in her anxiety to leave, Ruth had left one or two items in sheds and in pots and feeling slightly better, felt the need to retrieve them.

Gareth took her back to the bungalow without hesitation and briefly wondered what would happen over the extension. He imagined Hugo might be dispatched to finish things off, as in the circumstances there was no way he could finish the job. On the other hand, the fundamentalists might opt to pay Tony off and bring in another contractor. His boss would not object to this. The fundamentalists were not the most punctilious payers and were well behind with their remittance at the moment. This suggested that in order to preserve this negligent attitude towards payment, they'd leave things as they were.

Arriving at the bungalow, Ruth found an envelope containing an uncompromising note. She was given seven days to find alternate accommodation, an indication that the police had moved swiftly. The fundamentalists were obviously au fait with Ruth's visit to them and this defection was enough to bring about her immediate exclusion from the sect. Gareth doubted if they could do this by law, but neither of them cared. Ruth wanted out and thanks to Mam's willing acceptance of her, she could almost relax and attempt to forget her appalling experience for a while.

CHAPTER NINE

Hugo viewed the brightly coloured goldfinches through his binoculars. He was pleased that someone had provided a separate bird feeder for them, for goldfinches needed one to themselves and now that the bungalow was unoccupied, he'd make sure to bring the correct bird food for both them and the other birds whose feeder was suspended near the ornate bird table.

He moved the glasses to focus on the fruit bearing mulberry tree which intrigued him and decided he would not choose to stand beneath it in a white shirt. He knew of a friend who had done just that and with the berries fully ripe and dropping, suffered the consequences from stains which were difficult to remove.

As predicted, Hugo had changed places with Gareth when, despite the upheaval at the bungalow, the fundamentalists had rung Tony and requested he finish the extension. Hugo thought Tony a canny old bugger; one of his stipulations for continuing being that the timorous sect bring their outstanding account up to date and not fall behind again. Hastily, they complied and the wise move to install Hugo for Gareth showed Tony to be an altogether shrewd operator. If left to finish the job, Gareth might be questioned as to the whereabouts of Ruth and this way it could be a long time before the fundamentalists found out where she was. On the other hand, they may have washed their hands of her and unless Elisha returned determined to wreak further vengeance, Tony reckoned Ruth had little to worry about. Elisha's re-emergence seemed unlikely. He was now a wanted man and as Shiela, Hugo's pragmatic partner, commented in her blunt 'south of the river' way "E'll either get caught 'n get what 'ee deserves, or we wunt see 'im again.' She added a postscript which involved herself and the application of a pair of scissors to a certain part of his anatomy which made even hardened Hugo wince, and this graphic description of what would be a horrify-

25

ingly rudimentary operation evinced a certain amount of humorous comment from ribald topers in the pub, who would otherwise spend their drinking time boring each other with bad jokes.

Hugo was no saint and had once or twice strayed during their fifteen-year partnership, but had been persuaded to toe the line with similar threats to his masculinity. He'd become reconciled to his lot and was now satisfied that he could do worse than to stick with Shiela.

The more he surveyed the garden, the more he became impressed. In one way he thought it sad that Ruth had had to leave. Gareth, who currently talked of no one else, had informed him that the well-kept plot was Ruth's sole handiwork and Hugo was particularly taken with the lily pond that had attracted moorhens, plus one or two ducks and who knows what else in the way of pond life. His binoculars picked up dragon and damselflies and what would be lurking in the pool's depths in the way of fish would be interesting to find out.

'Excuse me!'

Startled out of his reverie, Hugo swivelled round to confront a bearded, indignant individual whose glare of obvious disapproval earmarked him as some bigwig in the fundamentalist hierarchy. His sudden appearance did not serve to make the muscle-bound builder the slightest bit uneasy. He was more than a match for any balding, late middle-aged adversary and letting his binoculars fall at ease round his neck, he bid the newcomer a basso profundo 'good morning'.

This flustered the elder for a moment. He was father-in-law David and he ran an unsteady hand through his receding hair before managing to utter what was a rhetorical enquiry.

'You work here?' And then somewhat sarcastically, 'That is, when you're not otherwise occupied?' This undoubtedly a reference to Hugo's apparent tendency to make time for his bird and wildlife watching propensities whilst on the job.

Deadpan, he answered the question in the affirmative.

David wanted to know more. 'What happened to the other man?'

This, thought Hugo, was typical of the fundamentalists. He'd latched on to their odious creed pretty quickly and interpreted it as a sort of religious apartheid. In their eyes, unbelievers were rank low life. You tolerated them when it suited, employed them when necessary, but seldom bothered to find out their names. And this David seemed a particularly purblind and bigoted example of the fundamentalist species.

But Hugo wasn't having any. Belying his assumed macho persona, he could switch to talking a fair version of the Queen's English if he chose and he wasn't disposed to let this condescending elder ride rough shod over him.

'By the other man, I assume you mean Gareth?'

'If that is what he is called.'

With difficulty, Hugo constrained himself. Much as he'd like to take this pompous and obnoxious creature down a peg or two and leave him in a ditch somewhere, it might not look good in the *City Times* if he were to be done for grievous bodily harm! He wondered why the elder was showing an interest in Gareth and it dawned on him that though contemptable, David was pretty acute and had sussed who might have aided Ruth's swift departure from the bungalow. Find Hugo's mate and conceivably find Ruth? Hugo wasn't going to reveal anything and, well aware of the next question that would be forthcoming, was determined not to answer it truthfully.

Disconcerted and vacillating, the elder pulled an expensive looking fob watch out of his waistcoat pocket, studied it briefly, returned it to its recess and continued in his efforts to try and extract information out of Hugo.

'Uh, you wouldn't know where this – uh – Gareth happens to live?'

Hugo played along. He was an old hand at fabrication and not adverse to indulging in it now.

'I should do, since he's also a good friend of mine. Unfortunately, he lives in a not very salubrious bedsit in Meerschaum Wood.' Meerschaum Wood was a suburban area not unlike an inner city and the perceptive builder knew this would probably stop the elder from enquiring any further.

But father-in-law David persisted.

'Oh well, does he live on his own?'

'That's right.'

Hopefully this monstrous lie would put the older man right off the scent. Hugo still did not understand why the fundamentalists would want to know where Ruth had gone, unless it was a fear that she'd open her mouth too much and Elisha's despoliation of her be too readily exposed from the horse's mouth.

But it must be too late for that, and from what Gareth had told him, the police had already labelled him a fugitive and instigated a manhunt. Posters would be put up and they would make use of social media. The *City Times* would have a big spread and Elisha's defection might even make the TV news and do the fundamentalists a good deal of harm. The paparazzi could well come sniffing round the industrial estate where the sect mostly operated and from what Hugo had learnt, the fundamentalists would probably clam up and threaten their employees with dismissal if any of these slightly despised minions expressed deprecatory opinions of their employers to the press.

Realising he wasn't going to get any further, the bearded elder gave Hugo a brief ungracious nod, turned on his heels, exiting the extension and striding imperiously round to the front of the bungalow where he'd left the car Hugo hadn't heard come, fired it up and departed. Perhaps it was just as well he hadn't witnessed the basic sign Hugo favoured him with before resuming his interrupted pastime. Hugo was now viewing an unusual bird that had just alighted on the bird table.

Maybe a brambling, with similar markings to a chaffinch. Not that uncommon, but he hadn't seen one on a bird table before. He'd have to ask the guys, the twitchers, who were meeting tonight in the pub for a swift one before going for a look at what birdlife might be found in Helmont Woods.

CHAPTER TEN

Weeks passed and the hue and cry over the wanted man died down. All leads had hit the buffers and the fundamentalists had weathered the storm caused by publicity in the press, some exposure on the TV news channel and had girded their loins over the possibility of an investigation of their sect by 'Panorama'.

Mam and Ruth's relationship had blossomed, and they'd ventured into town several times, confident that the fundamentalists no longer posed a threat. It seemed that Ruth had been put on the backburner as far as they were concerned, and encouraged by Gareth, she gradually began to embrace the benefits of the twenty-first century. She bought a copy of a magazine that promulgated tasteful make up tips, this serving to enhance her natural beauty even further, making Gareth's forbearance where sexual matters were concerned all the more worthy. He had to keep reminding himself that her experience with Elisha must have been unimaginably horrific and hope, as in the case of some women, it would not put her off further intimacy for life.

Mam knew of this café which had opened to support veterans in Broad Street. It was a pleasant place near the cathedral that she liked to patronise, and where they would be unlikely to encounter anyone from the fundamentalists. The guiding light in this purely voluntary venture was a jolly and welcoming lady called Marianne who could not be said to be exactly sylphlike. Portly might be a slightly underestimated description of her and like most ladies of her ample proportions, her inclination towards generosity matched her physique. She made a sponge cake for which most would die and gave Ruth, as a protégé of Mam's, preferential treatment. Ruth had been admitted to the gossiping circle of mainly no-longer young ladies as Gareth's 'young woman' and gradually assimilated the technique of talking about other people without being particularly bitchy. The ladies were obviously curious to know more of Ruth's background, but Ma determined not to enlighten them, and since the police had kept

29

secret the reason they sought the errant Elisha – to the media's annoyance – no one save her new 'family' and the fundamentalists knew of her involvement as the victim of the crime.

Today's meeting of the garrulous 'memsahibs', as usual, was engagingly lively and more contented than she'd been for some time, Ruth sat by the wide picture window contemplating the glorious cathedral over the road. People sat on seats before it consuming salad boxes or other things edible in the sunshine, and a good number of the passing pedestrians were accompanied by dogs. She'd often longed for a pet of some sort and had taken to Mam's Barnaby, who had decided her affection would not be unrequited and spent a lot of time occupying her lap. The fundamentalists did not allow pets of any sort, for what biblical reason she could not imagine, and for the umpteenth time she reminded herself how lucky she was to have escaped their clutches.

But this assumption could well be premature. Ruth went deathly white as she glimpsed the severe looking woman currently passing by the window. The woman paused and maybe out of idle curiosity glanced in and hesitated before wending her way. Ruth was sure the woman – her mother-in-law – had spotted her, and not aware that the ceaseless chatter of those around her had faltered, tried to comprehend what the lone voice of Mam was saying. It was definitely mother-in-law out there: there was no mistaking the chignon and the accusatory expression.

'You all right, girl? You've gone ever so pale. Dew, what's the matter?'

They all began clucking with concern and Marianne hovered nearby with a glass of water.

CHAPTER ELEVEN

A woodpecker was unusual. A flash of green and red, commandeering the bird table and putting the other birds to flight. Hugo didn't need his binoculars to regard this marvel, but his contemplation of it was cut short as the sound of a rather loud and unhealthy engine negotiating the drive to the front door attracted his attention.

He supposed he should investigate, but before he could rouse himself to do so, a car door slammed, and a figure came quickly round the side of the house to the annex. Dressed in a besmirched t-shirt and jeans with holes in the knees, his hair in dire need of shearing, the young man addressed Hugo cheerfully.

'Hi, I'm Simon, work for the "funguys" down at the warehouses. Come to tidy things up. Know where the key's kept? They said it'd be under a pot by the back door. That right?'

Hugo looked critically at the young man's right arm, which a tattooed snake adorned, and caught the eye with its venomous presence. Hugo loathed tattoos, especially on women, but refrained from commenting.

'Just a minute. You say you work for the "funguys". Is that an impolite way of referring to the fundamentalists?'

The youth was nothing if not confident, though a little surprised at the massive artisan's command of the native tongue.

'Sure, you know, the po-faced lot. We've got various names for 'em. Mind, some of their women are pretty fit an' I wouldn't mind...'

Hugo could not help being amused. 'And I don't imagine you indulge in that sort of talk in front of them?'

Unabashed, Simon shrugged. 'No, we ent allowed free speech where they're concerned. Just shut the fuck up 'n get on with the job, that's all they want. Mind, they don't say a lot to me. I'm too useful to 'em. I kips their machines goin'. Cost 'em a lot more t' get someone in every time summat goes wrong.'

Yes, thought Hugo, this was probably typical of the fundamentalists. Use people in the wider world when it suited; humour those like this Simon, whose 'dress code' would normally never pass muster, and rule less able employees with a rod of iron!

'D'you know why she went? I know 'ee did a runner and the p'lice are still after 'im. I don' know what 'ee did but the joyboys 'ave clammed up. They ent sayin' nothin'!'

'No to all that and if you like to go in there and do whatever it is you've come to do, there'll be a cuppa char available in about 'alf-an-'our. Why are you doing it anyway? Shouldn't be too bad. From what I can see, the girl looked after it pretty well. Is someone else movin' in?'

Hugo was still apt to drop his aitches, despite every effort his refined mother had made to cement them in place. His physique came from his father, his intellect from his mother, and he always felt grateful to them both.

Simon didn't waste words. 'Some of their sort from up north somewhere. 'Ee ent very well and they need a' 'oliday, so ol' Solomon says.'

'By ol' Solomon I take it you mean the late occupier's father, David. And when are this couple moving in?'

'Don' know,' Simon became animated, 'but look, I'd better be getting' on with it. I'll come back fur the tea in 'alf-an-'our.'

'You do that.'

It would have been useful to know when the bungalow would be re-occupied, though Hugo realised that his bird-watching activities might have to be curtailed because of it. The couple might not be so well disposed towards him as Ruth had been to Gareth. The fundamentalists also liked their pound of flesh and although the annex was near to completion – just a little more painting and floor laying to do – he knew his movements would be watched for any sign of slacking.

CHAPTER TWELVE

As befitted their status as leaders of the sect in the city, David and Sarah inhabited a tall, gabled house situated on the hill leading up to British Camp at Dinedor. The significance of the ancient hill fort was lost on them. Like most fundamentalists they were almost wholly blinkered by the Bible and did not acknowledge any other religion as having any relevance whatsoever. How they would have coped in dispute with a determined and cogent atheist or an intellectual Sikh, or even a Christian of another persuasion, would have been interesting, but since such confrontations never occurred, it remained a matter for conjecture. On one occasion, a member had rebelled and become an agnostic, his creed of 'I don't know' getting short shrift, resulting in him being thrown out and exiled from his family with remorseless lack of sympathy.

This evening there was to be a meeting of the elders and Harvey, the prominent leader from Manchester, had been invited to attend. The high-backed chairs were distributed round the long oaken table and the seven august fundamentalists took their places with David at the head of it, Harvey to his right and the others distributed in order of seniority. One surprising quirk of the fundamentalists allowed for alcohol to be drunk at home and both red and white wines were being liberally partaken of by the assembled hierarchy. A lot of church business was dealt with in a comparatively short time and thanks to David's astute chairmanship, 'any other business' could be afforded more time than was customary. David brought up the sensitive matter of his son and the allegations Ruth had made against him. He suggested that they should take a different stance, invite Ruth to retract her accusation and thus enable Elisha to return to the fold.

There were several objections to this. One elder didn't see how they'd persuade Ruth to recant, particularly as they'd banished her, and her present domicile was unknown. Furthermore, another said, how would they notify Elisha that it would be safe to return if, likewise, they had no idea where he was?

At this, David produced a wry smile and to their astonishment, declared that he knew precisely where his son was living. Gasps of amazement greeted this statement and Harvey, their Mancunian guest, deemed it prudent to intervene.

'I'm sorry, Brother David, but are you telling us you know where your son is and haven't told the police, who, I understand, have been trying to find him for weeks? Don't you think that dishonest?'

To fortify himself, David re-filled his glass with red wine, and addressing his guest made to answer the question.

'Brother Harvey. We did not go to the police. I think it was my errant daughter-in-law that did that. I wanted to deal with the matter internally. There are times when the biblical teaching overrules the law of the land, and I also think there was another factor that caused my son's flight. I think my daughter-in-law was unfaithful to him and this made him possibly behave a little more irrationally than he normally would.'

An elder with a more liberal outlook on things, Amos, saw fit to intervene. 'Are you telling us you knew where your son was all the time and for the good of the sect you chose to keep quiet about it?'

The leader had a prompt answer to this. 'No. As a matter of fact he rang me only yesterday and this is why I am glad we are having this meeting tonight. I have several, I hope, God-given answers to deal with the situation and I would like to submit them for your endorsement and approval. My son is living with a friend, an ex-fundamentalist, in the small seaside town of Balbriggan, north of Dublin. I—'

'Just a minute,' interrupted Harvey brusquely. 'You state this friend is an ex-fundamentalist, and is it not a sin to fraternise with those who have lapsed from among us?'

'Just so, but I have been in touch with the senior elder for All-Ireland – his phone number is in our world-wide directory – and explained the circumstances. He thinks it distinctly possible that both Elisha and his friend could be re-admitted if they show true repentance for any sins they may have committed, and Daniel Tovey approves of their re-instatement.'

Daniel Tovey was the supreme leader of the UK and his permission and approval would clinch the matter.

'But,' persisted David, at the same time looking round the table to make sure he had their full attention, 'the only way we are going to achieve this as far as I can see is to get that wretched girl to withdraw her accusation. And this is what I propose…'

What he had to propose provoked heated argument. Nothing like it had been done before and the implementation of it stretched the boundaries of biblical interpretation. To give him his due, David was prepared to put his neck on the block over it and after a lot more dispute, the elders voted in favour of their leader's plan by four votes to three, with Harvey permitted a vote by general consent. It remained to be seen if Sarah and Harvey's wife, Hannah, would not baulk at the part they were being asked to play in it and it fell to Amos to remind the company that, being female, they would have no choice in the matter, though this was one sexist rule of which he furtively disapproved.

CHAPTER THIRTEEN

The inspector was puzzled and talked to his sergeant about it.

'Why would they want to know where she lives when they've not long shown her the door?'

Sergeant Morrisey sucked through his clenched teeth, a habit he had when about to dispense a certain amount of rustic wisdom.

'Dunno, boss, but I wouldn't put anything past that lot.'

Inspector Halliday needlessly adjusted several objects on his desk before replying. He'd had this phone call from the fundamentalist leader asking if the police knew where the girl now lived. He thought it odd, since they hadn't exactly been co-operative over the quest to find Elisha. Although this was possibly understandable. They wouldn't want the publicity engendered by his trial, and in some ways might be relieved if he was never apprehended. On the other hand, he was the son of the leader and au fait with their considerable financial clout, the inspector knew that they could deny any transgression on his part by quoting the Bible: not a plea that any jury would necessarily ignore. It would be his word against hers and as the alleged violation was within marriage, should it come to it, the fundamentalists could afford the very best of lawyers, and who knows what the outcome would be?

Not that he wasn't firmly on the girl's side. He'd been looking at the sect's activities and history on the internet and been surprised to find that they were not without blemish. He anticipated that his sergeant, a wily old character and a light under a bushel, would tell him more.

'You don't seem impressed, sarge?'

The inhalation through the teeth repeated itself.

'Big case in the States, boss. They were killin' sacrificial lambs in a not very pleasant way. American Supreme Court ruled it unlawful and they 'ad to stop it, but for all we knows, it might still be goin' on illegally, even in this country. Then they was givin' funds t' the right-wing Australian government and makin' their members vote for 'em whether they wanted to or not. Biggest scandal was when their world leader 'ad an affair with some young woman and got kicked out...'

The inspector raised his arm in a gesture which suggested he'd heard enough.

'OK, sarge. You're confirming something of what I've been reading online.' Still waters run deep, he thought. You never knew what the deceptively intelligent sergeant was likely to come out with, and his surprising general knowledge had come in useful on more than one occasion.

Deep in thought, Inspector Halliday briefly studied the photo of his family on his desk. They were an uncomplicated lot, not apt to stray or possessed of anything other than minor faults, and he thanked the Lord for that. He labelled himself an agnostic and attended his local church in Tupsley, a western district of the city. It didn't do any harm to being seen there and his wife liked to go, declaring in her cultured ex-Malvern Girls' School tones that the vicar was an 'awfully nice chap' and they should make the effort to support him. The other Sunday he'd been surprised to see Gareth, the girl's supposed new amore in church with an older couple he assumed must be his parents. He'd not seen the lad since he'd come to the station with the girl and aware she was now living in Whittern Way with his family, hoped the fundamentalists would not discover her whereabouts. Unfortunately, given what the sergeant and he knew of their devious ways, he didn't think it would take them much effort to find her. She couldn't remain a recluse forever and had been seen in town by more than one of his officers who'd been told to keep a close eye, and he just hoped he could prevent any harm coming to her in the near future.

CHAPTER FOURTEEN

Harvey had objected at first, but not that well, and had finally given way.

His wife would have special dispensation to discard her chignon for the purpose of entering the veterans' café in Broad Street. Having departed from the sect before the visiting Hannah had arrived, Ruth would not recognise her. An outgoing personality, in all probability the Mancunian fundamentalist would be able to quickly forge an embryonic friendship.

Sarah took her into town in the Volvo and they arrived in Broad Street just as the cathedral clock intoned the hour and ponderously chimed eleven times. Wednesday was the city's traditional market day, though in the opinion of many of its inhabitants, the cattle market itself had long since been mistakenly moved to a site out of town. A mixture of stalls, livestock and lively auctioneer's banter, the old market had been a colourful place where most things could be purchased and many cash deals clinched between robust farmers. Good meals and good company could be had at the old established farmers' club and in the interests of commerce, the pubs stayed open all day.

The famous giant-killing football club played at nearby Edgar Street, somehow contriving to play a home match most Wednesday nights and after a day in the market and the hostelries, many a worse-for-wear Mid-Walian farmer would declare he didn't have time to go home and return for the match. Therefore, to solve this minor difficulty, he would disport himself in the 'Welly' – the Wellington Inn – or some other pub until near kick-off time. He would then make for the turnstiles in a hurry, hip flask secreted within the folds of his overcoat, and now adequately equipped with well-lubricated vocal cords, proceed to chastise the referee over nearly every decision the poor official happened to make against the home side!

Nominally a follower of Christ and his teachings, Hannah donated a few coins to the beggar who sat disconsolately outside the library, and given a photograph of Ruth on the girl's wedding day, felt sure she would recognise her without difficulty.

Sarah had gone off to park the Volvo and could be rung if required. She would stay in town to shop and wait until summoned by Hannah, whether the mission had been accomplished or not.

As it happened, nothing could have been easier. Hannah had simply walked into the babble of noise generated by the gossiping women, ordered a coffee, smiled at one or two of them and sat down next to the instantly recognisable Ruth. She'd seen a photo of her and was not mistaken.

Full of unrestrainable Welsh curiosity, Mam leant across the table to address the newcomer.

"Ello and welcome. You new to the area?"

Unlike most of her kind, Hannah was perfectly prepared to be gracious to those who were not of her persuasion. She didn't see why she should treat unbelievers as lesser mortals. She reckoned they were disadvantaged enough without being condemned and frowned upon because of it. In her opinion all humans were God's children, and she was happy to leave any assessment of them to God. She hadn't dared to express this viewpoint to the menfolk in their church, but she had the feeling that Harvey, afflicted by a potentially terminal illness, might well be persuaded to take a more broad-minded attitude.

The Welsh inquisitor was exceedingly garrulous and introduced the young woman as 'Rosamund, my son's friend', a statement that both mildly startled and then relieved the listening Ruth, who felt irrationally disturbed and a helpless spectator of this verbal exchange.

In turn, Hannah had no qualms about falsifying her background. She informed Mam that they'd come to the city from Bolton. She said her husband was not well and they'd sought somewhere more conducive to live. Frantically trying to conjure up the name of a suitable suburb, Hannah came up with the somewhat undesirable estate known as Meershaum Wood. She'd heard it mentioned on a local bus she'd caught, and plucking it from some recess in her mind, did not realise that the place could hardly be described as 'conducive' and was not somewhere where the retired and indisposed might choose to settle.

Mam did indeed look surprised, but aware that there were some nice spots on that rough estate, assumed that this new acquaintance and her husband had found one, and were evidently content with what they'd acquired.

It did not take long for Hannah to become fully accepted as a member of the circle or to achieve her goal, with generous Mam soon handing over a note of her address and extending an invitation for Hannah to call 'any time'. Knowing what would feasibly transpire from her complicity in David's plan, Hannah could not help accepting it with a degree of guilt and the non-participant in this exchange, Ruth, had a gut feeling that Mam's gesture could be premature and possibly misguided.

CHAPTER FIFTEEN

Harvey and Hannah enjoyed the prospect before them. The lawn, with its surrounding rowan trees, sloped down to a ha-ha, and beyond that, a few token cattle grazed peacefully in a meadow which gave way to a dark, brooding wood.

Unlike most of their inhibited sect would have chosen to do, the couple had encouraged Hugo's bird-watching propensities, invited him to lunch, and displaying a surprisingly liberal approach to most topics encouraged him to expound his theories on a wide variety of subjects.

Harvey's slowly advancing illness had prompted him to reassess his thinking. He'd decided to resign his position as senior elder of his northern church and the awesome fact that he might not be in existence much longer had imbued in him a far more tolerant attitude to mankind and life in general. He already regretted his compliance with what he saw as David's underhand machinations and with chagrin, realised that what he'd agreed to was, in his case, verging on the edge of hypocrisy. If anything, his reluctantly involved wife now felt even worse about assisting in the action to be taken and wished she had not agreed to set it in motion.

'And you're saying Amos is trying to attempt this abduction. Knowing him, I'm surprised. Isn't he the one that nearly always tried to temper a lot of the harsh judgements the elders make?'

'Undoubtedly, but I think David has something on him. He has to do as he is told if he doesn't want it revealed to all and sundry. Besides, he does have help, though they've been unsuccessful so far. Two big lads, the nearest the fundamentalists have to internal police with their Old Testament strictures. They are constantly watching the house, but the girl never seems to leave unaccompanied.'

Hannah was intrigued. 'You mean to say these two are on the pay roll to maintain law and order within the sect and what could David possibly have on Amos?'

Harvey started to chuckle, but it turned into a cough and his wife handed him the glass of water which stood on the cane table between them amongst various samples of current church literature; the attempted perusal of which had filled Hannah with increasing disinterest.

Her nose for interesting scandal well and truly alerted, Hannah questioned him further.

'And what might Amos's transgression have been?'

Recovering, Harvey ruminated for a while before answering. He liked to think they had no secrets from each other, but if Amos's alleged sexual deviance ever came to light, the elder would be finished.

'I'm told it only happened once or twice. She was fifteen and a bit of a madam by all accounts.'

This revelation did not unduly disturb his wife.

'Was this recent?'

Harvey shook his head. 'No, Amos was apparently quite young when it happened and according to David, he hasn't strayed since, but as David sees him as the best vessel to carry out this so-called abduction, Amos is not going to refuse for fear of being exposed.'

Hannah expressed her obvious disapproval.

'Good heavens! Talk about double standards. The more I hear of this duplicitous local leader, the more I dislike him. And if Amos and his brace of thugs succeed in abducting this girl, where are they going to keep her? I'm beginning to think the whole and idea stinks and wish I hadn't agreed to help.'

Harvey had to conquer a frequently recurring bout of coughing before he responded.

'I'm afraid you didn't have much choice providing I concurred. I did voice my objections at the time, but we are purely guests here and it would have been churlish to show dissent.'

*

Hugo busied himself picking up the ripe mulberries from the dust sheet he'd put down for them to fall on. They'd been dropping for a couple of weeks, and he'd already taken quite a number of bowls to Hannah, some of which she'd frozen and on one occasion used as an ingredient in a delicious summer pudding. Hugo was savvy enough to know that trying to pick the berries off the tree would result in a lot of squashed fruit and that his method of leaving them to descend in their own good time would prove more successful.

He'd nearly finished the annex and were it not for the fact that he'd been commandeered by Tony to help with one or two unexpected hitches they'd encountered in the barn conversion, he would have completed it. He could not deny that his growing relationship with the unusually amenable fundamentalist couple in the bungalow, coupled with his slight tendency towards a little procrastination, had slowed things down and he had to admit he'd miss their company when he'd finally finished. There were very few days when he'd not been invited in for lunch, tea was plentifully supplied and apart from having to stoutly resist any inclination to reveal the former occupant's whereabouts, he found both Harvey and Hannah engagingly normal.

They'd obviously been told by the devious David that Hugo had not been working there in Ruth's time, but his predecessor could well have been the cause of her questionable downfall. However, they hadn't pursued the matter and for that Hugo was mightily relieved. His loyalty to Gareth was rock solid and it was great that he would no longer have to lie through his teeth to them. Thanks to Hannah's incursion into the Broad Street veteran's café and her acquirement of Ruth's true address, Hugo's lie over Gareth's non-existent flat being in Meershaum Wood had been exposed but did not cause David to do anything about it. He wanted the annex finished and though furious with Hugo, was now concentrating on the attempt to abduct Ruth and would deal with the errant builder later.

You couldn't see the annex from the living room, and that part of the garden containing the mulberry tree was only just visible round the side of the bungalow if you went to the window.

This Hannah had just done, and seeing Hugo collecting the berries, announced to her husband that she was off to the kitchen to brew some more tea.

CHAPTER SIXTEEN

To reach the pub they'd taken the road through the lammas meadows, crossed the small bridge over the meandering Lugg and were now sitting in the hostelry's well-tended garden. This was a novel experience for the still partially traumatised Ruth, and with twilight embracing the inn and its environs she found it soothing and relaxing. They'd had an excellent meal, traffic on the busy main road had decreased, and apart from the muted conversation from imbibers seated at other tables, not much could be said to disturb the scene's tranquillity. An odd dog barked intermittently and occasionally one of the patrons with whom Gareth was familiar would pause at their table in passing, most likely intrigued by the stunner who accompanied him than by any desire to engage him in conversation. He seemed to be well acquainted, a regular at the establishment, and Ruth was more than content to leave their polite enquiries to him.

The wine had helped and the port and lemons which followed had increased her feeling of well-being, making her glad that alcohol was the one supposed vice the fundamentalists had tolerated.

The couple with whom they had just exchanged pleasantries moved on and Gareth gave her a quizzical look.

'Apart from the obvious, girl, somethin's been botherin' you lately. That's why I brought you out 'ere. Thought it would 'elp. Care to tell me?'

Even in the encroaching late August gloom, she found his small-boyish and concerned face irresistible.

'No– no, not really. Nothing more than normal. It's wonderful out here. I love it and really appreciate your thoughtfulness. You are a dear.'

He leant forward and took one of her hands in his, at the same time giving her one of the gentlest kisses imaginable. Sated, he then drew back and raised his eyebrows in decidedly inquisitory fashion.

'I 'aven't known you long,' he said, 'but you're a bit of an open book. One thing 'bout the way you were raised. You were taught not to lie and that's surely one good thing that lot instilled into you. So, come on, out with it. I'm only trying to 'elp.'

Ruth hesitated, then decided it would do no harm to divulge her misgivings.

'It's just that about the third time I went with your mam into that café...'

Gareth looked alarmed and hastily interrupted.

'Mam? What's Mam done?'

It was her turn to put a reassuring hand on his.

'Nothing, please listen. That time we went into the café, an elderly woman came in and sat down next to me. All your mam's ladies and Marianne, the proprietor, were very welcoming. The woman was immediately accepted, but there was something about her that made me suspicious.'

Gareth looked puzzled and shrugged his shoulders. 'Why?' he said and reverting to his fading Welshness, a result of the increasing time he was spending amongst the native population of the border county, he continued, 'Look you, I think we'd better go back inside. Dark it is getting out here,' and him smiling, 'perhaps we could find a quiet corner an' 'ave a cwtch?'

They moved inside the ancient old inn and found a nook to themselves, with Gareth first going to the bar to replenish their glasses. Ruth was glad to observe he was contenting himself with soft drinks and when eating she'd consumed most of the wine herself. Gareth appeared decidedly sober, but she still thought it fortuitus that they hadn't far to travel home.

Settled on what amounted to a bench in a corner, he looked enquiringly at her.

'So, this woman. What was so sinister about her?'

Ruth shook her head from side to side.

'Oh, heavens. No, she was to all intents and purposes quite normal. Except that she reminded me of the women in our lot.'

'Your lot? You mean the fundamentalists?'

Ruth looked slightly bewildered, taking a sip of what had now become a preferred cup of coffee. She, too, had had enough alcohol.

'Yes, but of course she can't have been, yet she was a little too forthcoming. Your mam wrote down our address and invited her to call anytime and it worried me. Fortunately, the woman hasn't been in the café since, but your mam mentioned her the other day and for some reason it's disturbing.'

Suddenly enlightened, Gareth began to fondle her hair and unobserved as they were, she did not attempt to stop him.

'Listen, my love, wouldn't this bogey woman character have the standard thing in her hair that all the fundamentalist females are stuck with, and you had before you left them, see?'

Ruth's face contorted, a happening scarcely serving to make her face any less beautiful.

'You mean the chignon? She could have taken it out temporarily. They could have seen Mam and myself patronising the café and sent her in to try and find out where I was living…'

It was Gareth's turn to look bemused. 'But, dew, why would they want to contact you so soon after throwing you out?'

'I don't know, but maybe Elisha's returned in secret and preposterous though it may seem, they want me to withdraw my accusation. He'll never escape a trial otherwise, and according to the Bible – or their interpretation of it – he's not in the wrong.'

Gareth remained perplexed. 'An' how they goin' to get you to change your tune? Why would you do that just to save that bastard? It's a no-brainer. If I 'ave anythin' to do with it, you won't go anywhere near the scum. I can't believe that's what they're scheming and anyway, did the woman give Mam her address?'

Ruth was enjoying the feel of his gentle hands through her hair which, now emancipated from the restrictive symbol of her former religion and unfettered, hung gloriously down her back and in Gareth's not too romantic words, 'kept her arse warm'.

'No, she didn't. She just said they'd come down from up north and bought a property up in Meerschaum Wood. I could tell your Mam didn't think a lot of that but was too polite to say so and the woman declined to reciprocate with her address, saying they were still in a mess from moving and she'd see Mam again when things had settled down.'

Gareth had a sudden illuminating thought and feasibly jealous of the attention he was giving Ruth, Bella, the overweight pub canine, came across in an obsequious manner, being inclined to seek attention wherever she could. This did not distract the besotted Gareth from caressing the girl's plenteous locks, but not to be denied, the dog put her snuffling nose in Ruth's lap in anticipation of having her ears scratched and was not disappointed as Ruth duly obliged.

'I think a combination of a lack of alcohol and your close proximity has befuddled my brain,' stated Gareth, 'and I don't know why I didn't mention it before now. Days ago, Hugo told me this couple had moved into your old bungalow and now I come to think of it, the woman sounds just like the one you've been describing. He says they're pleasanter than most fundamentalists tend to be. They invite him in, give him lunch and I wouldn't mind betting you they're your couple that supposedly live up Meerschaum Wood! They come from up north and she's a fading blond with no make-up, just like you describe!'

Ruth started to feed Bella some of her crisps and hoped the landlady couldn't see her doing it. You don't feel overweight Labradors processed potatoes, but unused to the empathy you can have with animals, when it came to resisting the portly creature's overwhelming entreaties, she was helpless and could not get enough of it.

'So you think this woman – the wife – is the one that came in the café?'

'Definitely,' asserted Gareth.

'And how do we find that out?'

'Simple, see. I take you out the bungalow and you stay in the car out the way. I knock on the door and with luck she answers it. It most likely be 'er 'usband won't appear. Hugo says he's unwell and bein' careful not to reveal yourself, you take a quick look and cower down on the back seat. She won't know me – I left before they came and Hugo won't let on – and I ask for directions to Hoarwithy, which she probably won't know. She could try and consult Hugo, but he'd hear my old van come and scarper into the wood. He can always use the excuse that he's seen a rare bird fly into it and from what he says of them, they have a lot of time for 'is bird-watching tendencies and will understand.'

Ruth smiled, and hoping they were not observed, gave him a passionate kiss, an action that seemed to bemuse the still adoring Bella, who ponderously backed away before returning to beseech the amorous couple to supply her ample stomach with further edibles.

The embrace concluded, Ruth caught her breath and in a pseudo-facetious manner said, 'My Welsh hero. You are a genius! But doesn't this place ever close? Shouldn't we be getting back?'

Gareth stood up and pulled her to her feet. 'No such thing as closing time these days and this pub stays open later than most.' He took her hand and escorted her to the door, acknowledging the landlord's farewell and the farewells of others he knew in the bar.

A rather forlorn, though hardly undernourished, Labrador followed them, her extra-mural ambitions over consuming taboo victuals not entirely fulfilled, and only a stern admonishment from her slightly sozzled 'lord and master' prevented the dog from accompanying the couple to their car.

CHAPTER SEVENTEEN

Inspector Halliday took the call from Sergeant Morrisey, who, before handing the receiver over and whilst talking to the caller, had indulged in a good deal of teeth-sucking. When engaged in this habit, it could reliably indicate the gravity of the information being imparted, and if its repetitive nature suggested something pretty serious, then the sergeant had reluctantly to cede his own preference to settle the matter to higher authority.

'Inspector Halliday here. Can I help?'

The caller was very ''ereford' but as is the case of most indigenous mortals of the Marches County, came quickly to the point.

'I wants t' report suspicious activity where I lives.'

'And where would that be?'

'I lives in Whittern Way an' there's this car that comes and goes at different times with these two blokes in it. Sometimes they just sits there for a long time. They don't live round 'ere. I knows most of 'em uz lives round 'ere an' these two sometimes comes two or three times a day an' at night. I reckons there up t' no good.'

The inspector sighed. Probably nothing could be implied from this, yet Morrisey had a nose for potential trouble from unlikely sources and wouldn't have handed over the phone without trying to appease the informer himself.

'And d'you know the make of car?'

'Yes. I's a 'ybrid 'onda, quite new. Wine coloured, reg number WVJ ...'

Inspector Halliday had heard enough, and mentally kicking himself, wondered why the penny hadn't dropped sooner. Whittern Way was where the girl now lived, and the fundamentalists wanted to renew their acquaintance with her. On the other hand, would they really employ a couple of 'heavies' to try and kidnap her? And what would they want with her anyway? He almost dismissed the possibility out of hand, but something told him not to take any chances. He didn't want clever clogs Morrisey ending up saying 'I told you so' and perhaps it wouldn't help to send a patrol car up there to investigate at intervals.

He re-addressed the caller, who'd been rabbiting on regardless in the way the locals had of repeating themselves and asked for the man's name.

'Wayne 'Iggins,' obliged the caller, 'an' I'm only trying to 'elp.'

'Of course you are,' reassured the inspector. 'And you can help us by ringing back if you spot the car in question and we'll send a patrol car up to investigate. However, as these two characters haven't as yet committed any noticeable crime, we can't make any promises, but thank you for calling and do get in touch if you see them again.'

He put the receiver down rather abruptly and turned to meet the expectant gaze of his subordinate.

'Sarge, I thought you were wasting my time at first, but had it not occurred to you that Whittern Way is where the girl Ruth now lives? After we received that call from the fundamentalists, as you know, I instructed a patrol to keep an eye on her, but they wouldn't have passed by very often and I still don't know what the fundamentalists could want with her after they initially banished her.'

Mollified that he hadn't put two and two together himself, Sergeant Morrisey became unusually subdued, and the inspector took advantage of his taciturnity to continue.

'So I think whether or not that upright citizen that just rang us does so again, we'll get the patrol lads to spend a bit more time up there, even though it might be a complete waste of time. Better be safe than sorry and I still can't get my head round the fact that a so-called religious sect might be up to no good where that girl is concerned.'

The teeth-sucking at this juncture not evident, the sergeant simply said, 'You know what I thinks, Inspector. Wouldn't put nothin' past 'em. Rum lot they are; an' my ol' granny would likely as not tell 'em t' go 'n jump off the end of Weobley Pier!'

With some difficulty, the inspector contrived to summon up his severest expression. The fact that there might be a pier at picturesque black-and-white Weobley, a village entirely surrounded by land, was news to him, but not a local, he still recognised it as one of the sergeant's not infrequent leg-pulls.

'I thought your granny long dead, Morrisey, and even if the sea did penetrate as far inland as Weobley, I don't think such a drastic action would meet with the chief constable's approval, especially as he inhabits the same village!'

CHAPTER EIGHTEEN

'Oh, don't look now, but a patrol car has just pulled in up by the shop!'

Joseph deemed this nothing to worry about. A large example of humanity, he just read his Bible, tried to live by its doctrines and did what he was told. Not so Mark, of similar build but not inclination. Alarmed, he was all for leaving town. Agitated by the sudden presence of the law, he felt the urge to put his foot down and get to hell out of it before trouble descended upon them. Unfortunately, he wasn't in the driving seat, and he knew Joseph couldn't be persuaded to budge once he'd made up his mind. Mark flinched as the patrolmen approached and one of them tapped on the driver's window. Joseph duly obliged, pressing the button to let it down, at the same time casting an innocent look at the officer.

'Yes, Constable?'

'Sorry to bother you, sir, but we've received a report that you've been seen in this area several times a day recently, and though I'm sure you're engaged in legitimate business, it would help if you confirmed what it is. We can then go on our way without bothering you further.'

Joseph didn't do facial expressions. With slightly obvious distaste, he contemplated the young policeman for a moment and said, 'Can I ask who this person is that allegedly reported us for no apparent reason?'

A relatively new recruit, the officer looked decidedly uncomfortable and appealed to his colleague, who duly obliged. 'We can't reveal that, sir, but maybe if you could perhaps tell us what you do and whether you live round here, we'll say no more and bid you good day.'

Mark might well resemble one of the bruisers employed to keep out or eject the undesirables who tried to inhabit the clubs and alehouses in Commercial Road on a Saturday night, but he was certainly not 'tuppence short of a shilling'. Seeking a chance to intervene, he did not stick to the rules as readily as Joseph and thought a white lie might well help the situation.

'Umm, as a matter of fact, we're looking out for a former member of our faith who's made off with some church valuables and we've been told he's gone to ground round here.'

'And what church do you belong to, if I may ask, sir?' The first patrolman again, seeming decidedly sceptical at Mark's doubtful response.

His doubts were confirmed when Mark replied, 'the fundamentalists'. Both police officers were aware of this, had been apprised of Ruth's defection, knew the house where she now lived and realised that Mark's hastily contrived deceit was a cop-out.

The senior patrolman contrived to put on his sternest expression and realising that the police might know more of Ruth's whereabouts than they were letting on, Joseph glared at Mark and waited for the inevitable admonishment he anticipated was about to be administered.

It was not long in coming. 'I'm sorry, sir, for reasons best known to us, I believe what you've told me to be untrue, and I think the best thing you can do is to disappear without delay. Also, a word of warning. If we catch you loitering in this area again, we'll take a more serious attitude. So we'll bid you good day and hope not to see you here again.'

The patrolmen walked briskly back to the patrol car and with reluctance, Joseph turned the ignition key of the Honda which, being a hybrid, was barely audible as it slowly moved off.

Joseph decided they needed to reassess the situation and turning left at the end of Whittern Way, drove over the hill by the Cock of Tupsley Pub and parked in the old road, which now did duty as a layby.

CHAPTER NINETEEN

Elisha liked to visit the beach, which could be reached by walking under one of the railway arches. Here could be had a view of the centuries-old harbour and that strange anomaly, the Martello tower. The tower had been constructed by the British, supposedly to defend Ireland from invasion: an unlikely happening in those days, since Napoleon was having enough difficulty in merely attempting to subdue England. Another prominent landmark was the disused lighthouse which had once served to guide the ships that navigated Howth Bay.

Fingal County was a glorious part of the world and the fact that his old friend, Matthew, had a whitewashed cottage on the outskirts of the town had been a godsend. It had been simple to keep in touch with Matthew by email and fortunate that Ruth, as a woman, had been denied access to his computer.

Another defector from the sect, Matthew had simply become wearied of the straight-jacketed, purblind life he'd been leading and fled to the Emerald Isle. He was now enjoying a questionably immoral existence with a delightful local girl called Mary who, even more delightfully, did not recognise immorality as anything tangible and was currently trying to encourage the dour Elisha to form a relationship with one of her friends: a spirited young lady called Maeve.

Mary worked in a local bar, and when his innate indolence could be overcome, Matthew helped out in the same busy establishment's restaurant. They'd also secured a place there for Elisha, and to his surprise no questions were asked. He was 'off the books' and keeping his mouth shut, found he quite enjoyed the work. He'd been warned not to appear too 'English'. Memories were long in this part of the world. Balbriggan had been raised and set fire to by the British auxiliaries in the original Troubles and any display of superiority in this town would inflame the populace and arouse not quite buried enmity. He'd so far resisted the enticements of Mary's friend, a very pretty example of Celtic femininity, and now ensconced on the beach, he idly contemplated his future. He flinched as the Dublin–Belfast express thundered over the archways behind him and cast his eyes in meditative fashion to the steely-hued waves where a solitary sailing boat inched across the bay. He had soon become enamoured with Balbriggan and its inhabitants and did not fear possible apprehension by the Garda. To change his appearance, he'd grown a beard and providing he kept his head down, thought it unlikely the Garda would be efficient enough to find and deport him.

His arrival had been entirely uneventful. The big cross-channel ferry had made its ponderous way up the Liffey, with the customs officer showing complete disinterest in his person and outside the terminal, Matthew had awaited him in a battered old Volkswagen. The drive to Balbriggan had been about thirty kilometres and it soon became clear that the town had suffered from the excesses of the period of time when the 'Celtic Tiger' had arisen: an era of false prosperity in the nineties and early new millennium which ended with Ireland in a state of near bankruptcy.

Hundreds of houses were constructed in Balbriggan during that time and after some years of recession, things had gradually improved and most of the town's populace – numbering some twenty thousand – were again able to enjoy a reasonable standard of living.

Despite sometimes being visited by a feeling of near-contentment, Elisha often thought of Ruth and the depravity to which he had resorted. Nevertheless, the comparative tranquillity of Fingal's sublime landscape and the untroubled existence he was leading was slowly enabling him to regain confidence. He'd already contacted his father over his possible return to the fold. Hardly the prodigal son, his defection and association with the exiled Matthew were obvious stumbling blocks, but David had been very reassuring. It all depended on Ruth recanting her accusation and he was egotistical enough to be almost certain that she would. There was no way he could return to join the fundamentalists without her cooperation unless he decided to come back regardless, and if that happened, the police would surely arrest him and the subsequent trial might well go either way.

He would have to wait for further news and no way would he inform Matthew of his future plans. Disillusioned with and wholly emancipated from the fundamentalists, Matthew would probably hustle him into a local bar, persuade him to partake of too great a quantity of stout and allow the persuasive Mary to harangue him over his complete resistance to her friend and temptress, the desirable Maeve.

He had been grateful to Matthew for his kindness and unstinting hospitality but found it impossible to disavow the dictates of a lifetime. If he did become re-accepted, he'd have to try and temper his belief and somehow persuade the fundamentalists to adopt a less strict regime. He'd had a taste of the outside world, finding it far from being the potential Sodom and Gomorrah the sect depicted it to be, and considered there must be room for compromise.

A few yards away from him on the beach an attractive young girl was shepherding a bevy of small children. He'd noticed her constructing sandcastles for them earlier and she seemed very capable: probably a nanny or a big sister. She was now reading to them, and he had to admit he was taken with her delightful interpretation of 'Goldilocks and d' t'ree bears'.

Emitting raucous feline shrieks, seagulls soared overhead and his growing attraction to this invigorating vista was slowly starting to make him a creature of unaccustomed indecision.

It must be near teatime and he'd go to his place of employment – Shaun's bar in Erin Street – where they'd always give him a meal even though he'd not been doing a shift. He was not a fan of Mary's home cooking – God bless her – but providing you did not take advantage of Shaun's generosity too often, the bar was a place of great conviviality. Here the inevitable Irish banter abounded and if you wished, you could talk about nothing whatsoever for hours on end: for the slightly disturbed Elisha, an invigorating experience.

He nodded at the young girl, received a dazzling smile in return and an enthusiastic farewell from the waving youngsters. Children. That was another thing, and he pondered this as he trudged a trifle disconsolately over the beach and under the railway arch.

CHAPTER TWENTY

Six-thirty and the two fundamentalist henchmen were parked in the unofficial layby over the road from the back of the Tupsley Pub. They would later take a walk down Whittern Way and were not at all optimistic that they'd see Ruth emerging from the house on her own. As far as they could ascertain, she never ventured forth unaccompanied and now prevented from appearing in the daytime, they thought the advent of September's slowly enveloping darkness might just help the chances of catching the girl unawares.

Joseph offered Mark one of his sandwiches and between mouthfuls, outlined a possibility that he thought might well enable them to apprehend their unsuspecting quarry.

'You know that old van of his?'

'You mean the one that he parks outside the house?'

Joseph sometimes wondered about Mark. He might have a degree, but things didn't always sink in that readily. A recruit that, unusually, had joined the fundamentalists from the outside world, his convictions and common sense were not, in Joseph's opinion, particularly acute or in evidence a good deal of the time.

'Yes, you numpty, and who have we seen come out of the house with the girl on at least two occasions when we were there in the daytime?'

'Why, the young man with the pony tail that you told me used to work on the annex to her bungalow.'

Joseph sighed. 'So wouldn't you say Elisha had a good reason for treating her like he did?'

Mark was obviously not cognizant with what had happened. 'Uh, I don't know, how did he treat her?'

Exasperated, Joseph explained. He'd thought the alleged violation was common knowledge amongst the fundamentalists, but it had obviously not penetrated the brain of his intellectual though dozy companion.

Mark looked shocked at the knowledge Joseph imparted, but it had at least aroused some interest in him.

'Surely what you described borders on abuse and rape and why aren't the police treating it as such? They're not revealing the real reason for Elisha's defection. They're just labelling him a missing person and the elders aren't saying anything, and since you infer Elisha's treatment of Ruth is now common knowledge in the church, why hasn't the truth been told to the press?'

Joseph despaired. He put his hands together and genuflected skywards.

'Spare me, oh Lord, and forgive me if I have not the patience to tolerate my obtuse colleague!' Determined to get through, he put away his sandwiches and turning towards Mark, almost spat out what he had to say.

'Look, can you not see the reason the police have not revealed this so-called crime is because they didn't want the paparazzi to congregate all over the girl, and the reason David doesn't want the public to know is because he doesn't think what Elisha did is a crime!'

Mark protested. 'Rape is a crime...'

'Not within marriage, it isn't...'

Showing a bit more spirit Mark riposted with 'Who says?'

Joseph became contemptuous. 'That book you don't peruse half enough, sonny. You know, the one that begins with Genesis and ends with Revelations: the book you're supposed to study and don't seem to; the scriptures that should rule your existence...'

Surprisingly for him, Mark firmly interrupted. 'And where in the Bible does it say rape is not a crime?'

Briefly flummoxed, the private sleuth turned evangelist, soon recovered. 'It doesn't, but it does say it can't occur between man and wife.'

Showing a persistence of which Joseph thought him not capable, Mark simply said 'Where?'

This almost defeated Joseph, but his lack of response to the question was sidetracked by the appearance of two headlights over the brow of the hill. These were attached to an unhealthy sounding vehicle which turned into the layby before indicating and going down a driveway which led to Tupsley House, a large hotel where weddings and other functions were held. Even though the rapidly descending dusk made exact recognition uncertain, Joseph thought it might be their lucky day.

'Mark, my boy,' he said. 'You should have more faith. Sometimes prayers are answered and it's up to us now!'

CHAPTER TWENTY-ONE

Saying he wouldn't be a minute, Gareth had gone into the hotel to see about fixing a job for Tony. He intended visiting the pub in Lugwardine afterwards, and it was just unfortunate that he'd left her alone at the wrong time. With a reaction akin to sheer terror, Ruth recognised them immediately. She'd seen them in church and at other fundamentalist gatherings and protested violently as they dragged her away from the van. To stop her screaming, Joseph put his hand over her mouth and bundled her into the car. Struggling violently, she tried to wrestle her way out and Mark could not prevent her nails molesting his cheek and drawing blood.

Joseph swivelled round in his seat and snarled at her.

'It might be an idea if you came quietly girl! Where you're going we can do things one of two ways and I don't like to think what might happen to you if you get it wrong!'

Distraught, Gareth went back into the hotel, shortly to re-emerge with Henry the owner and some of his concerned staff. They comprehensively searched the grounds by torchlight, and a positive character, Henry persuaded Gareth not to delay in calling the police, who did not take long to arrive.

With the patrol car came DS Angela Smith, the young police-woman who'd dealt with Gareth and Ruth over Elisha's violation, and not long after, Inspector Halliday – who already had his suspicions -arrived with the 'uniforms'.

Gutted and not able to fully concentrate, Gareth attempted to answer the questions the young sergeant was putting to him. Yes, he had noticed a car in the layby as he turned down the drive to the hotel. No, he didn't have the registration number. Why would he? He'd been talking to Ruth and with its rear end towards him, how could he identify the make? Particularly as nightfall had been swiftly descending. Turning left he'd only had a brief glimpse and to his unjustified chagrin, he tormented himself for not being more observant.

It just so happened that the two young patrolmen who had arrived first on the scene were the ones that had 'moved on' Joseph and Mark in Whittern Way barely seven days previously, and not made inspector for nothing, Halliday sprang into action. Leaving Morrisey to organise the search, he had the patrol car whisk him down to Lotherwas as quickly as possible through the city's congested rush hour traffic (their progress further impeded by an accident on the Asda roundabout) where upon arrival, he intended to interview that sanctimonious and devious senior elder of the fundamentalist church, David.

There was no doubt in the inspector's mind that Ruth had been abducted by the fundamentalists and prompt action over the matter would likely spare the poor girl further distress. He still didn't understand why they wanted her back, unless in his blind arrogance, leader David thought he could get her to withdraw her accusation over his son. But from what he'd heard on the grapevine of the blossoming relationship between the young Welshman and her, Halliday thought that highly unlikely.

Upon arrival at the fundamentalist church, Halliday found it fully lit and a service in progress, and heads craned as he and the young patrolmen entered the rather plain and purely functional building. There was no altar and currently, the congregation were being subjected to what could only be described as an Old Testament harangue from an extremely vociferous and highly animated David.

Utterly indoctrinated, his audience were giving him their rapt attention. Any improper thought of dissent was out of the question and Halliday recalled the statement of a very old Jew he'd met when a young man. Prior to the Second World War, Benjamin had attended a Nuremburg rally and had described Hitler's oratory as hypnotic. Bizarre as it might seem, the inspector thought there might be similarities between the evil dictator and the verbose and frantic religious leader. Hitler had held the adoring masses in the palm of his hand and was not David doing the same thing? Was he not a religious dictator, a dangerous animal throughout history, and with the power he wielded, could his evangelistic tyranny not be used to deliberately mislead the people? Being an agnostic did not mean you had to eschew all the

Bible's contents, and hadn't Jesus said something relevant about deliberately distorting his message? Halliday hated bigotry and preferred the convivial company of those relatively open minded, simple city dwellers who attended St Paul's, Tupsley. The vicar, Reverend John Moseley, personified this open-mindedness and the inspector had never heard him pronounce judgement on any of his flock who might be said to have gone astray. On the contrary, he was more likely to find an excuse for them and his attitude towards those of differing sexual persuasion was refreshingly accepting.

David droned on, a constant note of asperity in his voice, and Halliday sensed that his two young officers felt uncomfortable and restless. Their discomfort was not helped by the occasional slightly hostile glances they were receiving from members of the gathering, and when this obvious disapproval was pointedly directed at him, Halliday made sure to deflect their gaze with an equally blatant response. They were lucky he'd shown patience, hadn't broken the service up and having done so, confronted the volatile and obnoxious David without further ado.

The patrolman on his left, PC Ben Eldridge, leant to impart something into the inspector's ear.

'They're here, sir.'

'What d'you mean?' Halliday made no attempt to keep his voice down, a little irritated that he didn't know what Eldridge was on about.

Undaunted, the patrolman continued. 'Up there, sir. Up in the gallery. The two heavies we moved on last week.'

Halliday felt he was slipping. He hadn't observed the gallery, also full of the faithful, a structure supported on piers that ran the length of the church on the right-hand side.

The fiery sermon did eventually terminate, and its perpetrator was not fazed when confronted by the senior police officer. Young Eldridge hadn't been able to identify the two assumed abductors without disrupting the service and the inspector sent them back to their patrol car to wait until needed. He didn't think the heavies would disappear anywhere – an action that would almost confirm their guilt – and he was amazed at the cool and unperturbed way the fundamentalist leader denied any knowledge of

Ruth's disappearance. David was courtesy itself. He expressed his pleasure at meeting Halliday, having previously only spoken to him on the phone and even sent a minion to fetch Joseph and Mark, who with blatant mendacity denied any knowledge they might have of Ruth's whereabouts and furthermore suggested that there might be a simple reason for her absence and hoped she'd be found soon. This did not explain why they'd made up the cock and bull story over their daily vigils in Whittern Way, but as Halliday knew the answer to that, he let it go, being more concerned to find out where she was now and where they had almost certainly concealed her.

CHAPTER TWENTY-TWO

Dublin had seduced Elisha and without him realising it, Guinness and Ireland were slowly but relentlessly destroying his convictions and his faith. He sat in a bar in Moore Street with Matthew, savouring the atmosphere and listening to the cries of the market traders, a barrage of witticisms aimed at their customers as these startled mortals endeavoured to make purchases from the veritable cornucopia of goods on display.

Either side of this bountiful and mouth-watering prospect, the often run-down properties were inhabited by mostly oriental businesses; but paying lip service to modernity also housed odd nailbars, hairdressers, a bookie and a number of cheap eating places. In the early hours fresh foods and other goods were still brought over the cobbles by horse-drawn carts, a timeless means of delivery that had been taking place since the mid-eighteenth century.

It had not taken Elisha long to appreciate how ignorant he was of Irish history. This included his complete lack of knowledge of the important role the Celts played in promulgating early Christian belief. His interest had been mainly aroused by Matthew and Mary who, despite their apparent tendency to flout the rules, were nominal Catholics and had no problem when it came to attending mass. The father would have preferred them to marry but, a wise old 'fart', he'd become reconciled to their liaison, listened to their confessions and each time satisfied himself by imposing on them a few Hail Mary's 'to be going on with'.

Elisha had been examining the bullet holes in the fusilier's statue in exotic St Stephen's Green when his new mobile had rung with a momentarily alarming call from his father. He'd been tentative when giving David the number and hoped his father had not supplied it to other fundamentalists. He'd resisted the temptation to purchase a mobile upon arrival in Ireland and had made his initial call to his parent on Matthew's landline. But he felt he could not continue to impose on his friend's generosity and succumbing to the inevitable, bought his own phone.

Trying to concentrate on what was being said, Elisha found it hard to believe. David had managed to locate Ruth and was evidently negotiating with her over retracting her allegations. He thought there was a good chance she would co-operate and when she did, he felt sure it would be safe for Elisha to return to the fold. What he didn't care to say was what the police would do. Having spent a vast amount of time and considerable manpower in their efforts to find both Elisha and Ruth, they might not be too happy, and it was also possible that they'd think that Ruth had been cowed and bullied into changing her mind.

Elisha had refrained from putting his latest thoughts into words during David's call, but now felt an unexplained disquiet usurping the tranquillity he'd been recently experiencing.

'Another?' Matthew reached for Elisha's empty glass, his intention just to take it back to the barman, who would take his time in supplying fresh drinks. You didn't rush the stout and to both Englishmen, it surely tasted better when drunk in its homeland. At first, Elisha had had qualms about drinking in a bar, gradually becoming accustomed to it and adding it to the growing list of taboos he'd jettisoned since coming to this easy-going country. Another taboo could well be shattered in the person of Maeve, a fatal attraction of another kind, slowly blotting out his vision of Ruth: a frightening situation he'd never envisaged, and one becoming increasingly hard to resist.

An altercation had broken out in the street. Not an uncommon occurrence when you had the hard-bitten Dubliners vying for trade and the not unknown sale of under-the-counter tobacco and other dubious substances being proffered indiscriminately to all and sundry.

And here they came. The Garda. Not much to worry about according to laid-back Dominic the barman. They'd soon clear things up and be in for 'a drop of d' black stuff' themselves, either in his or O'Hagan's bar a little further up the street.

CHAPTER TWENTY-THREE

Amos hadn't wanted to undertake the task of jailer, but didn't see he had much choice. The girl had been brought to the isolated and slightly run-down cottage blindfolded and restrained. Very cunningly, David had consigned this task to two other young brothers, releasing Joseph and Mark to be at church when the police were likely to waste no time paying a visit. He'd received a call that the duo had captured her and in the time they'd taken to get from Tupsley to Rotherwas, he'd expeditiously arranged for the car he'd equipped with everything she'd need to take her, with Amos and the new young minders, to the place of incarceration.

Hillchurch Common is not the most accessible part of the county even in daylight, and Ruth had no idea where she'd been taken. Despite the shabby décor, she found the cottage comfortable and with a great effort, somehow managed to overcome her apprehension and nervous tension. Allowed into a surprisingly well-tended garden, a suntrap bordering on what looked like an impenetrable copse, she found the constant company of one of the young men, Ephraim, oppressively onerous, but had little alternative other than accepting it. Ephraim was baby-faced and incapable, or just not motivated to carry on an intelligent conversation, and like his fellow minder, Peter, appeared to be completely devoted to the fundamentalist cause.

Contrastingly, the highly-strung and strangely gracious Amos did everything he could to make her captivity conducive. His manner was almost apologetic, and he stressed that her present confinement would only be a temporary measure until she agreed to rejoin the fundamentalists, a definite no-no where she was concerned, leaving her in a wholly undesirable state that could be said to be between a rock and a hard place. She riled at the mere suggestion that she might accede to their demands, but still found it difficult to lay the blame for her enforced imprisonment on the obviously disturbed and mild-mannered Amos. She was fully aware that he was only the monkey, not the organ grinder. She'd picked up that expression from Gareth, who she desperately missed, and was fully aware that the devious soul who controlled things was father-in-law David.

After a couple of wearisome and tension-filled days during which Amos attempted to unsuccessfully bring about a reconciliation, he'd headed off somewhere in the car: re-appearing shortly, accompanied by a spry and quasi-benevolent looking David, who even had the gall to wave as they approached.

Sitting on the old-fashioned sofa in the drawing room with her minders on either side, Ruth tried to calm herself in preparation for what she knew would be David's inevitable inquisition.

At first, he was almost all Machiavellian charm. He knew where Elisha was, and Elisha wanted to come home. Ruth had only to withdraw her accusations, and all would be well. The couple could be reunited, and Ruth could resume her devotion to the fundamentalist cause, magnanimously forgiven for straying from the path of righteousness.

The girl's first reaction to this preposterous assumption that she'd rejoin the specious and hypocritical sect, took her captors completely by surprise. Before they could prevent it, she arose quickly from the sofa and stepping determinedly forward, dealt her father-in-law a hefty blow across the face with all the strength she could muster.

Utterly shocked and affronted, David's demeanour dramatically altered. He instructed his two young men to restrain this impudent 'creature' and take her to her room. She must be detained there until she relented, and they were to make sure the door was locked at all times. Distressed and hapless, Amos protested in vain, and David poured scorn on him, particularly when he objected to the instruction that a chamber pot be provided for Ruth to perform her basic functions.

The senior elder then proceeded to vent his ire on the threadbare carpet. He began a ceaseless peregrination of the room and Amos watched helplessly as the startled Ephraim and Peter forcibly took the sobbing girl upstairs.

Amos attempted to be the voice of reason. 'But surely, you can't treat the poor child like that. I don't think it's very …'

At the mention of the word 'child', David came to a halt and shoved his face into that of Amos.

'Child! The woman's a vixen!' he exclaimed, a small amount of his saliva landing on his fellow elder, 'and unless she wants to end up in hell, she has to learn a lesson!'

*

An unmarked police car had followed the leading elder when he'd been picked up from home on Dinedor Hill and taken to Belmont, where he'd entered the Tesco supermarket, spending some time in the restaurant before exiting via a back way into Farringdon Avenue. Here another fundamentalist vehicle had whisked him away to Hillchurch where he'd again been dropped off, only to be picked up by the waiting Amos.

The officers in the unmarked police car had expected the original fundamentalist conveyance to re-emerge from Tesco's car park sooner or later, and after a long patient vigil, it eventually did so. Frustratingly, it drove past without the object of their surveillance inside it, he having ostensibly vanished elsewhere.

Not daunted and very thorough, the police, led by DS Angela Smith, did comb the supermarket for the elder, but uncertain what they could have detained him for, had to acknowledge he'd outwitted them. Having followed him with the idea that he might lead them to Ruth on at least three occasions, they began to think trailing him something of a waste of time, but had to do as instructed, yet knew their lack of success was making Inspector Halliday extremely agitated.

CHAPTER TWENTY-FOUR

An upset Mam was trying to console Gareth, at the same time chastising him for calling upon the Lord to bring upon 'the bastard fundamentalists' famine, plague, pestilence and eviction from the shire by the county council.

With the intention of taking his mate to the pub, Hugo had called and proposed that before visiting it they called on the unusually liberal fundamentalist couple who now inhabited Ruth's former bungalow.

A coiled spring, ready to unleash at any possibility that might restore Ruth to the bosom of her new family, Gareth did not see how that would help. But to everyone's surprise, a voice from the corner of the kitchen, seldom heard in any serious context, chose that moment to intervene, playing the sage. The *Daily Mirror* was discarded and an awakened Da bent forward from his rocking chair, eager to contribute advice.

'I should go with 'Ugo, boy,' he said quite matter-of-factly: a simple and convincing statement which, emanating from the usually reticent Da, did not fail to make an impression on Gareth. An opinion on politics or maybe a guffaw over the antics of Andy Capp might sometimes constitute Da's contribution to any conversation, although he had always shown an interest in Ruth, who'd several times declared to Gareth that she thought his Da a 'sweetie'.

Ma could not allow her authority to be undermined for long and was quick to seize upon Da's unexpected intervention. Despite her normal dominance of the household being a fact of life, when Da made one of his rare contributions, a vestige of old-fashioned female submission surfaced and when it came to really important decisions, she usually gave way.

'Did you not go up to the bungalow to find out about the woman that came into Marianne's, boy?'

'Marianne's.'

'You know, the café, Marianne runs it.'

Gareth hadn't been aware that the portly Marianne ran the veteran's café in Broad Street, but he did know of Ruth's doubts concerning the lady that had entered it for a coffee and stated that she resided in Meerschaum Wood. It was less than a week since he'd discussed her with Ruth, but an excess of overtime had meant they had not had time to carry out their intended visit to the bungalow in order to see if she was the same lady. Gareth explained what they'd had in mind and taking his cue, Hugo asserted he thought it vital that he and Gareth should implement this proposed visit to Harvey and Hannah without delay, and the fact that he seemed to be on first-name terms with them augured well for any knowledge they might have over Ruth's disappearance. Hugo thought it unlikely they'd know who Gareth was and even if they did, he had a gut feeling they'd be quite sympathetic over his plight.

Da made another comment.

'No time like the present, boy.'

'Dew, that's right. Go with 'Ubert now, Gar', there's a good notion, see?'

Mam obviously approved and clapping his friend on the back, Gareth proposed that they leave right away.

*

There were moments on the train when Elisha questioned his own sanity. The four of them were having a 'night out' in the capital and he wondered how he'd come to agree to it. The more he lingered in this seductive land, the more he felt his faith waning, slipping away, consigning him to the pit or, with questionable enlightenment, to a world of the present, earthly pleasures and a disregard for what might come after.

He knew he would not be able to disregard the enchanting Maeve much longer and his father's blandishments and hearty reassurances on the phone over Ruth's willingness to resume the marriage seemed hollow and probably without foundation. He could even admit to himself that he'd been in the wrong and hoped it would be sometime before David gave him the all-clear to come home: a summons he was increasingly unlikely to answer.

That Saturday afternoon they'd been out to see Brin na Boinne, a gargantuan necropolis on the banks of the River Boyne, erected before the pyramids and translated into English as the Boyne Palace. The passage of tombs was reckoned to be one of the most extraordinary sites in Europe and convinced Elisha that spirituality and religious beliefs were not the exclusive property of narrow-minded Christians. He understood from Matthew that ancient sites and menhirs were prolific in Ireland and an awesome fact that there were probably more per square mile than anywhere else on the globe, mightily impressed him.

Leaving the train, they'd 'hopped' on the double-decker that toured the city and were now in Kearney's Bar, just out of the fashionable Temple Bar and consequently, not so expensive. The pub had been named after Peader Kearney, a republican who'd written the lyrics of the 'Soldier's Song', now the Irish National Anthem, and Elisha found himself joining in with the rebel songs that were rendered by the lively folk group, lustily accompanied by the well-lubricated punters.

Matthew pulled a face at the group's sole attempt to bring off a mediocre Ed Sheeran number – no pop lover he – and the more stout Elisha consumed, the more emboldened he became, to the extent that he found himself grasping Maeve's willing hand: her not resisting and him slightly alarmed at what might transpire as a result.

*

Nothing of note had happened for a few days and Ruth found that her guards were becoming increasingly bored and perhaps a little lax.

Ephraim and Peter had only shrugged when Amos had proposed letting Ruth out of her room. David had not stopped long, had calmed down and Amos had achieved one small concession when the leader had agreed she would be allowed to visit the toilet when required. One of the 'boys' was supposed to station himself outside the toilet door when she occupied it, but finding it embarrassing, usually left her to her own devices.

A phone call would let Amos know when David wished to

visit. He'd have to be fetched from down below and torn in two by conflicting loyalties, Amos half-hoped one of the householders on the scattered common would notice this unfamiliar car which arrived, deposited its passenger, and went on its way. They'd almost certainly know of the isolated cottage sited at least a mile and a half from its nearest neighbour and in true country fashion, feasibly harbour embryonic suspicions.

Like the ones in her room, the toilet window had been fitted with bars and she quickly dismissed the idea of escaping through it. Some other opportunity might occur and now that Amos had not insisted she stay in her room all the time, it was a distinct possibility she could contrive some other means to free herself.

Intrinsically modest, she nevertheless knew she was certainly not unattractive and the way that the fair-haired Peter flushed when she addressed him might signify that he could be willing to help her.

Hugo's ageing but comfortable Astra pulled into the driveway and caused the bungalow's safety light to come on. They had hardly removed themselves from the car before the front door opened and a lady stood awaiting them in what Gareth hoped was a welcoming attitude.

Recognising Hugo as they mounted the two steps, she thrust out a hand to Gareth and invited them inside.

'Did you leave something, dear?' She was all fussy concern and ushering them into the high-ceilinged front room, invited them to take a seat. Gareth was introduced to Harvey, whose pallor indicated that all was not well with him, and a fit of violent coughing confirmed it, so that Hugo suggested they perhaps took their leave and come again at a more convenient time.

Harvey quaffed some evil looking concoction from a glass, gave them a weak smile, and evidently recovered, motioned them to stay where they were. He enquired whether this was just a social visit or was there something else he could do for them, and after first enquiring about their preference where beverages were concerned, Hannah excused herself and went off to make coffee.

Hugo hoped Gareth would keep quiet whilst he answered Harvey's query. He and his friend had discussed en route what they might say or not reveal and had decided the time had come to tell the absolute truth. Only they and the fundamentalists knew why the police had instigated a manhunt for Elisha without making public his alleged crime. To protect her from the media, they'd not mentioned Ruth's involvement, but now she'd gone missing, prised from Gareth's protection, the young Welshman was at his wit's end.

Hugo was convinced that it was the fundamentalists who were responsible.

Hannah re-emerged with the coffee, a worried expression on her face.

Hugo explained about Ruth's decision to live at Gareth's and whilst Harvey's eyebrows momentarily flickered at this revelation, Hannah made to interrupt.

'What is it, dear? Hugo hadn't finished…'

Hannah went over to the sick Harvey who, though distinctly ailing, felt he ought to object to her bad manners. She took his hand in hers, at the same time addressing the two young men.

'I'm sorry, dear, but I have to tell them…'

Harvey appealed to her, fixing her with his rheumy eyes, both of which were extremely bloodshot.

'D'you think that's wise…?'

Undaunted, Hannah related her experience in the Broad Street café and her acquirement of Gareth's address, establishing that Ma's young female was indeed Ruth: knowledge she'd passed on with evidently disastrous consequences. She apologised abjectly for what she now considered a serious error on her part and wringing her hands, did not see how she could in any way rectify her mistake.

Trying to console her, Harvey maintained that it would have been difficult to defy the autocratic David but admitted that he should have done so.

Pre-empting a question from Gareth, he swore that he had no knowledge of Ruth's whereabouts at present; Hannah and he had not been informed of any abduction, but they were pretty certain the fundamentalists were involved in some way. David was a canny operator and would have kept the knowledge of her possible incarceration close to his chest. Only those who had picked her up and taken her to some unknown destination would know where she was and keeping a tight ship, David would threaten hell and damnation to anyone in the know who didn't have the sense to keep their mouth shut.

*

After the two young men had departed, the fundamentalist couple looked at one another in dismay.

'And now, I suppose those two will go straight to the police and tell them of your part in this whole sorry episode?' Harvey looked distraught.

'I'm sorry if you think I was wrong, dear, but it's been playing on my mind, and I had to tell them.' His wife held his hands once more, quickly removing one to hand him the foul liquid as another fit of coughing ensued. He squeezed the one delicate hand that he loved and still possessed, then disengaged in order to pull her closer, before managing to address her.

'No, I'm just as much at fault. There's something vital I haven't told you. Something only the elders know. We were all sworn to secrecy by David.' He hesitated, then deciding he should have no secrets from his wife, continued. 'You see, David shocked us by announcing that he knew where Elisha was and hoped to get Ruth to change her tune over the alleged violation.'

His wife was horrified. 'Never! But that's dreadful. Wasting all that police time and even if Ruth co-operates wherever she is, they could still prosecute him under the law…'

Harvey nodded his assent. 'I know that, and you know that. There's only that dubious bit in Corinthians that claims a man cannot abuse his wife…'

'Even so, but what amazes me is the arrogance of the man. It's pretty obvious he's captured and secreted Ruth somewhere and even though it's probably somewhere very remote, she's bound to be found sooner or later and it's quite likely one of his minions will give the game away. As for Elisha, shouldn't we go to the police over that?'

Harvey was reluctant. 'We could, but since I was sworn to secrecy, it would be something of a betrayal, and once public knowledge, it would be all over the media and the fundamentalist cause utterly discredited.'

Hannah gave a derisory chuckle. 'Would that necessarily be a bad thing?'

Harvey returned her smile, though it could be said to be more of a grimace. He made to stand, stumbled slightly, and heavily resumed his seat. His wife's face displayed unconcealed anxiety. It wouldn't be long now. They'd offered to take him in but he'd refused, and it alarmed her to be aware that the inevitable would soon happen. Let him have his way and perhaps it would be better if they went back to Manchester before it did. The trip to these pastorale climes had been meant to invigorate him, but only seemed to have exacerbated his condition and they could well have done without the intriguing circumstance into which they'd become involved.

*

In the pub, Gareth and Hubert were debating whether they should go to the police or not. Playing the oracle, Hubert didn't think they should.

'That couple 'ave enough trouble without us adding to it. The fuzz knew about the car that parked in your road for several days and they know of David's original phone call to them requesting Ruth's address: an odd thing after they'd only just kicked her out of the sect, and I don't see it would help to land Hannah in it. It's pretty obvious who's got Ruth...'

'Ych a fa.' Gareth muttered imprecations in Welsh under his breath but could see his friend's point. He'd liked the couple in the bungalow and could see why it wouldn't be essential to have them involved.

He gave the voracious Bella another crisp and made a further attempt at his pint which, understandably, wasn't going down very well.

CHAPTER TWENTY-FIVE

Superintendent Ingram came over from Worcester to have a conference with Inspector Halliday and his officers.

The conference room in the city police station could only be described as grim. It had seen interviews with a rum selection of criminals over the years, including the last one to be hung and the last to be given the birch. Apart from various ex-chief constables frowning disapproval from framed photographs, the room had little to commend it in the way of decoration and a plain rectangular table surrounded by half-a-dozen uncomfortable chairs, did nothing to relieve the overall impression of drabness and neglect.

The local force attributed this to the merger that had occurred some years previously between the county, Worcestershire and Shropshire, and to some extent was still resented. Nevertheless, Superintendent Ingram was a no-nonsense type of law officer, fair minded and prepared not to be too hard on supposed shortcomings before he'd investigated them himself. He'd just recovered from a dose of Covid and a trifle wearily surveyed the officers who, in turn, were furtively eyeing him.

Ingram tried to ignore the noise emanating from Sergeant Morrisey, whose teeth-sucking indicated his apprehension at what the great man from HQ might choose to say or whom he might criticise.

The others present, Halliday and attractive DS Smith did not seem fazed by the presence of Ingram and were confident they'd done everything they could to solve the case.

Ingram paused to consult the laptop Halliday had put in front of him. He studied it for a while and then pushed it to one side. He was not a great advocate of modern technology. For him it was unnecessarily complex and although he could appreciate its vast benefits, on some occasions he preferred to resort to pen and paper. He had a flawless memory and granting the company a faint smile which brought his bushy eyebrows into prominence, he addressed them in his even toned, slightly nasal midland accent.

'To re-cap. This male fundamentalist violated his wife and did a runner. She came to the station with the young Welshman who'd been working on the annex to the bungalow. She informed you of her husband's abuse and disappearance and, Inspector Halliday, you informed HQ, and the knowledge of his disappearance was communicated to national and European forces without delay. Because we decided not to reveal the nature of his alleged crime and against whom it was perpetuated to protect the victim from the media, the fugitive may only have been regarded by some forces as nothing more than a missing person. Therefore, I am not convinced that the search for him has been as concentrated as it might otherwise have been.'

'But sir...' Inspector Halliday protested. The superintendent stood up and wandered round the table until he came to the inspector, putting a conciliatory hand on his shoulder.

'Not getting at you, old man. If you think about it, no matter who they are, all forces are going to give priority to highly suspected criminals rather than just missing people. True, I know they are aware of his supposed rape. But rape within marriage? Might that be questionable? It's not that long since a law was passed making it an offence and the posters we've displayed, or social media appeals do not indicate to the public at large that the alleged offender is anything other than a missing person.'

The superintendent resumed his seat and hardly able to contain her anger, Sergeant Smith stood up. She'd gone a deep shade of crimson and Ingram was taken aback.

'You wished to say something, Sergeant?'

Not noted for underwhelming timidity and armed with the ability to orate with disarming frankness, Angela Smith let him have it both barrels.

'Please sir, I think your assessment of the efforts made by us and other forces to find the two fundamentalists most unfair...'

The superintendent put up his hand in an attempt to staunch the flow of the young woman's grievance.

'OK, OK, Angela. Point taken. I admit I may have been unappreciative and as I said to your inspector, it's not this branch I'm criticising...'

Inspector Halliday attempted to pour oil on troubled waters.

'If I may suggest something, sir?'

'Of course, James. I seemed to have stirred up a hornet's nest and maybe I should go and sit on the naughty step!'

This produced a ripple of laughter from all present, making the atmosphere less strained, and Halliday waited for it to subside before continuing.

'It's just that since the abused girl has now, we think, been abducted, there is little point in withholding the entire truth about her disappearance and that of her husband from the media and the public. I feel it would help rather than hinder our search for both of them. I'm pretty certain this weird sect has her confined somewhere and feel that unhampered publicity might now be a good thing.'

Just then a tap on the door heralded the entry of a petite PC with a tray of coffee.

'Ah,' commented the superintendent in what he thought was his best grandfatherly mode, 'that's most welcome, my dear. Perhaps we should take a break now – and Morrisey, for God's sake stop sucking your teeth and drink your coffee!'

Sergeant Morrisey looked as if he'd been shot and having forgotten he'd given it up, and in a panic, absentmindedly put three lumps of sugar in his coffee.

After further discussion, the superintendent bid them farewell and left Halliday to set the revised wheels in motion, something the inspector was only too keen to implement without delay.

*

Being a Friday, Simon knocked off at noon and went home to his cottage at the bottom of Hillchurch Common. Currently there was no one to go home to except Stubby, his devoted spaniel, who spent his days with Mrs Barton, the old girl next door: an arrangement that suited Simon, who did the heavy work in her garden and generally kept an eye on her.

Girls there had been, but their residence never lasted long and he sometimes felt he'd be better off not bothering with them. Mostly bimbo types seemed attracted to him. He imagined they depicted him as 'a bit of rough' and was not at all sure he wasn't insulted by such an unflattering description. He rather fancied some of those fundamentalist girls. One or two of the wives might be a bit frustrated. They didn't have much of a life and were pretty restricted. There was some fit totty amongst them and given a chance…

On the way back from town he stopped to look at a poster on a telegraph pole. He'd passed it every day without realising who it displayed. He was not a reader and, in any case, knew the score. General knowledge it was. Driving through 'Clonker' – as the village of Clehonger was known – he tuned into the car radio and picked up 'Radio Hereford and Worcester'. The news was on and it startled him. It appeared the girl had gone missing, believed abducted, and the police now wanted Elisha for alleged abuse of her and portrayed him as a dangerous individual who might be responsible.

Simon knew the tale. You don't work in a busy warehouse without picking up the gossip. Elisha had supposedly raped her (could you do that to your own wife?) and she'd gone to live with the young Welshman. Initially, the police had treated his 'doing a runner' as just that of a missing person and knowing what an egotistical bastard Elisha could be, Simon was puzzled as to why they had taken so long to reveal the truth. He thought maybe they'd wanted to protect her from the media, but now her disappearance would be all over it and knowing his employer pretty well, Simon wouldn't mind betting that the odious David was at the bottom of it all. He knew they'd wanted her back and was acute enough to have worked out why. He'd deduced that the obnoxious elder wanted her to change her tune. David would be unable to understand why anyone should want to forsake the creed they'd been indoctrinated with since childhood and if Ruth could be made to withdraw her accusations, then all would be well, and Elisha could return from wherever he was now exiled. Preposterous though it might seem, David might even harbour a hope that the couple would re-unite, and aware of the state of play that according to the grapevine existed between Ruth and the young Welshman. Simon thought pigs would fly before that happened.

The only organisation that'd be more than a bit miffed would be the boys in blue. In theory they could still prosecute Elisha for wasting police time, although this too was an option they probably wouldn't take.

Reaching his cottage at the bottom of Hillchurch Common, Simon pulled into the garage, switched off the engine and sat in contemplation. There was always the possibility that Ruth had gone off to join the missing Elisha, a notion he immediately dismissed without further thought. That would be crazy, and getting out of the car and locking the garage, he went to fetch Stubby.

His neighbour's cottage had a latched door, and despite Simon's oft repeated entreaties, old Mrs Barton never locked it. ('Er'd bin livin' yer nigh on forty year an' didn't see the need t' change things.) Snuffling behind this easily accessed entrance, Stubby heard the car pull in and had been ready and waiting long before his master had opened the garden gate prior to striding up the path in his usual purposeful manner.

The same amenable door opened directly into the low-ceilinged kitchen, wherein the lady of the house sat surrounded by photographs of sundry grandchildren, a bulky dresser, and a table festooned with papers opened at the competition pages. Her main companion was a disgruntled tabby called Poston who resented the regular visits of Stubby but was made to endure an uneasy truce with the aid of a rolled-up and indiscriminately wielded newspaper. Adding to this volatile scenario, a noisome and extremely menacing green parrot was apt to regale all present with some utterly profane language. Having served in the Royal Navy, the late Grancher Barton had been responsible for inciting the bird to indulge in these obscene outpourings and after being treated to several renderings of 'The Good Ship Venus', it was not surprising that the startled vicar had chosen not to call for tea as often as he had.

Receiving his usual joyous greeting from the excited Stubby, Simon sat down at the table and accepted Mrs Barton's inevitable offer of a cup of tea. An unwritten law decreed he was obliged to do this and bracing himself to digest the latest local gossip, he granted the old lady his full attention. It was surprising how much she managed to learn from her confined environs and Simon had long since concluded that Ted the postman and Reg the milkman were responsible for most of her information. Delivering in the Golden Valley could involve driving anything up to twenty miles a day and with quite a proportion of the inhabitants not receiving a great deal of company, dropping off letters and milk, eggs and newspapers had to be combined with a good deal of socialising. Both occupations were surely vocations, hazardous in inclement weather and not suitable for any deluded souls that might envisage keeping to schedule and finishing the round at the same time every day. Other sources of local scandal were imparted by Mrs B's neighbour on the other side, who usually wobbled round in precarious fashion to chew over the fat and slate all and sundry, and another gossipmonger was George from Dore-Dial-A-Ride, who took her into town and to Peterchurch Day Centre every week. But the icing on the cake was the indispensable *County Times*, which Reg delivered on a Friday.

The first bit of news Mrs B related concerned Hilltop Villa and she delivered it in that slightly truculent way that most of the old natives adopted in this part of the world. If you were an incomer, it took some getting used to, but you soon realised they meant well and once established, you came to accept it.

'That car come down the 'ill this mornin'.' Mrs B knew all the vehicles that belonged on the hill and all the owners, and this beige coloured one that had appeared recently intrigued her.

Simon waited patiently for further elucidation which he knew would be forthcoming and did not dare to interrupt.

'It went over the crossroads, past the church and come back up a bit later with that same man uz I've sin before.'

Her listener felt it might advance things if he tentatively posed a question.

'The same man?'

'Yes, Mrs D'arcy – her other neighbour – reckons they goes up t' 'illtop villa, though what sort of a state that place is in I don't like to think. Ant bin lived in fur years!'

Normally an example of the male species that wasn't any more than mildly concerned with other peoples' business, Simon still enquired further.

'What did these men in the car look like?'

The lady considered this question as if it weighed on her mind and after a pause during which she leant forward to scratch the irresistible Stubby's ears, deigned to answer.

'One 'az a beard – the one az is picked up – an' the other azn't an' neither of them iz that young. Not only that, before the car comes down the 'ill, I allus sees another un come from 'erefurd direction and turn left at the crossroads. I think it 'az the bearded man in it and it comes back out a while later and goes back along the road to town without 'im. I reckons 'ee must be picked up near the church by the 'illtop car and taken up there.'

Two things impressed Simon about this statement. He was aware that his elderly neighbour must spend a lot of time at the small, latticed kitchen window which gave an uninterrupted view of the crossroads and that whatever her slight issue with mobility might be, there was nothing wrong with her still acute mental capacity. Anxious not to show disinterest, he had to admit this revelation did arouse a small amount of curiosity in him and to appease the old girl, he'd perhaps take Stubby for a walk up Hilltop way over the weekend. This seemed to satisfy her and gathering up Stubby, he took his leave.

CHAPTER TWENTY-SIX

Elisha and Maeve were walking on the beach. He found himself holding her hand and internally remonstrating with himself for doing so.

A bunch of clouds were trying to obscure the sun, hadn't yet succeeded, yet it would only be a matter of time before it fully merged and became a whole. Inevitably, it would then rain, and the couple would have to seek shelter.

On a mild day the sea looked untroubled, with several ships and small craft crossing the bay. Some were, doubtless, bound for Drogheda and the port of Bremore, and others to Dublin or Dun Laoghaire to the south of the capital.

Elisha was learning a lot from his hosts and Maeve about British history and the occupiers' treatment of Ireland in particular, and the more he imbibed, the more appalled he became. To him, Maeve was fast becoming an enchantress. An unapologetic blonde – there must be some Norse blood in her somewhere – she still had that fresh-faced highly becoming Irish demeanour. She was not a slave to fashion and with her unruly and often tangled tresses, looked unquestionably beautiful in anything she cared to wear. She had an untroubled, uncensorious attitude to life and just accepted what it chose to throw at her, warts and all.

Hardly realising it, the couple soon arrived at the old lighthouse with its distinctive white tower, and finding an external door situated on the side of it, discovered that its unlocked state enabled them to gain furtive access.

Elisha had refrained from informing Matthew of the true reason for his defection from the fundamentalists. He did not know how his friend would react to what Elisha knew in his heart had been a crime. As far as Matthew was concerned, Elisha had just become disillusioned with the whole straight-jacketed way of life and, as he had, decided to quit. As for Ruth, that was a different matter, and since the latest news concerning her disappearance in the UK would not be of particular interest in the

Republic, there'd been no mention of it by the Irish media and it was doubtful if there ever would be. Like the European police forces, the Garda had almost certainly been supplied with details of Elisha and more recently, Ruth, but sporting his newly grown beard and with an improving ability to assume an Irish accent, he was confident that the somewhat laissez faire local police would not apprehend him. He was still being cajoled and kept informed of recent events back home by his father on the phone and had to thrust the alarming news of Ruth's incarceration to the back of his mind lest it arouse too many unwanted feelings of guilt and tarnish his relationship with Maeve.

The question of whether he wanted to partake of the bewitching Maeve was becoming a quandary he was on the cusp of resolving and a moment later, she decided it for him. Her sudden action in fervently embracing him took him by surprise. He tried to resist, finding it impossible. She pressed hard against him, and he reciprocated.

'D'y' not want me?' Her voice was beguilingly sensuous. Mesmerised, and finding it difficult to reply, he eventually found his voice.

'But – uh – aren't you a good catholic girl?' He tried to sound slightly facetious and this only induced a laugh, with her squeezing that part of his anatomy which was most vulnerable.

'Ah, sure, aren't y' d' funny one. Not all catholic girls are good, y' know, and don't y' tink if they were, there'd not be so many of them?'

'But in here?' The ancient building smelt musty and utterly flustered, he hastened to observe that there was nowhere comfortable, and in any case, he was not prepared.

'By Jaisus, not to worry now. It's d' right time of d' month and have you not ever done it standin' up?

He hadn't, but did, and after they'd finished, he was momentarily haunted by visions of Ruth.

The rain was now hammering down and sheltered from this customary Celtic storm, he continued to caress her naked breasts and wondered why he'd managed to lead such a monogamous existence for so long.

CHAPTER TWENTY-SEVEN

The full story of the missing couple now being revealed, the media had been re-awakend and David was furious. Besieged by reporters, he'd put Joseph and Mark outside the office at the warehouse and leaving his poor secretary to answer the constantly ringing phone, decided to go home to Sarah.

The police were now calling it a crime and even if he succeeded in persuading Ruth to withdraw her accusations, he had an uneasy feeling that would not be the end of the matter. His action in keeping her virtually imprisoned had not caused her to change her stance. If anything, it had hardened her determination not to accede to David's demands. Fortunately, none of the small number sworn to secrecy over Ruth's whereabouts had spilled the beans, but the whole episode was rapidly becoming a nightmare, and in a dilemma, he quite unusually sought his wife's opinion. For once heeding her advice, he decided to call a meeting of the elders. He was sick of being questioned by them over Ruth and having to deny all knowledge. Then there was Inspector Halliday renewing his questioning with a vengeance. Albeit apologetically, he relentlessly probed and almost certainly did not believe the senior elder's firm denials for one moment.

Increasingly nearer to leaving the oft quoted Shakespearean mortal coil, Harvey was invited but unable to attend the meeting of elders, and he was not one those brought to attend in the minibus by Joseph, deputising for Simon, who'd flatly refused to do it on his day off.

Another notable absentee was Amos. Harvey's absence was easily explained, but David had to concoct a story to excuse the missing Amos, who hadn't been seen at his usual post in the neighbouring factory for quite a while. Deceit having become an unfortunate necessity for the senior elder of late, he informed the brothers that he'd dispatched the missing elder to help out the fundamentalist community in Cheltenham, where Covid had struck particularly badly and they were struggling to cope.

An intake of breath from the corpulent Micah, who could sometimes assume the guise of a modern doubting Thomas, caused David to look enquiringly at him.

'You perhaps have a query, Micah?'

'Not really, it's just ...'

Impatient and on a short fuse, David was not in the mood to accept dissent.

'Come on, man, spit it out!'

Micah wished he hadn't said anything. He thought perhaps he'd been mistaken but took the plunge. 'It's just that I was in the large original bookshop in Hay with my wife the other day.'

'And why were you in a bookshop in Hay...'

Micah was even more inclined to wish he'd not embarked upon what might turn out to be a revelation with a perfectly simple explanation but determined to stick to his guns. He'd merely been looking at the religious books, seeking the alternative gospels which intrigued him and thinking it likely that of all places, he might come across the odd copy here. He attempted to explain this to David, who expressed his usual purblind disapproval and wanted to know what it had to do with their current business.

'Micah, you must be aware we do not accept any of the alternative gospels or the Apocrypha. You should stick to the Bible as our founder decreed and...'

Ignoring the disapproving looks he was receiving from his fellow elders, Micah took another deep breath and boldly interrupted.

'The point is, when we were walking up to the large car park at the top of the town to head home, I'm sure I glimpsed Amos as he drove out of it before heading off in the direction of the Golden Valley. I can't be certain because we weren't that far up the hill, but my wife also thought it was him.'

'Nonsense.' David's response to this was a little too dismissive and caused one or two of the others to raise their eyebrows, encouraging Micah not to cede ground to his intolerant leader.

'I'm sorry. I'm pretty sure it was Amos and Amos's car. I may be wrong, but I don't think so.'

David spread his hands in a resigned gesture. He decided he'd better not refute Micah's assertions further and resorted to bringing into play his inherent guile once more. He declared that he'd ring the leader in Cheltenham and find out the truth of the matter. As an old friend, the Cheltenham leader would play ball if required, and yet another falsehood could be contrived to explain Amos's apparently mystifying sixty-mile trip to the World Capital of Books.

David, of course, knew full well why Amos had been spotted in Hay. He'd simply been buying provisions for the captive and captors who were ensconced in Hilltop Villa. Assumed to be in Cheltenham, he'd been instructed not to come into the city to shop and to go instead to Hay. Ironically, it was unfortunate that Micah had chosen to go there in his quest for alternative gospels, and David only hoped his devious fellow elder would not check the facts by ringing someone in the Cheltenham brotherhood.

Assuring himself that he could once more make his explanation plausible, he planted both elbows on the table and bestowed a weak smile on Micah.

'Right,' he said, 'I'll give Edward in Cheltenham a ring later tonight and I'll let you know the outcome in the morning. Don't want to bother now. We've too much other business to settle.'

*

As he ascended the hill with the vibrant Stubby scampering through the fallen leaves ahead and disappearing at frequent intervals, bent on the trail of some woodland creature he aspired to catch and never would, Simon pondered the conundrum of Ruth's disappearance and more than ever, attributed it likely to have been plotted and carried out by the sanctimonious and hypocritical David.

Even Mary and Maeve did not know of Elisha's true identity. He'd been introduced to them as 'Alan' from 'd' six counties' and that is how they, workmates and friends now knew him. A lot of English lived in the north, particularly Belfast, and though times were now nominally peaceful and the Troubles over, you didn't ask questions.

Matthew and he were discussing things in a small bar in

Balbriggan. A Saturday afternoon hurling match meant that the place was quiet, and Matthew was not surprised to know that Elisha had come to a decision over his future and was not intending to return under any circumstances. Nevertheless, he was worried about his identity. He'd need to become legitimate and 'on the books' and Matthew assured him that he knew people in Dublin that could fix an insurance number, tax record and even a European passport without difficulty. As an Englishman who'd moved to the Republic as an ordinary unblemished individual, he'd been free just to walk in just before the UK implemented Brexit. He hadn't needed false documents, but he knew others that had who were now thriving and didn't see there would be any snags where Elisha was concerned. The only thing that would not be easy to inform his father he'd not be returning, and Elisha did not look forward to what would be his inevitably outraged reaction.

During a break, there was no way David could prevent Micah from taking 'a breath of fresh air' and Micah had walked a little way down the hill before consulting his smart phone for Edward's number. He'd met the Gloucestershire elder several times on exchange visits and upon learning the truth about Amos – the Cheltenham leader denying all knowledge – he made his way back to David's in a slightly apprehensive, but almost triumphant mood.

*

Simon and his four-legged companion reached what could be called the summit of Hillchurch Common and he paused, wondering whether to walk down the overgrown track which led to Hilltop Villa. It would be just possible to drive motor vehicles down it, though it wouldn't do the suspension on them much good, and a fading sign declared the villa to be private property: non-residents must keep out. To Simon this presented both an affront and a challenge he could not resist. Accompanied by his ever-faithful spaniel, it did not take him long to walk down through the oaks and beeches to the villa. It turned out to be a four-story construction that had seen better days that was almost obscured by the trees and undergrowth that had been allowed to proliferate in front of it. The onset of an early autumn and the trees starting to lose leaves meant it was partially in view and his curiosity now fully aroused, Simon continued to follow the track which managed to penetrate the density – it looked like someone had recently cleared a way through – and came across what appeared to be Mrs B's beige car, mud-spattered and parked in a weed-infested yard.

There was no sign of life, and deciding he didn't like the idea of trespassing, he re-traced his steps.

Simon didn't really know Amos. The elder was someone who worked in a small adjacent factory that made sticky tape. Amos may have visited David in the office, but not when Simon was around and since Elisha had skipped it, Simon had been delegated to oversee his forsaken enterprise and life when at work had become extremely hectic. With the press and media constantly moithering Joseph and Mark, Simon had proposed they simply tell the marauding reporters to 'fuck off'. The aghast expression on the faces of the two sentinels had been worth it. Indoctrinated from birth never to indulge in bad language, they were appalled, but were relieved when Simon did it for them and it did have some effect.

And that beige car, why would it be bugging him? It was not a rarity. There were a few around. But what of Mrs B's description of the characters in it? The man with the beard and the other car that brought him? He had no answer and arriving at the bottom of the hill, he bundled the eager Stubby into the car and drove off to have a pint in the Nag's Head at Peterchurch. They'd probably have the football on, and he could do with something to divert his thoughts away from things that might not have any basis whatsoever for action on his part. Not taking long to arrive, he sank his first pint and joined the locals in extolling the virtues of the side they inexplicably favoured and heartily decried the one they deplored. The ale descending smoothly, this wouldn't be the first time he'd drive home over the limit. Policemen in the Golden Valley were as rare as hen's teeth and providing he didn't overdo it, all should be well.

David had gone as white as a wraith and for the first time in living memory, experienced the feeling of being backed into a corner. They wanted to know it all and Micah's disclosure aroused their fury.

Nominally David's second-in-command, the aspiring Benjamin sensed an opportunity and, in this instance, set no store on loyalty. Unusually for a fundamentalist, he was a closet vegan, and this perhaps accounted for the fact that he resembled a walking cadaver, thin as a rake, but perfectly healthy. His questioning of David was relentless and bizarrely, the whole interrogation could be likened to the fall of Caesar, except that his downfall was a mental rather than a physical one and a reference to Shakespeare probably anathema to the fanatical Bible entrenched sect.

From her eyrie in the upper storey of the villa where she'd retired to get away from her captors for a while, Ruth had banged frantically on the window. But the wind and distance the young man had been away brought no reaction. He hadn't lingered and his abrupt departure had filled her with despair.

And now baby-faced Ephraim had arrived and wanted to know why she'd been assaulting the window, a noise they'd heard downstairs. She knew who the interloper had been but was not going to divulge his name. She'd recognised him as jack-of-all-trades Simon, known to all the fundamentalists and without whom David would struggle to cope with the practical side of the business. Simon had not been slow in allotting her lecherous glances when she'd occasionally encountered him whilst picking up Elisha from an all-male gathering where alcohol was permitted, and Simon had done duty as a waiter. She would have forgiven his past lasciviousness if only he'd looked up and, like some Arthurian figure, rescued her from captivity. However, she did make the mistake of telling Ephraim of the incident without revealing the interloper's name and with his customary show of bland efficiency, he proposed to rouse Peter and head off in pursuit without delay. They would leave Amos to guard Ruth and set off, a proposition that Ruth declared would be a waste of time. Simon would be well ahead, and not letting on that he was known to her and them, she fervently hoped that with curiosity aroused, he might shortly return to investigate further.

CHAPTER TWENTY-EIGHT

Hugo had finished the annex some time ago, but out of the goodness of his heart, still called in before and after work to help the now solitary Hannah. Harvey had been admitted to the hospice, was holding his own, and with skilled professional attention, was putting up spirited resistance to the insidious disease. Hugo saw to the bird tables, had a look round the garden and very often brought odd bits of shopping from town. Only that afternoon he'd spotted a great tit, not a common visitor to the hanging nut baskets, his enthusiasm for all things avian helping Hannah survive and deal with the adversity of her situation.

All Tony's crew were now working on the inside of the barn conversion, so it wasn't a hardship for Hugo to call at the bungalow every morning and evening. Sometimes he brought a devastated Gareth along and Hannah tried unsuccessfully to console the inconsolable Welsh lad. It seemed that all his enthusiasm for life had departed. No news of Ruth had crushed his spirit and poor Mam, who'd been regularly communicating with the abject and regretful Hannah, was desperate to find a way to bring back her 'boyo' to the land of the living.

Another to be very kind was the Reverend John Mosely from St Mark's and members of the church, who'd all prayed for Ruth's restoration in their midst. Amongst them was Inspector Halliday, perplexed by his lack of success in finding her and equally disposed to commiserate at the gathering after the Sunday morning service.

Without being prompted, that lovely young police sergeant had chosen to visit several times, and it went without saying that Sheila, Hugo's 'rough diamond' missus, did her best to help.

The final bombshell had landed to further wreck David's scheming. He'd had to come clean with the truth of the matter and now they were in a dire situation.

Elisha had rung to say there was no way he was coming home and to his father's intense horror, had told him about Maeve and placed the elder in a cleft stick. Elisha's defection meant it was no longer necessary to keep Ruth confined, yet releasing her would mean certain exposure, feasibly gaol sentences for himself, and the fundamentalist cause in the city utterly discredited. He hadn't reckoned on his son deserting the fundamentalists in this manner and tried to fathom some way to plug what was rapidly becoming a broken dam. His frenetic belief that Ruth would somehow withdraw her accusations and Elisha come home, had blinded his judgement. Like most religious dictators, he could not conceive that he'd been deluded and numbed with unaccustomed shock that the entire ivory tower now looked set to fall, desperately sought a solution.

He had not objected when on learning of Elisha's dissent, Benjamin had decided to call another meeting. Benjamin had realised that it would be unwise to free Ruth for her to go running to the police, and the other elders, with Micah prominent, were in full agreement.

CHAPTER TWENTY-NINE

Inspector Halliday had received a phone call from an anonymous source. The caller wished to retain anonymity but had vital information concerning Elisha Penworthy, former member of the city's fundamentalist church. They claimed he was now a resident of Balbriggan, a town north of Dublin in the Republic of Ireland. The inspector wasted no time in contacting HQ in Worcester and in turn, Superintendent Ingram roused the Garda in Fingal HQ which, fortuitously, just happened to be in Balbriggan.

Sergeant Morrisey was sceptical.

'Hmm, 'scuse me askin', sir, but did that call come frum someone in this country or frum over there?'

Halliday had wasted no time in checking with BT and been informed that the caller had rung from an unidentifiable pay-as-you-go mobile, probably in this country.

Morrisey was moved to offer some unsought advice.

'Well, I reckon that un ent goin' to flaunt 'isself over there if 'ee's there. 'Ee's probably walkin' round in disguise right under their noses and knowin' them Irish…'

Halliday wasn't having this. He realised that in his ignorance, Morrisey was basing his judgement of the Garda on his experience of the Irish comedians who disparaged their own race before the 'woke' era served to eradicate such performances and deemed it perhaps appropriate to put his subordinate right on one or two things about a nation that had spawned such luminaries as James Joyce, George Bernard Shaw, Maeve Binchy, Iris Murdoch, Keats, Field – the composer that invented and bequeathed the 'Nocturne' to Chopin – Brendan Behan and 'Waiting for Godot'. Also Guinness, the Abbey Theatre et al.

Morrisey was not daunted. He'd just about heard of Maeve Binchy – his wife was an avid fan – and didn't see what all these people had to do with the Irish police who, he was given to understand by a nephew who'd spent a day taking a ferry to Rosslare and back, were not the most reliable of forces. How Morrisey's relative could have made this assessment after only a few hours on Irish soil beggared belief, but made weary through the years of having to endure his sergeant's wayward opinions, Halliday decided to let the matter rest.

Now that smart young patrolman had entered the station and was seeking his attention.

'Yes, Eldridge?'

'Sir, just called in to tell you we stopped that doolally elder in East Street for a defective brake light.'

'Doolally elder?'

Eldridge felt his superior officer was being a bit slow. 'You know, sir. That pompous git that preaches hell and damnation from the pulpit?'

Amused by the young patrolman's description of David as a 'pompous git', Halliday was still mystified as to why the minor matter of a non-functioning brake light should be brought to his attention.

'Well, Eldridge. I'm sure you were quite capable of dealing with it. Why bother me? I've got too much on my plate at the moment.'

'No, but sir, he seemed to be in a bit of a daze, not taking in what I was saying, so we breathalysed him.'

'And?'

'Negative sir, but he could have been drinkin' vodka or what about drugs? They're a funny lot.'

'Think that highly unlikely, Eldridge. We could always do a raid, I suppose. But where would we look?' He constrained a laugh. 'Behind the altar, under the bed?'

PC Eldridge proved himself to be very observant. 'That lot don't have altars, sir. D'you remember when we were sittin' in the church waitin' fur Moses to finish his sermon? I noticed it then …'

Not for the first time Halliday thought that Eldridge should be made plainclothes. He was a bright individual and the inspector made a mental note to recommend that this promotion should happen. Eldridge chuntered on. 'Nice motor, sir. Top of the range Aldi. Must 'ave cost a bob or two. Anyway, we let 'im go sir. But if you'd like us t' mosey on down there 'n 'ave a sniff around, I'm sure Clem'd love it.' Clem was Eldridge's patrolman 'obbo and might conceivably be the one who indulged his mate's love of Westerns and the vocabulary that went with them.

But since Halliday had more important matters to deal with and thought the fundamentalists hardly likely to be doing drugs, he decided to nip his young officer's theories in the bud.

'I don't think we'll concern ourselves about whether or not the cranky sect indulges in soft drugs at the moment, Eldridge. Thank you all the same. You've proved yourself admirably sedulous and it won't do you any harm. Now I suggest you get back on the job and it wouldn't hurt perhaps, if you called on that poor young Welshman in Whittern Way. It all helps to engender a favourable image and shows that we care. So off you go!'

Eldridge saluted and left without further ado. Sometimes the chief spoke a different language. The patrolman didn't know what 'sedulous' meant or 'engender', but resolved when he had a moment, to look it up on his smartphone.

Morrisey, who'd been present during this conversation between Halliday and Eldridge, waited for the patrolman to leave the building before offering some more words of wisdom.

'Seems that young man'll be after me job before long. Bright un, 'ee is!'

In response, Halliday grinned and went off to consult the laptop in his room.

CHAPTER THIRTY

Sitting in Benjamin's front parlour, David realised he was losing it. Ringing the police to shop his own son had been a treacherous action. If the Garda caught Elisha, he would be extradited and deprived of this new woman that had ensnared him. But without Ruth being released the police wouldn't have much of a case against him. They could have him for wasting police time, but without her being available to make the accusation of rape, the whole thing might turn out to be a damp squib.

Exhausted and hardly in his right mind, David had revealed virtually everything to his fellow elders. This included his knowledge of Ruth's whereabouts and although this gained him almost 100 percent agreement on the necessity for her to remain a captive for the time being, Benjamin, who had taken it upon himself to conduct the meeting with no objection from David, then stated that her incarceration would have to end pretty soon. It had aroused a degree of shame in him at the way she'd been treated, and he thought it inhumane and unchristian. She would have to be freed, but he could not see how it could be done without the 'Sword of Damocles' descending on all concerned. This classical reference only drew blank looks from the elders, who were not familiar with most literature that could not be found within the Bible: ignorance that enabled Benjamin to preserve his furtive interest in Greek and Roman mythology along with his covert veganism, both of which, if exposed, would undoubtedly be frowned upon.

Micah spoke up. 'What if we promise to release her if she agrees to take no further action over the so-called rape and her forced confinement on Hillchurch Common?'

His part in the abduction and incarceration now fully known, Amos had left Ruth in the hands of Peter and Ephraim and driven in to attend the meeting.

'With respect, gentlemen, that wouldn't work.' No longer subject to David's despotic rule, Amos had no hesitation in making his views known. He adjusted his recently acquired bifocals and met the senior elder's slightly vacuous gaze with one of his own that exuded newfound confidence. 'I have had occasion to talk to the young lady a good deal and she is a very disillusioned, but also a very determined soul. She has made it quite clear to me that she has relinquished her faith and sadly, if given the chance, might even attempt to bring the fundamentalist church and mission in the city into disrepute. Whilst fearful for her chances of eternity, I can understand her bitterness, and there must be some way we can make reparations for the way we have inflicted upon her what I see to be a great sin. I trust the Lord will forgive us and show us the way to make amends.'

Sitting with grave expressions on their faces, none of the elders were moved to say anything and pouring himself a glass of water from a carafe on the table, Amos quenched his thirst and with the bit between his teeth, resumed his unexpected oration.

'I would suggest to you that we free Ruth very soon and be prepared to take what comes. We fundamentalists have overcome most setbacks in our time and with the Lord's help, I'm sure we can survive and combat this one. It could mean some of us having to pay the price where the law's concerned, but it may be that when it comes to it, and if we are truly repentant, Ruth will see things in a different light, once more become one of God's chosen ones and nothing more will come of it.'

Apt to think himself divinely inspired, Amos beseeched them to repent and raised his right arm in supplication. 'Now can I ask you to join me by saying the prayer which Our Lord taught us? Our Father ...'

The only elder that didn't join in was David. In a brief moment of vindictiveness, he thought that now would be the time to expose the rebellious Amos's predilections for little girls. But he had other things on his mind. Not aware that he was an undiagnosed psychopath and having no sense of guilt, the elder was unable to acknowledge any wrongdoing on his part. To him the solution was simple, and he'd not be sluggish in resolving it. Tomorrow was Sunday and Sunday would be a good day for it. He'd assign the preaching to Amos. He'd excuse himself, saying he was not well. Benjamin would take the services, and Amos could have a better view of the little girls from the pulpit. No need for Amos to go back to Hilltop Villa. The young men could cope, and in any case, Ruth would not be there much longer. After he dealt with her, he'd see to them. He'd suspected them of having a foul relationship some time ago, it couldn't be allowed to continue, and he'd nip it in the bud once and for all.

*

Ruth was having a cup of coffee on the Formica top table in the kitchen at Hilltop Villa. For company she had the anxious and pallid Peter. Since she'd first been brought here, he'd gradually come out of his shell, and she'd almost become his confidante. He'd apparently had a tough upbringing. He told Ruth his parents were hangovers from even stricter fundamentalist days. Any slight misdemeanour would induce a beating and brought up in the oddly named village of Ocle Pychard, he and his siblings came into the city to worship. But the abuse inflicted upon them in their home was not discovered until Peter had the courage to inform a teacher, and they were eventually taken into social care.

Neither of her two custodians were quite twenty years of age and with an embarrassing flush on his face, Peter had confided to Ruth that he was not interested in girls. Neither it seemed was Ephraim, and putting two and two together, Ruth deduced that they were gay and furtively active. The fundamentalists did not practice overt homophobia, but any inclination towards homosexuality was actively discouraged. Physical relationships were outlawed and the 'solution', a 'cure' administered by a dubiously qualified believer who delivered it to those of 'unacceptable' sexual propensities in the form of a series of lectures. The legitimate medical authorities abhorred this practice and it had not long been made illegal. This ruling did not deter the fundamentalists. The threat of excommunication was a sufficient deterrent for those who objected to the treatment, and what went on in a small room labelled the 'clinic' was declared to be no one else's business.

Discreet in their relationship, Peter and Ephraim hadn't been found out as yet, but there were slight and growing murmurings about the fact that neither of them had a girl in tow. Ephraim still lived with his parents and Peter was admired for the excellent job he was doing in bringing up two younger siblings after his parents had ended up in jail for abuse: a happenstance that had not helped the fundamentalist cause at the time. Peter was anxious to get home where a generous aunty was tending to his brother and sister at the moment, but he dare not defy David who had insisted he stay where he was.

Despite his unfortunate upbringing, Peter still stuck valiantly to the fundamentalist creed and his possession of an illegal taser supplied by David alarmed Ruth and quelled any thoughts she might have of escaping. Peter still espoused the word with a fervour she found difficult to understand and her suggestion that he should turn his back on the church in order to freely indulge in his relationship with Ephraim, horrified him. In vain did she tell him his attitude was sheer hypocrisy, only to have him riposte with the lame statement that he could live with it and, in any case, God would be his judge. If he left the fundamentalists, he'd no longer be able to see or talk to his siblings, they'd be taken from his care and once vilified by the sect and living with Ephraim, he doubted if any court would grant him custody. He was only just eighteen and would also lose the company of his friends, all in all an imposition he'd not be able to contemplate.

Defeated by his obduracy, Ruth put the kettle back on and asked him if he'd like another cup of the execrable instant coffee. She resolved to ask the absent Amos if they could have an improved brand of the stuff, but didn't hold out much hope. In her opinion, Amos wasn't a particularly good shopper and pouring the boiled water into the cups, she eyed the unpleasant beverage with distaste before slumping back on to the chair opposite Peter.

CHAPTER THIRTY-ONE

Shaun's was busy. Sunday lunch was nearly always fully booked these days and the three of them were busily employed. Shaun had made noises about helping in Maeve's direction, but after an exhausting week as an assistant at the veterinary surgeon's, she politely declined. In common with a lot of establishments that had abandoned their drinks only policy some time ago, Shaun had opened a kitchen and his wife's excellent skills in it had done the rest.

The cuisine was superb, and the restaurant kept the place solvent. With the price of stout and other tipples sky high these days, this was no bad thing and kept the wolf firmly from the door.

The publican was also well in with the local guards and tomorrow he'd have to be stocking up for their annual shindig which would be taking place in the function room shortly. The Garda were on a par with the civilian population when it came to consuming copious amounts of alcohol and with a chuckle, Shaun reflected that Friday might surely be a good day upon which to commit a felony or other crime in what was the ancient settlement of Balbriggan.

Simon usually went to the Nag's Head at noon on a Sunday before having lunch at precisely two o'clock with Mrs Barton. She insisted on having his company and he had to admit she put on a positive and sumptuous feast.

Some Sundays he would have liked to stay at the pub, but if you didn't get back to Mrs B's at the appointed hour, you didn't eat. The lady was a stickler for punctuality, and it was foolish to get the wrong side of her. When crossed she'd be likely to let the bloody parrot out of his cage and the foul-mouthed bastard would dive-bomb you: an experience which Simon was always anxious to avoid. Reggie was the only creature, man or beast, that frightened Simon, and the prospect of having the fucking bird landing on your head to sample your hair with his razor-sharp beak, was definitely not one to be regarded with anything other than extreme apprehension. Thankfully, Simon went out of his way to prevent this happening and when it did, Mrs B always protested that the avian 'jumbo jet' wouldn't hurt, but brushing the marauding menace off none too gently, he was glad when Reggie transferred his attention to Poston the cat who, terrified, wasted no time in fleeing up the tumblehome stairs to the bedrooms.

Today the mountain bike boys from Kingstone were in the pub. They were a convivial lot and included the one with the extremely short close-cut hair who worked for the agricultural engineering people, and a posh doctor who'd seen to Simon when he'd had piles and was rumoured to only work two days a week. If they ever managed to abandon the pleasures of the pub, the bikers were going on what they euphemistically termed a 'short' trip to the Beacons, only they'd been delayed by a mechanical fault and noticing in passing that the pub was open, thought they'd call in for one before going any further. The one had become a couple and after a while, despite the charisma being generated in the place, Simon realised it was quarter to two and if he was to partake of Mrs B's generous repast, he'd better get his skates on. So he gathered up Stumpy – the spaniel gorged with snacks from the punters – and starting his car without difficulty, was well over the speed limit when passing the fortuitously unoccupied Peterchurch Primary School.

*

Sarah had gone to the Saturday night women's meeting and David took the opportunity to examine the object sitting in front of him on the dining room table. Never mind what Jesus Christ said, David gave just as much credence to the Old Testament. The Old Testament didn't condemn the action he contemplated if justified and there were endless times in the first books of the Bible when it had been. To reach the promised land had involved confronting those already in possession of the countries in between, who had to be vanquished before it could be contested and claimed. This assault bordered on genocide but was of no consequence to the Jews. Licensed to conquer this 'land of milk and honey' per favour of an omnipotent God, Moses and Joshua had not hesitated to do so. Not called to account for their actions, they were commanded to invade and displace the indigenous race who already inhabited this fertile country and David, still clinging to the notion that he was the Lord's chosen representative hereabouts, did not see why he should not protect what he saw as the unblemished reputation of the local sect in a similarly biblical way. The old prophets had decreed that might is right, and this could not be disputed.

Sarah had left a cold supper and whilst consuming it, he looked once more at the gleaming weapon. After cleaning it and checking that everything worked, he wondered how long it had been since anyone had used it. Grandfather Miller on his mother's side had been its first owner, had carefully preserved it and when David's father had died, it had been left to David, the other side of the family having long since rebelled against fundamentalism and emigrated to Australia. The reason for their flight was not talked about. Like a dyke with a slight natural culvert in it, the fundamentalists periodically lost members and were too similar to the New Testament zealots of old to realise why.

Grandfather Miller had two sons with whom he was never less than intolerant. Their ineffectual efforts to embrace the faith and reluctant attempts to evangelise angered him, and often during their violent upbringing it was not uncommon for them to have the strap brutally applied to their backsides.

The tyrannical old devil could not control his temper, and it was no surprise that when older, the brace of brothers severely turned the tables and headed off to the southern hemisphere.

This explained the heirloom on the table, and helping himself to more cheese and pickle, David re-filled his wine glass and with what he mistakenly took to be a feeling of relief, consumed the rest of his meal, looking forward to the morrow.

*

At the Fingal police HQ in Balbriggan, the commanding officer wasn't very happy. A file had come through from Dublin with a picture of a wanted Englishman. By all accounts, Dublin had had this guy's portrait from the UK police for some weeks and had only just chosen to circulate it, not really having a clue where he was. There was no definite proof that he'd made for the Emerald Isle and they were just making an assumption he may have fled there: a frequently chosen haven for the wayward denizens of 'perfidious Albion's' underworld. Furthermore, after some weeks, his car had been found abandoned in a back street of Abergavenny, Wales and the hunt for him concentrated in that area. It had taken the street dwellers of that friendly border town sometime to realise the car was not one of theirs and with acute prescience and a wife that came from South Wales, the Irish police chief knew that the Cardiff – Manchester train went through both Abergavennny and the Marches cities. Hence, Elisha could have cunningly caught it in Abergavenny and changed at Crewe for Holyhead.

Not prepared to let it go at that, Fingal's head honcho sent off an email asking the English why he had not been notified by the desperado's possible presence on his patch before now, and in reply they stated that they'd only just received the new information themselves through an anonymous phone call.

Great, thought the commanding officer, and sent a couple of his 'troops' to take a gander around the town to include one or two of the more likely bars where this unlikely fugitive might be apprehended. It could be like looking for a needle in a haystack. 'Yer man' might be anywhere on earth by now. This verdant land was full of fleeing Englishmen trying to escape the economic and political mayhem of their homeland and by now, the bloody ex – what was he? – fundamentalist, could be living the life of Reilly: drinking copious amounts of Guinness and shaggin' some delightful colleen in Athlone or Cork.

Simon had to admit that the Sunday roast was exceptional this week. Mrs B had a way of doing roast potatoes that melted in your mouth and intoxicated by the aroma emanating from the roast lamb, he was conscious of the obsequious Poston fawning round his feet in an attempt to be given a share of it.

Between mouthfuls and the profanities screeched by the indomitable Reggie, Mrs B was attempting to impress something upon her dinner guest.

'Don' you get feedin' that animal.'
'Fuck you, Winston.'
'That hanimal 'az 'is own own cat food. 'ee don't need.'
'Roll me over in the clover!'

Exasperated with Reggie's constant interruptions, Mrs B arose in surprisingly sprightly fashion, grabbed a large towel which hung on a small, improvised washing line over the Aga and threw it over the parrot's cage. This had the instantaneous effect of stopping the foul-mouthed bird's tirade and the lady sat down to hopefully enjoy the rest of her meal.

'As I was sayin'- d'you want some more mince sauce, love? – don't get feedin' that cat. Kick 'iz arse if 'e's a nuisance 'n I'll feed the bugger when we 'ave finished.'

Showing she was not averse to using a modicum of bad language herself, Mrs B passed the mince sauce and Simon helped himself. All the while this exchange was taking place and Simon was indulging himself as a grateful trencherman should, Stubby lay asleep in the corner. He'd been filled with crisps and cold meat from the simple but adequate food being partaken of in the Nag's and besides, he didn't particularly care for roast lamb and hoped that next week Mrs B would humour his tastebuds by cooking a big lump of succulent roast beef.

*

Not impressed with Amos's cooking or shopping, without it being expected, Ruth had taken over as head cook and bottle-washer. Amos had gone off somewhere yesterday and not returned and Ruth thought it might be churlish not to offer to get the Sunday dinner.

Her two captors offered to help, assistance she refused, and with Peter's revelation about their relationship now out in the open, a more relaxed atmosphere prevailed, although the dutiful fundamentalist kept a firm hand on the taser.

Whilst she prepared the food, they played chess, and even baby-faced Ephraim showed a degree of animation as he contemplated the prospect of winning.

'Shouldn't have done that,' he said, as he made the unequal

exchange; a knight for a pawn and his position strong, moved in for the kill.

'Coffee?' The dinner was well underway, and Ruth saw no point in not being amenable.

Over lunch Ephraim really opened up. At first hesitant, it was obvious he wanted to get something off his chest and Ruth tried to encourage him.

'You wanted to say something, Ephraim?'

Peter gave his friend a daunting look, but Ephraim was not to be silenced.

'Well, Ruth, uh-well, it's just to say we'd let you go, only we can't ...'

'You can't?'

Suddenly aware of what Ephraim was about to reveal, Peter chimed in.

'It's just that Ephraim and I.'

Ruth put a reassuring hand on his.

'I know what you're going to say, and you don't have to worry about saying anything, bless you. I do understand, and I think the attitude of the fundamentalists towards those like yourselves is monstrous.'

Peter looked highly relieved and she could see that there were tears in his partner's eyes. More animated than she'd ever known him, Ephraim hastened to explain.

'You see, if we free you, we'll get thrown out and Peter won't ...'

'I won't be able to see my family. They'll take my brother and sister off me and ex-communicate us ...' Peter joined in.

'And we won't be allowed to speak or eat with our families, and we'll have to find somewhere else to live and some other way to earn a living.'

Ephraim was openly crying now, and it was then they heard the car coming down the track. The noise became louder and ceased as the vehicle reached the yard. The motor was switched off, silence prevailed for a minute, a car door slammed shut and footsteps were heard coming towards the front door.

A moment later, David burst in upon them.

CHAPTER THIRTY-TWO

The two young Garda assigned to enquire and show the photo print round the town paused when they came to 'Shaun's'. The place was frantically busy and they didn't think their presence would be welcome. And glancing through the bar window whilst providing diners at one of his tables with horseradish, Elisha saw them and came out in a cold sweat. He was known to Shaun and the regulars as 'Alan' but didn't like the fact that the Garda had entered the smaller 'Dubliner' bar opposite. They looked as though they were after someone and for some irrational reason, he thought it might be him. It worried him that, just to be neighbourly, he'd been in the Dubliner bar with Shaun and Matthew in the early beardless days of his arrival in Ireland and although he'd been introduced by his assumed name, if the Garda now had a photo of him, he might be recognised and 'shopped'.

His worse fears were realised when things had quietened down and he entered the kitchen and found the staff deep in conversation. That the Garda were now seeking one 'Elisha', wanted by the British police for alleged rape and believed to be somewhere in Fingal, had been on the local radio news. Matthew had heard it on one of his sorties to fetch meals from the kitchen. The radio in there was always on and alarmed by this news, Matthew had decided to apprise Shaun and Shaun's wife Kathleen of Elisha's true identity. He also explained that the allegation of rape had been made by Elisha's wife and convinced them that Elisha's denial was genuine, and he needed to be assisted in evading the Garda.

Elisha had been a good, reliable worker and Shaun wasn't going to betray him to the guards. Shaun had an uncle who kept a hotel in Dublin and when contacted thought it best that – possibly with Maeve – Elisha depart and be employed by himself without delay. There were patrons of Shaun's who had known Elisha when he first appeared in the town and although he was now heavily hair suited, someone might recognise him from the posters the Garda might display or see a photo of him they'd post on the internet.

Shaun was soon on the phone to Uncle Dermot who was in any case short-staffed, who readily agreed to take the couple under his wing and would not ask any questions. When not sleeping with Elisha at Matthew's, Maeve had a room at Shaun's and would doubtless want to go with Elisha. The matter of Elisha or 'Alan's' forged papers being well in hand by persons unknown in Dublin, Shaun thought it best if he left as soon as possible. The Garda wouldn't have a photo print of Elisha as he was now and off the scent, would probably never succeed in finding him in the dense conurbation that was Dublin. As for patrons asking where Elisha/Alan had gone, that too was no problem. Shaun had had East Europeans and all sorts working in the restaurant. They came and went, often lured away to Dublin, and it was no hardship to inform his customers that Elisha had done the same thing.

No time was wasted, and the fugitive was transported to Uncle Dermot's in Matthew's beat-up old Volkswagen that same night.

The one snag concerned Maeve, who honourably chose to work out a fortnight's notice at the vet's and didn't see it as a problem. She'd leave when it was done and perhaps work at Uncle Dermot's hotel until she could find employment in her own line. Dublin was a vast city and it shouldn't be too difficult.

CHAPTER THIRTY-THREE

Amos had not had much opportunity to preach before. David was such an egotistical bastard, he privately thought, that no one else – not even the erudite Benjamin – got much of a look in. Amos admired Benjamin, who conducted the worship in a sincere, slightly apologetic manner and allowed the worshippers to raise their voices in several choruses; a concession that the almost omnipotent David rarely allowed.

After the service, and with David absent and at Micah's behest, the remaining elders were to have a meeting to discuss the senior elder's future. It would have to be ratified by the national leader, but Amos was pretty certain that they could depose him. A series of phone calls last night had established that without exception, they agreed that David's leadership should come to an end. They all felt he'd lost it, was no longer fully in command of his faculties, and that his wholly dictatorial reign should no longer be tolerated.

Amos surveyed the fresh faces before him. Perhaps perversely, he'd almost been tempted to take a text from the Book of Ruth, but had dismissed the idea as soon as he'd thought of it. Despite recent disturbing events, he still possessed a sense of humour, but did not wish to be accused of having a macabre one. Besides, the Biblical Ruth being depicted as fond of her mother-in-law, bore little resemblance to the twenty-first-century one in that respect, and Amos felt a pang of conscience as he steeled himself to deliver a homily on the words of Christ.

'Do unto others as you would have them do unto you.'

David's misguided notion that Amos was a predator where little girls were concerned was without foundation. As a young man of nineteen, Amos did not deny that he'd seduced a girl of nearly sixteen who looked much older, and he knew that if nothing was done to curtail the senior elder's now discredited allegations, Amos's sole lapse would be used against him forever. Now fifty-odd, he noted the bright young girls sitting amongst the worshippers with nothing remotely akin to a predatory instinct and with something that might be described as a paternal smile, bid everyone good afternoon and commenced to preach.

'Just goin' next door for me ciggies, Mrs B. Left 'em there. Won't be a mo'.'

They'd finished their main course and rice pudding was on the menu as a dessert. It irritated her that Simon liked to smoke between courses, but as he did such a lot for her otherwise, she was inclined to overlook it.

When he'd gone, she took the opportunity to look out of the window and was just in time to see a sleek black car turn in and head up the track.

Simon was not long in returning. He hadn't the same view from his kitchen window, which was at the back of his property, and only vaguely heard a car – it could belong to anyone on the hill – going up the track.

As she was dishing out the rice pudding and not one to prevaricate, Mrs B observed. 'A black car just went up th' 'ill with that bearded man in it…'

Suddenly, something clicked within her dinner guest.

'A black car? An expensive lookin' one?'

'Yes.'

It might not be; on the other hand David had an expensive top of the range black Audi and to Simon it was falling into place.

'Sorry, Mrs B. I'll have to go. I'll explain later.'

'What about yer puddin'?'

'Sorry. Come on Stump!' Collecting a half-somnolent Stumpy and ignoring the obscene language being directed at him by the now uncovered Reggie, Simon moved swiftly through the door, and shadowed by the excited spaniel, made for his garage. He hoped his old motor would start without dissent and was mightily relieved when it did. He flew up the hill and disregarded the bumps he would have avoided on any other occasion. Abandoning the vehicle when he reached the forbidden ingress to Hilltop Villa, he assuaged Stumpy's feeling of rejection with a few doggie treats and resorted to shank's pony. It would not do to arrive fortissimo in a crescendo of engine noise and squealing brakes. If David had Ruth closeted in Hilltop Villa, Simon wanted to catch him by surprise. There would probably be one or two of the elder's henchmen in attendance and Simon, who didn't believe in God, nevertheless prayed for His assistance and was thankful that he'd taken judo lessons and was a more than competent exponent of it...

At first all oily persuasiveness, David tried to convince the unresponsive Ruth that they'd free her if she promised not to say anything about her captors or her captivity. He'd concocted a cock and bull story she could tell the police about her supposed kidnappers who would be completely unknown to her: taking her to a destination where they tied her up and kept her prisoner in a small room. He suggested she make herself very dishevelled and he would take her somewhere on the outskirts of a village where she would surely be picked up and eventually arrive back in the fundamentalist fold. Her excuse as to why the abductors freed her would be because she'd convinced them her family had no money, a rather weak explanation which, even so, David thought would suffice.

Throughout this blatant attempt to gain Ruth's cooperation she sat stony-faced and inwardly seething. Either side of her, Peter and Ephraim gave nothing away, though Ephraim had produced his illegal taser and was nervously fingering it.

It was then that Simon burst in upon the scene and without preamble, made to accost the startled David. But the elder wasted no time in producing the gun, a cumbersome old firearm which in deadly and tragic fashion, proved itself effective as everything happened at once. Almost confirming his fellow elders' contention that he'd become completely deranged, David had obviously decided that as his attempt to win back Ruth's allegiance had failed, he'd take her somewhere very remote and terminate her existence. But his attention was diverted as Simon made to lunge at him and out of the corner of his eye, he somehow noted valiant Ephraim's intention to utilise the taser. This caused him to redirect the gun, to fire it and watch, a fascinated voyeur, as the young fundamentalist disciple fell to the kitchen floor, a slow trickle of blood emanating from his chest.

David did not wait as Peter bent over his partner in great distress, sobbing and inconsolable. A shocked automaton, Ruth removed the mobile phone from Peter's back pocket and dialled 999 and Simon tried to impede the murderer as he made to take flight, finding him surprisingly agile, the pursued getting away by slamming the door in his pursuer's face and reaching his car before he could be caught. Several bullets embedded themselves in the house door, and lucky to escape their deadly impact, Simon emerged into the yard just in time to see the black Audi hurtling along the driveway. He felt torn in two, wanting to run to his own vehicle, yet highly concerned lest the ultimate tragedy had occurred back in the house. He thought Ruth would have requested both the police and an ambulance and deciding the latter course would make more sense – he'd be foolish to try and chase an armed man – he returned inside. Immediately confronted with the fact that Ephraim was already beyond help, he put an arm round Peter and Ruth found a coverlet to put over the recumbent figure of his former partner.

Perhaps having doubts about his faith, and between convulsive sobs, Peter was trying to ask Ruth something.

'What is it, love?' Ruth stroked his plenteous blond hair and tried to comfort him whilst Simon kept his arm firmly in place.

'D'you think there – there is somewhere else, Ruth?' Peter beseeched.

Trying to control her grief, Ruth said, 'Yes, of course there is.' She no longer knew but thought it essential to comfort the stricken Peter.

It was not long before the ambulance arrived, shortly followed by a police car. The medics soon confirmed that Ephraim was beyond help and with Peter accompanying him in the ambulance, he was taken off to a chapel of rest. The police were taken aback to find Ruth had been incarcerated in Hilltop Villa and put in the picture by Simon, alerted HQ over David, who was now a wanted man himself.

After the police had left, taking Ruth with them, Simon got in his car, soothed an agitated Stumpy and going down the hill, called in at the alarmed Mrs B's to explain things. As requested, he then drove into the city to the police station. There he found Ruth, Inspector Halliday and DS Sergeant Angela waiting, and a long interrogative session ensued during which Ruth declared she wouldn't want to press charges against the stricken Peter. She refrained from mentioning Amos and as he hadn't been around at the nightmarish scene when David arrived, she could forgive him and save all her ire for the new fugitive. Only the elders and Peter knew of Amos's involvement and Ruth thought it best to keep it that way.

At the same time as the horrific events had taken place on Hillchurch Common, the elders had convened to hold their after-service meeting.

If they'd been at all doubtful of their decision to oust David from the leadership, their misgivings were completely vanquished by the news brought to them shortly afterwards by the police.

Ephraim dead, Ruth found, and David wanted for alleged homicide. It was almost too much to take in and Benjamin prayed they'd be able to survive it all.

*

A few days later, sad tidings came that Harvey had passed away. Benjamin, Micah and others had visited him in the hospice – David hadn't – and Hugo and Gareth, the latter unbelievably elated now that Ruth was safely back at Whittern Way, were helping with the funeral arrangements. With Hannah's approval, there was to be a double internment for Harvey and Ephraim, the ladies of the church would do the after-service refreshments and with a marked sea change to acknowledge her growing friendship with the new widow, Ma had been invited to help.

The chief protagonist of the abduction was still at large, and the two original abductors, Joseph and Mark came forward and admitted their part in things without having to be apprehended. To Inspector Halliday's initial consternation, Ruth did not wish to charge these two villains, but the inspector affirmed his belief that forgiving them would be carrying forgiveness too far. He opined that since they had given her rough treatment when capturing and conveying her to David at Lotherwas, they should not get off lightly and the police would press charges themselves. He impressed upon Ruth that when (not if!) they hauled the notorious David in, as witnesses the two heavies would drive further nails into his coffin, and realising he was referring to the box people were about to be buried in, hastily apologised for his insensitivity.

During all the broo-ha-ha caused by the revelations pertaining to the fundamentalists, the media depicted Ruth as a heroine, a role she studiously denied. It was not long before the press found out where she lived, and even when stalwart Hugo had been given time off by his long-suffering employer, the vultures were not put off by his presence outside the house. Eventually the police had to keep a permanent watch, and things calmed down, though Ruth flatly refused to appear on the TV news.

An exhaustive and extensive search was being made for David and Inspector Halliday had a hunch that they would soon succeed in capturing him.

'Jeremiah' Morrisey, pessimistic as only he could be, was not so certain. The news that Elisha was somewhere in a relatively small geographical area of Ireland had not succeeded in revealing his exact whereabouts and the unhelpful sergeant intimated that the same failure might apply where his father was concerned. It seemed to run in the family.

CHAPTER THIRTY-FOUR

With remarkable disregard for the fact that he was a wanted man and with ample funds in cash, David had made for Monmouth. Showing his inherent guile he did not take the obvious route, but went over Cockyard, down to the Abergavenny road, and via Pontrilas, Garway and Broad Oak to Welsh Newton and Monmouth. He'd had a brief fright when a police car came up the Hereford road towards him, but as his number plate and make of car had probably not registered with other police forces yet, he still breathed a sigh of relief as the South Wales Constabulary vehicle passed by. He knew that Roddy would probably give him refuge. Roddy would have not forgotten the time they were boys and attended Redbrook School together.

Before moving to the city, David had been brought up in what could be described as the hybrid village of Redbrook: a community partly in Monmouthshire, Wales, the rest in Gloucestershire, England and on the fringes of the Forest of Dean. The glorious River Wye dissected it and a redundant yet still standing railway bridge enabled the villagers of Penalt opposite to cross the river and its children to attend the school. The railway had gone through some of the most breathtaking scenery in the country which included the gorge that could be viewed from Symond's Yat and Tintern with its famous abbey. David had enjoyed his childhood there, strict as it was, and also his surprisingly permitted friendship with a boy in the village.

David's parents had reluctantly enrolled him at the village school, but he was not allowed to take part in any of the activities that went on in the village otherwise or mix with what his parents called unbelievers. They insisted on imposing the rigid rule despite the fact that the quaint church had a welcoming young vicar and there was a small but flourishing youth club which David was forbidden to attend. Then a decree came from fundamentalist H Q that all members of the flock must move to urban areas. Until this edict came, they'd attended a small fundamentalist church in Chepstow and Mother did the shopping in Monmouth, an attractive town two miles up the road which David would have liked to spend more time in but was never allowed.

The one child in the village that formed a friendship with David was Roddy. At first this liaison was banned by David's parents, but faced with Roddy's persistence and engaging personality, they eventually gave in. David's mother was more soft-hearted than she cared to admit and confronted by Roddy's charm and obvious neglect, couldn't help taking to him.

Roddy and his folks lived up above on a shambolic farm called 'The Heights'. The famous Offa's Dyke, built by the Mercian king to keep the Welsh at bay, ran right through the farm and like almost everywhere else in this part of the world, the escarpment afforded superb views up and down the river.

Moving to the city, David had missed Roddy at first, but gradually and unavoidably became embroiled in the fundamentalist movement as he grew up, steadily imbibing its ingrained intolerance.

One exception to this strict code of conduct was made when David took Sarah to see his old friend, who had changed considerably and now ran the farm more efficiently than his deceased father had done. Offered refreshment by the hosts, the fundamentalists found the entire encounter excruciatingly devoid of any rapport and hopelessly tongue-tied and embarrassed, left after only a short while, never to repeat the experience.

In desperation, the farm was where David headed for now and he marvelled at the bosky river basin, the still prevalent tints on the trees and the slightly ethereal mist that veiled the river. A landscape that had witnessed many a bloody battle, seen Henry V bestow borough status upon Monmouth and hunt from what had once been the small forest township of Newland. Newland had once boasted an age-old grammar school and its glorious church, known as the 'Cathedral of the Forest' was still an eminent tourist attraction.

He turned left on the outskirts of Redbrook and confident some time would elapse before they'd seek him in earnest-he must be at least an hour ahead of pursuit-drove up the steep and winding road to the Heights.

An almost statuesque figure standing in the yard in his overalls, his pork pie hat secreting his baldness, Roddy gaped as the sleek Audi skidded to a sudden halt in front of him. Bucket in hand, he'd come out to feed his chickens. He'd just heard the news of the murderous incident on the radio and despite the fading light, recognised David immediately. He gasped at the import of the situation and prepared for the worst as his old friend got out of the car to face him.

David was all almost hysterical bonhomie and Roddy stood open-mouthed as a tirade of obsequiousness issued forth from this former, and now frightening friend of former years.

'You see, you see. It- it would not be- for- for- long. I have this trouble, this necessity to lie low for a while, and- and…'

David continued to rabbit on in this querulous fashion and standing stock still, expressionless Roddy studied and regarded the intruder impassively. Roddy might be considered by those who didn't know as a prototype village idiot, but further recognition of his character and undoubted intellect would make books and covers come to mind.

'You wait there. I'll see what Dulci 'as t' say.'

'Is that necessary?'

Roddy's intention to consult his wife was forestalled when the lady herself came out of the farmhouse and stood by her man.

'Somethin' the matter?' she enquired, and the knowledge that she recognised David, who she'd only met on one occasion, led her to continue. Not a person to prevaricate unduly, she walked up to David and simply said, 'Oh, it's you. Never thought we'd see you again after the last time. What d'you want comin' yer at this time on a sun …'

'It's just that …'

David was not accustomed to being confronted by assertive women and, his mind in a turmoil, was almost grateful when, in his turn, Roddy interrupted.

'You better come in. Dulcie'll make a cup of tea an' we'll decide what to do.'

Roddy knew exactly what he was going to do. His wife had

been upstairs when the news had come on the radio and he'd gone out to feed the chickens before she came back downstairs. He'd not had the chance to tell her about the murder and showed a remarkably cool head when David, the supposed murderer, with extraordinary nerve, now sought refuge.

Assessing the situation quickly, Roddy had decided he'd invite David in and contact the police on his mobile upstairs. He'd excuse himself by saying he needed the toilet and although this meant leaving Dulcie with David briefly, he was aware that it would not be in the fundamentalist's interest to harm her, and Roddy hoped he could keep him occupied until the police arrived.

This turned out to be a bad miscalculation on the farmer's part. Dulcie had made the tea and, inviting David to be seated at the pine table to drink it, Roddy announced with what he thought a deceptive smile that he needed to visit the toilet. But he had not allowed for David's nous. Half-crazed, the elder trusted no one.

'I wouldn't do that if I were you ...'

In vain, Roddy tried to play the innocent.

'I'm sorry, but I'll have to go. What's your objection?'

'Uh, you know what my objection is. Put your phone on the table and sit down.'

'I'm sorry, I'm not having you tell me what to do in my own ...'

Roddy was made of stern stuff, but quailed when David produced the gun and Dulcie let out a horrified scream.

The gun wavered in the elder's unsteady hand as he pointed it at the farmer and Roddy could not help noticing that the man seemed to be a nervous wreck. There was a hint of menace in the neurotic fundamentalist's voice as he made it clear he'd not tolerate dissent.

'You must think me ingenuous. You were going to sneak into the bathroom to ring the police, weren't you? News travels fast, doesn't it? I- I can't stay here now. I can't trust you.'

With sudden movement, he re-directed his weapon at Dulcie who, with remarkable courage, did not flinch or avert her eyes from him.

'Stand up and come with me,' he commanded, and her instant

refusal inflamed him. He became almost incandescent and arose in order to place the gun to the side of her head.

Fear was not a feeling to which the stoic farmer willingly ascribed, but he was trembling with it now.

'Do as he says, Dulcie, do as he says!'

Keeping her covered with the gun, David compelled Dulcie to walk to the door and forced her to accompany him across the yard, causing the safety light on the house to illuminate the dark tenebrous night. He motioned her to get in the car just as her husband emerged from the house, and risking all, she ran back across the yard to him.

A shot rang out and the deranged elder did not even pause to see where it had lodged. He flung himself into the driving seat of the Audi and made another reckless descent which easily matched the one he'd made earlier from Hillchurch Common.

*

It was still there. The old shed with the double doors they'd played in so many years ago. It had only ever contained bikes, tools, redundant furniture and serendipity belonging to the people that lived in the big house set back a couple of yards up the road. It had never been locked – people were more trusting in those days – and he and Roddy sometimes went in there on one of their rambles to muck about. They'd never disturbed any of its contents, save to make use of a dartboard complete with darts to which Roddy introduced his friend. They were never disturbed during their intrusions and at the time it had not concerned David whether or not playing darts was an activity acceptable to fundamentalists.

Something prompted him to pull in and investigate. He parked at a slight angle and his headlights shone on the doors of the shed which looked as though they hadn't been touched by a paintbrush since his childhood. He switched the lights and engine off and removed a small torch from the glove compartment.

The doors were stiff, but he managed to open them, shining the torch inside which revealed the shed to be empty. He calculated that the Audi would fit in quite easily and hoped nothing would come by as he drove his car inside. He mentally congratulated himself on his ingenuity. He'd have to spend the night here and walk up to the shoots at dawn. What did it say in one of the psalms?

'I will go unto the hills from whence cometh my salvation.'

He settled down on the back seat and said a prayer. He'd always been able to say an impromptu one without difficulty, but of late it had become a tiresome obligation, rather than a fervent attempt to commune with his God. The fundamentalists did not have a prayer book. They proclaimed whatever moved them and with some of them apt to speak in tongues, a strange atmosphere could sometimes prevail at worship meetings: one that an outsider might interpret as belonging somewhere between Heaven and Hades.

CHAPTER THIRTY-FIVE

Patrolman Ianto Evans had a day off. A day off was no more than he deserved. They'd been covering the tortuous A466 between the roundabout at the entrance to Chepstow up to Tintern with instructions to take the odd trip up to the high ground beyond. Here the riverbed was really a cutting formed in primeval days. Sometimes they'd gone beyond their patch and met the Monmouth boys at Llandogo. They'd even ventured over Brockweir Bridge to quite covertly have a chat with a Gloucestershire patrol who were parked outside the pub.

You had to do something to break the monotony and so far, they'd had no luck. It shouldn't be difficult to haul in a new Audi with the information the farmer, though traumatised, had provided. He'd had enough savvy to memorise the number plate, but this weirdo had somehow managed to slip through the net.

Ianto had hoped that his lovely spouse, Eira, could have had a day off at the same time as him. Eira was secretary of Trellan Primary School. The school took pupils from all over the high and wide plateau on the Welsh side of the river, was oversubscribed and made casual leave of absence a definite no-no.

Very much twenty-first century man, Ianto had cooked the breakfast to satisfy the healthy appetites of his 'pigeon pair' and to give Eira further help, also made the sandwiches. Eira had not expected him to do this after his night out trying to apprehend the odd and dangerous religious freak who was making the headlines on all the news channels. But as her doting mother was always saying, 'He's a one-off, girl. You don't get many of those these days.' A tribute that didn't say much for her indolent father, who spent most of his time propping up the bar down at the Ship in Tintern.

Although struggling to take a load of things for school to the car, she still managed to ruffle his thick wavy hair in passing, and he promptly arose to open the back door for her.

A witness to all this early morning activity, Maurice the

retired police dog Alsatian sat servile and pleading, watching the children's every mouthful and eagerly accepting the morsels they allowed him when they thought their father wasn't looking.

Breakfast concluded, Ianto helped with coats and scarves, admonished seven-year-old Briony for picking her nose, bundled them into the car and waved them off. He'd decided he'd take a walk with Maurice through Cuckoo Wood, then visit one of his favourite places, Cleddon Falls, known to the locals as 'Niagara'. He thought it very unfair that this part of Gwent was not only the most affluent, but also contained the county's most fabulous scenery. His parents hailed from Abertillery, had moved to Monmouth when he'd been very small, and that had ensured that, despite his very Welsh name, he grew up with an accent more akin to that of neighbouring Herefordshire. Driving down from the forest, you could travel through three counties in the space of about three miles and the population of Monmouth had the flavour of all three within its borders. It had two public schools, state schools where the pupils had to learn Welsh, something which did not bother Ianto, but did concern quite a number of children that came to the comprehensive from over the border in Gloucestershire.

This time of year, dawn took longer to arrive, but a bright start this morning heralded the first frost; the sky uncluttered with ominous clouds: the ideal day for donning his walking boots and inviting the intelligent Alsatian to accompany him.

Not that Maurice needed an invitation. The sight of Ianto removing his boots from under the stairs was sufficient for the dog to quiver in anticipation: whining and hastening to fetch his lead from the hall.

'Ready then, boy?'

They stepped out into the morning and pausing only to hail old Mrs Jenkins who lived in the semi next door as she put something in her recycling bin, went on their way

*

It had been a cold night in the Audi but thanks to the heavy ex-Swiss army coat Sarah had acquired for him from a charity shop, he had managed a little sleep, and a meagre breakfast of cheese biscuits and an apple had partially assuaged his hunger. He'd brought a couple of water bottles with him and where he was going, he would be able to replenish them with the purest water you would find anywhere. He was glad that he'd always made it obligatory not to go anywhere without sustenance and brushed aside Sarah's complaint that the car sometimes resembled a rubbish tip of empty crisp packets, chocolate wrappers and broken biscuits. He wondered how she was, and though a dutiful wife, had agreed not to share his bed for some time. She'd be looked after by the sect and as they'd grown apart in most ways, he didn't think she would miss him.

He sat on the seat which overlooked the tumbling shoots and marvelled at God's creation. Just a stream initially, the waters came to the edge, and with a jarring suddenness, plunged and plummeted (some would say bounced) down the steep acclivity on its unstoppable progress to the Wye. Some rough steps from the seat enabled the sure-footed to clamber down to be nearer this awesome sight midst the trees and David contemplated doing so before he'd return to the car.

Not far away stood Cleddon Hall, once home to the great philosopher and atheist, Bertrand Russell; human anathema to the polarised religious fundamentalists who had once declared that if he got to heaven, he'd tell God that he should give mankind more evidence of his existence!

As if the opulence of nature hereabouts and the view of the river valley was not truly breathtaking enough, the names given places within it were fascinating and perhaps entirely apposite. Bargain Wood, Farmhouse Mews, Ninewells, Dengely Wood and others of often unknown origin. A forest walk ran through stately oaks and beeches and the riverside Wye Valley Walk was much utilised by enraptured tourists.

*

Ianto Evans never forgot a face. Recognition was instant. But David saw him as just a man walking his dog. An exchange of pleasantries would suffice, and the young man would surely go on his way. Gifted with that canine sense that enabled the old police dog in him to somehow smell trouble, Maurice growled and bared his teeth as they approached. There was no question in Ianto's mind that this was the man being sought nationwide. This oldish character with a beard, balding on top and a slightly arrogant expression: a distinct birthmark on his left cheek.

David deigned to smile as Ianto and the dog approached and the young policeman saw no reason not to return it. Nevertheless, this was going to be difficult, but he was confident that with the dog's help, he could make an arrest. He took a deep breath and drawing level, firmly addressed the fundamentalist.

'Good morning. You are, I believe, David Penworthy, wanted on suspicion of murder. I am an off-duty police officer and am entitled to arrest you, advising you to say nothing that may prejudice…'

Glinting through the trees, the sun shone on the gun as the shot rang out.

*

Putting out her washing, Mrs Jenkins started as an agitated Maurice came into the garden. She'd been nervous of him at first, but soon came to realise he was just a big softie, though still wouldn't like to get the wrong side of him. She knew no one was in next door. She'd acknowledged Ianto's hearty greeting as he went off with the dog for his walk and wondered what Maurice was doing back home without him. The dog was whining in a very distressed manner and kept going down the garden path to the open gate and returning, almost as if he was trying to lead her somewhere.

Just then her husband hailed her from the open front door. 'What's the matter with him, Hayleigh, and why's he back 'ere without Ianto?' Alwyn Jenkins was a fit sixty-five-year-old and coming out, bent down to fondle the Alsatian's ears. Maurice did not tolerate this for long and padded to the gate once more, still emitting a piteous noise. Alwyn followed him and the dog started off down the path into the woods, a right of way he'd taken earlier with his master.

Jenkins turned to address his wife. He had a powerful voice and there was no question that, despite her partial deafness, she wouldn't hear him.

'Don't like this, Hailey. Reckon 'ee's tryin' to take me somewhere. Reckon somethin's 'appened to Ianto.'

Something had indeed happened to Ianto, and following Maurice, Alwyn arrived at the falls to find forestry worker Bill Higgins bent over the recumbent police officer, trying to staunch a wound from which blood was issuing in a slow trickle. Good fortune had decreed that Bill had been nearby when the shot rang out and he had quickly made his way to the falls to investigate, by which time the intelligent dog had left the scene and there was no sign of an assailant. Well known to Alwyn Jenkins, Bill had done all the right things but was worried as to how the medics would get a stretcher up to the falls. However, both men were pretty sturdy and a quick decision found them carrying the afflicted young policeman down to the car park below, which had been made to stop indiscriminate parking in the busy tourist season.

*

The estate agent had shown the prospective clients round the large villa set back from the road and was taking them a short way down it to view the large, shed belonging to the property. Not that there was much to see except a sleek, black abandoned motor: its owner a notable absentee.

CHAPTER THIRTY-SIX

They were having a civilised argument in Mam's house – it was always Mam's house, never Da's – and arguments were usually debates that Mam won. Right now she was concerned about the 'young ones' going to the Drover's Arms for what they maintained was just a harmless drink. In truth, she was so glad to have Ruth back in the bosom of the household; this lovely girl who she now looked upon as a daughter, that she was worried when she went out anywhere.

Gareth tried to reassure her.

'But Mam, 'ee wouldn't dare come back over by 'ere. The cops would 'ave 'im in a flash!'

Mam wasn't having any.

'You don' know that, boy. 'Ee might want revenge. Anyway, the girl's comin' with me tomorrow to lunch in the church 'all. That'll be safer.' Trying not to intervene in this mild altercation, Ruth nevertheless thought going to the pub accompanied by Gareth, Hugo and Shiela could be a lot safer than attending the weekly old folks' nosh-up with Mam. A not always silent observer, the oracle behind the newspaper spoke up.

'Don' see why she shouldn't go to both. That man'll be miles away by now and 'iz son could be anywhere. Peking or Moscow maybe!' Proving that although his geographical knowledge may have been gleaned from the *Daily Mirror*, it was a bit limited in that it had not apparently informed him that Peking was now Bejing, but they were all amused when Hugo stated that, even so, Da was not just a 'pretty face'. Hugo went on to aver that he was firmly in agreement with Da and with everyone except Ma in favour, the establishment's matriarch gave way.

'Dew, dew, if it is that what you think, is it? Then I'll 'ave to give way. I don' know. But there now, 'ave it your own way …' Not slow to take advantage of this rare capitulation, Gareth gave his mother a hug and fetched Ruth's coat. He helped her into it and promising to take every care, followed Hubert and Shiela out to Hubert's car where Shiela got into the driving seat. She'd ostensibly drawn the short straw and could look forward to an evening on the J2Os or some other bland form of liquid refreshment.

To Gareth's slight amusement, Ruth had decided to go to the pub in faded jeans, a different hairstyle and a pair of dark glasses. Her reasoning for this partial disguise was that some bright spark might ring the press, and they'd descend on the Drover's Arms like a pack of wolves.

She could see the headlines.

'EX-FUNDAMENTALIST VICTIM LIKES THE CIDER.'

'RUTH PREFERS THE TRUTH. STOWFORDS NOT STRONGBOW.'

And now there was further news on the intrusive tele of another suspected attempted murder. A young police officer had been shot and found lying near a well-known beauty spot and was now in a stable condition in Neville Hall Hospital, Abergavenny. This added to a statement made to the police by an alarmed Redbrook farmer, and the discovery of David's Audi in the shed, only pointed the finger one way. To the deranged elder. But there was no sign of him. He'd eluded the police and if she'd heard the latest news, Mam would probably be having kittens.

Things in the pub became pretty boisterous until right at the end of the ten o'clock news there came a newsflash. Quiet descended. A body had earlier been found by a woman taking her Chow for a walk. Wedged in the culvert which took the stream under the road into the Wye at Llandogo. There was practically no doubt who it was, and Hugo wasted no time in holding forth on the subject.

'I reckon he realised what he'd done and decided to call it a day. Very dramatic. I've bin there and if you're goin' to end it all, there couldn't be a more spectacular place to do it.'

'You mean he deliberately jumped?' This from Gareth, who couldn't conceive how anybody could do such a thing.

Ruth spoke up. 'God rest his soul,' she said softly, and added, 'if there is a God.'

Hugo was having none of it. 'Good riddance to bad rubbish!' he said, and Shiela admonished him for speaking ill of the dead.

'Besides,' rejoined the unabashed Hugo. 'Looks even more like that young police officer they found by the falls got shot by the bastard! Thas probably why 'ee jumped. Realised what 'ee'd done. That an' killin' the young fundamentalist.'

Ruth turned big accusatory eyes on him. 'That, Hugo, I fear we shall never quite know.'

'For once I don' agree, my love,' reasoned Gareth. 'It all fits. David kills poor Ephraim, flees to that farm, bolts from there, puts iz car in that shed an' it looks like 'ee went up the falls. The off-duty lad tried to arrest him and got shot for his trouble.'

'But why would he be there in the first place?' questioned Ruth.

'Per'aps 'ee intended to end it all anyway. 'Ee would have bin caught sooner or later and per'aps 'ee didn't fancy spendin' the rest of 'iz life in jail?' Hugo was nothing if not positive.

'An' 'ow is that young copper anyway?' asked the concerned Shiela. 'I sin a picture of 'iz wife an kiddies in the paper. Lovely girl an' lovely kids. Would 'ave bin a tragedy if 'ee'd popped 'iz clogs.'

'Oh', said Gareth. 'We get the Welsh news on our telly. Mam likes it. Apparently he's 'ome now. The bullet didn't hit anything vital. Only a flesh wound, though pretty deep, but they managed to extract it and he's well on the way to recovery.'

*

In the city police station, a similar debate was taking place and the indomitable Sergeant Morrisey was holding forth.

'So what it amounts to, Inspector, we ant got nobody to prosecute now that the main man az kicked the bucket. Unless, of course, the Irish catch 'iz son, an' I can't see 'em doing that.'

'And why have you such a low opinion of the Garda, sergeant?' Inspector Halliday found it difficult not to be impatient with his jingoistic subordinate.

'T'aint that, sir. She don't want to charge 'im and we could, but might not 'ave a very good case without 'er givin' evidence. They knows all about it over there. A lot of what goes on 'ere gets on their TV an' in their papers.'

The inspector tried hard not to go to sleep.

Proof of what the English police sergeant had being trying to impress upon his superior was in a report Elisha was reading in the august *Irish Times*. Somewhat timorously, it was giving the whole story in full. It included pictures of the young Welsh policeman's family, a photo of David and mentioned that his son was still somewhere in Ireland, wanted for alleged rape. This last piece of information made Elisha uneasy, although he felt less vulnerable in Shaun's uncle's posh and exclusive hotel than he did in the hothouse of gossip that was Balbriggan.

Famous client patronised the 'Independent Hotel' and with these luminaries to look after, and a melting pot of humanity to control in Dublin, the Garda must have few resources to spare for the capture and extradition of a renegade Englishman who may or may not have committed a serious crime. Aside from all this, the hotel had once been a bolthole for senior members of the IRA during the Troubles and always ready to espouse a cause, when learning of Elisha's 'plight' (made worse by a certain amount of Shaun's mendacity) Uncle Dermot had been only too happy to help.

His break over, Elisha put the *Times* back in the rack in reception. He didn't think staff were supposed to purloin and peruse it, but nobody ever said anything, and it did help to relieve his unrelenting toil. He hoped nothing would happen to put a spanner in the works or mar his relationship with the adorable and vivacious Maeve and went out of his way to give satisfaction both at work and in bed.

*

'I know it's a sensitive subject, love, but what about your ex? The fuss over him seems to 'ave died down, but I suppose it will end now you've withdrawn your accusations.'

Shiela was not a 'silk purse', but neither was she a 'sow's ear' and had an enquiring mind.

Ruth was denied an answer by Hugo's eagerness to get yet another word in.

'Yes, and when they bring his dad's corpse back to the fundamentalists, will that pious lot forgive 'im and give 'im a funeral?' And he went on facetiously. 'We've already got a funeral for two of 'em coming up, one more won't make much difference.'

This made Ruth angry. 'I don't think that's going to happen for one moment, Hugo. Much as I now despise them, I think Benjamin is an honourable and reasonably sincere man and I can't see David having more than a few words said over his coffin before being cremated.'

'And where will he go?' sneered Hugo. 'Up there or down below where 'ee belongs?'

'I've no idea,' replied Ruth with a sigh: at the same time resolving not to tell Mam that she didn't really believe in anything anymore.

The real surprise of the evening came when a smartly attired and well-groomed Simon emerged from the secluded dining area accompanied by DS Angela Smith, and both parties took a double take. It was a job to tell who was most taken aback, Simon or Ruth and Gareth. The couple had first met Angela on their initial visit to the police station and Simon had been interviewed when following the patrol car with Ruth in it from the horrific scene at Hilltop Villa. He'd had the enormous temerity to ask the sergeant for her phone number and for some reason she'd been able to disregard his unkempt appearance and when he later rang her, she couldn't refuse him. He thought the Drover's would be an ideal inn to take a classy girl like her and well away from the city, not likely to attract trouble. Hugo and Shiela were introduced and sensing a pair of newcomers that might not know the rules governing the excessive feeding of overweight Labradors, Bella waddled across to see what she could cadge.

CHAPTER THIRTY-SEVEN

The funeral procession was an impressive affair. Eight cockaded black steeds, four to a carriage, set out from the funeral parlour and arrived at the church to find it full, with a strong police presence outside to control the paparazzi, and cameras belonging to both the BBC and independent television, eagerly awaiting to relay pictures of the sad occasion.

Now free to decide her own stance where the fundamentalists were concerned, Ruth had asked her unofficial 'ambassador', Hugo, to sound them out, and their response being overwhelming in inviting her to attend. She decided to attend, though strictly on the understanding that she was not returning to the fold. She made it clear that she'd only be coming to support Peter and Hannah, would not be staying for the wake and refreshments: leaving that to Gareth, Hugo and Mam. It was quite something that the strictly exclusive fundamentalists had issued invitations to 'gentiles' at all, but they'd been shamed into doing so by the determinedly forward-thinking Benjamin who, in cahoots with Amos, was espousing a movement for change. The new leader had thanked his God for Ruth's forgiving nature with all his heart.

She had informed Benjamin of her decision never to return to the fundamentalists. Not one that, taking account their treatment of her, would by any stretch of the imagination be anything less than perfectly understandable. But her declaration that she'd grave doubts about the existence of a creator and was inclined to embrace agnosticism saddened him. He prayed for her immortal soul and hoped that her liaison with Gareth would prove enduring and acceptable in the eyes of the Lord. The Irish police had not found Elisha and in some ways Benjamin hoped they never would. After so many years, the marriage of him and Ruth would be annulled and observing her and Gareth together, he hoped this would happen. When removing David's body from the stream, the police had found no trace of a mobile phone on him – it was probably drifting down the Severn and into the Bristol Channel by now – and an examination of his laptop did not reveal a phone number or email for Elisha. David had been a canny operator and no further information over his son's whereabouts had been gleaned from either his office or personal papers. This meant Elisha could not be informed of his father's death, although it was probable it had been noted in the Irish news media.

It all went off well. To avoid the clamour out front, Ruth had taken a taxi via a circuitous route to the back entrance of the church. Welcomed by the skeletal and humble Benjamin, she'd made a point of hugging both Peter and Hannah; this inducing a murmur from the straightlaced fundamentalists and undeterred, she took a seat next to Gareth, Mam and Hugo. Hannah sat with what were obviously her married offspring and their spouses who'd come down from Manchester to stay during the last stages of Harvey's illness, and brave Peter was seated next to his young siblings, his uncle and aunt and Ephraim's haunted looking parents. Ruth could not imagine how they felt and Micah's passionate eulogy to their son may have done something to assuage their grief.

Benjamin extolled the virtues and goodness of Harvey, lamenting his passing with comforting aplomb and Amos, still not comprehending that Ruth had forgiven him and would not reveal his complicity in recent events, gave a little homily to those in mourning. He proclaimed his faith in Jesus Christ and even the sometimes derisive Hugo was moved to kneel when Amos led the people in prayer. A senior elder from the Mancunian church added his tribute to Harvey; just one of the large contingent that had travelled down from the north to pay their respects.

Hannah had decided to stay in the bungalow. There were too many memories to disquiet her in Manchester and with Benjamin's approval, she'd take in and try to help any misfits within the church who needed succour and spiritual help.

Ruth left before the coffins were transported to the cemetery whilst Gareth, Hubert and Mam, a little awkwardly, stayed on for the wake – to Hugo's surprise, not the non-alcoholic oasis he expected it to be.

The media had obviously decided they'd stand more chance of

seeing Ruth at the funeral and for once, there were no reporters outside the house when she returned to Whittern Way. Left with an unperturbed Da and Barnaby the cat, Hugo's Shiela, who'd volunteered to fend off any inquisitors during the family's absence, had only received a couple of phone calls and in her blunt Herefordshire way had not hesitated in giving the callers short shrift.

The only notable absentee from the funeral was Simon. He wanted no part in what he termed their superstitious rituals and marvelled at Ruth's capacity to forgive. He'd go on working for them and was glad that their former leader, a dangerous psychopath, was no longer at large. He also had other things to concern him. Like how he was going to introduce a nice girl like Angela to Mrs Barton without that fucking parrot sounding off with every profanity under the sun! Perhaps not to cross bridges before you came to them. And one thing at a time. Angela had already been introduced to Stumpy and Nag's Head – Stumpy adored her and they were now walking up Mrs B's garden path to encounter her, the stand-offish Poston and the execrable Reggie. A thought: maybe there was a God and if Simon prayed hard enough, perhaps the fucking feathered bastard parrot would be struck dumb!

CHAPTER THIRTY-EIGHT

Conscience stricken over his participation in the abduction and not wanting Joseph and Mark to carry the can for everything, Amos went to the police. Inspector Halliday was very sympathetic and fully understood. He'd been perplexed over how they'd explain what happened after Ruth had been snatched by the fundamentalist heavies and though aware that David was the main culprit, thought there might be others besides Ephraim and Peter involved.

When learning of Amos's confession, Ruth wanted to drop charges against Joseph and Mark as well and forget the whole thing, but Amos was adamant that he wanted to stand trial with them. The one concession he pleaded for was that Peter should be exonerated. He felt that the young fundamentalist had suffered enough with the demise of Ephraim and the inspector readily agreed, with some pleading from Ruth, to keep his name out of it.

None of these negotiations could prevent the case making headlines in the newspapers and other media, however, but a dignified statement to the press – quite unprecedented from a fundamentalist leader – did much to repair the damage. Impressed with Ruth's testimony, one of complete forgiveness, the judge did not see it would do any good to impose prison sentences. Aware that the main perpetrator of the crime could not stand trial for his actions, he ordered his minions to serve varying lengths of time in community service: something which did not dismay Benjamin or any of the other elders, it being now their new policy to engage with the general populace on a more broad-minded basis.

Largely due to Mam's standing at St Mark's, Amos found himself serving tea and coffee at the Senior Citizen's Club and in an unprecedented happening, Reverend Moseley was invited to preach at the fundamentalist church. The relationship of Gareth and Ruth blossomed, and Mam turned a blind eye over the fact that the spare room was no longer inhabited solely by Ruth.

Hannah was currently hosting Peter and his young siblings to give them a break, and great excitement was generated when a visiting Hugo spotted a very rare hoopoe in the garden.

Reformed sartorially, Simon became enslaved by the gorgeous PS Angela, who somehow had a calming effect on the belligerent Reggie, who took to sitting on her shoulder and with a possible attempt to usurp Simon, cooed sweet nothings in her ear. Mrs B wholly approved of the young police sergeant and of her cooking, which she declared was nearly on a par with her own. They often entertained the old lady to Sunday dinner and at times, despite one or two of the punters being a little nervous of having a member of the 'fuzz' amongst them, they visited the Nag's Head.

Predictably, in the police station, Sergeant Morrisey was sucking his teeth over something. He didn't seem very happy and was giving the caller short shrift.

'You say you found this cat?'

An interminable torrent of words from the other end of the line came in reply to this question.

'You say 'ee 'az an address on 'iz collar?'

More lengthy verbosity from the other end of the line.

'Well, if it's in 'erefurd, why can't you ring the number and get the owners to fetch 'im?... You've tried that?... But isn't Windsor Drive just round the corner from you? ... Oh, you left an answer phone message ... What's that? ... You can't take 'im back yourself cos your bowels are unreliable? ... Well, why not ring the RSPCA? You 'aven't got the number? Wait a minute.' Looking up the number, Morrisey groaned and wondered why he'd become a policeman.

EPILOGUE

Patrick was the senior partner in the veterinary practice and the sort of guy most women could not resist. Mature, wry and endowed with film star looks, she'd declined his lunch invitations at first, but had eventually succumbed. They never went to the same place twice or anywhere prominent and on this occasion, were sitting outside a small bistro just off O'Connell Street.

Warmed by the effulgent spring sunshine, they were engrossed in one another when Mary walked by. She was in the capital for the day and discreetly continued to make her way down the street, her mind a maelstrom of conflicting thoughts.

To tell or not to tell? She was certain Maeve had not seen her and by the time she had finished her retail therapy and got back to the station, she'd made up her mind. She told Matthew of her experience and begged him not to inform Elisha. But out of loyalty, he insisted on doing so. There might not be anything in it, he said, but Mary had grave forebodings.

With Elisha engaged on an evening shift at the hotel, Maeve busied herself doing various chores in the rather dingy apartment they rented in a not very salubrious part of Dublin.

At about ten she decided not to wait up and went to bed, only to be awakened at around midnight: the bedroom door being furiously flung open, and the light switched full on.

What happened next was horrific and her assailant did not wait to contemplate the consequences of his assault.

FINIS

BYBROOK IMAGES
More things in heaven and earth

INTRODUCTION

This is my literary tragedy, so those not disposed to imbibe this not particularly cheerful tale may choose to go no further. On the other hand, I think it is a great love story and as it contains moments of humour, it could merit a little perseverance.

Stephen Constance. The last throes of summer, 2023.

PROLOGUE

Diminutive in his short trousers, the small boy clutched his mother's hand as they approached the great oak. His father had gone off to Spain to fight and why he should have done this the boy could not comprehend, but he longed for his father to return unscathed. He had been an affectionate, diligent parent, a good provider and a constant source of fun.

Left a virtual widow for the duration, his mother tried to do her best and today's walk was supposed to be a half-term treat, though the weather did not make it the enjoyable experience it would have been during the height of summer. The trees were now fully devoid of their leaves and from the chimney pots beyond the common, smoke eddied languorously upwards, denoting that the harsh season had truly begun. A repetitious barking dog irritated the small boy and accosted his nerves. He hadn't wanted to come to this place where his granny, a suspicious old gap-toothed witch of a woman, intimated strange and mysterious things happened. But she insisted he be taken to see the 'faery ring'. A circle of fungi, the faery ring was said to be the habitat of the little people. Here lived the elves, the fairies and chillingly, the devil himself, and it did not do to disturb them by stepping into it. Legend had it that through abusing this ancient stricture, those that kept stock had their cows' milk curdled by Lucifer and some innocents, upon profaning the circle, vanished altogether.

The couple circled the great oak, an activity said to make wishes come true, and even at his young age inclined towards scepticism, the boy made to jump in the circle. This horrified his mother, who dragged him away from it in none-too-gentle a fashion and admonished him.

The dog had stopped barking and as they wended their way back down to relative civilisation, the eerie stillness seemed to contain an atmosphere of menace: permeating the boy's mind and hastening his progress.

A BEGINNING

The Whippet Inn stands at the bottom of Pope's Hill, the road to it climbing down off the plateau that is the Forest of Dean to join the busy Severnside thoroughfare connecting Gloucester with South Wales. The unpretentious public house commands a fine view of the River Severn, boasts a warm welcome, and cocking a snook at those who disapprove, pays scant respect to recognised opening hours.

The inn's regular cliental are a pretty mixed bunch. Some work at Rank Xerox, others on the land; there are a couple of postmen; a schoolteacher; the vicar of Bybrook and a slightly myopic lorry driver called Dan, who keeps a smallholding on top of Pope's Hill.

Dan is both a philanthropist and an opportunist. As a boy he'd been apprenticed by his parents to the local smithy, and all had gone well with this arrangement, until the day a man had called to have a horse shoed when the blacksmith was absent. The blacksmith had gone off to fit some wrought iron gates to a manor house and left young Dan in charge. By now well into his apprenticeship, Dan coped with the situation competently enough, and when he had finished, the horse's owner had thanked him and proffered a tip of half-a-crown. The man also offered the boy a job on his farm at three shillings a week, and since Dan thought this infinitely preferable to his parents paying out one-and-sixpence for an apprenticeship and him working for nothing, he accepted the offer on the spot. Shrewdly, he decided to pocket both his wages and the one and a tanner from his parents, and it was months before the timorous blacksmith, now burdened with work, found time to apprise them of the situation.

Even a larruping from his dad would not induce the unrepentant Dan to return to the smithy and he spent most of his pre-war years following the plough. Only the intervention of the Second World War managed to interrupt this idyllic existence, when a bout of patriotism persuaded him to join up, and the latter stages of the conflict found him involved in the fierce altercation at Monte Casino. He emerged from this tenacious battle without a scratch and coming home to his parents' smallholding, promptly proceeded to marry a local 'wench', calmly and without asking bringing her to live in their small cottage. Unfortunately, a habitat with only two up and down, one kitchen and a WC fifty yards down the garden, is not calculated to promote domestic harmony and a serious fracas between mother and daughter-in-law persuaded Dan to move out. But with the advent of children and modern sanitation, Marleen and the grandparents soon became reconciled, and the grandchildren, Kevin and Charlie, were a ready solace for the old couple, now living next door in their declining years.

Dan resumed his lorry driving and when not spending nights away, spent a good deal of the time reviving his not too infrequent habit of visiting the Whippet Inn. Like a lot of ex-warriors, Dan missed the camaraderie of war time, and the Whippet was a congenial and convenient outlet for indulging in blatant nostalgia without the presence of a nagging woman to silence one's drink laden tongue. Akin to fishermen's tales, small wartime anecdotes became significant events and as the night wore on were magnified according to the amount of alcohol the narrator had consumed.

Sitting on a stool at the far end of the bar, collarless and unsmiling, the one man who could probably have told greater tales kept his own counsel. He'd been on a hill in Korea not long ago and had mental scars to prove it. Although he chose to keep quiet, his glass was seldom empty. An offer of replenishment would receive a nod and a polite smile in response, so that Fred Duberley was kept permanently in drinks and there was not one man in the Whippet who resented it. A disability pension did not stretch far and by the end of the evening Fred would be swaying on his stool in an euphoric haze. All thoughts of the 'yellow Chinese devils' would be eradicated, and the whimpering of the wounded erased from his subconscious.

Not a small amount of this liquid largesse came from Dan who – by virtue of his dual roles as haulier and smallholder – was not short of a bob or two. Dan believed in working hard and spending hard. The clasp on his wallet needed no lubrication. It opened readily and a moth would no sooner seek refuge within its generous linings than 'a camel would go through the eye of a needle', a quote supplied from the scriptures by the vicar who, at the time, was probably well into his cups.

Guinness glass fuelling his educated patter, the vicar was holding forth to the helpless Fred who, uncomprehending, sat unsteadily astride his bar stool and nodded politely. That he was breaking an age-old taboo had not occurred to the well-lubricated cleric. He'd not noticed the frown on the face of the landlord or the uncomfortable silence that had settled on the company. He took another swig of the stout and said, 'No, what Christ was referring to was a small door within one of the gates of Jerusalem. The main gate would be closed at night and to gain entry, a late-night arrival would have to slip through the door. Obviously, if the traveller came on camelback, it would be difficult, if not impossible for him to be admitted ...'

'What about a donkey, vicar?' The raucous voice of Dan interrupted.

'A donkey?'

'Yes, thou's got a donkey uzz your little uns d' ride, 'asn't thee? An' thou's got a bit in the bank, I reckon. Twouldn't do for thee not t' get through thick pearly gates. Oi daime (I imagine) thas why thou kips a donkey 'stead of a camel!'

Laughter greeted this dubious example of rustic theology and the vicar looked somewhat discomfited. He tried to answer in a jocular pseudo-egalitarian manner – a mistake he frequently made – but only sunk further into the mire of his own making.

'I can't see,' he protested, 'why owning a donkey makes me a rich man. I don't suppose I stand more of a chance of eternity than you fellows. You imagine if you were God looking down at the human antheap ...'

But the incorrigible Dan was well into his stride by now; aided by the alehouse's strongest brew, he returned to the attack. 'Oi d' knoaw where oi be a'gwowin,' he said bluntly. 'That is if their bist room in thick churchyard of thine. Oi be gwowin' six voot under an' their oi'll stay until their yunt none of me left!'

The vicar seemed unabashed. He pushed his glass across the

bar, pulled a purse from an inside pocket and after meticulously counting out one and three pence for another bottle, turned to challenge Dan.

'So you believe in oblivion then, young Daniel?'

'I did see it,' replied Dan baldly. 'I seen enough corpses in the war, vicar. An' thaiy certainly 'and't gone nowhere. D'yud thaiy wuz an' lookin' scared shitless by the look on their vaces before thaiy died.'

The landlord deemed it time to intervene. Dan had overstepped the mark. You did not speak to a 'mon of God' in that fashion, no matter how much you disagreed with him. Apart from the crackle of the log fire, the bar had gone silent again, and one or two of the regular punters had shown signs of drinking up to leave before closing time; an unheard-of heresy which mien host was anxious to nip in the bud.

'Tha's enough, Dan.' The landlord leant over the bar in determined fashion. He was a big man and had never been known to allow too much dissent.

This caused the vicar to be cheerfully accepting. He patted Dan on the shoulder and favouring him with the smile he granted not-so-affluent parishioners on Sundays, said unctuously, 'Tell you what. How about you and I havin' a talk about it at the vicarage sometime? You could come and discuss things. It seems a pity for a fine, upstanding fellow like you to take the attitude you do …'

'No thank you, vicar.' Dan quaffed his ale and clung tenaciously to the mantle of stubbornness which sometimes lies immovably upon his tribe. He'd been brought up to respect the cloth, regretted his bad language, but was determined not to give way.

At this point in the verbal contest, having imbibed too readily, poor Fred Duberley parted company with his stool. Everyone rushed to put him right and after much discussion, and with palpable consternation the vicar offered to take him home. Wisely, the landlord detailed Dan to assist, and having walked down to the pub, Dan was glad of a lift home. He and the vicar staggered across the car park in the not-too-prevalent cloud-impeded moonlight, supporting the burden that was Fred and arriving at the clergyman's somewhat ageing Wolseley with, by now, the vicar breathing quite stertorously. They opened the rear door and with some difficulty, managed to manoeuvre the inebriated Fred onto the back seat. Perhaps unable to realise that the gesture might not help matters, Dan produced a packet of woodbines and offered them to the vicar.

'Smoke, vicar?'

The vicar hesitated and the offer, though maybe just psychologically, seemed to allay his temporary discomfiture.

'Don't mind if I do,' he eventually said. He took what he normally perceived as an 'evil panacea', climbed into the driving seat and invited Dan to sit beside him. They smoked for a while and listened to Fred snoring on the back seat, now dead to the world.

'Fred d' live in a cottage right on top of th' 'ill,' said Dan in an effort to break the tension, which hung in the air midst the stench of stale alcohol and cheap cigarettes.

'I was aware of that. I do visit, you know.' The vicar emitted a slight sigh: he grew tired of people thinking he was only active on a Sunday.

Dan kept quiet as the engine reluctantly fired and pinking badly, the Wolseley turned right out of the car park, taking a steep bend to the left and protesting as it climbed the sharp incline to the upper reaches of Pope's Hill. Most of the hill consisted of common land dotted with ubiquitous small cottages, and from here in daylight you could see the conurbation of Gloucester further on up the Severn and gracious Cheltenham beneath the Cotswolds.

The vicar threw the stub of his woodbine out of the driver's window and brought the car to a halt alongside some white palings; his headlights having picked them out upon their approach.

'Just thought I'd have a look at Wendy,' he said.

'Ah, thick Jenny,' commented Dan. 'You got 'er off Sir Crispin down the abbey.' This was stating the obvious. ''Im yunt a bad owld stick. Oi wuz doin' a bit o' fencin' for un last wik round the ol' deer park. Bad state it wuz in,mind. 'Im wants to let thaiy donkeys loose out there in the spring. 'Im musta 'ave near ten on 'em down their in the stables. Funny owld thing for un t' do, I reckon. Taike in owld donkeys. 'Im's as mean as dirt about zome things. Mind, thick young 'oman-thick Thai girl they brought back with 'em when 'er was a babby, d' do most of the work with 'em.' Here he was referring to the now beautiful young Buppha, who, upon leaving his post as British Ambassador to Siam, Sir Crispen and his wife managed to bring back to Britain. The child soon thrived in her new environment and was a constant solace and aid to her adopted parents in helping to manage the slightly run-down Grade 1 listed mansion that had once been a Cistercian abbey. She was now thirteen and showed every sign of being an absolute heart-stopper.

Well into his verbal stride, Dan continued to apprise the vicar of facts about Sir Crispen's family and circumstances of which the poor orally accosted man was already aware.

"N' young Fred 'ere, 'im 'elps when 'im can in the orangery an' the garden. Only light stuff, mind you, but what 'im doesn't knoaw about gardenin' and voreign plants yunt worth knoawin'. 'im worked at the abbey til 'im got called up an Zir Crispen be only too glad to 'ave 'im 'elp when 'im can. Anyway, I tried t' get my two boiys int'rested in 'avin a donkey, but thaiy yunt interested in much more than vootball an' 'oodin. Still thaiy be doin' well at school, zo I ent grumblin'.'

To give him his due, the vicar listened to this somewhat lengthy discourse with an air of patient resignation. A regular visitor to the former abbey, he let Dan finish before making any comment.

'Well, Sir Crispen seems quite an authority on donkeys and we're grateful for his advice over Wendy. She's doing well and will be an attraction in the churches come Christmas.'

Dan did not quite comprehend. ''Er'll be in church?'

'Yes, that's right,' continued the vicar. 'I expect we shall have the usual nativity plays – there are two schools in my domain – and she'll be traditionally ideal for Mary to arrive on. Anyway, if you don't mind, I'll just go up to the shelter to see if she's OK.'

He removed a torch from the glove department, got out, and with surprising agility, vaulted the palings, making his way over to the right-hand side of the sloping meadow where stood a sturdy three-sided construction next to a small shed. The shed contained barley straw and inside the shelter, a contented donkey, happily munching away at her preferred repast. Barley straw formed the basis of any healthy donkey's diet and too much lush grass was not an option, so that during the summer months, the vicar's children would hopefully tether her under the two big conifers that grew at the bottom of the vicarage garden. Here nothing else grew and some time under these trees would limit the time she spent in her lush pasture.

Checking that she had enough to eat for a couple of days, the vicar bestowed a little fuss on the amiable creature and returned to the car. With Dan's help, he would drop Fred off at the small domicile where the ex-Korean trooper lived with his mother, perform the same service for Dan who lived nearer the top of the hill and then make his way to the vicarage to be greeted by his wife, who always scolded him over these weekly nights out. But these were pre-breathalyser days and this was the only time he drove when more than a little under the influence. The vicarage was a large, looming property at Elton: a scattered community that could scarcely be called a hamlet, situated a country mile down the road from Pope's Hill. Although well into March, with a plentiful show of daffodils in bloom to brighten the daylight hours, the vicar would not venture to walk home in the dark after closing time and looked forward to high summer when he would be able to do so.

Tomorrow he would be meeting Sir Crispen in the small Victorian church which had been built to replace the medieval one that had once been attached to the abbey. The original had been desecrated and destroyed by fire at the time of the dissolution and an in between one had suffered the same fate in the mid-eighteenth century.

Sir Crispen and his wife were a strange couple. During her time in Siam, she had embraced the Buddhist creed and still practised it while he firmly stuck to his family's age-old loyalty to the C of E. Furthermore, he'd become one of the vicar's churchwardens for the little parish church of St Felicity, and yet this disparity in beliefs did not seem to mar their relationship. They were devoted to each other and the former diplomat, Sir Crispen, was equally devoted to the delightful Buppha, who was about the only human being that could twist the gruff and slightly despotic knight of the realm round her little finger. Sir Crispen's relatives maintained that his marriage had survived through each of the partners entirely ignoring what the other was saying at any one time: an unlikely recipe for marital harmony, but an apparently successful one. Sir Crispen was a good employer and made no attempt to disparage his wife's devotion to the Buddhist way of life. He readily assented to take her and Buppha to the Quaker meeting house in the nearby town of Westham, which sat picturesquely, a legacy of a bygone age, on a promontory overlooking the broad and winding Severn near the town church and steeply ascending graveyard. The Quakers had always had a reputation for broad-mindedness and their willingness to accommodate the small local bunch of Buddhists was but one example of their generosity. Another example of the liberality of both Quakers and Buddhists was the stance taken by Buppha. Whilst firmly attached to the creed of her forebears, she was perfectly happy to attend services in her benefactor's church, and though accepting that she would stop short at confirmation, the vicar was willing to go along with things as they were. He even let her play her 'Khaen' in church, a type of seven-note mouth organ that made an ethereal sound that did not seem out of place in the holy surroundings.

Tomorrow's meeting with Sir Crispen would largely concern Easter, and lacking a choir, the vicar had decided to invite a quartet from Westham Brass Band to accompany the main service. The forest was blessed with a number of brass bands and though not strictly within it, Westham had a fine one, and some of its instrumentalists had agreed to play in both St Felicity's and nearby Blaisdon church. Sadly, this did not meet with the approval of the local organist, a certain Arthur Barnet, who lived on an extraordinary smallholding with his ancient mother in the village of Blaisdon. Arthur was generally reckoned to be suffering from what some censorious mortals deemed as a loss of 'some of his marbles', but in truth, was just a victim of a condition which as yet was light years away from being acknowledged by the medical profession.

Arthur could milk a cow and tend a few sheep, but with no culinary skills whatsoever, he and his mother depended on a kind relative and meals-on-wheels to survive. However, mother was remarkably healthy, even if not fully cognizant of what went on and, spent most of her waking hours ensconced on a hard chair in the spacious kitchen surrounded by a near-cohort of invasive felines that she admonished when they tried to appropriate the table for their own purposes.

There was no recognised way up to 'Plumb Farm', other than to climb a steep meadow without a recognised pathway. The property had no electricity or sewage – though septic tanks were prevalent in the main village – and the Barnets' needs being satisfied where that was concerned in a very primitive way, it would probably be inadvisable to describe them in detail!

Though encumbered with more than his fair share of disadvantages in life, Arthur did have one outstanding talent. When completely focused, he was a brilliant musician. He could coax more out of the small organs in both Bybrook and Blaisdon churches than both their congregations thought possible. In those days most organs were still hand-blown, and it needed a cool head to manipulate the bellows handle up and down and to make sure the tell-tale did not linger on empty. A piece of string with a small brass weight attached, the tell-tale denoted how much wind was in the bellows: full when down and – sometimes disastrously! – empty when up. Thirteen-year-old Buppha had recently been coerced into wielding the bellows handle at St Felicity's and her air of serenity had made an instant impact on the disturbed figure who sat on the organ bench.

Buppha had helped the vicar pacify the dissenting Arthur over the importation of the brass groups at Easter, and the gesture the organist made of buying the young girl an expensive box of chocolates was just a prelude to him inviting her to Plumb Farm for a visit. Understandably, the elders at the mansion were not too keen on this idea. They were willing to concede that Arthur's reputation for spasmodic unreliability had declined since he'd known Buppha, but were slightly apprehensive about allowing their precious charge to visit the Barnets on her own.

Fortunately, a solution was found; one proposed by the vicar.

He was aware that Fred Duberly had also been eating out of the hand of the serene Thai teenager for some time and that Fred often took her round the orangery and gardens, displaying his knowledge of the plants and in the summer months, defining and explaining the insects that alighted upon them. He was proud of his know-how and when not plagued with images mainly experienced during the hours of darkness or freed from the temptations of alcohol when working at the abbey, could be a perfectly sane and companiable person.

Accepting the vicar's assurances, Sir Crispen chose a Saturday to collect Fred and picking up Buppha on the way back, took them to Blaisdon.

Upon arrival, he had second thoughts about allowing them to walk up the steep incline alone and experienced something of a culture shock when they arrived at the damp and neglected farmhouse. And the reception they received from the farm's owner could not be said to be that welcoming. Sir Crispen sensed Arthur might even be a little jealous of Fred, and wondered what might transpire between this unlikely triumvirate when he left. He resolved not to be long away and after making Fred promise to look after the vulnerable Buppha, departed with more than a few misgivings.

Engaging with old Mrs Barnet proved not to be a problem for the vivacious Thai girl. She somehow accepted all the imposing felines and even tolerated the invasive chickens that were obviously accustomed to visiting the kitchen, and she did not flinch when confronted by the flitch that hung head down from a hook in the ceiling. Her Buddhist principles did not prevent her from partaking of Arthur's homemade cider and it was also not a drink the eager Fred chose to spurn.

Fred did not care for Chopin rendered by the organist on a slightly out-of-tune piano, but Buppha was enchanted and wondered if Arthur would give her lessons. There was a Bechstein grand in the spacious library at the abbey and the notion that she could sit at it and someday play the music of the great composers greatly appealed to her.

Unfortunately, though she'd restricted herself to one glass of Arthur's rough cider, Fred hadn't, and by the time Sir Crispen came to collect them, the part-time gardener and ex-soldier was incapable. This unaccustomed state of daytime intoxication did not impress the owner of the abbey and he had to enlist the services of Arthur to help get Fred down the slope to the car. It was fortunate that the smallholder did not drink his own product and following behind, the tolerant Buppha found it hard not to feel distressed. She knew of Fred's proclivity to spend a good deal of his leisure hours in the Whippet Inn: this information supplied by a rotund village woman called Dora who doubled as the abbey's virtual housekeeper and incurable gossip.

Even so, and to the young Thai girl's certain knowledge, Fred had never come to work the worse for wear and only her intervention prevented the furious Sir Crispen from instantly terminating the lad's part-time employment. She seemed to have an understanding of Fred's mental state not granted to others. She'd tried to introduce him to meditation, but it was something he hadn't been able to comprehend, and the strictures of Lord Buddha were beyond him. Sir Crispen's wife – having become Bhuppa's adopted mother some time ago – had turned the old nursery in the mansion into a mini-temple wherein she lit joss sticks and knelt before the figure of an imported life-size Buddha. Sir Crispen had learnt to become well tolerant of those of his wife's persuasion when in Siam and had humoured her over her desire to convert the nursery into a place of adulation, but steadfastly refused to have anything to do with it. He had long since given up hope of them producing their own offspring and was resigned to the lovely Bhuppa being a more than adequate compensation.

A day or two after the fateful visit to Plumb Farm, Dan came down to continue his attempt at putting the deer park and surrounds in order, and Sir Crispen saw this as a perfect opportunity to have a word about Fred's excessive alcoholic propensities.

Using it as an excuse to down tools and accept one of his part-time employer's strong Gitane French cigarettes, Dan took his time before answering Sir Crispen's questioning. Having finally sorted out his thoughts on the matter, he implied that if Fred was discouraged from seeking the company of those of his companions that imbibed in the public house at night, then Dan could not vouch for his continued ability to cope with life. The appalling experience of the hill in Korea had left him with these recurring images. Images of yellow hordes descending upon the besieged Glosters. He'd been lucky to survive and already hampered by a slight medical affliction – a condition those responsible for his call-up did not recognise – his mental state was dealt a further devastating blow through witnessing the horrifying massacre of most of his colleagues.

'There is an alternative,' stated Sir Crispen.

Dan feigned incomprehension. He could not imagine what that could be. The answer was succinctly provided.

'Coney Hill,' said Sir Crispen matter-of-factly. Coney Hill was the great edifice of a mental asylum that straddled a large campus on the outskirts of Gloucester.

The look on the smallholder's face conveyed what he thought of that idea, but Sir Crispen was in no way put off by the response to it.

'He'd be well looked after, tended on the spot by medical experts and most assuredly weaned off the booze.'

Dan was still resistant. 'I reckon it'd kill 'im goin' in thick plaice. An' if 'im d' need t' gow in thair, what about thick Arthur Barnet? 'Im yunt the vull ticket, mind. 'Im should be their if any mon should!'

Sir Crispen pondered this for a moment, then said, 'I don't agree. He's just an eccentric and they manage up there. He'd definitely be a fish out of water in Coney Hill and his mother would be lost without him.'

Dan persisted. 'Zo would Fred's! 'Er does 'er best an' 'er'd be devastated if 'im were put away!'

A stalemate on the issue was reached and something of an egalitarian before his time, Sir Crispen let the matter drop. He asked Dan to keep a wary eye on the unfortunate former member of the 'Glorious Glosters' and suggested he requested his fellow topers in the Whippet to restrain their generosity to some extent, and with the good-natured ex-trooper fully willing to acquiesce, left him to his own devices.

The piano lessons were a great success. To give these, Arthur mounted his pre-war Raleigh sit-up-and-beg bicycle weekly, and despite having to contend with its usually under-inflated tyres, duly arrived with enthusiasm and strict punctuality to teach the ardent and grateful Bhuppa. It was not long before she could play her first 'party piece' – Beethoven's 'Fur Elise' – rendered faultlessly for her adopted parents who, imbued with pride and visibly moved, rapturously applauded her sensitive performance.

Invited in to hear this attainment, Fred was less than impressed. He felt that Bhuppa was his protégé, and here was his rival gaining plaudits for teaching something Fred did not really understand. Possibly because he was tone deaf, music did not appeal to him, and surely what he had been informing the Thai girl about nature and wildlife in general was more important and deserved far more recognition than this jumble of meaningless noise? Ergo, and sadly, the great composer's 'Pastorale Symphony' would almost certainly be lost on him.

Part Two

The inhabitants of the small town or large village of Eastdean were suspicious of and mystified by the 'Chinese takeaway' that had opened in the old chippie on the high street. The Chinese couple that had opened it were ahead of their time.

As practising Christians, Li and Chia Hao had fled from the persecution of their homeland's communist regime and without many questions asked, settled in the UK. Quite by accident, they'd one day motored down from Birmingham to the Forest of Dean, discovered the empty fish and chip shop and managing to raise the mysterious finance that enables such things to happen for those of eastern lineage, soon moved themselves and their children to live above it. At that time there were only around thirty-odd takeaways of a rudimentary kind that pandered to stodgy British taste by offering purely standard dishes like chow mein and chop suey and – very cannily – traditional British fish and chips and predictably indigestible meat pies. Like a goodly number of the second city's population, Chia Hao had been working in one of the mind-destroying car plants and with the notable enterprise that typifies his race, did not even entertain the idea that his new venture might involve an element of risk. Originally from Hong Kong, his grandparents had settled in the Chinese quarter of Limehouse in London in the earlier part of the twentieth century, had passed away before it was obliterated in the Second World War, but had kept in touch when still alive, and their acquisition of UK nationality had partially smoothed the way for the eventual settlement of Chia Hao and family in the country. Apprehensive about Japanese in Hong Kong during the war, Chia Hao's parents had moved south to Shanghai, had accepted the new communist regime at the end of it and, to their son's dismay, abandoned their religion, but respected his intention to leave China before it became entirely repressive and religiously intolerant.

The young Chinese couple were fortunate in that the giant organisation that was Rank Xerox had chosen to locate in Eastdean very shortly before they arrived, and whilst most of their trade was still done in fish and chips, the fact that Rank's attracted employees from a large area meant that quite a few of the more discerning customers were willing to sample the Chinese menu, and this relatively novel attempt to appeal to the normally resistant Anglo-Saxon palate soon succeeded and grew in popularity.

It so happened that the small parish of Benhall lay just up the hill from Eastdean, its rather insignificant nineteenth-century church sited at the end of a short lane that led to it from the sinuous narrow road that wound down the hill to Bybrook. At the bottom of the hill stood the old mill where the road forked left and right. You turned left for Bybrook and the right fork took you to Little Dean, but not before you encountered the quaintly named settlement of Green Bottom, a collection of houses situated just inside the all-pervading woodland, and giving the impression that it would be at home within the covers of a classic Thomas Hardy novel.

Although blessed with the natural unspoilt opulence that might be a balm to most of its residents, the bosky and untroubled landscape hereabouts could not be said to include an abundance of what some might conceive to be the essentials of modern living. Bybrook had a village hall of sorts: a wooden construction in which not a lot took place. Freezing in winter, it could be boiling in summer and apart from its limited facilities being used by the small gallant WI once a month, there was little interest in other activities and the main social event in those straitened postwar days took part in the church after morning service. The congregation included a goodly number of those that inhabited dwellings on Pope's Hill, who mainly came via the steep footpath which wound its way down to Bybrook from the summit and saved having to take a circuitous route by road.

Seeking somewhere to satisfy their spiritual needs, Chia Hao and Li had decided to attend Mattins at Benhall in preference to St. Michael's, Eastdean, where the rector had proved to be rather austere and not particularly friendly.

The locals were initially hesitant in their acceptance of these 'aliens' of the human species, but soon came round, and thanks to the vicar, the Reverend Charles Emsworth – he of the donkey and the inclination to patronise the Whippet Inn – they soon fitted in. And the delicate Li produced brief smiles on homely faces when asked to read from the Bible in her very cultured but mixed accent, which had shades of Brummie, Mandarin and Forest in it.

Not long after their first attendance they'd encountered Bhuppa, who'd eventually emerged from behind the organ at the end of the service and was immediately attracted to the Chinese family and in particular, their two children. This led to the Chinese being invited to join all the other congregations in the Reverend Charles's parishes to a combined service at Bybrook which sadly caused the one jarring note in proceedings. This was caused by the enigmatic Fred who, though reluctant, had been persuaded to join the congregation by way of the same sloping footpath that enabled a short cut to be taken to the church.

Somewhat alarmingly, the Chinese family's entrance had caused Fred's swift exit. A glance at Chia Hao's countenance had revived within him the dreaded scenario that, without success, he constantly strove to forget. Was it possible that one of those fiends had followed him here? He left in a lather of dread that bordered on sheer terror and despite subsequent attempts at reassurance by both the vicar and Sir Crispen, he ceased to attend the church and quite irrationally tried to think of ways to rid the locality of this sole haunting Chinaman.

It was not long before Sir Crispen's wife, Annie, who was possessed of even more egalitarian views than her husband, invited the Chinese family to visit, and momentarily forgetting the part-time gardener's aversion to Chia Hao, took them for a tour of the garden. Inevitably, this resulted in them bumping into Fred, the sudden encounter bringing about that terrified mortal's instant retreat to the potting shed wherein he stayed put; only being persuaded to emerge after their departure.

Knowing of his fondness for Bhuppa, they tried to get her to use her influence on him, but her attempts to probe and question him met with little success. Her solicitude only made him very agitated and after a while she gave up, and in this her parents backed her up. Thinking it all too stressful for a thirteen-year-old, Sir Crispen forbade any further effort on her part to solve the problem and resolved to consult his family doctor over the case.

One mellow autumn Sunday the Chinese family came to dinner after church at Benhall and abandoning her usual Sunday roast, and with Bhuppa's assistance, Annie decided to utilise the culinary skills she had acquired in Thailand. Thai food is not all that different from Chinese and her 'tom yung goong' (hot and sour food) consisting of pork and broth with lemon grass, kaffir lime, galangal, fresh lime and chilli, went down well with her guests. There is a certain type of Buddhism that vaguely permits the consumption of meat and with Sir Crispen to feed, his wife found it convenient to put a more liberal interpretation on things and though inclined towards vegetarianism, nevertheless earned her husband's gratification by often including meat as a staple part of the family diet. Around the table, talk eventually turned to religion, and still with some incredulity and knowing of the set-up in the abbey, the Chinese were amazed that two different creeds could be espoused within the same family. Religious tolerance was something more or less unknown to the Chinese and when Annie brought the Quaker fraternity and their kindness in allowing the Buddhists to use their meeting house into the equation, they were dumbfounded.

Also present at the meal were the vicar and his family, and his strongly ecumenical attitude did a lot to dispel the Church of England's perceived take on things. He opined that his church was currently hidebound and would soon have to change pretty rapidly to accommodate the pace of life in the mid-twentieth century.

Out of this new friendship came several other welcome benefits. After being schooled at home during her primary years, Bhuppa had refused attempts by Sir Crispen to arrange private education for her and when attaining the right age, had insisted on attending the newly built secondary school which had been constructed in a meadow opposite the Church Lane in Benhall. This had made it easier for the Chinese couple's eldest girl, aged twelve, to settle in there during the summer term without the same slight racial disparagement that Bhuppa had had to endure from one or two unenlightened pupils upon her enrolment. At the time, and probably stirred into prompt action by the knowledge that she was the adopted daughter of the chairman of the governors, the school settled the matter with admirable alacrity. The culprits were soon apprehended and punished and nothing adverse was directed at Ah Cy when she too became a pupil. She was soon assimilated into the limited social scene that UK teenage girls inhabited in the early fifties and if there were sometimes minor hiccups that afflicted scholastic progress, it was usually her efficacious new Thai friend that stepped in to sort them out. The two of them soon became firm friends and it was perhaps mildly amusing that Bhuppa introduced young Ah Cy to the 'Tipitaka' or Bhuddist holy book and such things as 'dharma' or truth, and the beads used for meditation. All symbols her parents had rejected in favour of Christianity years ago.

 Sometimes the vicar's children would invite them to ride Wendy, and Bhuppa was looking forward to Christmas when she would be Mary and at the vicar's request, ride a donkey into St Felicity's. The other churches would be visited by his daughter Rachel on Wendy, and as she fully accepted that Christianity was the main religion of her adopted country, Bhuppa had no qualms about taking part in this celebration of Christ's birth.

 Like nearly all the donkeys that Sir Crispen took in and nurtured, Wendy had been a poor undernourished creature and when nursed back to health, had been given to the vicar's family in return for a donation to the Donkey Preservation Society. All persons allowed to acquire a donkey had to be strictly vetted and agree to regular inspection by a representative of the society, and Sir Crispen would not part with one if he had the slightest misgivings about the prospective new owners and the environment the animal would be expected to live in.

*

It was 'Vicar's Night' in the Whippet. Happily attached to his bottled Guinness, the unsuspecting clergyman had no indication that Tuesdays had been dubbed this by its alcoholically inclined patrons, and once when a fellow cleric had intimated that his predilection for the famous stout was 'a marriage made in heaven', he did not dispute it and regardless, carried on with his weekly libations without further comment.

Except that on this occasion Dan was trying to engage him in conversation, and Dan in full flow was someone difficult to resist.

'Thou 'eard about the "Chinee"' then?'

Suddenly concerned, the vicar gave Dan his full attention. The proprietors of that now thriving concern were very much his business. They supported the little church at Benhall with enthusiasm and practical help, and if they were in trouble, then it was incumbent on him as their pastor to help. He replied in the negative and waited for Pope Hill's premier rustic orator to enlighten him.

'Bad do,' said Dan. 'Zomeone did braike their windas.'

Reverend Charles could not see why anyone should choose to do that. Vandalism was not something that was prevalent in the mid-fifties. It was not quite the era of Teddy Boys or, later on in the decade, bad behaviour induced by rock and roll, and the cleric could only put it down to racialism or mere excessive drunkenness.

Dan nodded in the direction of Fred, who sat morosely on his usual perch some distance at the end of the long bar counter. It was unlikely he could eavesdrop on their conversation.

'Oi az my suspicions!'

The vicar made a point of not casting his eyes in the same direction as the smallholder's. He was appalled at the veiled accusation.

'Surely not?'

''appened on zaturdaiy night.' Dan lowered his voice before re-commencing and a quizzical expression encompassed the vicar's face.

'You're not suggesting?'

Dan dismissed any doubts. 'Why not? 'Im d' catch thick last bus up t' Eastdean at vivish an' it d' get 'im their fur openin' time. 'Ee gets it in 'im zummat vairish an' thee cussent know what 'im'd do when 'im's 'ad a few.'

The Reverend Charles realised that Fred could well be the culprit. Thanks to a bus service that operated between Westham and Cinderford three or four times a day, and ambled through all the settlements in between – the benefit of having a sparsely motorised society – the haunted lad could get to the small town without too much trouble and did have this nightmarish vision of Chia as one of his former adversaries. Then a thought struck Reverend Charles that might well exonerate Fred from the misdeed.

'But Dan, how would he get back home?'

'Well, when 'im manages it, 'im walks. Though oi dairzay 'im az spent a vew nights in the church porch at St Michael's or on a bench in the churchyard. Oi picked 'im up with my wagon on my way back vrum somewhere one night an' 'im zeems t' survive some'ow.'

'But what about his mother? Doesn't she worry when he doesn't get home?'

Dan shrugged. ''Er don't worry no more. 'Er yewsed t' ring the "Garge" an' thaiy rung owld Jummy at the police 'ouse. But 'im allus come wome eventually, so 'er's given up bothcrin'.'

Reverend Charles tried not to get agitated.

'But what about these smashed windows? Is this- what d'you call him? Is this "Jummy" one of the local plods? I know PC James Worthington, but I don't know the sergeant very well and not a supposed "Jummy" at all.'

Dan laughed. 'Thou needs t' brush up thy vorest, vicar! Jummy bist vorest fur James 'n 'im's a lazy bugger. Oi d' reckon 'im 'oodn't try too 'ard to find out 'oo'd broken a bit o' glass. I daime (imagine) 'im d' spend too much time in thick bookies t' worry about zummat like that!'

The four-letter word beginning with 'f' was not yet in vogue, but the vicar still tried hard not to flinch at the swear word Dan had used. He moved along the bar to where Fred was still hunched, seeking further information and offered to buy him a drink. Fred never refused and the cleric determined to be only mildly inquisitory.

All this was observed by Dan who, with unusual discretion, began to address another former soldier, a conversation which could nearly always be guaranteed to last all night.

The Reverend Charles's first question was perhaps unfortunate and earned a sharp response.

'Did you go to Eastdean on Saturday?'

'No.'

The vicar could identify a lie when he heard one. He sighed and examining his conscience, told one himself. Looking at Fred with stern appraisal, he said, 'You know that's not true, Fred. Someone told me you were there. He was in the George and comes to Benhall on Sundays'

Fred became surly. 'What's it got t' do with thou what oi d' do when oi yunt workin'.'

Reverend Charles put a reassuring hand on his shoulder. 'Fred,' he said, 'I'm only concerned for your safety. We wouldn't like you to come to any harm in Eastdean, and perhaps if you attempted to drink a little less…?'

This admonition aroused slight amusement in the clergyman as he said it. Equating the small town with somewhere in darkest Manchester or the gorbals in Glasgow was a bit farfetched and inciting Fred to drink less when he'd just bought him one, a bit hypocritical.

Whatever, it elicited little response from Fred, but hoping that his words might have had some latent effect, the vicar returned to make further conversation with Dan, whose erstwhile companion had gone home to face the wrath of his Amazonian spouse; a force not to be denied. The landlord often received calls from irate wives of this nature and, a benevolent soul, contented himself with delivering the message and wisely keeping his own counsel. Most of those thus summoned who were not under 'petticoat government' simply ignored the relayed message, but Dan's mate Hamish, a rugged ex-patriot from Aberdeen, turned to jelly when contemplating the possible application of a rolling pin to his person. He'd not flinched when facing unremitting German fire at Arnhem, but to defy his enraged Lottie would take considerably more courage than he possessed. How Hamish and Dan communicated was a mystery. Indeed, how Hamish communicated with anyone in the pub was source of speculation to anyone who happened to speak the English language. The two dialects, Forest and Glaswegian, were irreconcilable and on more than one occasion, either the vicar or Sylvie, the rather well-spoken landlord's wife intervened, attempting to translate. When first installed in the area, the vicar had bought a book on 'Forest' by Harry Beddington, a mining superintendent, and he later purchased tomes by other authors; amongst them Keith Morgan and a Dr Tandy: the latter's description of what occurred in his practice reducing readers to tears of laughter.

Apart from being labelled behind her back as 'eye candy', the landlord's young wife was very intelligent and soon picked up the dialect; an achievement that led to one or two of the more erudite patrons adding to this description by furtively calling her 'the thinking man's crumpet'. How Joe the landlord had acquired her affections was not generally known, but '"im wuz a decent mon, an' per'aps 'er preferred a decent mon to a bit o' rough...'

Addressing the now disengaged Dan, the vicar said, 'I have an idea, but it'd need you to implement it.'

Dan was at a loss to know how the word 'implement' could be used in this context. He'd only heard it applied to machinery and waited for the reverend to explain.

The vicar lit another cigarette. No one as yet had told him smoking was a vice and whilst he had a suspicion it might inflict harm upon the 'temple' that was his body, he was sure the Lord would forgive him for enabling himself to endure the vicissitudes of existence by any means at his disposal. In his haste to assuage his own needs he'd omitted to offer his companion a similar panacea, and a slight cough and pointed look from that party caused him to hastily rectify the situation.

'Sorry, old man,' he said, 'now look, what I'd like you to do is go to the George on Saturday night in that pickup of yours and observe Fred who, unless contrarily motivated to drink elsewhere, will be well in his cups by the time you arrive. I have a strong feeling, a premonition if you like, that having just perpetuated one small crime, Fred might be tempted to commit another much graver one.'

Dan shook his head in partial disbelief and pulled a doubtful face.

'Thou d' really believe 'im broke thaiy windas?'

The vicar also shook his head; this more of an affirmative gesture.

'Call it divine intervention if you like, but I really think that such is Fred's irrational antipathy towards Chia Hoa, that the Chinaman and his family might be endangered.'

Dan wished the vicar would refrain from using so many big words, but despite this, managed to assimilate what he was saying.

'Zo, what it amounts to, iz thou wants oi t' kip an eye on 'im?'

The vicar smiled. 'You have it. You won't need to get there too early. From the information I have, Fred won't make a move until closing time, and you won't want to be inebriated just in case- in case-what d'you call him...?'

'Thou means Jummy the plod?'

'That's right, Jummy. He might stop you.'

'Can't zee uz 'ow 'im's goin' t' do that. 'Im spends most zaturdaiy nights a'gwowin' round the pubs 'isself. Zaiys 'im's only checkin' t' zee everythin's alright. But 'im az a pint in each on 'em, zo oi daime 'im wunt be in a vit state to arrest any other piss artiste!' Aware of this indiscrete bit of invective too late, Dan put an apologetic hand on the clergyman's shoulder. 'Sorry vicar, but thou doesn't know Jummy. 'Im yunt much of a law enforcer. 'Im's too vond of the good life: gamblin', drinkin' and not known at one time t' refuse the attentions of thick 'eadmaster's missus at the endowment school!'

This led to the bemused vicar wondering why this dilettante of a law enforcer had not been noted as a less than squeaky-clean officer by his superiors. He then recalled that the man's rather laissez faire sergeant, being of a similar mien, in his turn favoured the Lamb Inn where he assisted in flouting most of the rules governing public houses. Appearing not to notice or just ignore his constable's blatant flaws, he was grateful that even minor crime was not prevalent in the small community of Eastdean and serious crimes virtually unknown.

Dan had fully absorbed what the vicar had been asking and though not able to repeat it verbatim, in his own inimitable way showed that he knew what was expected of him.

'Zo what it d' amount too, thou d' want oi t' stick by un maike zure 'im don' do zummat drastic adder 'im leaves the pub?'

'You have it,' said the vicar, gratified, and took Fred's hand to shake it. He then proceeded to change the subject. 'By the way,' he said, 'how are your boys getting on?'

'Thaiy be doin' well,' replied Dan, proud of his offspring and further bent the reverend's ear by imparting the attainments of Kevin and Charlie which included Kevin's selection for Cinderford Juniors at football and Charlie's inclusion in Little Dean boys' cricket team.

The vicar listened patiently and took the opportunity to order another pint for Dan and a Guinness for himself.

*

Unknown to Sir Crispen, Bhuppa had been introducing Arthur Barnett to Buddhism. Quite often Sir Crispen and his wife were occupied elsewhere when he came to give her a piano lesson, and several times she'd taken him to see the makeshift temple which Annie had created in the abbey.

When learning of this, far from being gratified that the creed might gain a new convert, Sir Crispen's wife was becoming disturbed by the attention the eccentric organist was bestowing on the charming teenager. Nearing fourteen and developing rapidly, there was no denying that Bhuppa was extremely attractive, and Annie was concerned that the bizarre Arthur could put the wrong interpretation on the attention he was getting in return. Bhuppa was slavishly devoted to her piano, sparing every possible moment to practise and her gratitude to the owner of Plumb Farm might easily be misinterpreted by its somewhat eccentric owner. Annie hadn't like to frown upon a couple more visits Bhuppa made to the slightly decrepit farmstead in Blaisdon, but there was no question that it made her uneasy, and when at Bhuppa's instigation Arthur appeared on his bicycle for a meditation at the meeting house in Westham, she felt things had got out of hand. The smallholder had insisted that he sit by Bhuppa, had fidgeted and muttered throughout the meditation and at its conclusion, to their acute embarrassment, insisted on shaking hands with all present before leaving.

An appeal to Sir Crispen fell on stony ground. He dismissed

his wife's misgivings and said whilst it might be an idea to restrict Bhuppa's visits to Plumb Farm, he did not see any need to take any further action over what was probably an innocent friendship. Perhaps Annie could be around when the piano lessons were in progress, although he was quite sure Arthur would not engage in anything that was remotely improper.

This did not satisfy Annie and she insisted on accompanying Bhuppa when she took her piano teacher to the temple. She had to admit that he showed great appreciation and interest in the hallowed place, though whether he fully understood what it was all about, she had grave doubts. Then there was the fact that he was always presenting Bhuppa with small gifts. Bars of chocolate, fruit, and even cheap trinkets which, in her still slightly childish innocence, Bhuppa accepted: these offerings proffered with seemingly no base motives whatsoever. Not entirely convinced, Annie resolved to keep an eye open at the slightest indication that things were not as they should be and bring it to the notice of her husband once more.

*

The George was a large Victorian public house situated on the Cross in Eastdean: opposite the imposing church of St Michael and all Angels and very handily situated near the few shops and general post office. It was questionable which establishment – pub or post office – promulgated the hottest line in gossip. A visit to either of these places could make a body aware of local news and events within minutes and a trip to the small eighteenth-century town hall for similar information, though only a short walk away, would constitute a wholly unnecessary trip.

The George had two bars, and with the hands on the grandfather clock in the main one depicting nine o'clock, an unrelieved cacophony prevailed within it. This was partly due to the presence of Arthur Barnett who, in order to supplement his meagre income, was applying himself to a 'clapped-out joanna' with vigour, at the same time trying to not overly sample the contents of the tankards on the top of it, these provided by the punters who were bent on having a riotous evening at all costs. The village organist displayed a surprising knowledge of the popular tunes of the day and currently the whole bar was being inspired to join in with a remarkable rendition of 'Goodnight Irene' in full four-part harmony. This modulated smoothly into 'Cruising Down the River' equally well harmonised and was evidence – if any was needed – that as descendants of the Ancient British, Foresters were just as able to sing as any of those who hailed from the Celtic nations.

Fred had not been able to take up a position at the bar, for it was occupied from one end to the other with sturdy male drinkers, all of whom seemed to prefer to stand there, some with a foot on the brass rail beneath it, and all of them impeding attempts by potential imbibers to get served. The landlord had given up in trying to designate a permanent space at the bar for would-be customers and bearing in mind that most of the counter-hugging drinkers patronised the tavern during the week and not just weekends, he had to trust to their good nature, hoping they'd clear a path to let other people purchase their drinks without too much hassle.

Fred sat disconsolately at a table with two ancient devotees of the George who probably resented his presence, and during a comfort break taken by the willing Arthur, one of them took advantage of the comparative reduction in noise to address his companion.

'Bist thee a'gwowin' t' thick funeral on Wen'sdee, Clem?' Rummaging in his pocket for his tobacco tin and fag papers, the one addressed as Clem slowly deliberated, as if the question was a difficult one to answer and eventually deigned to reply.

'I reckon zo. 'Im wuza funny owld bugger, wuz Bindy, but 'im wa'nt a bad un, an' oi daime there'll be a bit o' bait t' yut adderwards.'

Obviously now a cadaver awaiting imminent interment, why the said 'Bindy' had acquired his nickname was a mystery. A local postman, he'd often stay in the George until long gone closing time-all the pubs in Eastdean totally disregarded lawful hours-and though worse for wear, he'd be at the small sorting office at 5.30 a.m. the next morning. Only the tolerance of the kind postmaster enabled Bindy to hang on to his job and his alcohol-fuelled exploits were legendary. Sometimes on a Thursday he would finish his round at 11.00 a.m. and if inclined, catch a Cotterell's bus to Ross where the weekly market ensured the pubs were open all day. He would then return on the same splendid hand-painted vehicle for a brief rest before taking his accustomed place in the George at night.

For him, Christmas was an especially hazardous time. Those he had supplied with mail throughout the year insisted on showing their appreciation by plying him with alcohol, and one particular Christmas, this generosity got the better of him. He had to give up and stagger home, and his mailbag was later found in a hedge by the previously mentioned member of His Majesty's Constabulary known as 'Jummy'. Not known for a particular inclination towards philanthropy, the police officer nevertheless finished the round for the errant postman and returned his bag to the post office. For once this did result in a severe dressing down from the normally tolerant postmaster, and Bindy did attempt to 'go on the wagon' for a while, but the demon drink returned with a vengeance and sadly, a newly dug resting place now awaited him in St Michael's graveyard.

Having rolled and inserted the roll-up into the accustomed place between his lips, Clem lit it and its smoke added to the veritable 'fog' that blanketed the bar.

'Oi taike it thou's gowin'?' he said to his buttie, an ex-faceworker known as Horace.

'Oi,' replied Horace, and obviously amused by something, emitted a throaty chuckle. Something had just occurred to him and served to lighten the grave prospect of their mutual friend's funeral. ''Ow owld be thou then, Clem?' he asked his companion with what could be described as a certain amount of irrelevance.

Haste was not an attribute that could normally be associated with Clem, but slightly intrigued by the question, he was for once not timorous in answering.

'Aighty-nine,' he said, and added, "ow about thee?'

'Aighty-seven,' obliged Horace jauntily.

Clem's face spread into a rarely seen smile.

'Well,' he said, 'oi daime zince we'll be in thick churchyard already an' we a' been born too zoon, it wunt be wo'th goin' wome!'

A fat 'oman's laugh was cut short and made inaudible as the restored pianist launched into 'Bless this 'ouse'; the bibulous chorus lustily harmonised and drowning out any further attempt at conversation.

The entrance of the law in the shape and ponderous gait of Jummy was not particularly heeded or remarked upon, apart from a few friendly salutations, and Dan's almost simultaneous appearance more or less received the same response.

Well known in the Forest, Dan had no difficulty in reaching the bar, and getting served, made his way back to the only chair available which happened to be at Fred's table. Fred did not seem glad to see him, but Horace and Clem were not similarly inclined and showed their approval by providing him with a ready-made roll-up. They were both resilient, hardened characters, who had left the mines to take part in the old war and unlike a lot of their fellow combatants who were loath to talk of it, were perfectly willing to relate their experiences. Lucky to have escaped the slaughter of the Somme, they were also happy to hear about the wartime experiences of Dan, the battle-hardened warrior of a younger generation.

Came the time at half-past-ten when the willing pianist had had enough and in passing the table containing Fred, Dan and the older couple, was shocked when springing to life, Fred assaulted him in the face with a stinging blow. Pretty fit, Arthur reacted in kind and after a short melee, during which both parties went at it hammer and tongs, Dan and PC Jummy – the latter for once alert – pulled them apart and restrained them. With some help from the landlord and others, the two antagonists were frog marched into the quieter lounge bar and made to sit quiescent whilst the police officer questioned them.

It appeared that Fred's unexpected aggression had been prompted by the belief that Arthur had allegedly been paying Bhuppa too much attention, an accusation that the musician bemusedly denied and became very upset about. It seemed that Fred was just plain jealous and despite Jummy's warning that if he caused further trouble, he'd possibly be charged with causing a fracas without provocation, he would not be pacified.

''Im's allus down the abbey, or 'er's up at 'iz varm, 'n it b'yunt right.'

Clearly something needed to be done to sort out the situation. The girl was far too young to be the victim of this dispute and at Dan's suggestion, Jummy would get his sergeant to telephone Sir Crispen, who, also a local magistrate, could be relied upon to assess and to arbitrate over the matter.

Given little choice but to accept this, Fred was escorted back into the public bar in a resentful lather, given ginger beer to drink and told to behave until Dan returned from transporting a shaken Arthur home to Blaisdon. They put the pianist's bike in the back of the pickup and Fred was told to wait for Dan's return in order that he too might have a lift home. This was a condition imposed by the unusually rigorous Jummy, who then departed, probably to see that all was well with his sergeant down at the Lamb on the lower crossroads.

The landlord of the George tried to keep an eye on the recent assailant, but this proved too much of a task as the local rugby team returned from an away match, heavily fuelled with alcohol, to add their boisterous presence to an already crowded bar.

Absorbed in a late radio documentary on the BBC Home Service which dealt with the repression being inflicted on the people of China, Li suddenly realised that Chia Hao had been gone for some time. He'd said he was only going to put waste in the bins and hadn't yet returned, though half an hour had elapsed. She would ascend the further flight of stairs in their flat to look in on their children, Ah Cy and nine-year-old Hoi Sang, then go down to the closed takeaway to see what had detained her husband. She was reassured to see her offspring slumbering peacefully, but there was no sign of Chia Hao in the silent take away. He must still be in the backyard and upon investigation and to her horror, this was a fateful correct assumption. He lay in a pool of blood against the dustbins, having taken what appeared to be some heavy blows to his person. The beam of light shining through the back window of the takeaway enabled her to see this and feeling his pulse, she wasted no time in returning inside to use the recently installed telephone to 999.

Totting up the day's takings, the bookmaker next door, who also lived in a flat above the premises, was disturbed by the ambulance's arrival and with his wife came out to see if they could do anything to help. This offer was a godsend to Li. She couldn't go with the ambulance and leave the children on their own, and since they'd got to know Mr and Mrs Brain, the neighbours, very well in the short time they'd lived in Eastdean, she had no qualms about leaving Ah Cy and her brother with them. Li was assured that it would be no trouble, and the couple would be glad to babysit until she returned. Cyril Brain had agreed to contact the police house, and hopefully Jummy would have returned from his peregrinations round the pubs, or the sergeant who lived a little way out could be persuaded to hasten to the scene of the supposed crime.

In the George, now empty and closed, Dan was trying to control his temper over the fact that Fred had apparently been allowed to leave. Jummy had forcefully stipulated that he must not be let out of the landlord's sight, and Ivan the landlord was protesting that he didn't have eyes in the back of his head. He maintained that Fred was not his responsibility and that if Jummy had wanted him kept secure, he should have had him shipped up to Cinderford and slung in the cell for the night.

They were interrupted by the arrival of Sergeant Pateman, a burly and troubled figure, who soon informed them what had happened. Liking a peaceful life, he looked decidedly moithered and had promptly contacted divisional HQ in Lydney who were soon on the case. Putting two and two together and correctly making four, it did look as though the disturbed Fred was the obvious culprit in what looked like a case of grievously bodily harm. There was no sign of the weapon which had been used to carry out the brutal assault and the A&E department at the old Gloucester infirmary in Southgate Street had thankfully stated that the victim was holding his own.

As it happened, they found Fred without too much trouble. This was mainly thanks to Dan, who'd found him asleep under the hedge down by the old mill on a couple of previous Saturday nights. He looked very peaceful when they found him, clutching his prized ebony walking stick with its ivory horsehead: an heirloom inherited from a grandad who had served in Rhodesia. It was revealingly spattered in blood and highly likely to have been the weapon that had been used to accost Chia Hao.

They took Fred to Coney Hill to await trial, and the sergeant reckoned that although there would be one, it would only serve to send him back there. Phrases like 'diminished responsibility' and 'whilst the mind was disturbed' were bandied about and the poor survivor of the Korean conflict would probably remain in the mental asylum for the rest of his life.

On the following Monday morning at a special sitting in Little Dean Magistrate's Court, though guilty, Fred was acquitted on the grounds of diminished responsibility. After a short spell whilst retained and examined by a doctor, he was sectioned as predicted and returned to Coney Hill.

It helped that Sir Crispen had been chairman of the magistrates, a position that could have disqualified him as an interested party, but his acknowledged status in the community ensured that no one would dare to question his involvement. The superintendent of Lydney Divisional HQ, who had initially resolved to have Fred put away, took one look at him, and confronted with evidence given by the new young commanding officer of the Gloucestershire Regiment, decided not to pursue the matter. There would be no committal to be tried in a higher court and with the doctor's prognosis of his mental condition accepted, it looked as though one of the regiment's surviving heroes would have to spend the rest of his existence confined in the mental asylum.

Full of foreboding, the Rev. Charles agreed to accompany him and his distraught mother in the police wagon. Traversing the stark corridors withing the grim building, they were taken to a secure ward where they were informed that Fred would reside until at some undefined point, he might be deemed fit for release. The ward had what could be called an 'airlock'. A door into it led to what was politely termed the foyer and here the tight-lipped young lady who'd been part of the escort, suggested that mother said her farewell. Now almost wraithlike, and not having come out with more than a few barely discernible utterances since his capture, the farewell did not register with Fred, but caused his mother to break down.

The abrupt departure of her with Rev. Charles could almost be interpreted as callous, but to utilise the old cliché, perhaps it is necessary 'to be cruel to be kind'. The door was shut firmly behind them before an inner one was unlocked and opened to admit Fred. The noise and scenario confronting him would not have been out of place as the subject of a canvas by Bosch. There were only two staff available to control a small sea of mostly uncontrollable humanity. They had a variety of afflictions and the senior male nurse, an amazingly genial and expansive West Indian displaying extraordinary tolerance would, when passing from his present existence, surely become a candidate for instant canonisation.

Outside in busy Southgate Street, the vicar's wife Isobel waited patiently in their pre-war Wolsey. Isobel could not be described as the power behind the throne, neither was she the meek little woman. She'd followed the police wagon to Gloucester, a clear-headed action that meant her far from flawless husband would not have to catch the bus back and make sure Fred's distressed mother caught it with him.

In an unobtrusive way, Isobel overseed most of the female things that went on in the three parishes and without undue stress, kept the children and the vicarage in order without them or her spouse realising. Gratitude was sometimes forthcoming, though she didn't expect it, and had to admit that Charles was the soul of generosity over Christmas and birthdays and never pretended to be what he was not. He rated himself an 'infernal priest' and reckoned his standing where perfection was concerned, fell way below that of his maker. He did not try to be all things to all men, and if he felt one of his flock deserved upbraiding for some misdemeanour or other, they were duly upbraided. The era when all were blameless through something occurring to cause them to err was fifty years away for the moment and the vicar believed in calling a spade a spade – you do wrong, you are berated over it. The horrors of twenty-first non-

171

morality had not yet arrived to befuddle the mind, and high tech was decades away from insidiously replacing humanity with artificial intelligence and faceless surrealism.

Part Three

CHAPTER ONE

A furious altercation was taking place between Sir Crispen and his wife: this unusual and upsetting spectacle brought about by the tearful Bhuppa's desire to visit Fred at Coney Hill. Sir Crispen's assertion that the mental hospital was not far removed from Dickens's notorious 'bedlam' was strenuously disputed by Annie, but his flat refusal to permit a visit was proving difficult to oppose.

In an effort to placate her, Sir Crispen had graphically described the scene he'd allegedly experienced when visiting Coney Hill with Dan. He asserted that they were not permitted to enter the ward, and when being conducted along the corridors he claimed to have glimpsed others of equally frightening scenarios and was adamant that it would not be a fit place for a young girl of Bhuppa's tender years to visit.

Upon their arrival, Fred had been brought out to a common room where the less afflicted were allowed to congregate and even the hardened soul that was Dan commentated on the almost unrelieved stench of tobacco and the impenetrable haze that accompanied it. It seemed that all the patients smoked and when asked by Sir Crispen whether anything was done to discourage it, a nurse shrugged and stated that, on the contrary, it was almost actively encouraged. The head medical honcho apparently preferred his charges to indulge in smoking. He disapproved of tablets like Valium and other addictive medicines and maintained that tobacco helped to assuage mental conditions and more than offset any physical damage it might do. When questioned over the probability that this policy could invite cases of cancer to develop, the same nurse lit a cigarette and stated he'd not known of one since he'd been employed at the hospital and just smiled when the inquisitory aristocrat questioned the veracity of his statement.

Annie was not prepared to back down, but a suggestion that Fred might be allowed out for a while and be taken by them to a quiet café somewhere in Gloucester, still met with stubborn resistance. Sir Crispen saw no way that the hapless man could be released back into the wide world, if only for a brief spell and furthermore, he had no intention to use his privileged status in society in order to try and bring this about.

Upset, Bhuppa had now left the scene and the strains of Beethoven's 'Pathetique Sonata' – albeit a little stumbling – could be heard emanating from the library. Despite centuries and a pedigree that practically went back to William the Conqueror, Sir Crispen was not a hard man and affected by the music, stopped in mid-sentence and enfolded his wife in his arms.

'Look Annie,' he said, 'I'll have a think. I do understand why Bhuppa would want to see Fred, but I really can't see there's any way at present that she can do.'

To his surprise, she kissed him lightly and sighed. There ought to be some way, but she knew it was useless to persevere with her protestations. She withdrew and thumped him playfully in the chest, indulging in some unusually ripe language as she did so.

'Right, you stubborn old bugger, isn't it about time you went to see to the donkeys?'

*

At the time enveloped in a drunken stupor; Fred had only been capable of giving Chia Hao two glancing blows. There was more blood than permanent damage and the patient was recovering well. His current visitor was the vicar, and the clergyman could not believe what the Chinaman was trying to say. He thought he had misheard and attempted to clarify what Chia Hao was trying to impart. Questioned by the perceptive and highly intelligent patient, the vicar endeavoured to explain what might have prompted Fred's vicious assault. He lucidly described the circumstances of the Chinese attack on the hill in Korea and it came as no surprise that the takeaway owner was fully aware of the appalling decimation suffered by the beleaguered Gloucestershire Regiment during this nightmarish encounter. Moreover, he could appreciate that this might give anyone nightmares and to Reverend Charles' astonishment, indicated that he would be prepared to forgive Fred and if it would help, meet him for an attempt at reconciliation.

To the representative of the established church's incredulity, Chia Hao went on to quote the New Testament. 'Turn the other cheek', 'Do unto others' and other pacifist incitements by Christ: he knew his scriptures and caused the Reverend Charles to vacillate, trying not to protest, yet being dumbfounded by the patient's capacity to forgive.

In vain, the vicar attempted to explain that Fred had been certified. In his opinion a meeting with Chia Hao would be highly risky. There was no knowing how Fred would react. Whilst the vicar thought Chia Hao's compassion admirable, he did not think Fred would be likely to make a volte face in return for forgiveness. He might still be obsessed and enraged and not comprehending Chia Hao's olive branch, indulge in further violence. This was a risk Chia Hao was willing to take, and the vicar intended to call in at Coney Hill after leaving the infirmary. He agreed to try and sort out Fred over the matter but was not very optimistic. He did not hold out much hope, for currently the former gardener only communicated in barely recognisable monosyllabic utterances and added to that, sometimes took a while to recognise those who came to visit him.

*

In order to see her injured man, Li usually caught a bus to Gloucester in the daytime and she was indebted to the sister of a couple who'd opened a takeaway in the city shortly before Li and Chia Hao had opened the one in Eastdean. With the aid of stalwart Elsie Brain, wife of the bookie next door, the girl would arrive for the lunchtime trade, catching a three o'clock bus back as Li returned in time to greet the children from school and prepare for the evening opening. She was never short of helpers in the evening as the people thereabouts mucked in and would not take payment for services rendered.

On Saturday mornings Sir Crispen brought Bhuppa in to assist and to the amusement of the locals, when coming back later to fetch her, he insisted on waiting at the back of the queue for his fish and chips. He resisted all their attempts to show him deference and when served, had no hesitation in inciting several children to take a chip when making his way back to the car.

CHAPTER TWO

Dan stood back and admired his handiwork. A truly rustic masterpiece: homemade with the bark stripped off the rungs. A splendid effort propped against the massive trunk and looking like it had been there for as long as the centuries-old oak itself. This was still an age when children were permitted to sample nature uninhibited: not confined by the constrictions of 'health and safety' or trammelled by the insidious encroachment upon their minds of computer games and the all-pervading internet. They were free to climb trees, play conkers, and maybe fashion bows and arrows from the proliferating willows that bordered the murmuring stream that flowed, pure and unpolluted, past the back of Bybrook Abbey.

It wasn't if Dan didn't have enough to do, but with typical generosity, he'd made the ladder long enough for the youngsters to reach the lower branches of the tree, and with their in-built lack of trepidation and inherent agility, they would be able to explore the upper regions of it with apparent ease.

So far, half-term had been blessed with reasonably clement weather – not always granted in June -and at present the children were in the donkey enclosure. The vicar's young son, Barnabas, had ridden Wendy down from Pope's Hill. His sister had held the bridle to ensure nothing untoward happened en route and they'd proceeded at a leisurely pace. A typical example of her species, Wendy did not object to this stately progress and in due course they arrived without mishap. Two newcomers to the juvenile fraternity were Kevin and Charlie, whose dad had persuaded them that they'd enjoy things at the abbey, were welcomed by the other children and soon absorbed into the general melee with alacrity.

The other children included Ah Cy and her brother Hoi Sang, aged nine, who'd quickly befriended Barnabas; both boyishly flamboyant and keen to try out the new ladder. In order to give the Chinese children's mother a break, they'd been transported down to the abbey by kind Mrs Brain the bookie's wife, who promised to pick them up later. Though not fully fit, Chia Hao had been allowed home to convalesce and what with looking after him and supervising the takeaway she had enough to do.

Currently in his study within the abbey, Sir Crispen was on the phone. He was trying to persuade the two errantly inclined twin brothers who inhabited a somewhat dilapidated cottage at the other end of the village to do more hours. He hadn't realised how much Fred had done in the formal gardens of the abbey, and where the orangery was concerned, the ageing Humphrey and Jeremiah hadn't a clue. They had both tended to resent Fred's presence on what they considered to be their patch, yet his now permanent absence had highlighted their inefficiency, showed who had been doing most of the work and left Sir Crispen in a quandary. He'd tried to persuade Dan to help more, but with scarcely concealed resistance, the truck driver and smallholder had declined. He declared that June was his busiest time of year. Besides hauling for George Read of Longhope, his in-season vegetables had to be transported to a wholesaler in Gloucester, and there was also the task of keeping the abbey's fencing and outbuildings in good shape.

With a wry expression on his face and employing inbred diplomacy, Sir Crispen had refrained from commenting that a little less time propping up the bar in the Whippet might help, and with so much to do – and virtuous though it was – why fashion a time-consuming homemade ladder for the children when there were one or two ready-made ones on the estate that would have been perfectly adequate?

Lighting a cigarette and silently stewing over his problems, Sir Crispen was startled by a tap on the study door. It opened to reveal Annie and an anxious looking Arthur Barnet, who stood behind her anxiously fiddling with his cap.

'Arthur would like a word, dear. I said you wouldn't mind.' She turned round to bestow a benevolent smile on the organist and continued. 'In you go, Arthur, and I'll get Dora to bring you coffee in a minute or two.'

Sir Crispen counted slowly to ten and having reached it, emitted a despairing sigh. He didn't like people invading his inner sanctum in the morning when he reviewed the holdings, answered queries from the tenants of several farms he owned in the county, chastised those that had not coughed up rents on time, and hated to be disturbed when doing so. And precisely what Arthur Barnet could want with him he could not imagine. Annie handled the payment for Bhuppa's piano lessons, and he was quite sure he could rely on her to sort out any problems that might arise. In any case, he understood that since the fracas between Arthur and Fred in the George, the former had become quite subdued. He no longer attempted to embrace Buddhism and had limited his interest in Bhuppa solely to teaching her the piano and complimenting her on her rapid progress.

Sir Crispen motioned the unwanted visitor to sit down opposite him: the big oak desk with its bass relief carvings serving to separate them. Cluttered with its owner's untidy papers, the desk had also to support an extremely heavy and archaic typewriter which, despite the layer of matted dust that lay upon it and permeated its inner workings, somehow managed to function when required.

Shunning the usual hunting prints that those of the conventional aristocracy usually favoured, Sir Crispen chose to display endearing and piteous photos of maligned donkeys on his study walls, and a large certificate behind his head proclaimed him to be some very important cog in the association that cared for these often deprived and ill-treated creatures.

'Good morning to you, Arthur. And what can I be doing for you?' Sir Crispen gave the organist an encouraging smile. Not long after making his acquaintance, the owner of Bybrook Abbey had read an article in the *Times* on the supposed mental illness labelled autism. What was known of it appeared pretty rudimentary. The study of it was as yet in a very embryonic stage, and wanting to know more, Sir Crispen used his facility in the German language to further his knowledge by acquiring a book by an eminent Germanic specialist on the subject. In it the author claimed that those suffering from a mild form of autism could often be more accomplished in their own particular subject than those of the so-called 'normal' populace. This sometimes brilliant proclivity could develop in various ways. In the case of Arthur

Barnet, music had turned out to be his forte, and as Sir Crispen had lately discovered, Arthur was no slouch where literary matters were concerned. A chance conversation upon delivering Bhuppa to Plumb Farm had revealed that Arthur was well versed in the classics. He'd apparently read Dickens, Hardy and the Brontes et al and – remarkably – also tackled the entire works of Wilkie Collins. To counterbalance this, he wasn't much of a farmer – Plumb Farm hardly befitted that description of it – and although not really equipped to deal with everyday things or able to write very well, according to the German author's theory, he did have the classic symptoms of those with Aspergers in that he would be obsessed with something for a while, then suddenly discard it. Which in some ways explained why Arthur had chosen to jettison his interest in Buddhism. What had replaced it, if anything, was not yet evident, but Sir Crispen imagined it would not be long before something did.

In fact, something had, and with a perplexed expression on his face, Arthur was about to explain. Concerned about Fred and his incarceration in Coney Hill, he'd been to see Chia Hao and they'd had a long discussion about the possibility of going to see him. Well aware of Chia Hao's remarkable capacity to forgive Fred, Sir Crispen was not at all sure that this unlikely collusion between the two of them would be a good thing. It seemed that Arthur had become a world authority on China and Korea overnight. He proposed to go with Chia Hao and attempt to explain to Fred that Chia Hao was a convinced and practising Christian and now had no allegiance to China and its oppressive regime. He was not a threat to Fred and if they could convince the patient of this, perhaps the authorities would release him to once more take his place in society.

Sir Crispen knew it wasn't as simple as that. People were not sectioned without good reason. Nevertheless, he was still very impressed with the case for clemency that Arthur was proposing and did not dismiss it out of hand. Informing Arthur that he would consult the vicar over the matter, he'd more or less concluded what he had to say when portly Dora, the inquisitive apology for a housekeeper, arrived with the coffee.

A hot day meant that all the windows in the abbey were open, and a sudden piercing shriek nearly caused Dora to drop the coffee. A hubbub of juvenile voices could be heard and alarmed, all three inhabitants of the study quickly made their way to the rear of the stately building from where the disturbance seemed to be coming.

It had all happened in a flash. Having availed himself of the new ladder to reach the lower reaches of the tree, young Barnaby had promptly parted company with it and landed in the stream amongst the watercress and surprised water creatures. He had been expeditiously pulled out by the older, quick-thinking Bhuppa, was unhurt, but very shaken and extremely sodden. Annie too, had been alerted by the shriek, and with Dan running from the stables where he was repairing a damaged manger, the adults were soon in control of the situation. Barnaby was taken inside, persuaded to strip and very embarrassed, sat in the large kitchen adorned in large towels, drinking a large glass of Tizer which Annie had managed to conjure up from somewhere. The primitive fridge provided welcome ice-cream for the rest of the children, and not one to stand on his dignity, Sir Crispen sat at the head of the bulky table – a worm-ridden monstrosity bequeathed by some long expired relative and enjoyed the treat with them.

Somewhat miffed by this unexpected disturbance to her routine, Dora displayed an air of slight truculence when told to forget the coffee and showed further disapproval by going off to 'do' one of the bedrooms with the aid of an extremely basic and noisy Hoover. This was a recent acquisition that partially banished her backache and did have another advantage in that it enabled her to skimp her work even more than she did before its arrival.

Debate was taking place over whether the new ladder should be removed before a further accident occurred, and whilst 'mother hen' Annie was in favour, led by Sir Crispen, the menfolk were not. The owner of the abbey declared that providing they took more care and all they risked was a ducking, they couldn't come to much harm and shouldn't be mollycoddled.

No one protested. Mostly easy going in his dealings with people, if the mood took him, Sir Crispen could be quite autocratic, and sensing his present stance would not allow for dissent, nobody objected to his ruling on the subject. Besides, he'd just thought of a way to implement Arthur's proposal over Fred and wasted no time in putting it to the entire company.

Amongst those in the kitchen, there were some who were opposed to this plan, but still aware of Sir Crispen's current despotic attitude, no one spoke against it. However, Annie's wise suggestion that those that hadn't yet attained double figures should not be subjected to what could be a disturbing experience was sensibly approved. It was felt that Coney Hill was not a fit place to take very young children and this being settled, Sir Crispen affirmed that he would contact the warden without delay.

CHAPTER THREE

The plan foundered before it could be carried out. A serious outbreak of scarlet fever meant that Fred and others were swiftly dispatched to small, isolated rooms in Blandley Hospital, near Stroud, an establishment especially designed to cope with contagious diseases. Thanks to a vaccine, scarlet fever rarely occurs in the twenty-first century and is not considered a serious ailment, but this was not the case in the early nineteen-fifties. It could be a killer and swift action had to be taken to prevent it becoming a serious pandemic. Cases had occurred in and around Gloucester; visiting Coney Hill was now restricted and poor Fred appeared to have exchanged the frying pan for the fire.

This did not prevent the concerned Bhuppa from organising a 'get well' card, signed by everyone that mattered; including Chia Hao and Arthur, who, confirming their stance of complete forgiveness, had no hesitation in adding their names willingly, with Chia Hao inscribing his in both English and Mandarin.

No one had been able to forewarn the hospital that the patient in room five might not take too kindly to the ministrations of a Mr Minze Wang. He was a physician who had trained in the UK before the war and stayed, rather than returning to endure the repressive communist government that now ruled his homeland. In reality, no one could have apprised the matron of Blandley over Fred's aversion to those of Chinese origins. Undoubtedly the warden and staff at Coney Hill knew the reason for Fred's incarceration but had no reason to think it remotely likely that anyone of Chinese extraction would be employed at Blandley. The fifties was a decade long before Filipino and other far eastern nurses graced the nascent National Health Service with their delightful presence and as Fred's aversion in any case did not extend to women of far eastern extraction, it would not have been a problem. Also, those at Bybrook Abbey, the township of East Dean, and the village of Blaisdon were entirely ignorant of the staff situation in the

183

isolation hospital, and with visiting prohibited, likely to remain so.

Which made what soon transpired truly remarkable.

Glimpsing Minze Wang through the glass protection screen, Fred's mind still managed to register and assimilate the Chinese physician's looks. Startled, he attempted to lean forward, his eyes staring, but the effort seemingly too much for his weakened state, he had to slump back against the pillow. Time and some unorthodox treatment eventually healed him and not now contagious, he was removed to a small ward to convalesce.

To the incredulity of those members of staff that knew his recent history, he became resigned to the presence of Minze Wang. It was interpreted by some as almost a miracle, but the matrons and those that supervised his medication knew better. Strengthened by the questionable treatment he was now receiving from Minze Wang, Fred had become quite lucid. He no longer saw devilish apparitions and the matron had reservations about some of the concoctions Minze was prescribing. She suspected the National Health would not approve of Chinese remedies, but as they seemed efficacious, she turned a blind eye.

Except in exceptional circumstances, visiting was not allowed, but when told of Fred's transformation, the vicar back in Elton cast aside doubts he might have and led his congregations in thanks for the patient's release from nightmarish images.

On the quiet, Annie at the abbey made supplications to Buddha and in his convenient role of worshipping both God and Mammon, Sir Crispen breathed a sigh of relief. Given permission by him, Bhuppa badgered Dan into selecting flowers for Fred from the orangery. These he somehow contrived to deliver on a trip for Read's to Swindon, a diversion he didn't want mentioned but found worthwhile when Bhuppa showed him a quite legible note she'd received from Fred expressing thanks.

CHAPTER FOUR

Sadly, though fully recovered both mentally and physically, Fred was taken back to Coney Hill. This was mainly through the obduracy of the police who, not convinced he'd been fully restored to health legitimately, feared a relapse. They had their doubts about Minze Wang, who evidently visited Gloucester Docks quite often and according to an informer collected unknown substances from foreign ships that berthed there. The bush telegraph had acquainted them with Minze's supposed methods at Blandley and despite his success, they were keeping their bloody-minded eye on him. Some Chinese drugs were definitely outlawed in the UK and they were biding their time before moving in to apprehend him when in the act of receiving goods. They could well have visited the isolation hospital, but two factors made them hesitate. One was fear of catching something contagious and the other the likelihood that they would catch both Minze and the suppliers exchanging the drugs and money at the docks.

Another possibility argued by a senior police officer was that if Fred was now fully compos mentis he could be charged again with the assault of Chia Hao. This was hotly disputed by an enraged Sir Crispen, who claimed that Fred had committed the assault when mentally ill and he would move heaven and earth to prevent a retrial, to which the divisional superintendent replied that you couldn't have it both ways. Fred had been sectioned and it needed a doctor to declare him fit to rejoin the outside world and if this happened, the police would have to reconsider their options.

As luck would have it, Dr Theodore Matthews, the chief medical practitioner at Coney Hill, was a man ahead of his time. He was not averse to alternative medicine and the prescribing of it and as a mason, was well acquainted with Minze Wang, in desperation had received help from him, and had no scruples if it helped some of the more pathetic cases in the mental hospital. He and Wang had no worries over their collusion. It helped that the chief constable was also a mason, so they had no worries on that score and could rely on his authority to quell any attempt by the police to terminate their activities.

The divisional superintendent had just received a phone call and wasn't a happy bunny. He had been instructed to leave both Minze Wang and Fred alone. No charges or arrests were to be made. Fred was being released and to his knowledge, the Chinese physician was doing nothing but good, the possible illegality of it should be overlooked and he and Dr Matthews should be left to mind their own business. The superintendent muttered under his breath. In his opinion this was just not right and maybe ... maybe he'd appeal to a higher authority or even expose the whole thing.

CHAPTER FIVE

The surgery in Eastdean was not in an obvious place. Built at a time when the motor car was not the dominant mode of transport, the surgery sat at the end of a row of houses opposite the modified primary school and had hardly changed in order to accommodate the relatively new National Health Service. The upper rooms were inhabited by the senior GP's family, not an ideal circumstance, but a long well-tended back garden afforded space for the children and provided a measure of comfort for Dr Pellew, a sometimes curmudgeonly soul, who had been opposed to the introduction of entirely free medicine and continued to make depreciatory comments about it. And now he was being asked to go along with the dubious treatment being handed out to Fred. He sat in his consulting room, the letter from Dr Matthews in his hand and wondered if the prescribed substance was in any way legal. On the other hand, if it was not on the list of banned drugs like cocaine or opium, who was to say it could not be prescribed?

He stood up and reached for a large tome which sat on a precariously fitted shelf – Dr Pellew was no handyman – and taking it down, he opened it at a section entitled 'Chinese Medicine'. He found what he wanted and having done so, supposed he would have to go along with it. Dr Theodore Matthews had been a fellow pupil at Marlborough and convinced that the nation's public-school domination of all things important should be maintained at all costs, Dr Pellew decided he'd oblige. The postal service was pretty reliable and as the stuff didn't smell, he saw no reason why it should not come per favour of Royal Mail. Another mason, Sir Crispen had agreed to pay for it (the Coney Hill doctor could not go on putting it down to expenses) and providing none of the other GPs were involved, things should go pretty smoothly.

Dr Pellew was not one for procrastination and reached for the telephone. He was put through to Coney Hill without too much delay and as luck would have it, the mental hospital's supremo was in his office and readily available.

Not for the first time, Dr Pellew reflected that the masonic movement had its distinct advantages, and he was glad that he'd taken the decision to become a member some time ago. However, he stressed to Theo Matthews that as a precaution, the drug parcel should be addressed to his wife. The flat had a separate mailbox, and this would prevent the receptionist or any of his colleagues opening it. Nevertheless, he would have to confide in Barbara. She'd been a doctor's wife too long not to know what was expected, and he had every confidence in her to know she would play ball. He also understood Sir Crispen would receive a perfectly legitimate bill and satisfied that all possible snags had been ironed out, he indulged himself by reminiscing over old times for a while and bidding (for him) Dr Theo a cheery farewell, put the phone down.

Apparently, Fred would be allowed home within the next few days. He seemed fully able to administer the drug himself; even knew why, and an initial appointment had been made for the following week. Patients just turned up at the surgery during opening hours and were seen in order of arrival, but to give Fred confidence, an exception was made. Dan, who lived nearby, had agreed to take him, and with an efficiency which the former military physician admired, all would be well.

CHAPTER SIX

The beginning of October could be quite benign, and the first couple of days were glorious.

Annie and Fred were in the orangery and in the background, they could hear the continuous uproar generated by the children. Released from school on Saturday, they were all there. As yet, no one had fallen in the stream; the ladder into the tree was being fully utilised and not at the moment being ridden, the docile Wendy was refreshing herself: the water in the bubbling bourn not yet polluted in the name of progress.

In little more than a month, the most pleasing thing that had happened was the reconciliation between Fred and Chia and, to a lesser extent, between Fred and Arthur Barnet. Fred had been to see Chia Hao and Li, had been given a meal, stayed to talk and sent away with something for his supper. He had resisted the temptation to visit the George, but a day or two later made the trek from Pope's Hill to Blaisdon in order to make his peace with Arthur at Plumb Farm. The reception he received was not effusive. Now that Fred had been freed and true to his contrary nature, Arthur's attitude towards Fred had reverted to being mildly hostile. Arthur still felt jealous over the place Fred had in Bhuppa's affections, but attempted to play the gracious host. He offered his guest some of yesterday's poorly made sandwiches which even the chickens had declined and was surprised when his homemade cider was rejected.

Fred tried to explain that he was on medication, but this was something the small farmer and musician did not comprehend. He had no time for doctors, had not experienced a day's physical illness in his life, and after several more abortive attempts to make Fred feel welcome, had watched, not really concerned, as his guest departed.

Enlisting Fred to help, Annie went inside, found the Tizer and some glasses, and carried it out to the children. Fred now seemed a different person and she only hoped the treatment he was receiving would have a lasting effect.

The children had decided to visit the donkey enclosure and as Dan was somewhere in the vicinity, she decided to make herself redundant. She felt the need to visit the homespun temple. For some inexplicable reason, she sensed that things were about to go wrong again, and a little spiritual help might prevent this from happening.

CHAPTER SEVEN

Walter had suffered a double whammy during the war. His mother had died in the little-known bombardment of Scarborough by the German Navy and his father, a rear gunner, had perished at the hands of accurate flack over Dresden. He'd gone to live with his gran who'd only died a couple of years ago and apart from a distant relative that lived somewhere vague in Derbyshire and sent a card at Christmas, he was very much on his own. Not that it worried him. He'd left school at fourteen, worked in the docks for a while, then took a job that suited him in that it wasn't so strenuous, at the isolation hospital. He now waited patiently as the narrow boat puttered slowly across the basin. Behind him his made in Gloucester conveyance, his old Cotton motorcycle, stood on its prop stand, its two empty panniers ready to be filled with the packages that boatman Seth Partridge would deliver.

Before going to work as a porter in the Stroud hospital, Walter had done a manual job in the docks and was familiar with the procedure for berthing a boat. As it glided into the quayside, he adeptly caught the rope that Seth flung at him, attached it to a ring bolt and made it fast whilst the boatman, a big bluff member of the well-known Partridge clan of Birdlip, wasted no time in jumping ashore to greet him.

The piratical looking Seth was never less than effusive. He possessed a beard that nearly descended as far as his navel, had a pair of fiendishly mischievous eyes and a handshake that, after its application, might induce those that experienced it to hastily make an appointment with a bone surgeon. He also had a pretty wife who went with him everywhere and a child who, educated by his intelligent parents, had been brought up on the canals and would never be able to cope with a more conventional lifestyle. The back cabin of a narrowboat was hardly the most spacious place to rear a child, but the craft had long been registered under a Gloucester number as fit for human habitation and Sarah had never complained about the limited facilities it provided. Unlike some boats, at least it had a water tank and the meals she concocted on board ranked with any that could be produced for a table on shore.

She observed Seth as he handed over two quite bulky packages which Walter expeditiously put in his motorcycle panniers. Minze Wang, who was not an unfamiliar figure in the city, had decided it would perhaps be judicious to keep a lower profile and for an acceptable sum, now paid his young colleague to collect and transport the 'goods' to the hospital. These exchanges took place about once a fortnight and seemed to Sarah a bit furtive, and an enquiry from her about the contents of these packages had resulted in Seth putting his forefinger to his nose and tapping it. She knew what this meant, and dismissing her suspicions, declined to question him further.

Calling in at Sharpness docks over the river, they'd transhipped a load of Scandinavian timber from a steamer that was too big to enter the port of Gloucester, at the same time collecting these mysterious packages that had come upriver from Avonmouth and were waiting for them. Sarah was not naïve and surmised that it would be too risky to send them by rail. An accidental spillage might reveal something incriminatory and having met Minze Wang, the prototype inscrutable Chinaman when he'd been coming to collect his packages in person, she suspected that the contents may have made their way to the UK from somewhere in the east.

She watched as Walter fastened his panniers securely, winced upon receiving the obligatory handshake, started up his precious pre-war vehicle, and roared off with his presumably precious cargo.

Sarah would have liked to offer the lad some hospitality, maybe a meal, but this was something those that plied their trade on the canals did not do. Your backcabin was sacrosanct and you did not allow anyone to get even a glimpse of its interior. To impose on this strictly private place was considered extremely rude. Despite this, the fraternity of those that crewed narrowboats and barges was extremely close knit and apart from the odd disagreement, they mostly enjoyed an untroubled existence.

When ashore, they sought one another's company in the pubs and cafes and on occasions, even attended the dockside chapel that had been built mainly to furnish the needs of those merchant matelots who were far from home.

Before unmooring and making their way to the timber quay to unload their small shipment, Sarah knew that Seth would take her and young Colin to their favourite 'greasy spoon'. Callum's café was situated near the Victoria dock where, according to her enthusiastic husband, could be eaten the best breakfast anywhere in the 'noble and ancient Roman settlement of Glevum'. She didn't wear much make-up, spent little time in front of the mirror and pausing only to sort out tousle-haired Colin, went ashore.

*

The black patrol car followed him down the Stroud Road, lights flashing, its bell sounding. In the knowledge that he'd done nothing except collect what he assumed were medical supplies for Minze Wang, he did the sensible thing and pulled in.

'Good morning, young man. We'd like to look at what youm got in those panniers.' Dead Gloucester, heavy browed and a bit intimidating, the constable looked as if he'd stand no nonsense. The patrol had been tucked away behind a crane on a routine visit to check for things illicit. They'd noted the exchange between Walter and Seth and not liking the look of it, decided to investigate.

Walter readily obliged and at the sight of the packages, the police officer hesitated, then consulted his colleague. The other patrolman was more positive.

'What's in the parcels, son?'

'Don't know,' said Walter truthfully.

'Where youm takin' 'em?'

Walter continued to play a straight bat.

'One goes to Coney 'ill and the other I takes to Blandley 'ospital where I works.'

The first patrolman raised his eyebrows. 'Blandley? That's the isolation 'ospital ent it?'

The two patrolmen were non-plussed. To them it didn't seem

likely that legitimate medical supplies would be entrusted to a hospital porter on an old motorcycle. Furthermore, why send them to the docks in a narrowboat and from where did the 'goods' originate? They toyed with the idea of opening the packages there and then but decided against it. Who knew what might be in them? And it would be best left to the boffins to sort out.

The second officer was the more positive of the two. 'Right, son. If you like to get on that lovely old bike of yours and follow us to the station, they probably won't keep you long.'

Walter didn't like the sound of this, but in his guileless, honest way complied and was soon inside Gloucester City Police HQ being interviewed by a slightly hostile detective sergeant.

Not really approving of the way things were being handled, the patrolmen were nevertheless sent on their way, and it was perhaps fortunate that the superintendent happened to emerge from his office to consult the desk sergeant over some matter.

'Who's he got in there, sarge?'

'Some lad they think might be deliverin' drugs.'

'Who's "they", sarge?'

'Jim and Dennis. Patrol, sir. Stopped 'im in the Stroud Road with these packages.'

'Is that his bike propped out in the yard?'

'Yes sir, and the lad's name is Walter.'

The superintendent took a moment to ponder this. 'Hmm. That's something in his favour. Keeps the bike well. My cousin used to be a grass track rider for Cotton's, you know. Good bike.' His face broadened into an expansive smile. 'Hmm, however, I think I'd better take a look at this myself. Don't want that bugger Watkins with his inflated ego giving the lad an unnecessarily hard time.'

It was no secret that DS Watkins was not a popular figure in the station, but it was surprising that the superintendent should express his feelings so demonstrably to the desk sergeant.

The superintendent strode into the interview room without ceremony and savoured Watkins' startled reaction.

'Super…?'

The superintendent took over. 'Think you can leave this to me, Watkins. Off you go. Ah, this is Walter, is it? Good morning to you, young man. This shouldn't take long.'

Inwardly seething, Detective Watkins left the room. Why the old man wanted to deal with this himself he couldn't imagine, but reluctantly went off to grab a resuscitating cup of coffee, more than ever determined to put in for a transfer.

The superintendent of course, was au fait with the probable reason for Walter's detention. It must be the stuff, part of which was being used to treat 'renaissance' man Fred, formerly of Coney Hill. Whatever it was, he'd been informed on the grapevine that it was doing the job, but that did not mean it could not have serious long-term effects. And if it became officially approved and generally available, who knows what could happen? The superintendent had recently perused the long list of approved drugs and whatever the medication was, he didn't think it was on it. The fact that Walter was delivering half of it to the Chinaman at Blandley confirmed that it was the mysterious substance that had received the nod from the precious chief constable and his masonic cronies. In a quandary, he was intrigued by the packages that had been brought into the interview room. He would have liked to open them but thought it judicious not to do so.

Having mulled it over for a while with Walter watching him anxiously, he decided the best thing to do was to let the lad go. If he decided to stand up to the powers that be and take it further, it might disastrously result in demotion, and as he was not far off pension age, he thought it best to let sleeping dogs lie

Before delivering the first package to Dr Matthews at Coney Hill, Walter decided to take a break and visit a milk bar in the Bristol Road. He knew some of his mates would be in there at this time of the day and slightly shaken by his recent experiences, sought a degree of friendly company before resuming his errand. He parked his bike at the kerbside and entered the slightly shabby premises a bit further up the pavement, noting that the windows badly needed cleaning and the Second World War utility tables needed clearing. A radio loudly churning out a Glenn Miller number made conversation difficult but did not detract from the vociferous greeting Walter received. He was not that naïve in that he did not realise the reason for his warm welcome might be an assumption by one or two of his idle friends that he was a soft touch. Usually bereft of any semblance of fiscal means, they could normally rely on the hospital porter to stand them a milk shake, but for once in his life choosing to look after number one, he was determined not to oblige. This did not impress his disgruntled mates and aware that he was not now flavour of the month, he downed his drink quickly and went on his way.

But it was most definitely not his lucky day. Arriving at the stark edifice that was Coney Hill, he undid his panniers, only to find the packages gone. Distraught, he nevertheless adhered to his honest attitude and confessed to Dr Matthews that they must have gone missing whilst he was in the milk bar. There was no way to lock the panniers on his bike and it had been remiss of him to leave the machine unattended and out of sight. He was abject in his apology and not impressed by his recent interview with them, was relieved that the medical chief would not be contacting the police.

CHAPTER EIGHT

There was concern all round by all three medical practitioners. Doctors Minze Wang, Matthews and Pellew all had patients dependent on the missing medication: the latter GP particularly worried over Fred who might revert to his former state without it. According to Minze, it might be a week or two before a further supply could be obtained and he just hoped that Dr Pellew had enough of the stuff to keep the abbey gardener on an even keel.

When informed of the situation, Sir Crispen was his usual phlegmatic self and those within his aegis displayed an equally calm attitude. Annie spent quite a lot of time in the temple and the vicar, who'd obviously noted Fred's change of temperament and been given an explanation, silently prayed that nothing untoward would happen.

Nearing the end of October, the weather had turned inclement, the nights were closing in and the donkeys spent a lot of time in the stables. They required a lot more attention where feeding was concerned and at Sir Crispen's kind suggestion, Wendy was taken back to the abbey for the winter where the vicar's children could come and ride and attend to her whenever they chose. This was quite a concession where the abbey was concerned. Once allocating them to new homes, he never invited them back, except in circumstances where there'd been an inspection and the new owners found to be unsatisfactory. But in Wendy's case he felt a bit soft-hearted. Pope's Hill was quite a jaunt from Elton and as there now seemed to be a firm bond of friendship between Buppha, the vicar's children and Chia Hao and Li's, he thought one equine mouth to feed would make little difference. Of course, he mused wryly, it might not be long before the Chinese children might pester their parents for one of their own and where would they keep it? He had a pretty good idea and why not?

Meanwhile Fred was seeking his attention. They were in the orangery and a demarcation line had been drawn here between Fred and the ancient brothers who claimed to oversee everything that went on in the garden. Sir Crispen had insisted that in keeping with his newly acquired attitude, Fred should be on an even footing with them and furthermore, be in sole charge of the orangery. The brothers spent some time being affronted, but reprimanded in a tone that would not tolerate dissent, went off to mutter under their breath about 'whippersnappers' who didn't know their place: this being expressed whilst taking an inordinately long time in the greenhouse smoking and trying to decide what, if anything, needed doing in there.

In the orangery a couple of cacti had been watered to death by the hasty and ignorant duo and thank heavens, they'd not meddled with the orange espalier that Fred had miraculously trained to grow along the back wall. The yucca appeared to be thriving, as were the begonias and the Australian 'fuschia' – the cornea – with its tubular flowers, looked very healthy. Sir Crispen had seen to the gathering of fruit from the orange and lemon trees and come the new year, a lot of pruning would have to be done.

CHAPTER NINE

The first week in November lived up to its name. A thick fog hung over everything and the children caught the early bus to school undaunted, but well wrapped up. Barnabus, aged nine, was dropped off at Blaisdon Primary School with Bhuppa and Rachel from the rectory going on to meet up with Ah Cy at the relatively new Benhall Secondary School. Ah Cy's brother, Hoi Sang, attended Eastdean Endowed and, unbeknown to his parents, enjoyed a recently acquired reputation as a purveyor of Chinese bad language! Most of these swear words were a figment of his imagination but were sufficiently inventive to convince his fellow Forest pupils that they were genuine and could effectively be used to berate their peers and thus improve his street cred.

*

In the Whippet Inn, Sylvie the landlady went about the business of cleaning with an air of distraction. This unaccustomed mien of hers had not gone unnoticed by her husband. Sylvie was normally an optimistic, affable soul and emerging from the cellar, her husband expressed his concern.

"Ast thou got zummat on thy mind, my love?'

Decisive, another of her characteristics, Sylvie abandoned her duster and sat down at one of the round tables. There were ten of these, all with decorative ironwork and a solid mahogany top.

Jo and Sylvie were complete opposites, but constituted a partnership that worked extremely efficiently, and sensing her unease, Jo positioned himself behind her and massaged her shoulders, an action that would have normally soothed the devil incarnate. Before becoming a publican, Joe had been a masseur at Gloucester Swimming Baths and had retained his skill.

Sylvie did not beat about the bush.

'It's Fred,' she said. 'He came in last night when you'd gone off skittling. He was a bit the worst for wear. I wouldn't let him have anything alcoholic. You know Dr Pellew rang up some time ago and told us in confidence that Fred was on a new drug. Not to let him mix it with drink. I think Fred had been elsewhere before he came here. I almost rang you at the Red Lion. It wasn't easy to cope with him, particularly as Dan wasn't here either. I did persuade him to go home eventually, but I didn't like the look of him. He's been soft drinks till now and God knows what'll happen if he's allowed to drink heavily again. No reason was given for his release from Coney Hill, but the bush telegraph being what it is round here, I don't think many people didn't know that it is some new drug that has kept him on an even keel.'

Her eyes displayed consternation and ceasing his massage, Joe pulled out a chair to sit opposite her.

'Why didn't thou tell oi this when oi come wome last night?' he enquired.

Sylvie considered the question and realising she hadn't an answer, shrugged her shoulders.

'Don't know really. It was late, you'd had a good night, and I suppose I didn't want to worry you.' Here she gave him a reassuring smile. 'Big softie that you are, it might have kept you awake.'

Joe was not all brawn and on more than one occasion he'd proved he had plenty up top and where he was concerned, books and covers came to mind. 'Oi d' think we should ring thick Doc Pellew. Zounds t' me uz Fred 'as run out of iz medication.'

'No time like the present,' prompted his wife.

In Joe's opinion, Dr Pellew wasn't very helpful. There'd been a hold-up over the supply of the new drug. Fred should have enough to keep him going, but the doctor would check this either by ringing the vicar and asking him to try and contact Fred, who had no phone, or he would ring the abbey where he might well be, and if all that failed, then maybe Dan would know where he was. Dr Pellew was not prepared to travel even the short distance to Pope's Hill himself and meanwhile would Joe ring round any likely pubs in the district to request they refrain from serving Fred alcohol under any circumstances.

To landlord Joe, this all seemed a bit hit and miss. It was a serious situation that needed urgent action. He quickly made up his mind and gently took hold of Sylvie's hand, giving her a peck on the cheek.

'Wun't be long, love,' he said, 'theese can manage for a couple of 'ours, can'st?'

This was the grim reality of being a landlord's wife. You were almost wedded to the punters when you were married to a licensee who had a marshmallow for a heart. She listened to the old A-40 van as it left the car park, turned left and mounted the steep incline to Pope's Hill. She would have to ring Dr Pellew again, tell him what was happening. The silly old fool should know how much Fred had left in the way of medication. But she learnt that an expensive education did not guarantee that the recipient of it possessed an overabundance of common sense.

CHAPTER TEN

For a brief moment Dr Minze Wang had become anything but the unflappable Chinaman. There had been a hitch. The supply would have to be renewed, and it would be likely that some of those dependent on the drug would be without it for a while. In an attempt to prevent this happening, he had contacted the Chinese quarter in Birmingham for an alternative supply and would employ Seth Partridge to meet a narrow boat at Worcester where the packages could be transferred from one vessel to the other. The doctor had contemplated other quicker forms of transport, but dismissed them as unsafe. A spillage in a guardsvan might cause all sorts of complications. The transport police could be involved, and not under the jurisdiction of the non-interfering Gloucestershire Constabulary, might well cause trouble. Road transport was an equally hazardous alternative and simply just posting such a considerable amount by Royal Mail would involve the railway again, an idea Winze had already dismissed.

*

Visiting Worcester was always a pleasant experience. It involved going through Tewkesbury with its decorous abbey, passing the pleasant towns of Upton and Pershore, before arriving at Diglis Basin. Before this there was the opportunity to cast eyes on the glorious cathedral opposite the quintessentially English cricket ground where the great Don Bradman had taken the county's bowlers to the cleaners on several occasions. The gregarious and graceful swans were another hazard, and it would upset young Colin greatly if one of these creatures had been hit, so they had to be given priority, no matter how long it took.

Pulling in to a jetty, Seth observed that there was no sign of the Birmingham narrow boat, the 'Solihull Queen' that he'd been sent to meet. Minze Wang had assured Seth that Roy Shakespeare and his boat had already set out and would probably already be moored before the Gloucester vessel arrived. Back in the day Seth had met the Birmingham boat's skipper and recalled how he'd been surprised at the man's surname. He later discovered that Shakespeare was quite a common 'handle' in the West Midlands, and this suggested that either William and his offspring multiplied profusely or there were other branches of the family who'd been equally fecund.

Joe hadn't stopped long at Fred's household. Fred's mother had informed Joe that she thought Fred had intended to catch the bus to Eastdean. He didn't say when he'd return, and she'd been worried that he seemed to have regressed. It didn't take much to work out where Fred was likely to be in the small town, and before briefly contacting his anxious spouse by phone per favour of Ivan, landlord of the George, Joe had learnt that Fred had left the premises only ten minutes prior to Joe's arrival. So it was decided that Ivan would ring Jummy or the sergeant at the police house to be on the lookout and Joe would continue to search for Fred, mainly in the other public houses in the area.

It appeared the Birmingham boat had been involved in slight collision upstream. Stepping on to the quay, Seth was approached by a member of the Worcester police force and was informed that it might be a while before Roy Shakespeare could rectify the damage and get to the rendezvous. The knowledge of this caused Seth to inwardly curse. Shakespeare had been indiscreet. On the other hand, what other way could he have relayed the news of the accident and hopefully, this young policeman would not be too inquisitive. Nevertheless, what he said next was quite alarming. Perhaps the police could help by contacting colleagues in Droitwich who might be able to arrange transport if the urgent goods were of reasonable dimensions?

Seth was just wondering how to respond to this surprisingly well elucidated offer (the force up here must be attracting better educated recruits) when he had a flash of inspiration. It would never do to let the police bring the packages to him. They would surely want to know what they contained and not like their Gloucester counterparts, who were restricted by orders from above, could blow the gaff over the whole thing. This would be a disaster of the first order and thinking quickly, Seth informed the helpful young policeman that he'd continue upstream until he reached Tardebigge Wharf where the accident had occurred and if he met 'Solihull Queen' recovered and coming down, so much the better.

Thanking the constable profusely for his assistance, Seth vaulted back on board and acutely aware that things were not going smoothly, Sarah made him a cup of tea with drop of the 'potheen' in it from the bottle that his brother, a ferry operative, had illicitly acquired during a crossing to Rosslare.

With a purposeful stride, Fred made his way to the Chinese takeaway. He'd not spent too much time in the George and knew he'd be able to enter the premises via a lane which ran parallel to the high street and along the back of the properties. But before turning down a short alleyway, he was just in time to see Hao emerge from the takeaway. Separated by no more than twenty feet, Fred followed him past the town hall and arriving at the junction where you turned left for Ross-on-Wye, tailed him as he walked through the nascent housing estate and out into the unspoilt countryside. The narrow road wound through a blissfully pastorale scene not far from the border with Herefordshire, and with an abruptness that took Fred by surprise, Chia Hao took the path up through the many-hued autumnal trees, his intention to take a constitutional on the mysterious upland known as Wigpool Common. Told to exercise every day to offset the trauma of his recent attack, this had become his favourite walk. Li fully approved, knew he would not be long away, and business in the dinner hour so brisk they now employed two young local girls to assist. His thoughts miles away and somehow absorbing the scenery as he proceeded, Chia Hao was not aware that he was being followed.

Possibly light-footed through the care he had to take in the orangery, Fred brushed aside the bracken silently and somehow managed to evade any obstructing tree branches. He determined he would not fail this time. One of the oncoming, howling mass of Chinese would surely die. There was no way now he could escape the wrath of the solitary British national serviceman. Fred felt the blade of the sharpened knife which nestled in his duffle coat pocket. He'd spent some time sharpening it and he was certain it would do the job efficiently.

*

For the second time in a short period, PC James Wainwright prodded himself to move swiftly. He'd been contacted by Ivan of the George whose call was shortly followed by the physical presence of Joe from the Whippet, who'd wasted no time in getting there. Jummy knew Fred might be wandering round the town bent on something nefarious and having been informed by bush telegraph of the situation over Fred's medication, was keen to make sure nothing injurious happened to the lad or anyone who came in contact with him.

Accompanied by Joe, Jummy strode down the high street and reaching the town hall, encountered Mr Gregory Wilce, the gradually fading part-time clerk. Well advanced in years, Gregory should have retired, but with Ranks virtually falling over themselves to employ everyone but the chairman of the council's three-legged cat or local prostitute Valerie – who reckoned to make more by following her own 'calling' – nobody else wanted the job.

The clerk was affixing a poster to the notice board and with his back to Jummy and Joe, was startled when addressed by Jummy. Turning round with a bemused expression on his face, he said, 'Oh, oh, it's you, PC Wainwright. Didn't see you. Nice day, can I help?'

Jummy knew that where Wilce was concerned, in order to produce a response, you had to make yourself very clear. It didn't help that after forty years of residence in the neighbourhood, Gregory was still unable to comprehend the dialect. The constable was aware that he would have to speak slowly and worse still, attempt to do it in something approaching correct English.

He cleared his throat and took the plunge.

'You ant sin Fred Duberley in town today, ol' but?'

This failed to stir the clerk's deteriorating grey matter into life.

'Fred?'

'Thou d' knoaw, 'im uz attacked 'im at the chippie a while ago. Thick Chinamon uz runs it.'

It took a while, but a vestige of enlightenment did dawn and despite the policeman's attempt to speak the nation's language in an acceptable way utterly failing, Gregory did seem to more or less digest and understand what he meant.

'Ah, yes. Let me see now. A few moments ago, I did see, at least I think I saw...' He paused to adjust his free National Health glasses, and this somehow gave him the will to continue. 'A member of the Chinese race did pass by. He seemed very preoccupied and didn't return my salutation. He was shortly followed by a stocky young man who I've seen around – you say his name's Fred. They both turned left at the junction, taking the road to Ross. I then lost sight of them...'

His last words were addressed to his interlocutor's back. Jummy had heard enough. He and Joe were haring off as fast as Jummy's beer-ridden paunch would permit. Turning left at the T-junction and playing a hunch, they decided to take the footpath to Wigpool. Hampered by the policeman's lack of fitness, it took them a while to mount the escarpment and en route they noticed the disturbed foliage and odd trampled bracken which indicated that the pursued and the pursuer had passed this way. And reaching the summit and running down the sloping common, they discovered the couple near the legendary great oak. All sorts of tales were told of the centuries-old tree and the mystical adjacent faery ring and making supplications in a pagan manner, people claimed to be cured of all sorts of ailments, from vanishing warts to things terminal; a place still revered by most old-timers hereabouts for its alleged and often unsubstantiated healing properties. Another more negative school of thought implied that stepping into the ring meant you were compelled to dance with the fairies forever and stood little chance of returning to the real world. The devil of Lucifer was another strong claimant of injudicious mortals who dared to step within the ring and was also reputed to be able to curdle the milk of the cows that grazed on the common.

It was obvious that neither of the present 'pilgrims' were there to be healed.

The Caucasian stood, immobilised, statuesque and indecisive in the faery ring. His right arm was raised, and his hand grasped a knife with a vicious looking nine-inch blade, poised and ready to strike.

Before him, the easterner cowered under the great oak, waiting for the knife to descend and praying for his Western God to save him.

CHAPTER ELEVEN

They didn't encounter the 'Solihull Queen' until they entered Tardebigge Wharf, the former entrepot on the canal which nowadays had a faded and underused look about it. Tardebigge consisted of a maintenance yard, a warehouse and a dry dock. The former worker's houses had long since been let or sold and the only other vessel at present moored in the Wharf was the dredger. This bizarre looking craft spent most of its time scouring rivers and canals for gravel over a wide area and unlike the few commercial boats that plied their decreasing trade on the waterways, would not have to cede defeat to faster road and rail transport.

It was soon evident to Seth that you would not need a magnifying glass to see that Roy Shakespeare's boat had been more than superficially damaged. Most things forrard were stoved in and how the narrow boat owner had managed to allow this to happen, Seth could not imagine. Roy was now standing on the quayside, engaged in conversation with a rough looking character who turned out to be the somewhat euphemistically named 'Harbourmaster'. Apparently there had been a collision with a lock gate and this had caused a virulent altercation between him and Roy, resulting in the police having to be called. Seth suspected that Shakespeare's unfortunate predilection for cloudy rough cider might have had something to do with it, but since he was anxious to collect the packages and be on his way only expressed perfunctory sympathy, and was relieved when his fellow boatman was able to produce them from somewhere in the undamaged stern of the boat.

By this time, darkness had fully descended and returning to Worcester through the innumerable locks would be a hazardous business. Despite the urgency of the situation, Seth decided that he could not risk another accident. They would bed down at Tardebigge and make the return trip in the morning. He was just glad that the police had not returned and witnessed the transference of the packages, and hoped they would not turn up again before he left.

After the interminable journey through the locks, Seth arrived in Worcester around noon to find a police car on the quay, and the same young police officer awaiting him. A character in a Gannex mac kept him company, looking such a caricature of himself that he could have played the part of a plainclothes cop in a Hollywood B-movie.

It did not take long for the lawmen to state their business. In his largely inebriated state, Roy Shakespeare must have opened his mouth and mentioned the packages to the police who attended the accident at Tardebigge. Perhaps it was understandable as he'd impressed upon him the vital need for them to be delivered as expeditiously as possible.

Hence the reception committee, although Seth was not unduly concerned by their appearance. In transporting the goods, he'd only been the monkey, not the organ grinder. He was well aware of what he was carrying and assumed that although it was not on the illegal drugs list, it must be borderline. Yet, as the doctors in Gloucester were prepared to prescribe it and the Gloucester Constabulary turned a blind eye, merely delivering it might not get him in to trouble.

But his self-assurance proved premature. The plainclothes gentleman was neither a refugee from a B-movie nor simply an ordinary member of the CID. He was the leading boffin of the Worcester Constabulary's newish forensic team, and at the young constable's insistence, Seth had to submit the questionable goods on the spot for them to be examined. And opening one of the packages up, the slightly supercilious forensic expert did a double take! He ran some of the mauve-coloured powder through his fingers and it didn't take long for him to identify it.

'Good God!' he exclaimed. 'Never thought I'd ever see this in this country. Banned in Shanghai before the Second World War. I worked for a clinic in the British part of the international settlement there. Extraordinary how the bloody Japs left us alone! There were also the ruddy communists and nationalists. Just as bad as one another. Anyway, I got out, but before I did, I was largely involved in getting this stuff banned!'

He made a face and resumed applying his fingers to the 'stuff', oddly attracted and repulsed at the same time. Sonli, he said, could have a disastrous long-term effect on those who took it. When first discovered it had seemed like an elixir, a panacea, but after about a year on the treatment, a large number of patients deteriorated. He was appalled that Sonli was being used in the UK and with a reinforcement in the form of a police car arriving at that precise moment, the packages were impounded, and Seth taken to Worcestershire Police HQ to be questioned. He knew it would be no good positing the argument that the Gloucestershire Constabulary were OK with the substance. The Worcestershire and their clever dick forensic head honcho obviously weren't, and despairing, he was taken away, leaving his beloved Sarah to cope with vulnerable young Colin and the narrowboat.

CHAPTER TWELVE

Both Fred and the potential victim remained transfixed as the breathless Jummy and Joe arrived on the scene. Fred still held the knife aloft, uncertain and seemingly stricken by some force that held him in the grotesque pose. Chia Hao remained rooted to the spot under the brooding oak, and approaching Fred from behind, the policeman made to restrain him. But before he could do so, the disturbed figure with the knife dropped it and collapsed into the faery ring, reduced to a crumpled heap of humanity: still extant, but no longer a threat.

Chia Hao cautiously came out from beneath the tree. He was shaking uncontrollably and not devoid of any compassion when it was required, PC James Worthington put a muscular and comforting arm round him. Eventually managing to control his trembling limbs, Chia Hao proposed they check Fred's pulse, which proved to be perfectly normal, though he remained unconscious.

The policeman knew he would have to summon help and although there was quite a degree of risk involved, Joe agreed to stay with the two adversaries whilst Jummy departed on a quest to find some.

A solitary house stood near the footpath leading up to the common and Jummy made his way back down to it fairly quickly. He just hoped that the family that lived there had a telephone and mentally castigated those high-ups in the constabulary who had been promising the simple 'plods' on the beat new CB radios for an age and had still failed to deliver.

CHAPTER THIRTEEN

There was no way the Worcester force could comply with Gloucester's tolerance of the use of Sonli, and after a brouhaha that caused ripples within both forces, the views of Quentin Wherefold, the forensic expert, were swiftly acted upon. The need for prompt action was strongly emphasised when Dr Matthews of Coney Hill reported that a patient who'd been prescribed the medication for six months collapsed with muscular and respiratory problems and was slowly being weaned off it.

Apparently affected in a different manner through running out of the medication, Fred Duberley had been returned to Coney Hill and both he and other affected patients were now under the care of Dr Matthews who, watching his back, would not let any of them be taken to hospital for treatment.

In an extraordinary turn of events, a sample of Sonli was taken on a train to the Chinese embassy in London. Despite his disapproval of the communist regime, the eccentric Quentin had a long-established 'friend' there and with the full approval of the Chinese ambassador, who was not wholly immune to the pleasures of living in a Western democracy, the 'friend' seconded Quentin's assessment of the debilitating medication and furthermore, a knowledgeable attaché confirmed that Sonli had been banned in China since the nineteen-thirties.

The question concerning the source of supply in the UK was solved by ciderholic narrowboat skipper Roy Shakespeare and yet another police force, Birmingham City. After a method of interrogation which could be said to be bordering on the scarcely permissible, Roy coughed up the information required, and the hardened big city coppers did the rest. A nest of soft drug dealers was unearthed within the Chinese quarter of the second city and for his cooperation in enabling these dealers to be apprehended, both he and Seth were released without charge.

As it would show the Gloucester hierarchy in a bad light, a decision was taken to keep the whole matter under wraps providing Sonli was consigned to the scrap heap, and at some point, a local MP who was also an obliging mason would have it banned on the pretext that he'd known of its increased usage and the resultant harm it would undoubtedly do to those that used it, which, of course, was no use to the stricken Fred Duberley. Back in the mental hospital, he was experiencing periods when the images were starkly prevalent, and other times when sanity prevailed. Unlike other cases, his physical health had not been affected and Dr Matthews was confident he could cope with his condition without assistance.

CHAPTER FOURTEEN

Weighed down with responsibility, Sir Crispen found an unexpectedly informed helper where the orangery was concerned. Mentored by Fred, Bhuppa had picked up more knowledge about it than her adopted parents realised. She somehow managed to fit schoolwork, assisting with the donkeys, piano playing and religion into her crowded schedule.

At first Sir Crispen kept an eye on her stewardship of the orangery, but finding her utterly competent, left her to it. This was to the chagrin of the two ancient brothers who had their respective noses put out of joint again but were left in doubt that where the tending of it was concerned, Bhuppa was in sole charge.

Nevertheless, another problem in the person of Arthur Barnet soon raised its unwelcome head. Far from being the once supposedly guileless country farmer, he was once again proving to be a too frequent presence where Bhuppa was concerned. With her fourteenth birthday imminent, she looked much older, and with Fred's renewed incarceration unlikely ever to end, Arthur was perhaps paying her more attention than he should have. It took some time for Sir Crispen to realise this, and having done so, he proposed that he confront the farmer, and that Annie give the still innocent Bhuppa a pep talk on the subject. He now suspected Arthur's motives were not entirely honourable. Like other men of his age and despite his eccentricity, he would still have certain needs and having been denied them for so long, might not be able to resist those urges, and therefore could not be trusted. There was a maiden lady in Longhope that taught piano, and with a heavy heart, Sir Crispen gently told Arthur his services would no longer be required. He was also instructed not to visit more than once a week, and at all times Annie must be in attendance to act as chaperone.

Unfortunately, he had not allowed for the rebellious streak that exists in most teenage girls and Bhuppa was no exception.

When informed of this new arrangement, Bhuppa flatly refused to comply. She would give up her piano lessons altogether and declared that the vicar would not be happy when she refused her services as an organ blower in his churches. She did not see how she would be able to confront the organist when he was almost non persona grata at the abbey. She became highly embarrassed when Annie, uncomfortable at having to perform the role, tried to explain Sir Crispen's misgivings about Arthur and the fact that he might have dishonourable designs on her.

She fled to her room, locking the door and in a fit of belligerence they did not know she possessed, eventually re-emerged to declare that she was renouncing Buddhism and would no longer tend the orangery. She would concentrate on her schoolwork and Sir Crispen could see to the donkeys without her assistance and she would not be riding one in the Christmas carol services.

Not unaware of the contrary attitudes of young girls, Annie assured her husband that this stance of Bhuppa's would not last and managing to engage the assistance of a pleasant village lady to do some days as head cook and bottle washer, did her best to help with the orangery and the donkeys.

Apprised of this recent development, that fount of rustic wisdom, Dan, was all concern and made it his business to offer advice. Bhuppa was fond of Dan, and though withdrawn and cussedly uncooperative where her parents were concerned, she would listen to him, seeking him out when he came to perform some task at the abbey, and Annie was convinced that his simple counselling would ultimately restore things to normal.

Up at Plumb Farm, Arthur was devastated. Much as he tried to deny it, he subconsciously had hopes of Bhuppa. He could not see that what he felt should be denied. All he saw was a very attractive young girl who aroused him, and hampered by sexual frustration and the demands of his position as an important cog in the church, his mind was a melting pot of longings and misgivings.

On a visit to the abbey, prior to his semi-banishment, he'd overheard two workmen who'd been engaged in doing something to its fabric. They had been discussing Bhuppa and referred to her potential in very crude terms. They labelled her 'jailbait', and although Arthur had no notion what that meant, he thought it must be a derogatory term and with difficulty resisted the temptation to accost them. In an entirely convoluted and illogical way, he laid the blame for his estrangement from the abbey at the hands of Fred Duberley, for where Bhuppa was concerned, Arthur still envisaged the hapless Fred as a rival. The fact that the former steward of the orangery was now constrained in Coney Hill, possibly forever, did not impair Arthur's confused thinking. Fred would have to be eliminated and Arthur would be the one to do it.

CHAPTER FIFTEEN

Dr Minze Wang, who'd been instrumental in introducing Sonli to the district, gradually had to decrease the doses he was giving to patients in the isolation hospital. Still in touch with fellow medics in China that continued to prescribe it illegally, he too carried on in a reduced way, administering it in increasingly reduced amounts. His patients who mostly had a rare, barely definable contagious disease which could prevail for months, had been making good progress, and aware that not all those who imbibed Sonli ended up expiring, he reckoned the chances of survival were pretty high but knew that if denied, two of the patients might well die, making it worth the risk. So he continued the treatment. Matron was in favour, maintaining that it was not yet illegal and providing everyone in this small out-of-the way hospital kept quiet about it, it should not be a problem. (When roused, Matron could metamorphise into a twentieth-century Medusa, and woe betide any member of staff who revealed that which she had declared must not be revealed.) A difficulty would be that Minze's new suppliers in Birmingham had been flushed out. He'd need to go back to his slightly unreliable supplier in Avonmouth. This might have its pitfalls, but should be possible to arrange without too much trouble.

*

The dormitory was quiet. All its occupants seemed to be asleep and the nurse in charge sat down at his station with relief. He hoped none of them would wet the bed or require other attention during the night. He'd only just been assigned to night duty and wasn't enjoying it. With luck, he could lean back and doze for a while. It was difficult to sleep in the daytime and unusual mealtimes were a problem. The new coffee machine in the corridor spewed out execrable coffee and having drunk a little more than half of it, he settled in a more comfortable position and nodded off.

Fred wasn't asleep. He had been, but plagued by the images he had awakened and got out of bed, He walked stealthily to the dormitory door and found that nurse Vincent had been very remiss. The door wasn't locked as it should have been and very cautiously, Fred opened it. Stricken by second thoughts, he padded back to the bedside and removed a pair of shoes from the locker. He wasted no time in removing his pyjamas and putting on his day clothes and made his way back to the door.

Emitting porcine grunts, Nurse Vincent didn't look likely to surface for a while and this enabled Fred to emerge into the dimly lit corridor without being observed. He knew of a back entrance to the gymnasium which might provide him with an exit from the hospital. They sometimes used to play football under supervision in the large recreation yard to which the door gave access. He traversed the lengthy corridors with care. Apart from the odd ejaculations coming from the acute wards, silence prevailed, and he reached his objective without further incident. By this time his mind had cleared. The images had gone, save one of Chia Hao, which stubbornly lodged itself within his psyche and incited him to rid himself of the solitary Chinaman once and for all. No longer restrained by Sonli, his temporary amiability towards Chia Hao had expired and finding the gym door locked, he employed the practical side of his nature to open it. A small screwdriver did the trick, and he was soon able to walk out into the night air.

Not unfamiliar with the city – he'd started after school as a butcher's boy in Gloucester – he found his way to Barton Street and negotiated the level crossing into the centre. He proceeded nervously through the dimly lit and almost deserted streets, fortunately encountering nothing but the odd late-night vehicle and hardly any pedestrians. Those he did see were mostly too far gone from excessive libation: the flotsam and jetsam from the ubiquitous taverns that provided solace for a goodly number of the city's steadily increasing population.

Half an hour later found him just beyond the western bridge at the curiously named settlement of Over, with its prominent vegetable market and its pub still dismissing reluctant topers into the wide world outside. As he drew level, one of these patrons hailed him in a hearty and friendly manner.

''Ello there, son. Oi d' d' know thou, don' oi? Oi've zin thou somewhere before, a'nt? Where bist goin'? W'as doin' out this time o' night, owld but? Do'st want a lift?'

Fred knew it would be unwise to ask for a lift to Pope's Hill. Once back with his mother, they'd easily find him, and he'd be whisked back to Coney Hill in no time.

'Bist goin' anywhere near Eastdean?' he replied.

'Just the ticket,' said his new would-be benefactor. 'Oi d' live in Drybruck. Be easy to drop thee off in Eastdean on the way.'

The car, an old pre-war Austin Seven, was parked near the pub entrance, immaculate and well-maintained, starting first time without demur.

The journey was slow but without incident, and turning left at Huntley, they drove through Longhope village and soon came to Eastdean, turning right at the crossroads into the town.

'Where do'st want t' be dropped off, young 'un?'

The driver had given up interrogating Fred enroute. His passenger hadn't volunteered much information, save to say he'd been to the pictures and hadn't known what time the last bus went from Gloucester.

Dropping Fred off at the darkened church of St Michael, the obliging driver made a noisy departure up the hill towards Drybrook. He'd pass a haven of wildlife called 'The Wilderness' on the way and on reaching the apex of the steep hill, it dawned on him where he'd seen the reticent young man before. The Whippet Inn at the bottom of Pope's Hill. Not a pub he'd patronised more than a couple of times in the past, but the face was etched on his memory. He did not forget a face and if his memory served him correctly, he'd had a brief and somewhat one-sided conversation with the lad in that pub some time ago. The driver cannot have read the local paper after the Chia Hao incident, not getting on with his estranged sister and his lone occupation as a deliverer of farm foodstuffs did not usually leave time for gossip. He had the occasional drink but was a member of the Drybrook Methodist Church and he tended not to partake too often, so as not to be frowned upon by the straightlaced non-conformists.

Fred entered the church porch and settled on the bench that took up one side of it. He could hardly see the notices displayed on a notice board opposite and found all attempts to sleep elusive. He arose and fingered the circular iron handle on the great Gothic oaken door. He felt it give way and entered the church without difficulty. Some light from the six main windows enabled him to locate the main aisle and turning right towards the altar, he picked up a kneeler and using it as a pillow, stretched out on one of the pews.

Sleep did eventually embrace him, but even here, supposedly in the house of the Christian God, they would not leave him alone. Multifarious Asian visages and his fellow combatants falling like flies in a hideous bloodbath. Him holding a last drink to a mortally wounded nineteen-year-old beseeching Fred to conjure up his mother and the sergeant-major grimly trying to incite them not to give way. This just before the devils broke through and a bayonet pierced the non-commissioned officer to reveal his entrails. Fred had ultimately survived by lying still and faking death: him and a few others. But the battle over, he had arisen prematurely, been captured and only escaped through the negligence of a Chinese guard who'd gone off to relieve himself.

And here they came again, riding donkeys, and he did not see why they should not be riding them. Donkeys had been part of his existence and there was nothing peculiar or untoward about it. The leading rider was Chia Hao, not looking his benign harmless self, transformed into a fiend with a bayonet and making towards the callow and helpless British soldier with grim and murderous intent.

He awoke screaming and sat bolt upright. He must have been asleep for hours. Dawn did not occur early at this time of the year, and it was barely light.

*

The relative that shopped and cooked so many days a week for the Barnets was not well and despite the fact that meals-on-wheels came on two days, Arthur was confronted with a near-empty larder. Push had come to shove where he was concerned and with the resolution he could sometimes display, he went into Eastdean very early on his bicycle in an attempt to rectify the situation. They were very obliging in the grocers. They advised and fetched everything for him, knowing him from his musical endeavours in the George and feeling temporarily emancipated from his duties on the farm, he decided he'd delay his departure from the town by visiting St Michael's. He'd never been in the church before, and he wondered what the organ might be like. He knew there was a regular organist – he'd never been asked to play there – but was curious to find out how big the instrument was, whether a two or one manual, and maybe if no one was there, he could have a surreptitious play on it.

Propping his sit-up-and-beg bike against a nearby tombstone and not concerned about the purchases which he'd bought from the grocers and put in two panniers that hung either side the back wheel, he made to enter the church. An overcast sky did not assist in brightening up the gloomy interior, but Arthur could see that the organ and choir stalls were beyond the chancel steps; the chancel leading to the altar. He had not gone more than a yard or two down the aisle before a gaunt figure rose in front of him.

CHAPTER SIXTEEN

Sir Crispen let the donkeys out every morning at about eight, even in winter. Their release into the old deer park today coincided with the emergence of an insipid sun. But the sun didn't have a chance. The ominous clouds would have no truck with this blatant intrusion and soon restored the dark mid-November status quo.

Still in her dressing gown and looking out from a back room window, Annie noticed that instead of showing a certain liveliness at gaining their freedom from the stables, the donkeys were standing around in what appeared to be an organised circle. They were very still, and to anyone else they might not appear to be tacitly communicating, but to Annie, a convinced Buddhist, it was obvious that they were. She knew what it meant. Someone was dying. She could not think who that could be, but this solemn gathering meant but one thing. Whoever it was would pass away and depending on their performance in life, would be reborn, either in animal or human form to continue their everlasting existence. Whether they would return as some high or low form had all to do with their past lives and the karma they had attained. Annie could not think who might be dying. It must be someone who lived in the abbey, was an employee or a regular visitor. The donkeys would not engage in the ritual for someone they did not know. She went downstairs to alert her husband about what was taking place in the deer park and her thoughts on the occurrence. Embroiled in paperwork, Sir Crispen was not very receptive at first, but at her insistence did abandon the office to cast his eyes on the strange equine activity. Often more open minded than people gave him credit for, he did not throw cold water on Annie's assertion that her temple and adherence to the Buddhist faith had brought this about.

Sir Crispen pondered this for a while, and not able to offer any other reason for the donkeys' strange behaviour, went back inside to his paperwork. He was slightly alarmed at the prospect of someone within his circle severing his or her 'mortal coil', but his phlegmatic C of E doctrine was enough to convince him that any such thing would be unlikely or simply pure coincidence.

*

The Reverend Samuel Jenkins received a shock when entering St Michael's to ready the church for a mid-week service. The recumbent figure by the font had obviously been grievously assaulted. His face was badly damaged, and blood seeped from a prominent gash in his neck. There was no sign of an assailant, the young man was still alive and the Reverend Samuel's first thought was to summon an ambulance, then return from the rectory to try and staunch the blood until it arrived. But upon exiting the church he encountered a parishioner he knew and left the startled man with the accosted one whilst he hurried off to make the urgent phone call.

At Coney Hill they searched the building and grounds and, failing to find the missing patient, informed the police. Nurse Vincent was castigated and threatened with dismissal, and only a chronic shortage of staff ensured his survival.

Sadly, it was all to no avail, for Fred died in the ambulance on the way to hospital and an examination of the meagre contents of his wallet enabled the hospital to inform the asylum without too much delay.

At the police house, Sergeant Pateman found himself temporarily in charge of a possible case of homicide. He was horrified at the prospect and hastened to enlist help from headquarters. It was not long before the big guns arrived and Eastdean had never known anything like it. Talk of likely assailants was rife in the George and enlivened further when it was known that even the rector had been interviewed as a possible suspect. That other notable clergyman, the Reverend Charles, swiftly visited Fred's mother on Pope's Hill and took her back to be cared for by his wife, Isobel, before going on to the abbey.

CHAPTER SEVENTEEN

Not surprisingly, when he arrived, all was not well. He found the aristocratic couple in a complete state of shock. There were grave problems and happenings that needed explaining and they didn't know what they were going to say to Buppha when she came home from school. Dan, who was also present, had already offered some homespun philosophy, but much as they normally admired his down-to-earth take on things, they were anxious to know what the vicar made of it all. Dan was assigned to make the coffee whilst Annie related her Buddhist belief and an explanation for the donkeys' strange behaviour. To her surprise, the Reverend Charles did not dispute what to him could have been an alien and heretical concept. He could not accept the idea of reincarnation but would never despise those that did. Advancing years had expanded his thinking. Whilst ascribing to and finding Christianity a perfectly satisfactory religion, he was rapidly coming to the conclusion that it was perhaps only one way to experience God and that there were other ways and beliefs that would find him. He dare not express these views to his traditionalist bishop but saw no reason why he should not covertly hold them himself.

The denizens that spent a good deal of their time in the Whippet Inn were astounded that Chia Hao had been named as a suspect, and it took Joe to explain why this might be. Those that had visited the takeaway thought him a "armless un' and it took Joe with the help of Sylvie to explain why the 'plods' might suspect him to be the perpetrator of the crime.

Joe put it in language they understood.

'Well, az oi d' zee it, Fred 'ad a go at Chia that night adder 'im 'ad bin in the Gaarge an' then we, Jummy 'n oi that iz, caught un on Wigpool with that blaide about to straike before 'im collapsed int' that vaery ring.'

'Yes,' said his articulate wife. 'So Chia had every reason to extract his revenge, though personally, I don't see there is any way Chia could be the assailant. He's a most gentle, mild-mannered individual and at one stage was even talking about going to see Fred in Coney Hill.'

'Thou 'az a point there,' said Lager Len, who'd never been known to drink anything else.

*

The vicar's suggestion that he leave before Bhuppa came home was rejected. Sir Crispen thought it might be helpful if he stayed, nor would the knight object to Dan's continued presence. They were both people the teenager cherished, and it would help to have them around when she arrived. Not comfortable with that idea, Dan made his excuses and returned to a task he was doing in the abbey's improved workshop, the overhaul of which Sir Crispen had sanctioned recently: a big improvement and a handy place to retreat to when unwanted problems demanded attention. Dan was not wholly adverse to a modicum of procrastination and felt that, in this instance, he could not provide further help. He noticed that the donkeys had abandoned their vigil and not for the first time, questioned his own view that Annie's faith was a load of nonsense.

Upon coming home from school and being confronted with the news of Fred's demise, Bhuppa was devastated. She clung to Sir Crispen, sat on his lap and entwined his neck with her arms. She sobbed, wept bitterly and could not be consoled. After some time had elapsed, she did consent to go with Annie into the temple to put her grief before the Lord Buddha. Annie wondered what Fred's karma would be. He hadn't led a blameless existence this time around and on balance perhaps deserved to return in some middle-of-the-road human guise. On the other hand, Fred had been a lover of all wild life, and no one had displayed more sensitivity when it came to appreciating and nurturing the plants and shrubs that adorned the orangery. She chastised herself for judging him and concentrated on trying to console Bhuppa. She could not imagine who would want to dispose of Fred and thought that in no way could it be the gentle and forgiving Chia Hao. In any case, the police had already dismissed the possibility that he might be the perpetrator of the assault. At the estimated time of the appalling incident, he'd been seen cleaning the take-away. He was fastidious about this and had so far received top marks from the hygiene inspector for his diligence. Besides, another early riser, Mr Brain the bookie, had tapped on the door in his customary fashion and been admitted to partake in what had become an early morning ritual: some of Chia's excellent coffee and an amiable chinwag.

The police medico that had examined Fred in the morgue had established that his attacker had struck somewhere between 7.30 and 9.30 in the morning, which firmly established Chia Hao's alibi. But another mystery was how the perpetrator would know Fred was in the church. Had they possessed adequate grey matter, the girls that did the early morning shift at the Co-op may have been able to shed some light on the subject, but not the brightest pebbles on the beach, it didn't occur to them to do so.

CHAPTER EIGHTEEN

Committing his foul deed had not appeared to have affected Arthur's existence in any way. To him it had been a simple matter. A problem solved. He'd eliminated a rival and by the look of things, got away with it. Made aware of Bhuppa's distress, he eagerly complied with her request that he be allowed to resume teaching her the piano. He was still deemed a friend and she vehemently contested the notion that he posed some kind of moral danger and with Fred gone, fervently made the case for Arthur's reinstatement. Somewhat reluctantly, Sir Crispen acceded to her pleading, the only proviso being that Annie was always present when the lesson took place.

There was a pond at Plumb Farm, fed from a stream that cascaded down from the hill behind it. The source of the stream was unknown. It must have bubbled up from somewhere, but as the hill was precipitous and not climbable, no one amongst the generations of Barnets that had occupied Plumb Farm ever attempted to find out from where it came. Nevertheless, its flow was pretty constant and because of this, the level of the pond seldom varied, and only a severe drought might cause it to do so. An outlet enabled it to continue on down the meadow where it tumbled into the broader Blaisdon brook at the bottom, near the narrow footbridge. The footbridge would not accommodate the passage of cattle or other stock. These had to be driven through the brook, not a difficult task, and one that Arthur did not have to perform that often. He hadn't a great deal in the way of stock and thanks to the Barnets' tendency to hoard money under the mattress – often to the detriment of their standard of living – he didn't need to be much of a farmer. A paucity of modern conveniences didn't make life easy, but as Mrs B was 'away with the fairies' a good deal of the time, she didn't complain, and life went on much as it had since Edwardian days.

As has been previously documented, Arthur liked to milk a cow, and when not musically engaged, had a predilection for ducks. When first trying to raise them, he'd been wholly unsuccessful. Plagued by crows and magpies, the ducklings did not survive much beyond birth and it was not until obliging Dan constructed a wire mesh pen for the expectant mothers of the species that things vastly improved. Not that wily Dan was without a vested interest in this aquatic enterprise. Thereafter, he often parked his pickup down by the footbridge and on the pretext of visiting to enquire how Arthur's mother was doing, usually left with half-a-dozen or so duck eggs.

Today was one of those days and having asked to use the toilet, which was housed in a small shack someway down the back garden, he performed what was necessary and hoped there were no creepy-crawlies there, ominously bent on exploring his nether regions. He had an aversion to spiders that could still be around at this time of year, and momentarily absorbed in a reverie, came out of it abruptly as he noticed the walking stick. An almost unique walking stick. He'd only ever seen one of these before and immediately knew to whom it belonged. An ebony walking stick with some African figurehead in ivory perched on top of it: besmirched with a brown substance he recognised as dried blood. Fred's walking stick had not been found with his belongings at Coney Hill or picked up from St Michael's when he'd been taken to hospital. Which meant…

It all made sense now. In a quandary, Dan took a deep breath and tried to compose himself. He availed himself of a portion of the *Daily Herald* – a substitute for toilet paper – and with no chain pulling involved made his way back to the Barnets' not particularly hygienic kitchen. Upon his entrance the invasive chickens fled in a flurry of feathers and squawking, and he sat down at the newspaper-covered table trying to stay calm. He forced himself to chat to Mrs Barnet and having done this for as long as his disquieted mind allowed, thanked the lady for his duck eggs and departed. Where Arthur was at that significant moment he did not know, and still highly disturbed by his alarming discovery, he didn't particularly care.

Driving along the backroads a bit faster than he would normally, he diverted to Eastdean and only just missed colliding with a new Studebaker, an American car, as it exited the car park of the George. His mind a maelstrom, he drove the pickup into one of the parking bays. He quickly vacated it and made for the pub entrance: anxious to consult Ivan the landlord as soon as possible. He could not understand why no one had sussed it before now. There had been that incident when Arthur had taken a break from playing when Fred had stood up and, unprovoked, hit Arthur, causing a fracas to break out during which Arthur gave as good as he got.

Not without some misgivings, Dan posited the possibility that Arthur could be the villain of the crime scenario and though not inclined to question it, the landlord did not see that a pub brawl could result in one of the contestants deciding to achieve vengeance by murdering the other.

'Oi don' reckon 'im meant to,' asserted Dan, but having second thoughts, Ivan was no longer sure. He'd quickly changed his mind. He now thought that the slightly unbalanced farmer could well have intended to murder Fred. He felt the farmer may have had other motives, and the local grapevine almost infallibly accurate, he knew about Arthur's piano teaching, a possible conduit for perversion.

The landlord was a strange convert to capitalism. 'Ivan' was not his real name. Dubbed that by those that knew him during the Second World War, his leanings towards communism had long evaporated, but the Russian appellation had not.

'What did thaiy doctors zaiy 'im 'ad bin 'it with? Musta bin zummat besides Arthur's visits.'

Dan knew the landlord was right, but reluctant to reveal his knowledge of the walking stick through some misguided notion that he did not want to condemn one of his ilk to life imprisonment or even capital punishment, he had not as yet mentioned it. He proceeded to do so, and Ivan poured them both a drink, a pint for Dan and a stiff short for himself. This was a revelation and he listened as Dan continued.

'These az a point ol' but. I wuz chopsin' to Jummy in the Whippet the other daiy 'n 'im zed the mon uz did examine Fred definitely zaid uz 'im 'ad bin 'it wi' zummat. Question is, what t' do over it?'

Taking in to consideration what Dan had discovered in

Arthur's toilet, Ivan now wondered why they'd been hesitating. He thought it would all come out in the wash eventually and they might as well tell all and save the police a lot of time. It was quite clear to Ivan that Arthur had had enough gumption to take the walking stick home with him, thus hiding vital evidence and showing intelligence they did not think he'd possessed. A light under a bushel: musician, literary buff and as yet, unrevealed murderer.

The George was quiet this time of day, and with Dan's approval, Ivan went out the back to use the telephone.

*

Where Dan's pickup had been an hour ago, there now stood a patrol car. A patrol car minus its occupants, which suggested that they'd gone up the sloping meadow to arrest the unsuspecting Arthur Barnett.

CHAPTER NINETEEN

The fortitude of Bhuppa was remarkable. Fred deceased and Arthur banged up awaiting trial could have made her go to pieces, but she determined not to dissolve into the stark world of unbridled grief.

She spent long periods in Annie's homespun temple and recognising that Fred's body would be consigned to St Felicity's churchyard, did not spurn the concern of the vicar. He did not try to influence her belief and was perfectly willing to tolerate the placing of one or two Buddhist symbols in the church at the funeral. She would also be allowed to perform what amounted to a lament on her Khaen and with extraordinarily wry humour temporarily brushing aside her deep rooted sorrow, pointed out that someone else would have to blow the organ on the day.

The Reverend Charles steered a tactful middle course. He impressed upon Bhuppa that as a confirmed member of the Church of England, he felt Fred should be laid to rest in the churchyard.

Privately he'd begun to have doubts about Fred's eternal destination. He admired the dogged and utterly convinced stance of both Annie and Bhuppa and did not question their right to follow the path they had chosen.

At first, Sir Crispen had baulked at the suggestion that Annie should read a passage from the Buddhist holy bulk, the Tripitaka. He was to read the positive passage from the Book of St John where Jesus Christ proclaims to his disciples that 'no man cometh to the father except through me'. It was Bhuppa that persuaded him to give his assent and since he was well aware of her hidden feelings and he could not resist her, with some input from the vicar, he gave in.

On the morning of the funeral, pretty rubicund-faced Rachel insisted on coming up to the abbey to saddle Wendy the donkey. Despite her parents' misgivings, she wanted to be there when the cortege entered the church. She would stand sentinel outside until the service concluded, and the coffin interred in the graveyard. She would be joined by Ah Cyr on Amos, her newly acquired jack donkey, and they would accompany the cortege as it came through the village. The two younger boys from the vicarage and the takeaway would remain in the abbey under the care of Dora the slapdash housekeeper. ''Er didn't like funerals an' 'er'd only be too glad to oblige.' The lads would stay there until the interment was over when a wake featuring a quartet from Westham Brass Band would be held.

In the deer park and displaying uncanny prescience, the donkeys were absorbed in what could be interpreted as equine meditation. They scarcely moved during the service and eyed one another with doleful expressions. Promoted earlier by some unknown and compulsive inner directive, Sir Crispen had decided that the grey November weather would be no barrier to them making an adjunct to the ceremony. He didn't normally let them out for too long during what he termed inclement weather, though his exposure to the Thai climate had made him an unreliable judge of what was 'inclement'. To him, any day that did not include the effulgent rays of the sun was almost a personal penance. He loathed the English winter and sometimes regretted his return to the land of his birth, but as heir to the abbey, he'd had no choice. The place was his responsibility, and he had also to carry on his broad shoulders the burden of being squire of the village, an unofficial post his family had held for generations. He was also the district's main magistrate, chairman of the school governors, church warden and arbiter of any petty disputes that varying antagonists who might not want to consult the vicar, nevertheless wanted settled.

He often wondered what would happen if some of his uncharitable and condescending fellow aristocrats were usurped in an uprising by the so-called plebians they mostly despised. In the wealthy Cotswolds he knew that most of the villages were still populated by those that rented or lived in tied cottages owned by local landowners and did so because they had no alternative. Postwar agricultural wages were still poor and a silent, scarcely perceived protest was slowly taking place. There were factories offering much higher remuneration in Gloucester and Cheltenham. Ranks were firmly established in the forest, and other concerns tempted those whose families had known nothing but the daily grind involved in tending stock and tilling the soil.

His mind demanding constant challenges, Sir Crispen often speculated. He could not see the phlegmatic English peasantry engaging in revolution. A Robespierre, he thought, could not arise in an Anglo-Saxon scenario and no way could he see the so-called peasants employing the guillotine! But given the chance, who knew what someone like the unbalanced Arthur Barnett would do if incited to revolt?

Reminded of that tainted mortal, Sir Crispen knew that Arthur would come before the magistrates tomorrow, a formality that would decide whether he would be committed for trial in a higher court. Sir Crispen had visited Plumb Farm to find a young cousin of Arthur's in charge. The cousin tactfully explained that when Arthur departed this life – a distinct possibility either sooner or later – the cousin and his wife were destined to inherit, and meanwhile they were happy to move in until that happened. Mrs Barnett seemed unaffected by Arthur's absence, and with the cousin's wife proving to be an excellent cook, was probably better looked after than she'd ever been. The cousin was very distressed about Arthur's pending trial and anxiously sought Sir Crispen's opinion on the outcome. On the one hand he'd been glad to get away from a not very salubrious area of Ross, though exchanging it for Plumb Farm had hardly improved matters. Whilst very compassionate where his incarcerated relative was concerned, he could not wait to set about improving the place; the state of which appalled him.

Satisfied that Arthur's mother was in good hands, Sir Crispen had left in a better frame of mind. Nevertheless, he did not know what the outcome of Arthur's trial would be. He hoped it would be de ja vie, like Fred, committed to Coney Hill: undoubtedly the best of three outcomes. The other options were life imprisonment and – heaven forbid – the death penalty. By any stretch of the imagination, Sir Crispen did not think the latter fate would be imposed. He knew that the dubious Chinese drug, Sonli, was no longer being sanctioned and hoped Dr Matthews in the mental asylum had learnt his lesson and was no longer using it. Sir

Crispen had been very au fait with the effect it had on Fred and did not know if what he'd heard about the Chinese advocate of it in the isolation hospital was true. As for Dr Pellew, he was an old fool and should have known better.

CHAPTER TWENTY

Walter knew that Minze Wang was still using Sonli and must have another source of supply. And frequently bored with his mundane occupation in the hospital, Walter wondered if he might get something profitable going by supplying his mates with it.

He approached the doctor with his proposal and found him quite amenable. Sonli was now coming up the Severn from Avonmouth again. Yes, it could be smoked and yes, Minze Wang had reverted to obtaining it from his original suppliers. Stressing it wouldn't be cheap, Minze insisted that if anything went wrong, Walter must not reveal from where it came. His voice during this insistence contained a hint of menace Walter had not experienced before and the doctor went on to mention that he had 'friends' in the city of Bristol, and betrayal by a lowly hospital porter would not occur without retribution being carried out. An enquiry by Walter as to where Minze thought the Sonli went that was stolen from the boy's motorcycle panniers was simply answered by the Chinaman. All sorts of substances made it into HM prison, Gloucester, and Sonli could be one of them. It could be sanctioned by a bent 'screw' or merely brought in by a visitor. Then there were the ubiquitous city pubs where various drugs were bartered, most having found their way from the port and likely imported from foreign climes. Sonli was a versatile drug. It could be smoked, taken in drinks, and as Minze used it, to treat the mentally and physically afflicted patients. He did not dwell on its debilitating effects. He now had a new, plentiful supply and if Walter wanted, he could become a distributor and be furnished with the names of feasible clients whom he could approach with care. Walter indicated that he'd probably start by approaching his mates and Minze though that might be a good way to start. Money was the Chinese doctor's god. He had a perfectly adequate salary but had no scruples when it came to supplying Sonli to those who would pay for it.

Walter had some vague notion that he could give up work when possessed of newly acquired wealth. He dreamed of a 'Life of Riley' away from the humdrum existence he led at the isolation hospital. Sonli would provide him with this. He would start by supplying his mates, then confident he could get away with it, venture forth into the city's underworld.

CHAPTER TWENTY-ONE

Unusually, it didn't take long for Arthur to be brought to trial and, sadly, committed to prison. His incarceration happened during advent when preparations for Christmas were being carried out and somewhat marred the occasion. His lawyer's plea of 'unsound mind' did not impress the jury. Arthur had answered questions perfectly lucidly – it would never occur to him not to – and he appeared surprised that anyone should think he had wanted to kill Fred. He'd been attacked in the George by Fred for jealous reasons and saw his chance in discovering him in St Michael's as an opportunity to extract revenge. Things had got out of hand, and he was very sorry. He'd been found guilty and because the judge believed there were mitigating circumstances, he was sentenced to life imprisonment and escaped the dreaded death penalty.

Burdened by the loss of Fred and the imprisonment of Arthur, it took Bhuppa a great deal of effort to return to living a normal life, something achieved with the help of her friends, and by resuming her care of the orangery and helping with the donkeys. She would not touch the piano and was not allowed to visit the prison. Sir Crispen labelled it an even worse place for a blooming young girl to visit than the mental melting pot that he alleged Coney Hill to be.

Having broken up from school, Bhuppa and the other children were helping to decorate the church. She did not see this as an incongruous thing for a Buddhist to do, especially as it was being done under the supervision of Annie, who, again, saw no reason why she shouldn't celebrate Christmas as the wife of an Englishman in her adopted country.

One or two ladies from the WI were also contributing and the vicar, easy going, left them to it, not interfering and concerning himself solely with such spiritual matters as the order of service and when riding a donkey, Bhuppa would enter as Mary. Bhuppa had no particular favourite where the asses were concerned and had opted to ride Vic, a reliable and less stubborn jack who she knew would readily co-perate. The other girls were not to be left out. Rachel would do the same thing at Blaisdon on Wendy and Ah Cy, to her parents' delight, would ride Amos into the small church at Benhall. To keep her further occupied, Bhuppa had been ferried later by Dan to help with decorative things at Blaisdon and Rachel had joined her. Also, all members of Chinese families dutifully helped with whatever business the family were involved in and Ah Cy was no exception. Having been a willing helper at St Felicity's, she was not expected to be one of the decorators at the other churches and as far as the boys were concerned, unwillingness and a craze for playing marbles explained their absence.

The vicar expressed admiration for the extremely large and tall Christmas tree that Dan had acquired and provided without charge. He could not quite accept that it had fallen off the back of a lorry and suspected the Forestry Commission were the losers, unaware that one of their carefully nurtured conifers had gone missing.

CHAPTER TWENTY-TWO

Walter had bumped into Seth near the chapel in the docks and the narrow boat skipper's appearance had given the hospital porter an idea. He suggested they sojourn to Callum's café to have breakfast and hungry after unloading, Seth gladly assented. Business had been gradually diminishing and the narrow boat owner was soon bemoaning the fact to Walter over the café's sumptuous breakfast. Callum didn't do things by halves and the matelots and dock workers who patronised the place were usually appreciative of his efforts. Sarah had taken young Colin into the shopping centre where the Bon Marche was playing host to Father Christmas, and whilst not entirely convinced that such a children's benefactor truly existed, young Colin was only too glad to receive the present he doled out to every child whose parents had coughed up the appropriate amount to visit his grotto.

At Callum's café midst a hubbub of accents both native and foreign, Walter tentatively put a proposal to Seth which the canal navigator immediately rejected. This caused the callow seventeen-year-old to wish he'd not made the approach. Apart from a couple of derisory sales of Sonli to his milk bar mates at a reduced price, Walter had not been successful at pushing it. Inclined to think that Winze was overcharging, he wondered if Seth could acquire and transport Sonli at a cheaper rate. But the sagacious Seth had learnt his lesson. He vehemently denied that he'd be able to acquire the drug for less and strongly advised the gullible hospital porter to leave it alone. Seth was not aware that the lad had already made several pathetic attempts to push it further and was desperate to make good the extortionate investment he'd made with the unscrupulous Chinese doctor. Seth lectured the now disconsolate Walter on the pitfalls he might experience by dabbling in the city's underworld and by the time he'd finished, the porter had taken to speculating over how he was going to dispose of the drug other than by dropping it into the canal.

Seth shovelled the last piece of black pudding in his mouth, drained his teacup and arose. He clapped his fellow diner on the shoulder and admonished him further, engaging in some insulting and friendly banter with Callum and the multi-national customers before striding out on to the quay. He resolved to keep an eye on young Walter and hoped the lad would not do anything rash; a bad mistake could easily earn him an undesirable police record.

Seth didn't like to be away from his boat too long. He often thought he was attached to it by some nautical umbilical cord, and walking briskly round the basin to where it was berthed, he quickly vaulted aboard. He could not imagine life without it, but with trade slowly declining, he did not know what the future might hold. The warehouses were seldom filled to capacity these days and if the demise of the docks happened, he hoped these great storage leviathans would not become derelict, eventually arising to enjoy a renaissance in some other capacity.

The small steam train that plied the dock's sole railhead was exiting just then and rumour was rife that it, too, would not be around much longer. With a degree of sadness, he watched it leave, then, pulling himself together, put the large, blackened kettle on the stove. Canal life decreed you could never have too many brews and some of the special tea that found its way into the docks tasted infinitely better than that you could buy in the shops.

Walter took the lift to the top floor of the Bon Marche. He'd needed the toilet and thought it odd that it should be on the fourth floor. The lift was still attended by a boy in uniform who declaimed the floors as they were reached and operated various buttons to stop and start the lift. Walter's favourite floor was 'Lingerie, knickers and brassieres', a pronouncement the lift attendant delighted in making, which induced varied reactions from his passengers: acute embarrassment in young girls; ribald remarks from young men; and disapproving frowns from frustrated spinsters.

The reason for the toilet's placement on the top level became obvious when passing the adjacent restaurant and Walter realised that the toilet's main usage would be by those who ate in this cafeteria. Having relieved himself, he paused at the entrance to the spacious dining area and observed a pretty Asian girl sitting at a table near the open door. She must be about sixteen and lifting her head from the book she'd been reading gave Walter a wan smile.

After a lot of cajoling, Bhuppa had persuaded Sir Crispen to let her do some unaccompanied Christmas shopping in Gloucester. Using her feminine wiles and aided by Annie, who thought a day out would ease some of her recent tribulations, Sir Crispen yielded and depositing her to catch a train at Blaisdon Halt, told her to be careful and to return on the three o'clock from Gloucester.

Although he'd not long since had a monster portion of bacon and eggs in Callum's, Walter could never resist further sustenance and would not deny that he had an ulterior motive. He hadn't much experience with girls, but with a great effort, he entered the restaurant and politely asked the Asian girl with the sparkling eyes and the book if he could sit at her table. At first this startled her, but liking the look of the polite and surprisingly good-looking young man, she momentarily conveyed an air of amusement before suggesting he order something to eat: at the same time making it plain that she'd not object to his company.

Dan could drive anything and was currently behind the wheel of a big articulated lorry, pulling into the premises of a busy organisation in the Bristol Road. Greeting a foreman he knew, he enquired how long it would take to load up and told that an hour would be required, decided to go and see how poor Arthur Barnet was coping in HM prison. He caught one of the frequent buses into the city centre and from there took the short walk to the jail where he found Arthur ensconced at a communal table in a bright recreation room, supposedly engaged in group therapy.

Dan sat down opposite Arthur and attempted to converse, not receiving an initial response, feasibly because of his part in finding the evidence which led to the farmer's arrest. But being eager for news, Arthur soon capitulated and wanted to know all the gossip from home that the vicar, who'd recently visited, might not have wished to relate. The vicar had kindly brought Arthur's mother with him, which had been a mistake, for she barely recognised her son in this strange environment and most of the time, just sat there with a beatific expression on her face. Arthur seemed pleased that the cousins were minding Plum Farm and quite convinced he would one day return to resume his old lifestyle, magnanimously pointed out that as the farm possessed four bedrooms, they would be able to stay put without there being noticeable inconvenience to himself. He was concerned that his pianoforte should receive its usual six-monthly tuning and requested that Dan get in touch with Ivan Constance of Ross. The Constances were an old, highly respected family who'd inhabited the village of Longhope for generations, and one of them, a rumbustious character called Theophilus, had been responsible for enhancing the summit of that notable landmark, May Hill, with its crown of trees. And with slightly confusing logic, Arthur wouldn't want anyone else but the one who lived in Ross to tend the piano.

And how was Bhuppa? Bhuppa was well but skirting round the fact that Arthur was responsible for Fred's demise – a fact that the farmer now chose to emphatically deny – Dan said that she was distressed over Arthur's imprisonment and maybe if he behaved himself, the farmer might be released for good conduct. Dan thought it more likely that pigs would fly. Arthur's crime was too grave, but it wouldn't do to deflate his optimism by saying so.

And no, Bhuppa wouldn't be allowed to visit. Sir Crispen considered the prison an entirely inappropriate place for a pretty young girl to set foot in. Confronted with the sight of her, there was no knowing what comments would be made by a lot of frustrated old lags and Dan wholly agreed that it would be distressing for her to run the gauntlet of their dubious remarks.

Consulting his wristwatch, Dan indicated that he'd have to leave. The artic with its load had to be in Manchester by nightfall and, as was inevitable, time did not stand still. Arthur was crestfallen over Bhuppa's non-appearance and Dan felt briefly sorry for him, then recalling the gravity of the crime, quickly bid him farewell, and went on his way.

Nascent and disturbing feelings were already beginning to arise in Walter and Bhuppa. Walter's innate shyness did not impede his ability to instantly fall in love with Bhuppa, and although made cautious through hearing of the sexual exploits of indiscreet fellow pupils in the bike sheds at school, Bhuppa had the usual yearnings that any fourteen-year-old furtively wanted fulfilled and looking at him from under lowered eyelids, she thought Walter might be the one to oblige her. Of late, her devotion to Buddhism had taken a knock. She seldom visited the meeting house in Westham and to Annie's consternation, had all but abandoned the abbey's makeshift temple. She still intended to ride the donkey into St Felicity's on Christmas Day in ten days' time but had relinquished her post as organ blower to a sturdy boy from the village whose see-sawing adolescent voice meant he could not sing in the small choir which the newly appointed organist had successfully founded. Arthur's replacement was a retired musician from Huntley, extremely competent, but who only played written voluntaries as opposed to the extempore ones with which the former resident of Plum Farm had regaled the congregation. According to some, the new man's playing was soulless, not something with which the vicar concurred, and only grateful to employ a replacement for Arthur so quickly, the Reverend Charles was pleased that the Christmas services could hopefully take place without any foreseeable disaster occurring.

    Walter was suggesting Bhuppa might like to ride pillion on his famous Cotton motorbike. They could go to Cheltenham and walk down the prom. They'd maybe have a cup of tea in the renowned Cadena café and listen to the resident trio that performed there. Walter did not like to admit his liking for classical music to his mates, but complied with their current preferences for people like Pat Boone and Guy Mitchel and Frankie Laine, and was even partial to this new skiffle thing that seemed to be taking over.

    Bhuppa mentioned she'd been learning the piano and had just given up and Walter wanted to know why. The girl gave him a dazzling smile and evaded the question. She wasn't sure about the motorbike, but she would like to see him again and perhaps they could go to the pictures at the Odeon, just across the way in King's Square. She didn't know whether this would be allowed, but bringing into play her rebellious streak, decided that what her adopted parents didn't know about wouldn't worry them. If, like a dutiful daughter, she caught the three train back today as promised, there would be no reason why they should not allow her to visit Gloucester when she felt like it. They need not be aware she was going there primarily to meet Walter, and what the consequences of this might be, she considered herself old enough to cope with.

Before returning to pick up his load, Dan remembered that his wife had asked him to buy some stamps from the GPO in King's Square and having purchased them, he emerged from the post office just in time to see the young couple coming out of the Bon Marche, holding hands and on their way to the railway station. Despite his former existence as a hard-bitten member of the forces, Dan had a certain attitude to what was right and proper, and the sight of Bhuppa and Walter together disquieted him more than he cared to admit. To him, at the age of fourteen, Bhuppa was just a child. True, holding hands was harmless enough, but where might it lead? He'd not exactly been unaware of girls whilst at school and he'd certainly indulged in one or two 'knee tremblers' with the more obliging ones, but the thought of his cherished Bhuppa falling from grace in that manner horrified him. Blessed with somewhat docile offspring of his own, he'd always taken an interest in her welfare, was prepared to help her parents in any way required and if such an animal could exist in the contemporary world, had once been described by a jocular Sir Crispen as an 'old family retainer'. And now he had an uneasy thought that he'd be damned if he did interfere and damned if he didn't.

Walter found the Hereford-Ross train without difficulty. It was steaming on one of the bay platforms. Almost a living thing, its Castle loco seemed to be pawing the rails, anxious to be off and awaiting the guard's whistle.

Greatly daring, Walter took hold of Bhuppa in a rather gauche manner and kissed her. At first alarmed, she quickly responded and anxious not to miss the train, promised to write to him at his hospital flat, but did not want him to reply by posting letters to the abbey. She suggested he sent them to Elton Vicarage C/O her friend Rachel. Rachel rose very early in the morning and Bhuppa would make it right with her and Rachel would almost certainly comply with this arrangement. Bhuppa would write first and this would give her time to make her friend aware of what would transpire before Walter replied.

Closeted in a compartment on her own and lulled by the soothing motion of the train, Bhuppa tentatively began to pleasure herself. Other girls at school had incited her to do this and at first thinking it immoral, she soon came to believe there was no harm in it and even took to musing what it would be like to do the real thing with a boy. Not just any old boy, one specific one, and the thought of doing it with Walter meant that she soon became damp, and had to admit she'd enjoyed it.

CHAPTER TWENTY-THREE

On the Sunday before Christmas and with a nice touch, the Westham Brass Quartet marched ahead of the donkey into St Felicity's. Unlike Arthur, the new organist did not object to their presence and had even made arrangements to accommodate them during the service. Complete with descant, 'O Come All Ye Faithful' nearly raised the roof and 'Hark the Herald' was not far behind. Vic the donkey behaved impeccably upon entry but removed by Dan for the duration of the service, wandered round the churchyard foraging the sparse winter plant life within it. An unaccompanied interval caused by Dan going over the road to greet and smoke a cigarette with an old non-church going buttie, implemented a disaster in that it left Vic free to sample the flowers that relatives had adorned the graves with for Christmas: a floral display not intended to disappear down a non-discriminatory equine creature's gullet! Complaints were later received and disregarded with the explanation that a donkey could not distinguish between one sort or another and you couldn't have it all ways. Tradition demanded that Mary entered St Felicity's on a donkey and there would be an outcry amongst the parishioners if she arrived in any other way.

Despite the arctic temperature of the decrepit village hall, tea and mince pies still managed to engender further conviviality to proceedings and though bothered by what he had witnessed in Gloucester, Dan munched a mince pie, decided he could just about tolerate another glass of mulled wine and would defer any decision until after Christmas. He noticed Bhuppa had – with or without permission – made herself up a little more than usual, if anything looked even older and was receiving admiring glances from some of the younger males present. This made him uneasy, but not wishing to mar the festive season with what could be unwelcome information, he was even more determined to stall by letting matters rest for a while.

The benign old canon from the cathedral who'd been the guest preacher made a point of talking to those of the younger generation who were present. These included Bhuppa who, at first wary in her response to him, soon found his enthusiasm for anything related refreshingly infectious. Not at the moment entirely enamoured with either Christianity or Buddhism, she nevertheless found the old canon very broad-minded. He was profuse about her role as Mary – she could even imagine him denying the virgin-birth – quizzed her about donkeys in general and expressed admiration for Sir Crispen's benevolence in housing them, restoring their health and arranging for their further welfare.

Christmas at the Whippet Inn did not provide a respite for the landlord and landlady. On Christmas Day, Joe and Sylvie laid on a sumptuous feast for those unfortunates who, for various reasons, lived on their own. These included the distraught mother of Fred and other assorted loners, but not those that adhered to the doctrine of preserving their single status come what may. Of these misguided mortals it was sometimes said in the vernacular, "Im or 'er was very nice, mind. 'Im d' kip 'im self t' 'imself an' doesn't bother no un!' Translated this meant 'im or 'er was bloody selfish and did little to enhance the well being of his or her fellow man or woman. This was certainly not the attitude of Foresters as a whole, but you did get some 'miserable old buggers' who couldn't appreciate which side their bread was buttered: a quote from that plain-speaking denizen of the public house, Dan, whose ire could be raised by their ungracious attitude.

Where his own domestic arrangements for Christmas were concerned, Dan complied with the usual penance of having dinner at home with his parents and invited in-laws. Playing the dutiful husband and father, he arose very early to ensure that the goose – preferred to turkey – was expeditiously deposited in the oven. This enabled him to extract a promise from his nagging wife that he could leave after dinner in order to 'help' at the Whippet. He continued to behave like a model consort during the preparations, and replete after the meal, willingly endured his partner's disapproving frown in order to enjoy the company of several old cronies in the public bar of the pub. His two boys,

Kevin and Charlie, were well satisfied with their presents: a football and a Wolves kit. They were quiet lads and in order to get away from their stifling grandparents, would be quite content to go 'oodin during the afternoon, only re-appearing when their stomachs signalled that it was teatime.

To solve his conscience, he did help Sylvie with the washing-up and during this laborious task, she noticed he seemed distracted.

'Something the matter, Dan?'

Dan deposited a dinner plate he'd been wiping into a cupboard and sat down on a kitchen chair. The noise from the bar indicated that a good time was being had by all and Joe's decision to hire Buster, a purveyor of dubious jokes and ditties, to entertain the mostly elderly company after lunch, was proving to be a stroke of genius. Performed in a broad dialect, it would probably be incomprehensible to any poor soul from the outside world, although the insidious invasion of the Forest by aliens from elsewhere had not yet come about. Second homes for affluent city dwellers were not yet a reality, and the idea that this glorious haven from normal civilisation would become overwhelmed and largely inhabited by outsiders was a daunting prospect.

'Don' know uz oi should zai?'

Sylvie took her hands out of the large enamel sink and wiped them on a towel. She turned to face Dan.

'Like a cup of tea?'

Normally fuelled almost exclusively by alcohol, Dan nevertheless thought that a cup of tea might not be a bad idea and expressed his thanks for the offer. On rare occasions he'd drunk Sylvie's tea and enjoyed it. It was a vast improvement to the slightly insipid brew his wife made. Sylvie made it the old-fashioned way. You warmed the pot with tepid water, emptied it and spooned in just the right amount of loose tea. You then filled the kettle with cold water, placing it on one of the rings of the gas cooker. An electric kettle was not yet an aid owned by the pub tenants, but like some banshee, a whistle on the steam kettle's spout informed you when the water was boiled. This was transferred to the teapot, allowed to stand for a while and stirred before being poured into the cups with the aid of a tea strainer.

The strainer ensured no stray tea leaves encroached into the cup and as to whether you put milk in before or after pouring the tea was still an age-old moot point and often caused controversial and heated discussion.

Dan made up his mind and somehow knew he could trust Sylvie.

'Oi did zee young Bhuppa in Glaster the other daiy with a byoy.' It came out blunt and to the point.

The landlord's wife did not seem to be alarmed by this brief revelation.

'Probably some lad from school,' she said, 'shouldn't think it's anything to worry about.'

Dan shook his head in what could be interpreted as a slightly contentious gesture.

'Thick lad yunt a schoolboy. Oi a' sin 'im in Glaster before now. 'Im 'az an' ol' motor bike an' oi d' reckon' 'im's a good deal older than 'er. Thee cussent know what might 'appen. 'Ers too young an' thaiy wuz 'oldin' 'ands, like.'

When opening her presents, Bhuppa did not seem her effusive self. This might have had something to do with the obligatory presence of two maiden ladies, sisters of Sir Crispen and not possessed of their brothers' joie de vivre. Though generous with their gifts, Bhuppa could not help but think of them as slightly racist in their attitude towards her. In her eyes they were two old biddies who would have been more at home as memsahibs in British India. To her they were kindly condescending, having to accept her status in the aristocratic household, but covertly stuck in a mindset that labelled her a slightly inferior being. It did not help that they lived in the highly scrubbed and filthy rich village of Painswick, played bridge with those of similar inclinations and were long-established members of the Cotswold String Orchestra. They didn't often visit, but Christmas was another thing. Very conveniently being pioneers of vegetarianism, they were easily satisfied, at the same time trying not to disapprove of the roasted bird broad-minded Annie provided for Sir Crispen and one or two single employees of the home farm that the abbey owner, not a bit class conscious, invited to his table.

The two ladies were inclined to enjoy making desultory

conversation, but a chance remark by Aunt Jonquil to Bhuppa, could be said to be anything but desultory. It was an unfortunate enquiry and one which made the poor girl blush and become consumed with unease. Although she had done nothing with which to reproach herself, she somehow knew her recent attachment to someone of the opposite sex would not meet with the approval of her adopted parents. Ergo, it now looked like the cat would now well and truly be out of the bag.

'My dear, did we not see you in Southgate Street the other day with a nice-looking young man? Is he a school friend or something? We'd just come out of Hickie's music shop and we thought it was you.'

Bhuppa had seen them and pretended she hadn't and hurrying on by with Walter, eventually disappeared with him into his favoured milk bar. Here his mates were apt to make questionable comments to her which she usually chose to tolerate for his sake. Her innate intelligence enabled her to field their remarks with surprisingly mature and mordant wit but, undeniably, the adopted aunts' revelation meant that the Sword of Damocles appeared about to fall.

Sir Crispen now displayed a face which implied he might be having a word later and Annie looked quite alarmed at the prospect.

Complete with driver, the Dormobile Dan had organised had arrived to collect some of the Christmas revellers from the Whippet and with their exodus, Joe and Sylvie closed down for the rest of Christmas Day. They were left with the sole company of Dan; ever the wizened regular, him expressing consternation over the Bhuppa dilemma. Opinion was divided. Sylvie thought maybe the vicar could be persuaded to have a word with the young girl, but her spouse adamantly disagreed. He felt this could be terribly embarrassing for both parties, particularly if the affair was entirely innocent. To which Sylvie expressed the opinion that it would be too late to interfere if it wasn't. On the other hand, how would Bhuppa react to the remorseless grapevine informing most of the populace of her trysts in Gloucester? Once more showing sagacity that outward appearance suggested he might not possess, Joe posited the idea that Dan might be the person to approach Bhuppa. Dan had been the one she had turned to during the qualms her parents had experienced over Arthur Barnet; a temporary falling out he'd helped to resolve and perhaps a quiet word from him might help to prevent the occurrence of anything untoward.

Whatever, all three decided that doing nothing could result in an undesired happening, and to prevent this, Dan should be the conduit of their concern.

*

Sir Crispen tried not to be heavy-handed and had insisted Annie be present when he admonished Bhuppa. Feeling distinctly uncomfortable, he outlined the law where under-age girls were concerned, and it needed Annie to reassure Bhuppa that they were not implying she was indulging in an illicit affair. But a relationship between a fourteen-year-old and a seventeen-year-old boy was not desirable and perhaps if they waited a couple of years...

Wide-eyed listening to all this, the rebel in Bhuppa was not strong enough to prevent her bursting into tears, and incapable of accepting condolences from a somewhat mollified Annie, she fled upstairs to the haven of her own room. Inwardly hating it, the rarely seen martinet emerged from within the Knight of the Bath. Bhuppa would no longer be able to visit Gloucester unaccompanied and all communication with the boy must cease.

As it transpired, he'd seriously underestimated the determination and resolve of his adopted daughter and would ultimately suffer the dire consequences of his restrictive measures.

CHAPTER TWENTY-FOUR

Forty-eight hours later, Walter walked into the milk bar and was handed a neatly addressed envelope by Giovanni, the amenable Italian proprietor. This was the first missive he'd received by this means, and without opening it, he just assumed it contained the date and time from Bhuppa for another meeting in Gloucester. The young couple had soon realised that post delivered to the city was quicker and more reliable. The isolation hospital where Walter worked had only one reception area where all the post was unceremoniously dumped in a heap, and although this too was a questionable way of doing things, it was obviously better than the postman delivering it to individual patients with contagious diseases. You had to sort through it to make sure you were not missing anything, and the patients' mail was sent to their rooms with their meals by staff wearing their accustomed masks.

A post box opposite Benhall Secondary School provided a convenient way to send letters for Bhuppa and Rachel was a good friend who, very willing to help, always arose early in order to pick up the post before her parents at the vicarage could do so. Bhuppa had been a little concerned about this arrangement, but Rachel assured her that her extremely busy parents would probably not comment on the odd letter addressed to Bhuppa care of their daughter. They had too much else to concern themselves with and not inexperienced through running a youth club in nearby Little Dean, were too savvy to bother about the foibles and impetuous actions of teenage girls.

Somewhat indiscreetly, Walter had shown the slightly perfumed envelopes he received to his impecunious and curious mates and in their intrusive and prosaic manner – which almost always included a swear word in every sentence – they beseeched him to open this latest communication from his loved one in front of them. Walter had received more than a few and though he'd rashly told them about this new girl in his life and they'd met her, he certainly wasn't going to reveal the contents of the letters she wrote to him. His reluctance prompted them to indulge in uncouth jibes and not prepared to put up with this merciless ribaldry for any longer than he had to, hurriedly finished his drink and without opening the letter, defied their protests and left. He rode his motorcycle round to the park, a not particularly attractive place in winter, and slumping down on a seat dedicated to someone completely unknown to him, proceeded to slit the envelope open with his Swiss army knife. At first alarmed at the recent events graphically described by Bhuppa, he read on and was reconciled to her proposal that they could contrive to meet up in the small township of Eastdean. He could ride his famous Cotton motorbike there and a good bus service would enable Bhuppa to meet him without too much hassle. Her other suggestion that she could meet him after school surprised and disturbed him. He'd never thought to ask her age and didn't like the idea of meeting a schoolgirl in uniform in a small town where she'd easily be recognised if they were not careful. They would have to be very discreet and meet in a back street on a Saturday or during holidays, being careful where they went. He resolved to write back giving his views on the matter and included a couple of dates when they might feasibly meet. He hoped she could find somewhere quite secluded and eagerly anticipated a favourable reply.

 Sir Crispen and Dan were doing running repairs to the roof of one of the stables. It had been leaking for some time and with both of them similarly attired in heavily soiled working overalls, it would be difficult to distinguish between the aristocrat and the artisan. Sir Crispen broached the subject of Bhuppa and her supposed visits on one or two Saturdays during January to meet up with school friends in Eastdean. Dan played dumb. He'd had to take the same stance when Sir Crispen had broken the news of Bhuppa and Walter before Dan had managed to have a word with her. He suspected his fellow worker and part-time employer had a devious and suspicious mind and Sir Crispen's next words confirmed it.

 Déjà vu, thought Dan. Here we go again. Another subterfuge similar to the underhand one he'd had in tailing the misanthropic, but late lamented Fred. He supposed he couldn't refuse. Particularly if it meant protecting the assumed virginal status of young Bhuppa. She'd apparently be visiting Eastdean this coming Saturday: catching the ten am Westham-Cinderford bus from the handy bus stop outside the church.

On Friday nights it was customary for Walter to meet his mates in a back-street pub. His mates were now the only ones he supplied with Sonli in small doses. His career as a small-time dealer in the substance had become a damp squib. He'd also forsaken his room at the hospital for a grimy but more convenient flat in the city. This enabled him to have less contact with his potential nemesis, Minze, who did not seem distressed at his defection and just supplied Walter's small needs, again with the stipulation that he would not reveal Sonli as a drug suitable for all and sundry. Walter imagined the unscrupulous Chinese doctor had bigger fish to fry and absorbed his complaisant attitude with something akin to relief.

The landlord of the Hen and Chickens didn't care about Walter and his under-age friends imbibing in the back bar. There were times when they became a little boisterous, but his wife – a raucous virago who could have stepped out of the cauldron of enmity that Dickens depicted in *Tale of Two Cities* – would sternly quell their high jinks with a frown and a fortissimo 'That's enough you bloody heathens!' This inevitably did the trick and providing the Amazonian woman did not notice them slipping Sonli into their drinks, they were allowed to stay until looming insolvency obliged them to leave.

Almost certainly under the influence of alcohol and Sonli combined, Walter had a sudden scintilla of inspiration over a matter that had been bothering him for a while. The last time he'd met Bhuppa he'd tentatively broached a subject that concerns any healthy young male from time to time: this as they sat in the little church at Benhall where they were likely to remain undisturbed. A clever ruse by Bhuppa to obviate recognition in Eastdean and a convenient hideaway for an exploration that, aware where it could lead, she didn't allow to progress too far. Her beau had been disappointed. Excruciatingly embarrassed, he'd taken up the offer of his barber of 'something for the ladies' and confronted with the prospect of fulfilling his desires, had been torn both ways. Her age daunted him: the pew they'd desecrated with fervent clinches hadn't been very comfortable and a censoring figure of Christ looking at them from a stained glass window plus Bhuppa's unwillingness to let him remove any part of her apparel, had acted as a disincentive and cause of frustration. But he now thought he had the answer. Sonli affected different people in different ways. It gave most of his mates a 'high' and he didn't see why it shouldn't have the same effect on Bhuppa. This Saturday could be different, and having scruples might be virtuous, but he was going to put his on the back burner. Under the influence of Sonli, Bhuppa would likely consent. They usually had a soft drink from a bottle in the church which he provided, accompanied by various unhealthy snacks, and it would be no trouble to add Sonli to the bottle with, he hoped gratifying results.

One of his mates dug him in the ribs. 'Come on, sunshine. Time youm woke up. Waz you off with the fairies or zummat?'

The fairies? He must have dozed off and why did the mention of the little people disturb him? He put it down to the Sonli and, conducted out of the pub on a frost laden night, ceased to worry about it.

CHAPTER TWENTY-FIVE

Chia Hao opened the door to the takeaway and turned the sign round. Business was flourishing and placidly content with his existence, he paused to admire the old motorcycle which he noticed carried a pillion passenger as it roared past. He stood contemplating it for a while, a cold mode of transportation, noting that both rider and passenger were well wrapped up to combat the elements. Both wore balaclavas and were enveloped in the currently fashionable duffle coats, seemingly an obligatory form of clothing for the generation who, unwisely, were not obliged by law to wear crash helmets.

Chia Hao watched the vibrant machine as it passed the town hall where the old codger was engaged in putting even more fatuous and unnecessary notices up on the display board, and saw it turn left opposite Rank's, probably heading for Ross. His attention was then diverted back inside by Ah Cy, who had taken to 'organising' him in the same way as her mother. He pretended to object to this, but confronted with Ah Cy's irresistible charm inevitably conceded defeat. This was how the delightful girl had persuaded him to acquire her a donkey, at the same time getting round the stern but equally malleable Sir Crispen to allow its stabling to remain at the abbey. They were off down there this afternoon for her to exercise the beast and as it was a somewhat inclement day, Chia Hao would take her in the car, rather than have her ride her bicycle. He did not object to this arrangement, as Sir Crispen would more than likely conduct him round the abbey grounds to witness latest developments and this amiable sojourn would most likely conclude with coffee taken in the capacious kitchen. Here Sir Crispen would initiate deeply philosophical discussion and at some point, Annie would join them, not loath to expound the dictums of Buddhism. Chia Hao did not dispute her beliefs and although a convert and strong advocate of Christianity, was prepared to concede that you could not dismiss other creeds and philosophies out of hand. Since his migration to the UK, he'd also become a devotee of William Shakespeare, and convinced that the great Bard had something to say on the subject, tried in vain to recall what it was.

At Elton Vicarage, another daughter was engaged in fielding enquiries from her parents. There was nothing devious about rosy-cheeked Rachel. Very pretty, with her high cheekbones and startling blue eyes, she could be termed an English rose, but her tomboyish nature sometimes defied such a description. She still enjoyed a friendly scrap with her little brother and only when he pulled her lustrous auburn hair did she stoop to pin him to the floor. Not of a particularly enquiring nature, she'd accepted Bhuppa's request to receive the oriental girl's post without dissent or curiosity and faithfully took it to school where she handed it over without comment. A letter had arrived at the beginning of the week, and for the first time, been intercepted by her father. He'd celebrated an early communion at St Felicity's, and before leaving had picked up the mail which, for a country round, came uncommonly early. He'd put the letter for Bhuppa on the hall table and until this morning refrained from commenting on it.

In an unaccustomed way, Rachel was now prevaricating and Isobel, who could not think why the letter should be addressed to the vicarage, was not satisfied. And almost for the first time during her relatively short existence on earth, Rachel told a white lie. She knew full well who the letter was from and was surprised her parents had not known of Bhuppa's trysts with Walter in Gloucester when the aunts' unfortunate revelation had resulted in it becoming common knowledge.

The Reverend Charles eyed his daughter with brief and rare disapproval.

'That won't do, love. We know all about Bhuppa and Walter. Sir Crispen made a point of telling me himself. That letter coming the other day suggests to me that the young so-and-sos are arranging to meet elsewhere. I don't think it was from a "pen-friend" and I'm surprised you tried to pretend it was ...'

Here Isobel intervened, putting a semi-restraining hand on his arm.

'Charles, don't be too hard on Rachel. I don't think she's

trying to be anything other than protective and loyal to her friend.'

Not the sort to become greatly upset when admonished, Rachel shrugged her shoulders. 'OK, I know the letter was from Walter. Bhuppa tells me most things. I knew she was meeting him in Gloucester, but I don't know if that recent letter was the acceptance of one he'd received with details of a meeting place elsewhere. She didn't tell me that.' Here she gave her elders an infectious grin. 'And I s'pose I'm an idiot for not telling the truth. You goin' to lock me in the attic with bread and water for a week?'

Her father came and put his arm round her, an action that did not stop him retaining his serious face.

'Course we're not, love. Just forget it. However, you must understand the perils and implications of Bhuppa's association with Walter. She's only fourteen and things could happen ...'

Unabashed, Rachel interrupted. 'Dad, I know all about that. There's a girl at school that was in "the club". She's left and we're told she's been sent away to have the baby. We were all given a dire warning. About sex and all that ...'

Reverend Charles wasn't sure he approved of this talk. Society had not yet advanced enough to realise that teenage girls needed sex education, and he would have to discuss it with Isobel when Rachel was not present. But Isobel forestalled him.

'Charles, dear, we have to face the facts. A little more knowledge might prevent a lot more upsets.'

'Yes,' said Rachel and continued with astonishing frankness. 'And I'm not sure about your Virgin Mary. She wasn't married to Joseph and can you really believe she got put up the duff by some ghost in a white sheet?'

The Reverend Charles tried hard not to laugh and Isobel could not control herself. Dan followed the bus towards Eastdean and was surprised to see Bhuppa alight at Benhall, where she walked down the lane to the church. He heard the motorbike come up the hill from the Lamb Inn at the Eastdean crossroads before he sighted it, and with his pickup largely concealed in the school car park opposite, watched as Walter turned down the same lane. He assumed the motorcyclist must be Walter, and hoping the couple would soon emerge from the church, hunkered down in the pickup with a much-needed cigarette.

It was only just eleven am and by a quarter-past the hour he'd had enough. He mulled over what he should do and discounting the notion that he might simply go up to the church to have an awkward confrontation with the young couple, decided to adjourn to the George: the inn handily placed in the centre of Eastdean. What there was in the way of traffic for those days nearly always had to come that way and a good view of the shops and church could be had from the public house's front bar. Dan was confident he'd see Walter's vehicle if it appeared and, in any case, would shortly return to Benhall if it didn't.

Dan could consume a considerable amount of ale in a short time and for what he thought half an hour, put the world to right with Ivan the landlord and a lot of early topers, most of whom were old acquaintances. By the time he deigned to consult his watch, he discovered that pub time – deemed by most drinkers to be different to its Greenwich equivalent – had somehow advanced to 12.15. Alarmed that he might not have noticed his 'quarry' ride through the town, he tried not to panic and bidding Ivan and his clients a rather frantic adieu, returned in haste to Benhall. Not prepared to hang around further, he drove straight to the church in the hope of finding the youngsters still in residence. Here he found his growing pessimism perfectly justified and inwardly cursed himself for his carelessness. He could not think where the youngsters had gone, but decided to return to town where, hopefully, some help might be obtained from the natives.

No assistance was forthcoming from the general stores or post office and with a sinking feeling, Dan decided to consult Chia Hao at the takeaway. There he struck gold, as Chia informed him that he'd seen the motorcycle that morning. He described what passed the town hall and turned left towards Ross about a quarter of an hour ago.

Dan thanked him, and with intuition normally only granted to the fairer sex, promptly drove off, turned down the Ross road and, half-a-mile along it, spotted the Cotton motorcycle on its prop stand, parked by the path which led to Wigpool Common.

His departure left the Chinese proprietor of the takeaway in a dilemma, and it was only his wife's intervention that persuaded him he must ring the abbey. Saturday meant that the 'chippie' – for that is what the good citizens of Eastdean mostly called it – was frantically busy and the situation was further complicated by the intrusion of PC Jummy, bent on purchasing a small portion of chips. But in some ways this was fortunate. 'Cometh the hour, Cometh the man' came to mind, and garnishing his chips with condiments prior to wrapping them, Li apprised him of state of play. In his bucolic and slightly ponderous way, Jummy decided to take the matter in hand. He asked to use the telephone and made the call to the abbey. A hubbub being prevalent in both the takeaway and the barely decreasing queue outside meant that Li could only hear one side of the conversation. Jummy was to investigate. He'd follow in the young couple and Dan's footsteps. He would make sure Bhuppa was safe and sound and they'd return her as soon as possible, most likely in Dan's pickup. The voice on the other end of the line sounded fraught, but the phlegmatic police officer managed to sound unusually reassuring. He didn't think Sir Crispen needed to appear on the scene. He was convinced the couple had only gone for a walk on Wigpool and with questionable sagacity, informed him that he'd sort it out without too much trouble.

CHAPTER TWENTY-SIX

Dan contemplated the statuesque figure in the yellow costume that stood underneath the great oak and near the faery ring. Taken aback, he thought he'd not seen a woman so beautiful. Dressed in this long, ankle-length robe, she could have been taken for a latter day Aphrodite. Her looks were classic and her demeanour ethereal. She declined to favour him with a smile and acknowledged his greeting with a barely discernible nod of her flaxen-haired head. A tremor of anxiety invaded him; the like of which he had not experienced since the hideous clash at Monte Casino. Able to absorb a great deal more alcohol than he'd recently drunk in the George, he knew it was not that which was affecting his mental state. He realised he must enquire, must ask this almost otherworldly being if she'd seen them. He can't have been far behind and they could not be far away.

A picture of a visit to this place as a child and his wicked granny's incitement not to step in the faery ring permeated his vacillating thoughts; until a vision of hapless Fred threatening Chia Hao from the centre of it loomed large. The gleaming knife poised and the ex-Gloucestershire regiment squaddie collapsing with Chia Hao, Jummy and Joe from the Whippet alarmed and looking on. Dan had not been present at this macabre scene, but the vision of it was vivid and not in the slightest distorted, invading his mind.

The woman had not moved and summoning up the courage, he made to address her.

'Thou ant zin a byoy an' a girl come this waiy, hast?'

'I did and they're not long gone.' His dialect hadn't fazed her. The voice was authoritative and matter of fact, and she did not offer any further information.

'Did thou zee where thaiy did gow?'

'I did.'

Dan was perplexed. 'Well, if thou zaw where thaiy did gow, can these tell oi where?'

A hand was placed on Dan's shoulder and a familiar voice said, ''Oo's that thou bist talkin' to, Dan?'

Dan swivelled round to confront PC Jummy.

'Thick lady over by the tree.'

Jummy's disbelieving gaze contained elements of pity and despair, as turning back round, the traumatised former soldier found it hard to accept that the woman had vanished. Conducted away from the scene by the unusually understanding policeman, Dan decided to stay mum over the beautiful woman. She must have been an apparition, and nobody would believe him if he revealed what was certain he'd witnessed and he, too, might end up in Coney Hill.

CHAPTER TWENTY-SEVEN

An exhaustive and extensive search for weeks after the couple disappeared proved abortive and at the abbey an atmosphere of disbelief and despair prevailed. Annie spent most of her time in the makeshift temple and Sir Crispen could not be persuaded by the vicar to resume his duties as churchwarden at St Felicity's. He 'abdicated' as a magistrate, gave up his role as school governor and spent most of his time ensconced in his office accompanied by a bottle containing something stronger than H20. Had it not been for the stoic Dan, equally devastated, but not prepared to give in or reveal his own experience on Wigpool, the donkeys would not have received the attention for which they were brought to the abbey, and thanks to his efforts and those of the tawdry brothers who had somehow been jolted into conscience-ridden action, the estate more or less continued to be run reasonably efficiently. Other assistance came from various tenant farmers who'd always been treated fairly by their now distressed landlord, and with resilience that sometimes only children can display, Rachel and Ah Cy spent much of their spare time helping at the abbey with the animals.

What could be described as a pall of disbelief lay over the village. Bhuppa had been a universally popular figure. She had managed to overcome any initial racial prejudice with her captivating manner and a tolerant attitude to all and sundry. Walter was almost an afterthought, and it was only the tax disc on his motorcycle which enabled them to trace his former address at the hospital. The matron there wasn't very helpful. She did not know of any relatives – including the possible uncle in Derbyshire – and investigating the boy's Gloucester flat proved unproductive. It was arranged that Dan should house the motorcycle until – and if – the couple were found, and Walter's meagre possessions would be stored in the lost property room at police headquarters.

Annie steadfastly refused to accept that the young couple were demised. She pointed out to her disbelieving husband that their possible extinction would have been preceded by the donkeys gathering in silent vigil, as they had done when Fred passed away. Sir Crispen's reaction to this assertion consisted of a weary shaking of his head: a negative response accompanied by the replenishment of his glass with whatever was in the opaque bottle.

In vain, the Reverend Charles tried to convey an air of optimism to his parishioners. His valiant attempt to project solace from the pulpit was almost heroic and he needed the booster of 'Vicar's Night' on a Tuesday in the Whippet even more than usual. Only a more liberal amount of stout and his theological training enabled him to adopt a priestly and comforting stance towards those sadly affected by the extraordinary and mystifying disappearance of Bhuppa and Walter.

With Sir Crispen adamantly refusing to grant interviews to the media, the vicar found himself thrust into the role of fending off the predatory national dailies and were it not for the support of his bishop, might not have been able to cope. Reasons depicted in the press for the youngsters' disappearance were manifold, often lurid, and in some cases, downright preposterous. Almost the entire gamut of the supernatural was explored and no solution found. It all sold newspapers and if it caused further distress to those involved, to those that inflicted it, it was a matter of no concern.

Sunday morning found Dan prompted into visiting the one almost forgotten former member of the locality who had been condemned to spend what could be the rest of his life incarcerated in prison. And Dan could not say his timorous visit was made without an ulterior motive. Disturbed and rendered largely sleepless for some weeks through speculation over what might have happened to Bhuppa, he could not dismiss the vision of the woman dressed in the yellow tunic and the rancorous, doom-laden rantings of his old, putrescent grandmother. She had always averred that the faery ring was forbidden territory. Some said Lucifer himself abided there and manifested evil upon those who ventured within it. And once again, Dan could not dismiss the old witch's notion that to dance with the fairies meant mortals could be held hostage for years, and it was true that not everyone enjoying the sometimes-dubious advances of twentieth-century existence decried the fantasies of an earlier age.

One of these was Arthur Barnett. He'd been born into an old suspicious West Gloucestershire rural environment and a family which did not disparage the old ways and beliefs. Arthur found Dan a willing listener to his explanation for Bhuppa's distressing disappearance. The former farmer and musician had obviously been fond of the young Thai girl and, nonsensical as it might seem, was anxious to find a way she could be induced to return to the land of the living. Dan wryly noted that Arthur did not include Walter in his wish for this to happen and though not entirely convinced that miracles were a thing of the past, nevertheless could not give credence to the likelihood of one occurring in this case.

Arthur went on to elucidate. He recalled his mother in her younger, more lucid days. Before what could now be recognised as the onset of Alzheimer's – not labelled as such in those days – she had been quite an authority on local folklore and particularly liked to tell him about the little people and those that allegedly inhabited Wigpool.

'Seven year,' he said, 'thou wunt see anythin' of thaiy for seven year.'

He pontificated further and Dan listened patiently until what had become a repetitive tirade irked him and he decided to change the subject.

'Any rowd,' he said, 'oi a' got thick motor bike safe in my garige. 'Im's worth a bob or two and Jummy did zaiy it were probably best oi kip un zaife until … until …'

He had been going to say he'd look after it until Walter reappeared, but being almost convinced this would never happen, he struggled to continue.

The allusion to PC James was, in any case, an unwelcome one to Arthur. He had no desire to be reminded of that particular police officer, who he figured was the main character in what he maintained was his wrongful imprisonment. Arthur had never shown any remorse over what he had done and was quite convinced he would be released in the not-too-distant future.

Dan had heard all this before and not disposed to display any sympathy towards Arthur's primarily self-inflicted plight, left the indignant inmate to wallow in his mistaken sense of injustice, himself making for the New Inn in Northgate Street. He hadn't enjoyed a pint in that magnificent and historical hostelry for years and felt a session there would provide a panacea for the unjustified rant he'd had to endure from the misguidedly adamant prisoner. It was still invading his mind and maybe the downing of one or two bevvies would soon serve to banish such unwanted thoughts.

CHAPTER TWENTY-EIGHT

With universal coverage in the newspapers and even on the BBC, you would have had to have been a recluse not to have known of the young duo's unaccounted for disappearance. Added to this, Walter's non-appearance for work, his absence from the notorious milk bar, and the fact that Seth had not seen him around only served to increase the level of Dr Minze's curiosity. The dodgy doctor had even visited Seth at the docks to enquire if he had any information, and finding him uncooperative, revealed that his visit had a twofold objective. The fuss over Sonli had subsided in certain quarters and after a relatively fallow period, Minze was experiencing an increased demand for it. He wondered if Seth would be able to help in fetching some supplies from Avonmouth. His present transporter would be away for a month and at a loss to know where he could find the time to travel there to fetch the stuff himself, hoped the boat owner would be able to help. This only succeeded in inducing a flat refusal. No way was Seth going to imperil his precious narrowboat by entering the Bristol Channel, and Minze tried hard to contain his annoyance. He was not used to being thwarted, but somehow managing to show restraint, did not hesitate when accompanying Seth to Callum's Café, where they both enjoyed the proprietor's renowned breakfast.

A frequent visitor upriver to Worcester, Seth was au fait with recent developments over Sonli. He'd learnt that a private member's bill would be considered in the House of Commons within days. He was aware that Gloucestershire Constabulary had a lax attitude towards it, and thanks to the clued-up boffin at their forensic department, Worcester didn't, and the bill was being submitted by that city's parliamentary representative. Gloucester would now have to comply with the other force's intolerance and that of the second city, which had soon moved to outlaw it. This wasn't entirely unsuspected news for Minze, but a gambler by nature, he'd long decided that if Sonli became a banned substance, he'd still continue to push it. To his nervous wife's consternation, they'd moved out of their hospital flat and into a luxurious bungalow on the outskirts of Stroud. He needed what would now be his illicit income to maintain his lavish lifestyle, and though his move aroused mild curiosity in his work colleagues, the complicity of Matron ensured that no one questioned it. Besides, Matron was also amenable in other respects. Her overbearing demeanour had rid her of two husbands, the second of whom had departed just recently; a circumstance of which Minze was taking full advantage. His relationship with his insipid wife had long deteriorated into two separate bedrooms and he could see the time coming when she would leave him, probably to live with her ancient, ailing parents. As she already spent most of her waking hours with them in their large uncomfortable villa near Stratford Park, he could foresee her moving there permanently: an occurrence for which he could hardly wait.

Part Four
Disintegration

CHAPTER ONE

It did not take more than a couple of years for Sir Crispen's health to fail entirely. His lack of response to Annie's plea to seek help over his addiction could have only one result. He would not eat and sat with his deadly, supposed liquid crutch, even when the Reverend Charles came to call, and did not respond to any of the concerned clergyman's attempts to help. The mentally beleaguered knight sat immobile, glassy eyed and perhaps beyond redemption. However, this was not a view shared by others and the persistent Dan did his best to inject some life into Sir Crispen by talking about the abbey, the estate and the donkeys, none of which, sadly, produced any reaction in the grief-stricken aristocrat. In the early stages of Sir Crispen's deterioration, bless them, the children visited, but as this only prompted him to momentarily emerge from his alcoholic stupor to mutter 'Where's Bhuppa?' Annie thought it judicious for them not to visit again. She judged it too upsetting for them and displaying great fortitude, they accepted this and when available, continued to help with the donkeys.

The end was inevitable, and the funeral was held at St Felicity's, with the Reverend Charles and the Bishop of Gloucester officiating. The powers that be had wanted it to take place in Gloucester Cathedral. They thought it would be more fitting, but Annie was adamant that it should be held in the local church and Sir Crispen laid to rest in the churchyard. As it turned out, half the 'county' attended, including such dignitaries as the Lord

Lieutenant, but Annie did not accord them special treatment. She was more concerned with looking after the devoted estate workers and villagers and did not give precedence to any of the alleged upper classes, quite a number of whom were only there to observe protocol. Extra seating had to be imported, and the coffin arrived on a bier hauled by a quartet of cockaded black horses. As one of the pallbearers, Dan had a lump in his throat and inveterate ex-warrior though he was, unashamedly wept during the service.

Bybrook village hall must have been a new experience for the aristocrats, but the catering was excellent and a down-to-earth character, the bishop did a good job in helping the diverse souls that gathered within for the wake. Annie did her best to circulate, all the while aware that she did not ascribe to the Christian definition of afterlife. Her grief was mitigated by her Buddhist credo. Convinced that she and Sir Crispen would meet again in some other life form, this future existence would also be granted to Bhuppa, whose right to immortality the newly made widow did not question.

CHAPTER TWO

Another year elapsed and Annie made a decision. The abbey and the estate had become hers. It should have been bequeathed to Bhuppa, and after her and if she'd no children, it would become the inheritance of a vague cousin of Sir Crispen's who had rarely visited and besides, had a vast estate in Scotland. Neither of Sir Crispen's sisters had shown any interest in the abbey and had perhaps viewed his decision to disregard any claims they might have with relief. In making the cousin next in line after Bhuppa or any offspring she might have, Sir Crispen had not envisaged it would ever become the Scot's inheritance and as it transpired, Annie's decision to have the abbey ceded to him turned out to be a disaster. Her motivation for this surprising move had more than one reason. Firstly, she found the running of the abbey quite onerous and something else within her was telling her to up sticks and return to Thailand. She had reached the stage where she no longer wanted the responsibility, and despite the Reverend Charles and others advising against it, determined to have her own way. It was all arranged with the family solicitor and the cousin and beneficiary came down from the Highlands to sign whatever needed signing. He immediately declared that he would not be living there and his notion that the abbey could be turned into flats momentarily caused Annie to have second thoughts. But within a month she was gone and to the chagrin of the rapidly growing children and Dan, the new owner of the abbey had persuaded the Donkey Preservation Society to reluctantly place the gentle creatures elsewhere.

Fortunately, it was agreed that Ah Cy's donkey could share Wendy's paddock on Pope's Hill and with a few modifications done by a willing Dan, the rudimentary hut was converted into snug and safe refuge for the winter.

Now sixteen and hampered by a boyfriend she didn't particularly care for, but was too nice to jettison, Rachel left a lot of the donkeys' care to Ah Cy, who didn't mind and was even making noises about her father acquiring a pony as a step towards a show jumping career. And all this activity took place against the ever-present mental wounds inflicted by the disappearance of Bhuppa, the deaths of Fred and Sir Crispen and the unexpected severance of Annie's move to foreign climes. Added to this, the abbey was no longer a place they were allowed to visit. True to his word, the new owner had delegated an estate agent to let it out as rooms. His original intention to convert it into flats was a no-brainer. It was a listed building, and no way would he get planning permission. Unfortunately, the estate agent was mainly concerned with his commission, and soon filled the place with a varied and dubious selection of the human race. Renting was still a cheap option at the time and not discriminating or enquiring too closely, he was not concerned that the abbey now housed quite a high percentage of dodgy inhabitants.

Most weekends the stately edifice was reduced to the status of what might be termed a fallen woman. Perhaps not a particularly apt analogy, but a description not that wide of the mark in that the abbey resounded to loud music, hosted the sale and purchase of illegal substances, and assailed the ears of the dismayed villagers into the early hours of the morning. The police came, and assuming an attitude that was to become all too common in future, did little to curb the residents' activities.

Suffering from an absentee landlord, the abbey began to show signs of neglect. Dan was no longer employed there, and the two ancient brothers were similarly discarded. The orangery became a haven for weeds and the stables, in the manner of most unused buildings, somehow managed to look forlorn and mourning for their previous existence.

One of the abbey's new inhabitants had at one time been a patient at the isolation hospital. He knew Dr Minze Wang and of the now illegal substance that the unscrupulous man still purveyed. The former patient was wise enough to sell it in very small doses which some of the gullible residents took in their drinks. In the pusher's jaundiced opinion the distribution of Sonli added greatly to the joie de vivre of the weekend parties, and on the increasing occasions when the law was persuaded to call by, an unusual villager who regularly attended and approved of the shenanigans would tip him off. Drinks were then hastily dispatched into the stream where the children's swing still hung, sadly suspended by just one of its ropes, and the police arrived to find the residents drinking innocuous Coca-Cola. Instructing the tenants to turn the music down, they went on their way and were perhaps glad not to have to take further action.

CHAPTER THREE

Seven years on and Eastdean was still not a place where the shops were permitted to open on Sunday, although this made it no different to other towns throughout the country. A humid, stifling June day already discouraged too much activity and apart from a stray dog and some indolent cats stretched out in advantageous nooks and crannies in order to enjoy the blazing sun, nothing much stirred.

It was still only ten am and the gradually dwindling numbers that attended St Michael's were not yet wending their way to matins and the same applied to those non-conformists who worshipped in the Methodist chapel down by the cross. A languorous atmosphere prevailed, enhanced by the lack of traffic, and there were those that approved of the sabbath day shutdown and others that didn't. However, it was almost certain that this state of tranquillity would not last all day. The pubs were due to open at noon and closing down again at two, would re-open from seven until ten-thirty. Over the border, the Principality of Wales stayed true to its non-conformist heritage on the Lord's day and the effect this had on the English border counties had turned out to be a mixed blessing. An invasion of deprived Welsh drinkers in coach parties and by other forms of transport, meant that English pubs near the border were often packed to the gunnels with Celtic revellers on Sundays. They were bent on having a good time and given to burst into fervent song at any moment. Eastdean was lucky inasmuch that it was not so close to the border as towns like Coleford, Ross-on-Wye and Monmouth. But the George in Eastdean did have a big car park and displaying an acute eye for business, Ivan the landlord willingly encouraged coaches to visit. Troubles sometimes broke out between the locals and the Welsh, but the newly appointed sergeant and his hard-bitten sidekick who had arrived to replace Pateman and PC Jummy a couple of years previously, were not prepared to tolerate any nonsense. They were usually about at closing time and to the relief of the townspeople, ensured that the visitors left in subdued and orderly fashion.

At present, the only figure to be descried in the high street on this fine Sunday morning was a tall, slim young lady who stood idly outside Chia Hao's takeaway, at times bending to fondle a large ginger Tom who entwined himself round her legs whilst emitting the soothing throbbing sounds that all felines tend to emit when content with their lot in life. The cat's attractive companion would certainly not fail to warrant the attention of any male admirers who happened to be passing and a description of her merely as 'Asian' would fail to do her justice.

The faery ring had vanished. Dressed to combat the ravages of the winter season, Bhuppa and Walter were bemused. They removed their outer clothing and stared at the greenery of the common which surrounded them. The trees were in full bloom and the old oak seemed weighed down with the abundance brought on by what seemed to the young couple as an extraordinary transition from the threadbare nakedness of November to the inexplicable plenitude of a glorious midsummer day.

When Bhuppa began to imply that they might have been company with the 'little people' for an indeterminate length of time, Walter ceased to mock her contention, and his scepticism diminished. Regardless, he thought their best option was to walk into town and despite having to carry their heavy winter apparel, they made good time. It did not take long to reach the T-junction, where they turned right for the town with the object of presenting themselves to Jummy at the police house and persuading him to ring the abbey. Surely confirming that it was indeed a Sunday morning, they were overtaken by only one car and encountered a single pedestrian who, after nodding at them in a cursory manner, hurried on his way. A large notice on the gates at Rank's now instructed workers to gain access to the factory through the rear entrance. This involved a drive through the town down to the cross, a left turn, followed by another before you took the right-hand bend to Longhope.

It was perhaps as well they did not stop in passing to peruse the town hall noticeboard, where the dates of meetings and other pending events would have undoubtedly disturbed their fragile equanimity. As it was, the biggest shock was yet to come. As they approached Chia Hao's takeaway, the fickle ginger Tom deserted what appeared to be his slim, elegant young mistress and came to greet them. And there was no doubting who the young lady was.

Standing there in her full length Quipao or Chinese dress, the girl was undeniably Ah Cy, but an older Ah Cy, with beauteous almond-shaped eyes and an odango hairstyle consisting of two buns fashioned out of her abundant dark hair.

It was difficult to assess which of the two girls was more shaken by the encounter. Bhuppa could not control her trembling and clung to Walter for support, whilst Ah Cy looked as though she'd seen a ghost.

'Bhuppa, is it you?' Ah Cy came towards her bemused friend and casting aside all restraint, encased Bhuppa in her arms. Both girls were reduced to floods of tears and aware that her concept of time had gone hopelessly awry, Bhuppa looked at her friend with utter incomprehension and Walter stood helplessly by, not knowing how to react.

Just eighteen, Ah Cy would be off to university shortly. She'd become an adult and was mature enough to recognise that Bhuppa had ceased to grow. This happened to some people for some reason and yet Ah Cy could not entirely convince herself that this was so, and it did not in any way explain the Thai girl's seven-year absence. Ah Cy had so many questions and wisely deciding that there were too many to answer, invited the young prodigals to step inside to consult her parents. Due to the fact that the couple had only ever been able to meet illicitly, Ah Cy had never met Walter, therefore his appearance was not a problem and his action in picking up Montgomery, the ginger Tom, marked him out as a decent lad. Montgomery was a contrary creature. Very few people of his acquaintance were allowed the privilege of picking him up. He was Ah Cy's cat and Walter must certainly have something about him to gain the creature's unreserved approval.

Walter mentioned that his motorcycle had gone missing. He would like to visit the police house to consult Jummy about it, but with a startled look, Ah Cy informed him that Jummy was no longer there. It would be best, she said, if they both came inside and talked to her parents. The police house had apparently been converted into a small, but proper police station. A new sergeant and constable manned it and perhaps Walter would like to call there after he'd seen her parents. Besides, Bhuppa was anxious to ring the abbey. She must let Annie know she was alive and well and she couldn't wait to see the donkeys... An indefinable invasion of her mind had told her that Sir Crispen had passed away. It was if it had become part of her past. A past she hadn't experienced, but it helped to mitigate her grief and subsequently bewildered those to whom she related it.

It was as well she could not see the look of consternation on Ah Cy's face as she ushered them inside to consult her astonished parents, with Chia Hao, much affected emotionally, striving hard to be the obligatory inscrutable Chinaman.

He and his family had been about to leave for morning service at Benhall and, bearing in mind the use Bhuppa and Walter had made of the church, the Thai girl later found this quite ironic. The Chinese family had faithfully adhered to their belief to the extent that Chia had become a lay reader and scheduled to help Reverend Charles with the service this morning, quickly rang him to tender apologies. Something urgent had happened to prevent his attendance and the takeaway proprietor would explain later. He could not imagine how the vicar could possibly take a service if Chia had informed him of Bhuppa's dramatic reappearance and reckoned it could wait until mattins was over without a slight delay doing any harm.

No overly fazed by the sudden appearance of the couple out of the blue, Li sat them down in the colourful kitchen with its picturesque Chinese wall-hangings and provided them with tea and sweetmeats. Bestowing on them his charming avuncular smile, Chia then proceeded to tell Bhuppa in his gentle measured fashion about Sir Crispen's death and was taken aback when though upset, to his bewilderment intimated that she already knew and had known for some time. She was appalled when learning of Annie's departure, the news of the abbey and the donkeys, but became almost elated when Chia revealed that both he and the vicar had Annie's address and phone number in Thailand, and they kept in touch. They'd received Christmas cards from her – her Buddhism did not prevent this – and if Bhuppa liked, he'd ring her once they'd discussed how they were going to explain the girl's extraordinary seven-year absence. Both Bhuppa and Walter were now fully convinced they'd been somewhere else for those seven years. It was still utterly inexplicable, but with Chia showing them the calendar, the date on his Sunday newspaper and other irrefutable evidence, all doubts about the veracity of their remarkable experience evaporated.

Bhuppa contended that the faery ring had something to do with it and, the beneficiary of thousands of years of Chinese wisdom. Chia did not dispute her theory. There were similar tales in Sino mythology and did not Shakepeare write 'there are more things in heaven and earth, dear Horatio, than you have ever dreamed of in your philosophy' and the Chinaman recalled his own terrifying experience with Fred and the fortuitous arrival of Joe from the Whippet and PC Jummy.

Ah Cy tentatively questioned them over where they may have been during their absence and what they might have been doing. To which Bhuppa shrugged her shoulders and pulled a face.

'No idea,' she said. 'It's as if we fell asleep one day and woke up the next, except everything has changed but us!'

CHAPTER FOUR

In Benhall church Reverend Charles found it difficult to concentrate. It was unlike Chia Hao to become involved in some sudden crises. He was normally Mr Reliable. The vicar had to persuade reluctant Isobel to read one of the lessons, a task she could do perfectly well, but not one for which her non-existent ego befitted her. She was more adept at assigning people to take their turn on the flower rota, or was humbly at home when toting the large green tea urn the ladies now used after service to promote sociability amongst the small congregation.

Reverend Charles had briefly thought of asking his feisty daughter to help, but she'd almost become a lost cause. Now twenty, she'd dropped out of college, still had the same indolent boyfriend and was inclined to pour scorn on what she termed 'organised religion'. She now co-habited with what was now termed her disreputable partner in a grotty flat in Cinderford most of the time, but at least had the decency to come home some weekends to see her parents. 'Living together' was still looked upon as undesirable and immoral, and the fact that the vicar's daughter was indulging in it was an embarrassment to him and a vehicle for much tittle-tattle in the village and surrounding areas.

After the Benhall service, the Reverend Charles sat at the dining room table to eat Isobel's hastily assembled repast. Those present included Rachel and a slightly truculent Barnaby, now seventeen and loath to admit to being anything other than the world's greatest expert on everything. Barnaby had suffered at the hands of fellow pupils through being the son of a clergyman and had tried to project a macho image by excelling at sport, to the detriment of more essential subjects. Unfortunately, his abilities were more suited to academia. He was only partially successful at athletic pursuits and to his parents' despair, showed no signs of realising his undoubted ability as potential wordsmith. Out of necessity, the clerical family usually had their Sunday dinner on a Saturday, so that Sunday's fare was a hodge podge of leftovers.

This enabled Isobel to attend wherever the main morning service was being held and her husband to dash off for the afternoon service in one of his other churches. They had just begun to savour the pudding – a make-do offering of tinned peaches and cold rice – when the phone rang and arising wearily, the vicar exited the dining room, padded along the tiled hallway, and lifting the receiver from the phone which stood on a small, solid octagonal table, enquired who might be wanting him.

His brow creased as he listened to the person on the other end of the line.

'Really?' he said with a distinct air of incredulity, taken aback and giving the impression that he could hardly believe what he was being told.

'No, as it happens, I've nothing until this evening – You'd better bring them here until we decide what to do what's that? You've tried ringing Annie? No, it's almost impossible sometimes. Yes, what with the language problem and operators that hardly speak English. Sorry, that sounds a bit jingoistic. No, I don't think it's a good idea to contact the police just yet. We must try and keep it to ourselves until we're absolutely certain what to do. You say they don't know where they've been for the last seven years? I find that hard to believe, that's preposterous! I can't accept that. Well, I admit, it does seem inexplicable otherwise. Oh no, that has to be an old wives' tale. Sorry Chia, although your English is excellent, you may not have heard of that expression. Good lord sounds though that ring wants exorcising, though I can't imagine the bishop allowing me to do that. Sorry, that's something else you might not understand. Anyway, bring them here as soon as you can, and we'll try and sort it out. I can hardly believe it and not a word to anyone else, mind you. Exactly, and can you imagine the brouhaha if the media were to get hold of this? It took ages for things to die down when they disappeared, and I dread to think what headlines and speculation there'd be over their reappearance.'

Reverend Charles replaced the receiver and sighed; wondering how he was going to break the news to his family.

CHAPTER FIVE

Like all other pubs in the district, the Whippet closed at two pm on a Sunday and with the police presence now governed by a new superintendent and a stricter regime in Lydney, the opening hours had to be rigidly observed, and lock-ins had become a thing of the past. Except that by employing her feminine sixth sense, Sylvie was almost certain Dan was worrying about something. He'd drunk very little whilst being strangely reticent, and having cleared the bar of malingerers, she invited him into the pub's living quarters to have a glass with her and Joe.

The décor and furnishings of the licensee's sitting room was a world away from that of the smoke-tarnished bars. Prints of French impressionists adorned the walls and small cabinets contained prized ceramics: Meissen, Crown Derby, Delf, Staffordshire and from other illustrious makers, an indication that Sylvie came from an affluent family. A Persian carpet further enhanced this impression of mainly Gallic opulence, and the presence of Hector, the pub couples' full-size, slobbering poodle, emphasised their predilection for things French. The only incongruous object in the room was a large mounted dead fish which modest Joe had caught and had framed, now hanging above the door. The landlord had never mentioned this to the motley clientele that patronised the Whippet, and he supposed his prowess as a fisherman – almost certainly to be disclosed by Dan – would now provide a subject for discussion at length amongst the regulars who inhabited and held sometimes complimentary and sometimes censorious court in the public bar.

Normally not reluctant to convey any titbit he'd heard in the pub to any mortal that would listen, Dan did not seem very receptive, but did revive when plied with an ample amount of Joe's best brandy. An enquiry as to who the distinguished couple were in the photo on the Pleyel baby grand piano informed Dan about something else he didn't know about Sylvie. The photo was of her parents, who were apparently French and went a long way to explain her action in creating a little bit of 'home' in the Whippet. Her flawless English had been honed through her majoring in it at Cambridge University and a photo adjacent to that of her parents showed her in full graduating regalia. This was yet another unknown fact which, when revealed to the punters, might induce in them something a little more respectable than the slightly sullied comments they sometimes made behind her back.

Brains and beauty can be a lethal combination. Sylvie had plenty of both and she did not find it difficult to prise what she wanted to learn from the disturbed forester.

'Something the matter, Dan?' Sylvie gave him a devastating smile. Not one he could easily resist. Flustered, he placed his empty brandy glass on the side table and Joe immediately re-filled it.

'T'yunt nothin' uz oi'd like t' chops about normally, but oi daime iz maiybe 'bout time uz oi did. Though thou might wunt t' ring up Coney 'ill adder oi d' tell thee. Oi d' reckon it must be more than a vew year since oi did zee thick 'oman, an' maiybe oi should 'a zaid zummat at the time. But oi daime no bugger would 'ave believed oi an' as it wuz, it were Jummy uz nearly 'ad me brought in fur questionin'. It wuz only because 'im wuz too idle and cusent be bothered, that 'im let oi gow.'

His somewhat garbled and self-conscious revelation was interrupted by the phone ringing and Joe quickly moved to answer it. Whatever the caller imparted caused the usually unruffled landlord to take a quick intake of breath.

'As a matter o' fact, vicar, 'im's 'ere. Sittin' right in vront of me.'

What the vicar said next induced a brief smile. 'No. them daiys yunt appenin' no more. Lock-ins iz a thing o' the past with thick Super down in Lydney around. 'Dan's just with we in are flat us'll come raight awaiy.'

He put the receiver down and turned to face his wife and Stan; an utterly bemused expression on his face.

'I take it that was Charles Emsworth?' said Sylvie in what could be called a slightly accusatory tone. 'What did he want?'

Joe took his time before replying. He helped himself to

another measure of brandy and proffered the decanter to Dan, who did not hesitate to sample some more of its contents.

Not usually one to show impatience, Sylvie was exasperated.

'For God's sake, Joe! What is it? What did he want?'

Before addressing her, Joe took another long swig of brandy. 'Thaiy 'a bin found,' he said. 'Thaiy bist at the vicarage. Thaiy walked in t' Chia Hao's, 'n 'im brought 'em to the vicarage. Vicar wunts uz t' gow there now.'

To Sylvie this was maddening. 'Who's been found? What are you talking about?'

'Bhuppa 'n thick byoy, thaiy a' just turned up.'

Sylvie became agitated. 'Sacrebleu! What d'you mean? Just out of the blue? For heaven's sake, where have they been for the last seven years? They can't have just ceased to exist all that time. What does Charles say? Shouldn't the police be contacted and what about Annie? Has anybody rung her?'

'Yes, but theiy yunt bin able t' make contact and 'im yunt rung the police. Dussent think it's a good idea t' get them involved. 'Im wants uz t' get over their to discuss it with 'im 'n Chia zummat vairish.'

Sylvie got fed up with Joe's protracted explanations in 'Forest'. He was perfectly capable, like a lot of his fellow woodlanders, of speaking what she called the Queen's English, but cussedly would not do so when others of his breed were around. He'd been educated at Monmouth School, been awarded the Latin prize and had flatly refused a place at a university. He'd taken what he called a proper job with the Alton Court Brewery in picturesque Ross-on-Wye, and after some years working there and meeting gorgeous Sylvie in a notorious back-street pub called the Hole-in-the-Wall, to everyone's amazement, persuaded her to marry him and became landlord of the Whippet Inn.

Dan, who'd taken no part in this verbal combat, was now on his feet.

'Zounds t' oi uz we should get t' the vicarage straight awaiy,' he said, and without dissent, they made for the door.

CHAPTER SIX

At Gloucester Docks Minze was in animated conversation with Seth Partridge. Someone had blown the gaff, and the Chinese surgeon had had an uncomfortable contretemps with the local police who came to interview him at the hospital and question him over his alleged possession and dealings in Sonli. The parliamentary Bill to outlaw the drug had not yet been passed, but it soon would be, and prosecutions brought over it could be retrospective. The police wanted to know where he kept his supply and turned the smart bungalow upside down in their quest to find it. Even though the drug was not quite illegal yet, he did not protest over their action and confident that his stash was safely deposited in the outhouse of a farmer that conveniently used the stuff himself, he just left them to get on with it and stifled a chuckle when their search proved to be abortive.

The wary Seth was in two minds. He was aware that Minze had given notice at the hospital and had pacified the matron with a large dollop of money, telling her he wanted a break and left her with a threat to inform her restored second husband about what had been occurring between Minze and herself if she welched on him. He'd arranged to lie low by skipping to the Chinese quarter of Birmingham for a while, with the ultimate ambition to ensure anonymity by returning to some country in the Far East, where his talents would make earning a crust comparatively easy. He thought that travelling to the second city by road or rail would arouse suspicion, he could easily be spotted by the forces of law and order and thought a journey on a private narrow boat would be less of a risk. When considering this, Seth had grave doubts. A narrow boat was a family home upon which outsiders were not encouraged to encroach. Carrying a passenger was not normally an option, but the sum the Chinese surgeon offered for casting aside this taboo was sorely tempting. Business on the canals had been steadily declining for some time and the contention that 'every man has his price' came guiltily to mind.

The reappearance of Bhuppa and Walter had connotations for Charles Emsworth. As a Christian priest he had already to contend with his own daughter's unmarried relationship and he could not believe that after seven years in some sort of exile Bhuppa and Walter were not now an item. Pensive, he had to admit that the Thai girl had always looked older than her age, but there was no way she could be taken for twenty-one. It had to be seen if she resumed growing, a bizarre situation, and the same applied to Walter. However, as a man of great compassion, Reverend Charles concluded that there was no way the boy could have consorted with the delightful young girl for such a long period without their relationship becoming physical. Bhuppa's birth certificate would denote her to be twenty-one and being irrefutable, he supposed there should be no reason why the couple could not marry: even though it was not something he felt wholly comfortable about.

The reaction of Rachel and Bhuppa to one another did much to dispel his doubts. Rachel was not the only one in his several parishes to shun the ceremony of marriage and much as he did not approve, he feared he would have to learn to accept it. There were already a couple of girls in the district who had not 'gone away' to have their illegitimate babies and were bringing them up on their own, defying convention with not a father in sight.

In her quiet efficient manner, Isobel had managed to rustle up some drinks and edibles and they all sat round the long table in the capacious kitchen discussing what should happen next. Opinion was not that divided, and including Bhuppa and Walter they all agreed that for the present, the police should not be informed of the couple's reappearance. Notifying the police would attract an avalanche of unwanted publicity and subsequent media harassment. As they did when the couple vanished, the media would have a field day, and the young couple and their friends would be hounded by the paparazzi from pillar to post.

Then there was the question of the abbey, which Bhuppa would have inherited. Now legally in the possession of the Scottish cousin and let to what seemed to be a motley collection of malcontents. Chia Hao did not see how Bhuppa could claim it back as hers.

Never imagining that the girl would return to the land of the living, Annie had despaired and, quite legitimately, bequeathed it to the cousin, and the fact that it was now inhabited by a hoard of mostly undesirables was unfortunate, but a fact of life.

To everyone's surprise, Bhuppa declared that she didn't want to take possession of the abbey anyway. It would be too much of a responsibility and in this, Dan, whose knowledge of the state of it was greater than that of any of those present, concurred. He pointed out that the abbey had long needed re-wiring, the roof wasn't that sound and well before Andrew the Scot had taken over, Sir Crispen's melancholia over Bhuppa's disappearance and his subsequent death had brought any restoration on the fabric of the old building to a standstill. Dan had not been re-engaged and as far as he knew, no one else had, and even if it were possible, he thought Bhuppa regaining her inheritance unlikely, and if by any chance it did materialise, could be a mistake.

Accustomed to chairing meetings and by profession an adept orator, Reverend Charles proposed that for the time being Bhuppa and Walter stay at the vicarage – it had six bedrooms – and he'd try once more to ring Annie. The young couple would have to be more or less incarcerated until a decision was made and with this in mind and as a temporary measure, he would contact his widowed mother who lived in an isolated cottage on the edge of Bodmin Moor. Despite her obvious loneliness, he hadn't persuaded his mother to sell up and to come and live at the vicarage. She'd probably be only too glad to accept Bhuppa and Walter as lodgers. It was very unlikely they'd encounter anyone they knew down in Cornwall and depending on what Annie-if and when they managed to contact her-thought, they might have to stay in the extreme south-western county for some time.

Discussion over the future of the 'prodigals' having terminated more or less satisfactorily, Reverend Charles tried once more to ring Annie in Thailand. To his surprise, he was put through with very little trouble and his news induced in Annie a state that could be described as tearful euphoria. Her elated response when handed over to Bhuppa was emotionally joyous and her proposed instant solution to the couple's future welfare was both practical and exotic. They both must have legitimate birth certificates which would enable them to be issued with passports and having been born in Thailand, Bhuppa should not find it difficult to become a resident there. Like everyone else, she was mystified by their seven-year absence and the explanation for it, but with admirable pragmatism and a refreshingly open mind where spiritual matters were concerned, was willing to accept there might be more to faery rings than meets the eye. She intimated that it could be quite a while before any possible move to Thailand could occur. There could be complications, and it would be advisable for the intending emigrants to be married before they attempted to enter the country. She did not see Bhuppa's lack of ageing as a hindrance to any potential nuptials and again, the birth certificates of both her and Walter would prove that she was now twenty-one and her intended, twenty-four. Their relationship must be very stable if it had survived seven years and what Annie cautiously termed co-habiting, and she saw no reason, providing they were willing, why the vicar should not conduct a marriage ceremony. To say that Reverend Charles had conflicting thoughts about this would be an understatement. He would consider the matter, he said, but had little doubt he would concede and with a brief word to the determinedly adamant Annie informing her that they'd be in touch, he handed the receiver back to Bhuppa and smiled at Walter.

'Did you get the gist of that, young man? And what are your feelings? A new life in the mysterious east or an uncertain future here?'

Walter had already put two and two together and made four. There was no doubt in his mind. He couldn't imagine life without Bhuppa. He adored her and if she so desired, would spend the rest of his life on the moon, living there as its sole, uncomplaining, besotted earthman.

The marriage ceremony was a simple one. It was conducted by the Reverend Charles in St Felicity's in the dead of night and only those in the know were present. This the vicar hoped could eventually persuade the police to take a lenient line on Walter's assumed original 'crime' in what may have been a sexual relationship with a fourteen-year-old girl and smooth the couple's passage in any attempt to settle in Thailand.

Dan, it was, who'd been delegated to make the trip to Cornwall and found driving the vicar's Wolseley a very satisfying experience.

They arrived at the homely cottage, an oasis on the edge of a bleak landscape, chillingly depicted in novels by one of Bhuppa's favourite authors, Daphne du Maurier. The weather was still seasonably warm, and the sun shone down unremittingly, brooking no dissent from the occasional cloud that traversed the otherwise uncluttered sky. The vicar's mother made them warmly welcome and seemed delighted that Bhuppa could name most of the flowers that flourished in her colourful and well-tended garden. She told them to address her as Celia and wasn't a bit of a prude. Without a trace of embarrassment, she showed them to the largest bedroom in the cottage and accompanied this by saying 'I thought you'd like this one, my dears. The bed's very comfortable and hasn't been slept in since my Henry was alive. I do miss him and I shall enjoy your company, though I understand you might not be here very long.'

CHAPTER SEVEN

Around a fortnight later, Seth made his way through countless locks between Worcester and Birmingham. No surprise had been expressed over the presence of a distinguished looking Chinaman on the narrowboat and Minxe had captivated young Colin with legendary tales of Cathay and the various dynasties. The odd person of a different pigment of skin had long been nothing to remark upon and lock keepers and various wayfarers they had encountered had shown no interest in Minze beyond granting him a brief salutation. They probably deemed him to be one of the oddballs who defected from foreign vessels and been employed on the canals with no questions asked.

Good fortune had favoured the surgeon in that the police had returned before he left and that he'd simply walked out of the smart bungalow after dark with a knapsack containing some essential possessions and caught a bus to Gloucester, where he found Seth waiting with the narrow boat. He'd known the journey would not be comfortable: he had to sleep outside on the cramped 'deck', and as they progressed, he'd been grateful that the small hours were still and warm. Seth had been happy to negotiate the broad Severn to Worcester at night, but they'd had to wait in the Digbeth Basin for daylight before attempting to take the tricky route to Birmingham.

In later years, Seth felt no remorse over what subsequently happened some way up the canal when he'd pulled into a landing stage on the bank to allow Sarah to purchase some essentials from a store which they knew to be nearby. Availing himself of the opportunity to stretch his legs, Minze had walked a good way up the canal bank and stumbling over some discarded detritus, had fallen in the water. Had he been able to swim, this would not have been a disaster, but Sarah and Colin having returned, Seth was anxious to be off, and three-quarters of an hour having elapsed, he decided to walk down the canal to see what might have detained his passenger.

He was just in time to witness a couple of burly characters, saturated and obviously distressed, engaged in pulling Minze out of the water. He rushed to their aid and having settled the Chinaman on the canal bank, felt his pulse. One of the rescuers produced a small hand mirror and this confirmed that Minze would play no further part in life. Not that much further upstream, a lockkeeper used his phone to summon help, and it was not long before the police and an ambulance arrived on the scene.

As he sat in the police station being questioned, Seth saw no reason not to answer truthfully. The corpse was Dr Minze Wang. As far as Seth was concerned, the surgeon was just visiting someone in Birmingham. Seth had not questioned him over the purpose of this visit and had just been paid a small amount to take him there: a response that slightly amused the interviewing officer. Didn't Seth think Minze could be taking something dubious to Chinatown and in that case, why hadn't he caught the train or used some form of road transport? Seth answered this by implying that Minze might have preferred the leisurely progress that people experienced on canals. Perhaps Minze viewed it as a break from his onerous duties. People nowadays liked travelling along the waterways as a relaxing experience and Seth cited the fact that pleasure craft were becoming an increasingly common sight on the canal network. This was a white lie. As yet, the age of taking canal holidays had not really dawned, but Seth's mild untruth served to answer an awkward question, and the police officer accepted it. Minze had also not told Seth he was doing a runner and even though inclined to suspect this might be the case, the narrowboat skipper could quite honestly deny any inference that he had any knowledge of it.

Satisfied that he'd not been able to implicate Seth in the demise of the devious Minze in any way, the police officer decided not to detain him and asked who he thought they should contact over the unfortunate happening. They hadn't found any indication of Minze's identity in the consultant's wallet – he'd craftily posted all his personal papers to the address in Chinatown – so Seth gave them the name and location of the isolation hospital. He managed to keep a straight face whilst imparting this information, for the highly efficient local grapevine had spread its vicious tendrils from Stroud to Gloucester, inferring that the matron and Minze were not physically unacquainted when it came to trying out mattresses, and Seth could not help thinking that the ignominious death of the Chinaman was a good thing. Minze had done far more harm than good, and with the hard-bitten attitude garnered by one who'd had a hard life, Seth could not feel the slightest bit sorry for him.

CHAPTER EIGHT

Standing in this fertile garden, Bhuppa was slowly managing to quell her feeling of unease. Lulled by the pleasant hum of bees on the riotous lavender and the rare sight of two cuckoos emitting their distinctive cry in their flight down the lane to the village, she was almost beginning to wish she could remain here forever. Torn several ways, she was aware of her strong desire to see Annie again, but wasn't sure she wanted to live in Thailand. Having enjoyed a largely unrestricted occidental upbringing, Bhuppa knew that the status of women in that country might not be as emancipated as it was in most European countries and was not sure she'd be able to cope with the restrictions imposed on her if she moved there.

Beyond the cottage, the great expanse of Bodmin Moor stretched out towards Brown Willy and Rough Tor. Smaller tors relieved the endless vista of moorland and rivers and streams flowed through the broad valleys: a taste of paradise that Bhuppa was becoming reluctant to leave.

Only a mile or so west, the village of Breward provided an oasis of civilisation with its church, ancient pub, silver band and, from all reports, flourishing social life. But Walter was all for Thailand and when she'd expressed doubts, he'd promptly dismissed them and been quick to remind her of the reason they were trying to abandon-in her case-adopted country, and his native land. Even if they stayed in this remote part of the world, they would eventually be found out and the resultant publicity would blight their lives. This did not seem to reassure Bhuppa, but the more Celia told them of Cornish folklore and legend, the more her tales of piskies, the 'dobel vaen' or 'little people' made her come round to Walter's point of view. Deep down and without acknowledging it, Bhuppa would have liked to have returned to live on the fringes of the Forest of Dean. She would be prepared to tolerate the furore their unexplained reappearance would cause and hoped that given time, it would die down. Her suggestion that they stay put and try to visit Annie at intervals received another negative response and she could only think it was different for him. He had no family and if they stayed, he would probably have to endure another mundane occupation, and the chance of a future in a country where the sun mostly shone must, to him, seem like a no-brainer.

Heeding a suggestion by Celia, they were about to take a walk across the moor to Rough Tor and Brown Willy, the mystical landmarks that to some had almost sinister significance. A crackpot society called the Athenian founded in 1954 and crazily advocating the existence of UFOs, deemed Brown Willy a sacred mountain, a preposterous astronomical unlikelihood that Celia, a convinced cynic, completely discounted. The fact that the highest peak in Cornwall had no evidence of prehistoric settlement did not imply that it may have been revered as a sacred place and a cairn on the summit suggested that someone of importance had been interred there. From the nearby and slightly lower hill of Rough Tor a commanding view of Brown Willy could be had and, on its slopes, the remains of primitive housing had been discovered.

The moor was littered with stone circles and crosses, and apart from the livestock that roamed, taking advantage of the free grazing rights, Bhuppa and Walter would only be likely to encounter the odd hiker or archaeology inclined holidaymaker en route. The moor had not yet become popular with conventional tourists. As yet, there were no designated walks, and Celia had stressed that the youngsters would come to no harm if they simply made for the two tors as the crow flies. She'd taken steps to assist their progress with a packed lunch and a plentiful amount of drink and her efficiency belied her age. The vicar's mother was a remarkable woman. Aged eighty-seven, she had all her faculties, but apologised for the fact that she could no longer walk vast distances and therefore, could not accompany them. Unlike her son, she did not ascribe to any religion, but as an agnostic – she explained to her guests – did not dismiss any of the main ones as entirely invalid.

As their residence in Cornwall continued, Bhuppa's misgivings about the county's folklore intensified. After their admittedly unproven experience with the faery ring, it seemed ironic that giants, mermaids and 'knockers' were said to exist. She particularly didn't like the prospect of meeting a 'knocker': a creature two feet tall and somewhat scruffy, who lied underground and was reputed to have meddled with the former tin miners' equipment. Bhuppa had told the old lady of the faery ring. Celia knew of the young duo's seven-year absence and did not attribute it to anything supernatural. She chose to be purely pragmatic about such things, declaring that the human mind was completely incapable of comprehending what went on in the never-ending universes and perhaps it was best not to bother with it at all. She accepted the brilliance of scientific discovery, at the same time questioning why the cosmos should exist in the first place, but debunked the Creationist theory as a convenient way of informing a primitive people how the earth began in a relatively simple manner.

To a large extent, she succeeded in quelling Bhuppa's apprehension over the 'little people' and bid the couple bon voyage as they set out across the moor. She then drove into the village with the intention of visiting the old inn. So far, she'd managed to control her addiction when Bhuppa and Walter were around and the village pub's recent decision to stock vodka would enable her to imbibe without breathing fumes all over the youngsters when they returned. What she'd told the young girl about her attitude towards Cornish myths and unworldly beings was the complete opposite to what she believed. As a woman, she was not allowed to be a Druid, but had furtively attended their gatherings and also thought it very likely that the young couple's seven-year disappearance had been caused by stepping into the faery ring.

And the first person she encountered in the pub was an old soak; an undistinguished reporter from the local Bodmin newspaper called Bill. It was not a chance meeting. She'd rung him and her drinking propensities currently making her a little short of funds, had seen pound signs for both her and him over what she was about to reveal. Of course, this was on condition he kept her name out of it.

CHAPTER NINE

How it started, no one knew. Feasibly one of the near-do-wells had gone to sleep and not extinguished his cigarette – or weed – or maybe it was an electrical fault. The fact that it happened in the early hours after a Saturday night rave cast suspicion on its assorted and often eccentric inhabitants, most of whom escaped from the subsequent inferno unscathed. Anciently structured using seasoned beams and precious oak panelling, the abbey was soon reduced to an empty shell. Fire fighters attended from Cinderford, Gloucester, Newent and Ross, but thanks to a disastrously timorous phone call, it was all too late. A bemused and probably drug-affected inhabitant had eventually made the call from a neighbouring house, but despite this, had to watch as the magnificent centuries-old mansion house played out its agonising death throes before his very eyes.

A spectator, who alongside everyone else viewed the spectacle with absolute horror, Reverend Charles arrived to try and give comfort to those who would not normally have given him the time of day. With considerable acumen, a quick-thinking person had obtained the key to the village hall, several ladies had got the tea urn into action and in these times when most of the population still tilled their own gardens, preserved fruits and made pastries, cakes and bread, the now homeless tenants from the abbey were swiftly given succour and sympathy.

Amongst those rushing to their aid was Dan, currently attending to a badly affected fireman who, sampling the proffered hipflask, was eternally grateful and did not take long to revive.

Visiting her parents for the weekend, gorgeous and enigmatic Rachel was an unlikely angel where some of the near-hysterical children were concerned and Chia Hao's family, when learning of the disaster, were not slow in coming from Eastdean. Steadfast, Isobel managed to pacify some of the more seriously traumatised and turned a blind eye when one or two of them, showing consideration she thought they would not have possessed, went outside to smoke the dubious contents of their roll-ups.

CHAPTER TEN

They halted by the stone cross and gazed towards their objectives, Rough Tor and Brown Willy, both the summits of which were now obscured by lowering black clouds. Undaunted, they resolved to continue on their way and did not realise that Celia had been negligent in not warning them of the perils of being caught in a storm on the moor; an experience to be avoided at all costs. Rain on the moor, usually accompanied by erratic winds, could quickly switch from vertical to horizontal, and the best place to be when it occurred was somewhere else!

Bhuppa paled as she cast her eyes on the faery ring. A perfect circle with its sentinel toadstools in attendance. An oasis in an otherwise sea of heather, just a few yards from the stone cross. And to her distress, standing by it, the familiar figure in the yellow tunic. A living magnet drawing her towards the ring. Uncontrolled, she was hardly conscious of her acquiescence and only Walter's frantic cry and restraining hand prevented her from stepping into it.

'No, Bhuppa, no!' he pleaded; not sure he'd be able to resist his own near-compulsive motivation to follow her.

The frightening apparition granted them a ghostly smile, speaking to them in an unrelieved monotone.

'Ah, I thought we'd see you two again. Why did you leave, and welcome back?'

Having been assured that Bill, the Bodmin weekly's all-purpose hack would contact a national newspaper without divulging his source and herself slightly the worse for wear, Celia drove home just in time to escape the storm from the moor which now looked likely to embrace the village.

They hadn't noticed the approach of the Land Rover from one of the moor's sidetracks. The driver, a big, bluff-looking local, and presumably a farmer, hailed them and motioned them to climb in which – after brief indecision by Bhuppa – they succeeded in doing. They had to endure a look that was almost menacing from the tunic-clad woman (which the Land Rover's driver didn't see) but Walter's firm hold on his girl's arm had persuaded her to take a seat in the vehicle and when she looked back, the apparition had vanished.

The kindly farmer was one of those who sustained his stock by letting them graze on the moor during summer. He was curious to know where the 'grockels' he'd picked up came from and admonished them for not taking note of the local weather forecast. Confirming his prediction of violently inclement weather, it was not long before the threatening storm broke. It buffeted the sturdy vehicle with great gusts of wind and the relentless precipitation hammered like stair rods upon its roof. Fortunately, this sudden mayhem did not appear to disturb the driver. He knew Celia and taking a not very distinctive short cut across the rough terrain, soon arrived at her cottage.

He turned out to be someone Celia knew quite well, but didn't rate. Her attitude towards them had noticeably changed. Her speech was more guarded, and they had the impression that she was suppressing something she didn't want them to know. She seemed a little unsteady on her feet, although there was no indication that she'd been drinking, and Walter concluded that it was just her age and fatigue that ostensibly accounted for her current indifference.

The next morning Celia went into the village to do some shopping, and her departure preceded the appearance of a small MG sports car driven by an ageing would-be Lothario called Clement Insole. He proclaimed himself to be a reporter from a big national daily; he'd been tipped off by Bill the local hack, knew exactly who they were, and implied it would be a waste of time them denying it. He had all the facts about their seven-year void and with perseverance and a good deal of reiterated knocking had persuaded Walter to open the door to him. He knew of the faery ring and all the varied explanations for their 'vanishing act' and much as they tried to deny it, he persisted with his invasive questioning until they could not help but let most of the cat out of the bag. Content with the revelations he gleaned, he promised not to distort any of the facts, bid them farewell, and haring back to Breward, found a phone box and reverse charged his sensational story to his editor in London.

Now becoming accustomed to making quick decisions, Walter used Celia's phone to ring the number on the card he'd been given by yesterday's rescuing farmer, who said he couldn't come but would send his wife with a car. Bhuppa hastily packed their rucksacks and not much later, an elderly Austin, driven by a typically dark daughter of Kernow, drew up outside. Dusky and generously endowed – and to those of less charitable nature distinctly portly – she lost no time in making their acquaintance and appeared not at all put out in receiving the short-noticed request to transport them to Bodmin.

'Only one query,' she said cheerfully. 'Couldn't Celia take you, though I suppose she doesn't like driving far at her age?'

Walter was non-plussed. 'Uh-well,' he stammered, 'she doesn't know we're going.' He mentally chastised himself for this unsatisfactory explanation for their abrupt departure and was rescued by the intervention of Bhuppa.

'It's an emergency,' she said, 'and we need to get back to Gloucestershire. Celia's gone to shop in the village and I've left her a note in the kitchen.'

'Fair enough,' declared the farmer's wife. She'd become well accustomed to being called on to provide the unofficial village taxi service. It wasn't legal, but nobody, including Petroc, the village bobby, ever questioned it and if they ever did, she was prepared to swear that she did not charge for the service and was aware the villagers would back her up. It could sometimes be a lucrative sideline and certainly helped in the struggle to keep the farm going.

Unfortunately, these two didn't look as though they had much and, taking a furtive glance at the meagre contents of his wallet, she didn't charge him much when they arrived at Bodmin Station.

CHAPTER ELEVEN

Receiving the phone call from his zany and not always accurate reporter, the editor of the execrable *Daily Fanfare* was not impressed. 'Clement, you numpty. You do realise the police have been looking for this couple for seven years and the lad is likely to be convicted for having relations with a minor? ... What's that? You say they're now married? That still might not stop the fuzz from prosecuting. I suggest you go to the nearest cop shop-is there a village bobby? And get him or them to visit that cottage and arrest that lad pronto! ... What d'you say? The fact that he's twenty-four and she's twenty-one now might not make any difference. The thing could be retrospective. Who tipped you off, anyway? ... You're not going to say? You might have to if the fuzz has anything to do with it ... Anyway, get your arse into gear and contact them right away. Then let me know what transpires. I shall hang on to your story for the moment, but once you've told the boys in blue, I shall probably be able to run it.'

Mollified by the harsh reaction of his editor and with a rare feeling of empathy, Clement Insole decided to return to Celia's cottage. He didn't like the idea of the pleasant young man being hauled in for having under-age sex with that lovely young girl that was now his wife, but upon arrival, found the cottage's elderly owner in a lather of indecision. She accosted him in a highly accusatory manner and finding her interrogation hard to refute, confessed that he may have been the reason they had decided to leave. She did agree to ring PC Petroc at the constabulary, who was out on business and his wife assured Celia that he would be told of the situation as soon as he returned. It would be another couple of hours before the flustered Petroc arrived on a bicycle to find both Celia and the convivial reporter having an amicable conversation in the picturesque garden. An empty wine bottle stood on the garden table and another one was about to be opened. In the Bedward law enforcer's opinion this did not auger well and his first enquiry as to why Clement had not rung the police station in Bodmin met with a barely apologetic reply. The reporter's often laissez faire attitude to things had surfaced once too often and Petroc's contention that the west country fugitives might be well away by now was a disturbing thought.

*

As it happened, Bhuppa and Walter had made it all the way to Taunton and showing considerable acumen, had bought hats and dark glasses which they hope would sufficiently disguise them and displaying further intelligence, they boarded a bus bound for Gloucester and taking a risk when arriving, caught the local train to Hereford, alighting at Blaisdon Halt before the hue and cry for their apprehension had really got going. It was not far from Blaisdon to Bybrook, and bidding good day to one or two walkers who fortunately didn't recognise them, they made for St Felicity's with the intention to take refuge in the church. But rounding a bend where the road divided at the old mill, they were horrified to cast their eyes on the charred remains of the abbey. Convulsed, and sobbing her heart out, Bhuppa clung to Walter.

'Why did no one ring Celia to tell us and why wasn't it on the news?' She was utterly distraught, but ever practical, Walter ushered her past the ruined edifice and into the church before he replied.

'The BBC West of England Home Service from Bristol would not be heard in Cornwall. It comes under South-West, with studios in Plymouth.'

Inconsolable, Bhuppa was not satisfied and through her tears she said, 'Why wasn't it on the national news and why didn't someone from here ring …'

'I don' know …'

He didn't finish what he was saying as the church door opened and the vicar walked in. It was difficult to say who was most affected by this chance reunion. Not a very tactile man, he was taken aback when Bhuppa flung her arms around him and placing her gently in a pew, he tried to gain control of the situation. He'd heard the news of the hunt for the couple on his car radio and could hardly believe it. The decision not to tell them of the abbey's destruction had been a consensus between Dan and himself. It was felt they might be impetuous and leave their hide-away to come back to Bybrook, thus risking their apprehension, but as the press had now exposed them anyway, he could see that they'd had little alternative but to return. Quite by accident he'd left some details of a sermon in St Felicity's and as it was still July and the nights hadn't drawn in much, he'd decided to go and retrieve them. He swiftly came to the conclusion that until some other solution could be found, they would have to come back to the vicarage. This could not be a permanent arrangement. The police would almost certainly eventually call on him and he could not envisage Bhuppa and Walter being hidden in the attic whilst as a man of God, he'd have to lie to ensure Walter was not arrested. An alternative solution was already forming in his mind and knowing the people who would have to be involved and well aware of their Christian sincerity, he was quite sure they would oblige.

CHAPTER TWELVE

Bold headlines left no doubt that the young couple who had been missing for seven years had reappeared, and as the *Daily Fanfare* put it in its inimitably crude parlance, had they 'DONE A RUNNER' and they were now once more being sought by the police. The disreputable rag then went on to speculate 'had they been in Cornwall all the time?' and only astute probing by 'ace' reporter Clement Insole had uncovered their whereabouts

For once not having to drive anywhere or do anything particularly urgent, Dan had used this as an excuse to repair to the Whippet and had brought the *Daily Fanfare* with him. The half-a-dozen or so clients who were amongst those that usually inhabited the pub at midday were ignited by the news and various questionable viewpoints were offered as to where the couple might be. Some had heard the news on the radio, but were eagerly awaiting the hour of one o'clock when it might merit a mention by the newsreader on the newly acquired television set. This recent innovation proudly sat, a small box in the corner used mainly by the publican to watch afternoon racing when the pub was shut. Viewing it in the evening was prohibited by the landlord's spouse, who reckoned that inns should be places to socialise and was concerned lest the new medium should destroy the pub's convivial atmosphere and upset the status quo. Despite her positive Gallic origins, Sylvie didn't entirely wear the trousers, but another instance of her persuasive nature was her insistence that the public's daily paper must be the *Manchester Guardian* and had Dan not walked in with the *Fanfare*'s as yet exclusive story, they wouldn't have been able to read about Bhuppa and Walter's flight the next day.

Dan despaired. He'd done all he could to help them conceal their tracks by taking them to the vicar's mother in Cornwall and couldn't see that the welcoming old lady had been the one to reveal their hideout to the press. Nevertheless, not for the first time he thought you couldn't judge a book by its cover. As an adherent of Agatha Christie's tales, he'd read enough about feeble old women to know that appearances could be deceptive, but even so, he somehow couldn't put Celia in the same category as the famous novelist's anti-heroines.

Whilst her cottage garden had been lovingly attended, the interior of the cottage left a lot to be desired and he'd seen enough to realise the place was well in need of decoration and some structural attention. Possibly, a lack of money prevented this happening and an approach to a newspaper might go some way towards alleviating the lady's slightly straitened circumstances.

Now called 'Ploughman's lunch', a late twentieth and twenty-first century version of what had once been simply called 'bread and cheese' had not yet become the usually overpriced meal it now is. The original, tastier and far more palatable version consisted of half-a-loaf of freshly baked homemade bread, a large raw peeled onion and a generous portion of cheddar or double Gloucester. You had to be a man and a considerable gourmet to devour such a plenteous banquet and when accompanied by a pint of excellent Alton Court ale, it almost managed to constitute a culinary nirvana. And all this was provided for not much more than half-a-crown: an offer Dan proceeded to take advantage of prior to keeping his appointment with the vicar that afternoon. He could not think what the clergyman would want of him. It was probably just something that needed attention at the vicarage. Dan was never left unoccupied for any length of time. He often wondered how he'd managed to do so much when the abbey was functioning and tried not to think of that period in his life too much.

Brought to him by Sylvie, when it came, Dan's repast was a veritable feast. Someone once said the way to a man's heart was through his stomach, though he knew that wasn't the landlady's motive where he was concerned. He wouldn't have minded trying it the other way round but knew the chances of that were non-existent. Sylvie also brought a message from the vicar who, well aware of Dan's proclivity to patronise the pub a good deal of the time, had rung up to say he'd fixed the problem and no longer required Dan's services.

CHAPTER THIRTEEN

The assistant chief constable of Gloucestershire sat in the office of Superintendent Mills, head honcho of Divisional Headquarters in Lydney. He was not particularly happy with the force having to try and track down the young couple for the second time. Superintendent Mills was inclined to agree and implied that the whole furore caused by their vanishing act was a colossal waste of time and manpower. Particularly as the superintendent knew of someone who, in all likelihood, knew where they'd gone to ground and wouldn't say.

The assistant chief constable showed slight surprise at this revelation. 'And who might that be?' The superintendent put his cards firmly on the table.

'An old friend of mine who, when relatively young, conducted my marriage ceremony at St Jude's in Gloucester and subsequently christened my children. The Reverend Charles Emsworth, now the vicar of three country parishes, including Bybrook, where the ancient abbey recently went up in flames. The girl we seek, Bhuppa, is the adopted daughter of the late Sir Crispen. I am surprised, sir, you didn't know that. You came to the funeral. An important man, Sir Crispen. Magistrate, chairman of this-and-that. School governor, wealthy landowner etc. Nice old buffer and quite radical in his thinking. Drunk himself to death. Couldn't hack Bhuppa's disappearance.'

The assistant chief constable wandered round the office desk and slapped the superintendent on the shoulder. 'Harrison,' he said, 'I believe I must be suffering from the first stages of dementia. I did know all that, and what d'you propose we do? You seem to know this Reverend Charles, this furtive clergyman pretty well. What say you approach him? D'you think he'd spill the beans?'

'No, sir. I think he'd opine that as they were now married in the sight of God they'd done nothing wrong, and he'd not be prepared to reveal their whereabouts. If we insisted on pressing charges the young man could well end up in prison and considering the amount of grief he seems to have had in his short life, I think it would be a sad conclusion to the whole affair.'

A tap on the door heralded the arrival of a trim PC with coffee. She had a thing for the assistant chief constable and blushed violently as he enquired how she was getting on. She was not alone in her admiration. Most of the female staff in the division found him extremely attractive and allied to a personality that evinced understanding and sympathy for their family circumstances, where the enamoured girls were concerned, he was close to being God almighty.

'Thanks, Judith, and how's that Labrador of yours? Could we make a police dog out of him? Though I don't think it'd work. Labradors are too soft.'

Reduced to putty in his hands, the poor girl had to explain that her dog was a bitch and expecting puppies, and after some facetious remarks, he bid her adieu as, extremely flustered, she left them to it.

Harrison Mills was tempted to say something about his senior officer not having lost his touch but thought better of it. He stirred his black coffee and waited for a reply to his opinionated take on the Walter and Bhuppa affair. He was an extremely educated man, fond of the arts, particularly literature, and could not help comparing the tale of the young couple to that of Romeo and Juliet, Tristan and Isolde, and other great lovers. And wasn't Juliette the same age as Bhuppa when she fell for Romeo? The superintendent had made up his mind. He'd like to advocate leniency. It would be simple. A sort of amnesty could be initiated. He could go see Charles Emsworth and inform him of the police decision. The media could then be told of it and the young fugitives would be free to live how they wished. They'd probably have to endure countless interviews, but they'd be advised to sell their story exclusively to one newspaper. The superintendent did not see why they should not benefit financially whilst they could. Their exploits would soon become yesterday's news and they'd be free to take whatever path they chose.

It was almost as if the assistant chief constable had read his mind.

'You'd like to let him off, wouldn't you, Harrison? And I'm inclined to agree with you. I'll leave it to you. Go and see Charles Emsworth and put it to him. I'm sure from what you say he must know where they are and will co-operate.'

'I'll go first thing tomorrow, sir. More likely to catch the man on the hop. Think he's certain to play ball and won't suspect us of anything underhand.'

The assistant chief constable frowned. 'Come on, now, Harrison. You're not going to ask him where they are with a view to an amnesty, then having found them, do the dirty and arrest the lad?'

CHAPTER FOURTEEN

It was scarcely light as Bhuppa crept down the stairs. Her nerve had finally broken. She could not see a future. In vain, Walter had stated that although he might eventually be arrested, British justice would see he'd be fairly treated. Even if imprisoned, he was convinced he'd not be there too long, but Bhuppa did not agree and maintained that even a small amount of time would induce unbearable loneliness. She was aware they couldn't remain with Chia Hao and his family indefinitely. Sooner or later they would be discovered, and she insisted that her proposed plan to terminate their distress was the only way. They would never be able to acquire passports for Thailand in their present situation and though upon being apprehended, Walter may only be incarcerated for a short time, what would they do after he was released? She could not see the other side of the coin. Their circumstances might generate a good deal of sympathy, but Bhuppa could only see the glass half empty, not full. She was adamant that her decision to call it a day was the right one and though internally bludgeoned by conflicting thoughts, Walter acquiesced.

On a Yale lock, the door closed silently behind them, and they began to walk down the street in the moonlight, the streetlights adding visionary assistance. The odd scurrying cat was the only creature about as they passed the town hall. They could make out the mostly out-of-date notices on the board outside it and further on turned left, taking the road to Ross. Early autumn meant that the full moon hung, a ravishing orange sphere, dominating the gregarious stars and bright enough to show that the roadside hedges were turning from summer green to the variegated hues of autumn. A persistent owl's cry startled them as they climbed the path to Wigpool, then stumbled down the slope to the great oak.

And there it was, and they wasted no more time.

On Pope's Hill the ageing donkeys Wendy and Amos stood motionless in the paddock. A young family with five children who had come to live on the hill had been only too glad to be given them by Ah Cy and Rachel; the one bound for university and the other living elsewhere. Prescient of someone's passing, the donkeys seemed to be in a trance and only came out of it when two of the exuberant new owners arrived to see them before going to school.

*

Isobel was surprised to see the sleek black limousine coming up the driveway at 9.30 am. Even more so when its driver got out and opened the front passenger door for the high-ranking officer to get out. Nearly always possessed of a calm disposition, she nevertheless could not imagine what he wanted and replied to his cheerful greeting with some misgivings.

'Mrs Emsworth? Is your husband in?'

'Afraid not,' said Isobel. 'He's at an ecumenical conference in Bristol for a day or two. Is there anything I can do to help?'

'Well, perhaps you have a phone number?'

'I've the hotel one. They may be able to help.'

Superintendent Mills came to a decision. 'No, thank you, all the same. It's not something that can't wait. I need to see your husband in person.'

Isobel looked alarmed. She had a pretty obvious idea what it might be about, but determined to play dumb.

'There's nothing wrong, is there? I can't imagine Charles would ...'

'No, no, of course not. I'll give you a ring tomorrow and meanwhile, if you can get in touch, tell him it's something rather important. But not to suppose we're trying to feel his collar – as it were – no pun intended.'

Now stoney faced, Isobel didn't appreciate the joke: she was aware her clerical husband had a more prominent collar than most and scarcely replied to the police officer's farewell as he climbed into the vehicle, which turned round and purred back down the drive.

Returning from his conference, Reverend Charles found his wife in a state of anxiety. She'd received a visit from an agitated

Chia Hao to say that the birds had flown the nest. He knew not where, and the clergyman resolved that it must now be time to contact the police on two counts.

It did not take long for this new development to become general knowledge and the media had a field day, with some censorious of Reverend Charles and Chia Hao for not revealing they were in cahoots when hiding the couple from the police: calling for some action to be taken against them.

Involved but not implicated, Dan was having a pint in the Whippet and trying to understand what Hamish was saying to him. Saturday lunchtime in the pub was usually busy. Some were playing darts, others shove halfpenny and a foursome competed for matchsticks in a game of crib. The place was rife with talk of recent events and the only one not enjoying the camaraderie of the pub was the man himself, Daniel Michael Woodman. Uncharacteristically sad and restless, he finished his drink, made what he thought was the correct answer to the unintelligible Scot and slipped away without engaging in too much of a farewell.

EPILOGUE

The owner of the cottage at the bottom of the path to Wigpool had only received a brief nod from Dan who, having parked his pickup, strode purposefully up the incline to the common. The cottage owner could not imagine why Dan was carrying the spade and deciding it was none of his business, went back inside to continue watching the 'Flowerpot Men' on his not long-acquired television set. He had his doubts about 'weed', but was almost certain they were all just good mates.

Dan ran down the slope to the oak and set about the nearby faery ring and its attendant fungi with his spade. He did not observe the figure observing him. A statuesque figure attired in a flavescent robe, a severe expression on her face as she slowly dissolved.

FINIS

ONE OR TWO NOTES...

The author did see two cuckoos careering down a Cornish lane emitting their distinctive cry. A very rare sight.

Wigpool Common exists, but not as I have described it. Nevertheless, it is a truly magical place.

In the prologue it is mentioned that the small boy's father had gone off to fight in Spain. Assuming Dan was born in 1922 and was ten years of age when visiting Wigpool with his mum, I have brought the Spanish Civil War forward by four years! This would make Dan twenty when he joined up for the Second World War. (Agricultural workers were not conscripted.) Since such illustrious authors as Thomas Hardy and others have altered history to suit their narratives, I make no apologies for following suit.
SPC.

www.ingramcontent.com/pod-product-compliance
Ingram Content Group UK Ltd.
Pitfield, Milton Keynes, MK11 3LW, UK
UKHW042117250425
457892UK00001B/44